台灣原住民的神話與傳說〈3〉魯凱族、排灣族、賽夏族、邵族

Taiwan Indigene : Meaning Through Stories : Rukai, Paiwan, Saisiyat, Thao

總 策 劃	孫大川	英文翻譯	文魯彬
故事採集	奧威尼·卡露斯／亞榮隆·撒可努	繪　圖	伊誕·巴瓦瓦隆／見維巴里
	潘秋榮／簡史朗		賴英澤／陳俊傑

社　　長	洪美華	責任編輯	謝宜芸、何喬
初版協力	曾麗芬、林玉珮、林宜妙	美術設計	蔡靜玫
	劉秀芬、黃信瑜	封面設計	盧穎作
		市場行政	莊佩璇、巫毓麗、黃麗珍、洪美月
出　　版	幸福綠光股份有限公司	總經銷	聯合發行股份有限公司
	台北市杭州南路一段 63 號 9 樓之 1		新北市新店區寶橋路
	(02)2392-5338		235 巷 6 弄 6 號 2 樓
	www.thirdnature.com.tw		(02)2917-8022
E-mail	reader@thirdnature.com.tw		
印　　製	中原造像股份有限公司		
新　　版	2021 年 10 月		
初版四刷	2024 年 6 月		
郵撥帳號	50130123 幸福綠光股份有限公司		
定　　價	新台幣 580 元 (平裝)		

國家圖書館出版品預行編目資料

台灣原住民的神話與傳說 (3)：魯凱族、
排灣族、賽夏族、邵族／亞榮隆·撒可
努等著 . -- 初版 . -- 臺北市：幸福綠光，
2021.10
　面；公分
ISBN 978-986-06748-7-3 (平裝)

863.859　　　　　　　　　110013522

本書如有缺頁、破損、倒裝，請寄回更換。
ISBN 978-986-06748-7-3

台灣

原住民的

神話與傳說 ③

Taiwan Indigene : Meaning Through Stories : Rukai, Paiwan, Saisiyat, Thao

魯凱族、排灣族、賽夏族、邵族

故事採集　奧威尼・卡露斯／亞榮隆・撒可努／潘秋榮／簡史朗

繪　圖　伊誕・巴瓦瓦隆／見維巴里／賴英澤／陳俊傑

總策劃　孫大川

英文翻譯　文魯彬

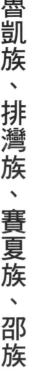

CONTENTS │ 目次

彩繪原畫欣賞

第三冊　魯凱族、排灣族、賽夏族、邵族

1. 魯凱族 Rukai

2. 排灣族 Paiwan

3. 賽夏族 Saisiyat

4. 邵族 Thao

非看不可的原住民資料庫

族語開口說
Learn the
Languages

造訪部落
Visit the Tribes

＊ 本套書共三冊，一、二冊目錄如後。

第一冊　泰雅族、布農族、鄒族

1. 泰雅族 Atayal

故事導讀：神聖的祖訓　Sacred Ancestral Teachings

1. 巨石傳說　The Legend of the Giant Stone
2. 神奇的呼喚術　The Magical Summons
3. 彩虹橋的審判　The Rainbow's Judgment
4. 部落百寶盒　Treasure Box of the Tribes

- 泰雅族的生命禮俗
- 不可失傳的傳統技藝
- 紋面文化與文飾
- 英雄戰鬥與出草傳說
- 泰雅族的食物
- 泰雅族的祖靈祭

2. 布農族 Bunun

故事導讀：月亮、百步蛇與人的約定　The Moon, the Hundred Pace Snake and Man's Promise

1. 與月亮的約定　Rendezvous with the Moon
2. 布農之女阿朵兒　The Story of Adal
3. 憤怒的百步蛇　The Angry Hundred Pace Snake
4. 獵人的信仰　The Hunter's Faith
5. 部落百寶盒　Treasure Box of the Tribes

- 木刻畫曆
- 祭典豐富的布農族
- 天籟八部合音享譽國際
- 布農族的分布與社會組織
- 布農族的傳統服飾

3. 鄒族 Tsou

非看不可的原住民資料庫

族語開口說　　　造訪部落
Learn the　　　Visit the Tribes
Languages

第二冊　阿美族、卑南族、達悟族

1. 阿美族 Amis

卑南族 Puyuma

3. 達悟族 Tao

非看不可的原住民資料庫

族語開口説
Learn the
Languages

造訪部落
Visit the Tribes

1996年，我回到母校繼續碩士學程。當時寫論文，為了什麼主題煩惱不已。指導教授提醒我，萬丈高樓平地起，既是決定未來往原住民族議題研究發展，應當從原住民族文化的文本分析奠定良基。

這套《台灣原住民的神話與傳說》，對於許多想要認識原住民文化的朋友，或者從事原住民研究的學生，甚至是原住民本身，這是最重要也是最基礎的入門書。

在電子出版蓬勃的時代，特別感佩幸福綠光出版社以精緻的重編再版這套叢書。期盼這樣的心意，啣來更多的新枝，豐富神的花園。

（伍麗華／校長立委）

原住民神話不只是原住民族文學心靈的泉源，也是延伸台灣人民共同想像空間的資源。這本書將原住民神話配以精緻的圖畫，不但可讀性甚高，而且提供很多延伸閱讀的資訊，誠為認識原住民文化的駿良入門書。

（吳密察／台灣史學者・國立故宮博物院院長）

神話與傳說乃人類歷史之母，口述的神話與傳說是台灣原住民歷史的脈絡，更是台灣史之根源。

身為台灣人不可不溫習自己的神話傳說，熟悉自己的歷史。

（胡德夫／民歌之父・原權會創會會長）

陳耀昌

《斯卡羅》掀起「探討台灣史」、「了解原住民」的全民運動，讓我們深刻領悟，台灣是「多元族群、同島一命」：

- 原住民了解白浪，白浪卻不夠了解原住民。
- 您知道嗎？台灣原住民是南島語族的祖先，台灣原住民是台灣帶給世界的禮物。
- 了解原住民，請從了解原住民祖先的神話與傳說開始。
- 何況，天啊！《魯凱族》的插畫竟然出自原住民大藝術家：伊誕·巴瓦瓦隆，太珍貴了。

（陳耀昌／醫師·名作家）

薛化元

每個民族／族群都有長久流傳的神話與傳說。

神話與傳說雖不是歷史，卻是民族／族群歷史記憶的展現。因此，神話與傳說也成為重要的歷史文化資產。

台灣原住民由於早期沒有文字，神話與傳說更承載了原住民的歷史傳承，而這也是這套書價值之所在。

（薛化元／政治大學台灣史研究所教授）

初版推薦語

總策劃序　**關心原住民議題的重要入門書**

這一套原為10冊的《台灣原住民的神話與傳說》，集合了原住民的作者與畫者，出版於2002年年底，初版、二版都刷了好幾刷，雖談不上暢銷，但長期以來，它仍然是關心原住民議題的讀者重要的入門書。

2016年，出版社更投入心力，封面、紙張做了更新。在族語語彙的拼法，無法全面改成和現行官方書寫系統一致的情況下，編者們設計了「開口說」的音檔，以掃描 QR Code 的方式（見目錄），直接讓讀者聆聽族語，用聲音拉近彼此的距離。

尤其，2001年之後，原住民各族的正名訴求紛紛獲得官方的認定，目前台灣原住民已經分為16族了，這是我們在人權上很大的進步。這些新認定的族群有噶瑪蘭族（Kebalan，2002）、太魯閣族（Truku，2004）、撒奇萊雅族（Sakizaya，2007）、賽德克族（Seedig，2008）、拉阿魯哇族（Hla'alua，2014）、卡那卡那富族（Kanakanavu，2014）等6族；連同近年來愈來愈受到矚目的平埔族各族正名運動，反映了原住民議題發展的新趨勢。我們真誠的希望親愛的讀者們，能注意這些變化，更深地了解我們原住民的族人。

我們十分珍惜這套《台灣原住民的神話與傳說》系列所積累的將近20年的文化資產記憶，幾經考慮，出版社決定重新編排再版，在不減損其豐富內容的前提下，將原本10冊的規模濃縮成3冊的形式，以降低書籍的成本，嘉惠更多的讀者。我們這次雖然仍沒有能力增補後來正名的6族，但這幾年也看到不少有關他們，包括平埔族，相當豐富的出版物，熱心的讀者應該可以從其他管道掌握與他們相關的資訊，彌補我們的缺憾。

要特別指出的是，這次我們在插畫的處理上做了重大的變革。經幾比對，我們發現插圖用黑白呈現，不但可以避免色彩喧賓奪主的情況，而且反而更能突顯整體畫面細膩的線條與素樸古雅的風格。不過，對彩色有興趣的讀者，仍可用QR Code找到原畫的初貌。尤其，更值得一提的是，我們這套書的英文譯者文魯彬先生（Robin Winkler），在台灣生活近40年，深入認識了台灣，並更走進了原住民的世界，他以極大的熱情重新潤飾他原來的故事英譯，還增加了「What's more?」和「Where did it come from?」等內容。我們希望有更多外國朋友，透過這套書打開的窗口，認識優美的原住民文化！

An Easy Book to Enter the World of Tribes

The "Taiwan Indigene: Meaning Through Stories," a collection of writings and paintings by Taiwanese indigenous peoples, was first published at the end of 2002. The original and many reprints of the series, while not a "best seller," is established as an excellent introduction for those interested in the indigene of Taiwan. The 2016 edition even included a QR code link for those wishing to hear the vocabulary of the indigenous languages.

Following the series' release in 2002, years of struggle by many of Taiwanese indigenous peoples bore fruit, and the ten tribes recognized when the series was first published, grew to 16 officially recognized tribes. The six new tribes and their year of official recognition are the Kebalan (2002), Truku (2004), Sakizaya (2007), Sediq (2008), Hla'alua (2014) and Kanakanavu (2014). The recognition of these tribes and attention given to the so called "plains tribes" all reflect the development of our nation's "indigene" dialog. We sincerely hope these stories will help our people to follow these trends and gain a deeper understanding of Taiwan's indigenous peoples and culture.

I treasure experiences over the past twenty years and was delighted with the publisher's decision to reissue the books with revised content and format. Without detracting from any of the original stories, the ten volumes have been combined into three so as to make the books accessible to a wider audience. As an aesthetic choice, we also decided to print this reissue with the paintings in black and white – the color paintings are available at our website. While no new stories were prepared for the six newly recognized tribes, we have included much new information about those tribes, as well as information for the as yet unrecognized plains tribes.

It is worth mentioning that the English translator for the series Robin Winker, has since the series' first release, spent considerable time immersed in Taiwan's indigenous culture, and for this series the translations have all been revised and new material has been added, notably the "What's more" sections. Through these stories we look forward to welcoming many more foreign readers to the richness of Taiwan's indigenous culture.

paelabang danapan

魯凱族
Rukai

▶小筆記▶

· 巴嫩公主嫁給蛇郎君的故事，正是台灣膾炙人口的傳說。

· 魯凱比鄰排灣，血統相近，皮膚都較暗；都喜歡檳榔、琉璃珠、陶壺，節慶盪鞦韆，吟唱古調、吹鼻笛，也是天生的藝術家。

‧貴族頭目世襲，但另從全體族人選出智慧勇敢者擔任實際的首領。

‧男女均以佩戴百合花為聖潔、榮譽象徵。

‧沈文程、梁文音都是魯凱族人。

故事導讀　　綿長的情絲

魯凱族和排灣族相鄰近，文化和血統錯綜交織，相互影響甚深。在情感的表達上，兩族皆深邃而幽曲、柔遠而細膩，從他們的古調吟唱和鼻笛的哀訴，即可見一斑。即使如此，兩族間的文化風格，依然清晰可辨。比較而言，魯凱族人比排灣族人更見含蓄、內斂。

美麗的慕阿凱凱被壞心腸的老人大惡勒擄走，威逼誘騙，強行將她嫁給自己的孫子。流落異鄉的慕阿凱凱，雖然滿腹憂傷，卻從不屈服於逆境，以其堅強的意志感動了自己的丈夫。最後在丈夫、子女的陪伴下，一家人循著檳榔樹和荖葉，返回家鄉，與族人重聚。而巴嫩的愛情和婚姻，雖屬自願，但比慕阿凱凱的異族通婚更加不可思議；那不僅是異類的情愛，還涉及詭異的幽冥世界。她和她的蛇郎君的跨界婚姻，當然要比慕阿凱凱更讓人心碎。

百步蛇郎君以笛聲和瀟灑的威儀，擄獲了巴嫩的心。迎娶前夕，大家都心知肚明，巴嫩這一嫁出去便再也不能回來；於是通宵樂舞，表達依依不捨的情感。次日，在送巴嫩至達露巴淋湖的路上，巴嫩殷殷致意、反覆叮嚀；揮手、回望，每一句言語，每一個身體動作，都充分表露了魯凱族人含蓄、曲折的情感世界。後來巴嫩託夢給自己的父母，告知她的兩個孩子即將來訪。果然有兩條小蛇蜷縮在靠窗的寢台，兩老欣喜莫名，以美酒、鮮肉招待；當夜兩個孩子亦託夢答謝。巴嫩的後裔代代都是如此探望親人，直到有一天因一個不懂事媳婦的粗心，才切斷了這樣的關係。但是巴嫩的思念卻沒有因此而斷滅；她幻化成白鷺鷥，那在天空迂迴、盤旋的姿態，便彷彿去而又返、周行不殆的情絲。

慕阿凱凱和巴嫩的故事，除了愛情之外，其實還有一個共同的主題：那是對親人、族人與部落的深厚情感。以巴嫩的例子來看，從揮別、叮嚀、託夢到變成白鷺鷥，真是千絲萬縷，纏綿、低迴，久久不去。

魯凱族人之所以如此重視親族的感情，主要或許是因為他們對祖靈的堅定信仰。以陶壺維繫的家族神聖紐帶，始終是魯凱族社會最最核心的價值。而雲豹帶領建立的家園部落，不單是蒙受祝福的地方，更是人和自然（雲豹）共同認可、捍衛的場所。此外，頭蝨家族對雲豹的貼心照顧，也再一次讓我們見識到魯凱族人綿長、細膩的情感。

　# The Long Unbroken Thread of Love

Whether we look at their culture or even lineage, the Rukai and Paiwan share many similar characteristics. Rukai and Paiwan are both profound and quiet, easy-going and gentle, as demonstrated by their ancient songs and the soulful sound of their nose flutes. Nevertheless, the two are clearly distinguishable, with the Rukai generally being more reserved and introverted than the Paiwan.

The beautiful Muakaikai was abducted by an evil old man and forced to marry his grandson. Muakaikai, now living in a foreign land, is full of sadness but never succumbs to adversity. Her husband, moved by her resolution, one day accompanies her and their children, returning to her childhood home. They follow the trail of innumerable betel nut trees that she had planted when she was first taken from her village. However, the story of Baleng's love and marriage, although voluntary, is even more incredible. Whereas Muakaikai married outside her tribe, Baleng married outside her species into a totally strange world, making her story even more heart rendering than the story of Muakaikai.

The hundred pacer snake/handsome prince captured Baleng's heart with his flute music and majesty. On the eve of the wedding, everyone knew that Baleng would never return, so the dancing and singing continued through the night, a demonstration of deep attachment. The full spectrum of the Rukai emotions were expressed by Baleng's waving, looking back, and all manner of gesturing to her relatives on the next day as the villagers accompanied her on the way to her new home at Dalupalhing Lake.

Baleng then communicates with her parents through dreams, telling them when her two children were about to visit. Sure enough, two little snakes appear curled up next to the window, and the old couple joyously fete them with wine and fresh meat, for which the two children thank them, again, through their dreams. Baleng's progeny visited her relatives in this way for generations. These visits continued until they were terminated due to the carelessness of an ignorant daughter-in-law. Nevertheless, Baleng's feelings for her relatives endured, and she is now seen as a white egret, hovering high in the sky above her village.

Apart from describing love, the stories of Muakaikai and Baleng share a common theme: the deep feelings one may have for relatives, or for one's tribe or clan.

The Rukai emphasis on their relations with family and tribe may be accounted for by their strong belief in ancestral spirits. The sacred bond of the family, shown by their clay pots, has always been at the core of Rukai social values. Their attachment to their home, such as in the story of the clouded leopard, shows it to be not only a blessed place, but also a place where the symbiosis of humans and the rest of nature (symbolized by the clouded leopard) plays out. And finally, the caring for the clouded leopard by the "head lice clan" once again reveals the subtle emotions of the Rukai.

美麗的慕阿凱凱

一陣強風捲走了美麗的慕阿凱凱，使得大貴族達拉巴丹痛失愛女，族人驚愕傷心。

原來是壞心腸的老人大惡勒把慕阿凱凱擄走，強行把她嫁給自己的孫子。流落異鄉的慕阿凱凱不屈服於逆境，並以真誠打動丈夫，奇蹟般的回家了。

這是一個流傳久遠的故事。達拉巴丹是從前魯凱族有名的大貴族，只有一個既美麗又孝順的女兒，名叫慕阿凱凱，不但得到父母的疼愛，族人也都非常喜歡她。據說，凡是看過她的年輕男子，往往像是喝了酒似的，陶醉在她迷人的風采中。

部落中有一個貴族的兒子，長得英俊瀟灑，名字叫庫勒勒爾樂。他家的地位比慕阿凱凱家低了一些，不過包括雙方父母在內，族人都認為他們是天造地設的一對，年輕人也幾乎都默認長大後會結為夫妻。但是，長大後的庫勒勒爾樂，不知為什麼父母遲遲不向女方提親，又著急、又擔心，深怕被別家捷足先登。

這一天，一年一度的獵人祭才剛剛結束，最歡樂的「被滿足之日」就要上場。期待已久的年輕人，一早就成群結隊上山，摘採野蔓藤，合力編成又長又粗又結實的鞦韆，懸掛在大貴族達拉巴丹家高大的百年老榕樹上。

 What's more?

大貴族（talialalaye，達里阿拉籟）：由於魯凱族的家族是長子繼承制度，最大者為大貴族，排行老二、老三則為二等和三等貴族。

達拉巴丹（Dalapathane）：是魯凱族的家名。魯凱人每一家都有家名，從家名就可以知道其社會地位、名分和人品。

部落（chekele，池歌樂）：只要是兩個家族以上聚集在一個地方，都可以算是一個部落。「池歌樂」這個詞對魯凱族人來說，不但是他們生活的中心，也是靈魂的歸宿。

獵人祭（kiapa-alupu，給阿巴阿鹿步）：獵人祭是為男孩子一生一次成年所舉行的生命禮俗，時間大約在收完小米的第二個月圓時，約每年八月中旬。

被滿足之日（taki-pakadralhuane，達給巴卡拉魯阿尼）：每年為男孩子舉行成年禮之後，會在另外一天為女孩子舉行佩戴百合花冠，下午並舉行盪鞦韆節目。其意義是「安慰或滿足」之意。

鞦韆（talaisi，達拉依西）：這是一種貴族女性特有的權力，每年舉行盪鞦韆儀式，以安慰族人一年的辛勞。

節目在午後開始了，全村的男男女女都穿上盛裝禮服，來這裡跳舞、盪鞦韆。女孩們一個接一個，爭取擺盪得最優雅、最美麗的誇讚；男孩們也輪流競逐，看誰擺動得最有力穩健、最高、最遠。

輪到慕阿凱凱盪鞦韆了，大家自然而然的停止歌舞，男孩們紛紛排列兩旁拉擺鞦韆，每邊超過百人；女孩們更是全神貫注，歡喜的目睹著慕阿凱凱的風采，由此可見大家愛慕及擁戴的程度。

一開始，慕阿凱凱就盪得又遠又高，在空中既舒暢又高興，情不自禁的彎著腰、翹起腳，順著節奏，盪得更遠更高，彷彿沒有極限。

在眾人歡呼聲中，她又以一扭腰、一翹腳的力道迴旋轉身，美妙的姿勢贏得所有在場觀看的人鼓掌、喝采，聲音響徹雲霄，庫勒勒爾樂心中更是如癡如醉。

What's more?

野蔓藤（vaedre，哇莪樂）：學名為山葛。魯凱人採集「哇莪樂」，將其捆成一束如胳臂粗的繩索，吊在樹上，底部編成環形以便套上一隻腳，中間繫著一條蔓藤以供擺動，便成為一座鞦韆。

榕樹（daralape，達爾拉柏）：在魯凱族社會，家屋外面前庭有榕樹，表示這是貴族家族，因此魯凱語所稱的榕樹有「貴族遮陽」之意。貴族的女兒要出嫁時，在惜別舞會上，就是用榕樹葉拭淚。

盛裝禮服（ngia-ragelane，依阿拉歌拉呢）：一種按照身分、階級刺繡傳統圖案的禮服，只在特殊場合，如婚禮和祭典中穿戴。

沒想到，這時候竟然有一個壞心腸的老人大惡勒，悄悄躲藏在不遠的草叢中，想擄走慕阿凱凱，給自己的孫子作妻子。壞老人暗暗的念咒：

「但願有一陣強風把妳吹走！」

於是，果然一陣強烈的龍捲風吹襲而來，把慕阿凱凱連同鞦韆都捲到空中去了。

強風過後，走避奔逃的族人回到大榕樹邊，只看到鞦韆由高空中緩緩飄落，卻不見慕阿凱凱美麗的身影，全場陷入一聲聲哀嘆哭泣，眾人到處著急的呼喚她的名字，卻仍毫無下落。

慶典只好黯然落幕，最可憐的是慕阿凱凱的父母，痛失愛女之後，終日以淚洗面，庫勒勒爾樂更是痛不欲生，族人一提起這件不幸，都紛紛搖頭低聲嘆氣，歡笑不再。

話說慕阿凱凱隨著龍捲風飄啊飄的，最後飄落在一個遙遠而陌生的地方。壞老人大惡勒早就在她飄落的地點等著，當慕阿凱凱在驚恐中飄落地面，還來不及看清四周時，大惡勒已經將她捆綁起來，並用布蒙住眼睛，背著她快步向神秘的森林走去。

慕阿凱凱慢慢從暈眩中恢復意識，發現自己全身動彈不得，用力睜開眼睛，竟是漆黑一片，不禁傷心又害怕的流淚呼喚：

「依娜！依娜！快來救我！」

What's more?

大惡勒（Taevele）：這個老人也是魯凱族人，因為孫子不被貴族女孩所接受、喜歡，心裡吃醋、嫉妒而後生恨，百般的想陷害慕阿凱凱。

龍捲風（alhilhaogo，阿里絡咕）：在這個故事裡指的是真的龍捲風，但有時候是用來形容天災，如瘟疫、農作物遭病蟲害而鬧饑荒。形容在短時間內且極有毀滅性的天災。

大惡勒立刻拿出預先包好的檳榔給她，並且假惺惺的溫柔安慰她說：「孫女兒啊！妳放心！我不會傷害妳！我要帶妳到一個地方，保證妳一定很快樂的。」

慕阿凱凱嚼著檳榔，但眼淚還是不停的流出。每到休息的地方，慕阿凱凱便把檳榔汁吐向左右，希望留下記號，好讓急著找她的父母知道行蹤。

據說，慕阿凱凱吐出的汁液，在右邊長出一種叫大拉牡安心的檳榔樹和一種叫咾威嗚的荖葉；左邊則長出另一種叫芭咕拉麗阿的檳榔和劣等的達哇嗚哇露荖葉。

最後，他們來到另一個部落郊外的榕樹下，大惡勒把綁住慕阿凱凱手腳的繩子鬆開，拿掉她眼睛上的罩布，她伸展雙手，揉著眼睛後慢慢睜開，發現眼前所見到的都是陌生的臉孔。

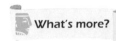

What's more?

檳榔（sabiki，撒必給）：在魯凱族的神話故事裡曾敘述：「突然有一道曙光由天窗照耀下來，隨後一顆檳榔滾落在所織的亂麻線上。她好奇的撿起來，並順手以食指沾爐火中的炭灰塗抹在表面，然後放進嘴裡嚼著，就懷孕生子了……」便可以理解「檳榔象徵男性」的概念。所以所謂「一夜情」，魯凱語就稱做「一口檳榔的情」。

依娜(ina)：魯凱語稱媽媽為「依娜」，故事中慕阿凱凱呼喊「依娜…！」聲聲哭喊求救。

荖葉（drangao，朗阿烏）：蔓藤類植物，葉子可以包檳榔食用，或將它的莖切一小塊夾在檳榔心，再加石灰就可以吃。

琉璃珠（silu，繫露）：琉璃珠有好幾個等級，從最高等級到最低等級大約有十幾種，一種項鍊可能有十個等級編製而成。

迎接慕阿凱凱的人已經在等待，尤其是老人大惡勒所設計配對的男子、也就是他的孫子，以及其他家人。可是慕阿凱凱無法接受這種強迫的行為，只是非常冷淡的呆坐著，對任何人都不看不聽，憤恨澎湃洶湧心中。

慕阿凱凱只愛父母以及青梅竹馬的庫勒勒爾樂、還有朝夕相處的族人，根本沒想過和任何外人共同生活。但是這個部落的大貴族和長老，每天不斷很有禮貌的向慕阿凱凱道歉，又很正式的拿出一大盒琉璃珠和一串串首飾當聘禮。舉目無親、又累又餓的她，知道自己已經回不去了，也沒有其他選擇餘地，只好無奈的被背著進入部落，嫁給了大惡勒的孫子。

慕阿凱凱被強擄到陌生地方，嫁給不認識的人，只能終日暗自垂淚。雖然丈夫對她極為疼愛，但慕阿凱凱日思夜想的都是故鄉的父母、愛人，以及呵護她的族人。每當早上晨曦從東方照耀的時候，慕阿凱凱總是對著陽光偷偷啜泣、祈禱，盼望有一天族人能夠找到自己。

日復一日，年復一年，已過了十幾個春天，慕阿凱凱也已經生兒育女。雖然難忘家人，但仍克盡本分的稱職持家，扮演著好妻子、好母親的角色。有一天，慕阿凱凱的男人終於說，非常感謝她這些年來的付出，為了體諒她對故鄉、家人的思念，決定帶一些貴重禮物，全家陪著慕阿凱凱返鄉。

興奮又畏怯的慕阿凱凱，在丈夫、子女相伴下，循著多年以前被擄的原路回娘家。沿路上，慕阿凱凱以前吐出檳榔汁而長出的檳榔樹和荖葉，都已長高、開花、結果。

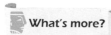 **What's more?**

聘禮（sabathane，莎巴丹）：有「用來替換女孩的生命」之意。傳統魯凱族的聘禮有：1.首飾；2.禮服；3.禮刀；4.項鍊；5.肩帶；6.陶壺；7.鐵鍋；8.斧頭；9.鐵鍬；10.鐮刀；11.背網袋；12.珠寶盒；13.切肉刀；14.一塊地；15.精神（一生的愛）。

長老（marudrange，瑪路朗）：長老是平民和一般貴族所選出來的領袖，來制衡大貴族以防範其為所欲為，或商討內部事務和對外的策略。

被背著：結婚是人生的大事，在魯凱族傳統婚禮中都是將新娘背娶回家。

故鄉的族人遠遠看見眾多外地人緩緩走來，好奇的靜靜觀看等待。當慕阿凱凱表明身分之後，馬上有人尖聲驚叫：

「她還活著！慕阿凱凱回來了！」

消息迅速的傳播開來，鄉親一一熱烈歡呼迎接，個個喜上眉梢。慕阿凱凱的父母聞訊，也疑惑的拄著枴杖出來迎接。

回到娘家，慕阿凱凱眼看久別多年的父母，已經是白髮蒼蒼的老人；見到家裡還留著當時因失去她而佩戴的喪布，百感交集。眾人相擁而泣，既對命運的捉弄不勝唏噓，也對重聚團圓充滿歡喜、安慰。

Where did it come from?
本則故事由作者的母親瑟妮特（Senethe）講述，採集自古茶布安（屏東縣霧台鄉好茶村）。

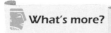

What's more?

喪布（kalhemeane，卡樂默阿尼）：如果家族和部落的任何人死亡，全家族的人或整個部落的人都要戴喪布（黑色的布），表示哀悼之意。

02

雲豹的頭蝨家族

頭蝨特別多的爾部祿家族，專責養育魯凱族的
神犬雲豹；由於雲豹巧妙的引路，族人才找到
古茶布安這塊新樂土，他們立起石柱，以天地
為證，祈求祖靈保護。

魯凱族人早已明白人為力量有限，接受自然、
仰賴自然、維護自然才是永續生存之道。

很久很久以前，大地才歷經大洪水不久。阿美族、卑南族、魯凱族三個族群還一起居住在東海岸的把那巴那揚。

其中，魯凱族群分為達魯瑪克、達德樂，以及在轉角處的古茶布安等三個小族群。

族裡有兩兄弟，哥哥名叫布喇路丹，弟弟名叫巴格德拉斯，他們都是部落中的首領。兩兄弟覺得希給巴里吉這處小小的溪岸沖積地，已經容不下逐漸增多的族人，為了後代子子孫孫考量，必須去尋找另一個較寬闊、可以長久居住的地方。

於是，兩兄弟帶著他們的獵犬雲豹，向族人解釋離開的理由後，依依不捨的說：「唉依！莎保！」

在祝福的道別聲中，快速動身出發。

 What's more?

把那巴那揚（Panapanayan）：即現在台東縣太麻里鄉美和村附近。

達魯瑪克（Tarumake）：指現在的大南部落，即台東縣卑南鄉東興新村。

達德樂（Dadele）：現在的屏東縣三地門鄉青葉村。

古茶布安（Kochapongane）：現在的屏東縣霧台鄉好茶村。

阿美族、卑南族、魯凱族：都蘭山（Tugngalan）的東北方是阿美族，都蘭山的東南方是卑南族，魯凱族則在肯都爾山（Kingdurn）一帶。

首領（ma-ililuku，馬依里路固）：「策劃者」、「帶領者」之意。頭目是從貴族中產生的，而且可以世襲。由於頭目並不一定代代都有能力來治理一個部落，所以每隔一段時間都必須選出一個新首領，來彌補貴族的不足。

希給巴里吉（shikipalhichi）：這個讀音是東排灣語，意思為「轉角處」，位在台東縣太麻里溪流域。

兄弟倆沿著太麻里溪谷溯源而上，沿路一面打獵，一面尋找他們夢中的樂園。

他們順著夕陽沉落的方向前進，每次都以為只要跨過高山上榕樹林台地，便到了世界的邊緣；誰知到了山頂，遙望西邊，才知道還有一望無際的山川和叢林。

如此翻過一座又一座的高山，兩兄弟疲憊不堪的來到一處人煙罕至的地方，口渴、飢餓，無法動彈。獵犬雲豹雖然也累得喘息不已，卻突然又矯健的消失在山林中。

眼看天色快暗了，他們正打算趕緊四處尋找水源解渴時，雲豹一身濕淋淋的縱躍出現在他們面前，一邊抖落水珠，一邊引領他們到一處溪谷——竟然是一潭豐沛又清澈的水源！

雲豹在岸邊舔水解渴之後，便躺下睡著了。不論兩兄弟怎麼呼喚，牠就是賴著不走，哥哥布喇路丹認為：

「可能神明的意思就是要我們在此定居。」

接著，兩兄弟謹慎的從溪邊走出來，詳細探勘周圍地形，覺得天然條件很好，便在西邊的鞍部，選了一個有自然屏障易守難攻的新家園古茶布安，也就是現在的舊好茶部落。

 What's more?

雲豹（Ihikulao，里古勞）：魯凱族人認為雲豹的花紋如雲飄渺神秘，所以「里古勞」也有超乎尋常的強者之意。

唉依！莎保！（Aye！Sabao）：「唉依」是「再見」之意；「莎保」是「辛苦」之意。在這個故事是「再會了，抱歉要離開你們」的意思。

打獵（alupu，阿鹿布）：以前的人是帶著獵狗背著弓箭在叢林中尋尋覓覓，因此「阿鹿布」有尋覓或尋找的意思。

神明（ku mubalithita，古慕巴里低達）：是指管理山的祖靈。

兩兄弟找到一塊長方形的石柱，合力把它豎立在鞍部的山頂，表示：

「我們擁有這一塊地！」

之後，哥哥布喇路丹吩咐弟弟巴格德拉斯由原路回到部落，邀請家屬及親友共五家，大約二十五人，遷移到這裡定居。

移民家庭當中有一家名叫爾部祿，受到族人的信任與委託，專職養育、照顧雲豹的生活。他們人品很好，又有愛心，更了解雲豹的習性與需求，和雲豹建立了深厚的感情。

養育雲豹的爾部祿家族，不管哪一代子孫，頭蝨都特別多，因此被稱為「頭蝨家族」；但是他們個個聰明、品德良善、郎才女貌，一向都是各族人人爭相嫁娶的對象。

居住在舊好茶部落下方，隘寮南溪對岸的外族，看到新來的移民在這裡拓荒，便不斷的侵犯干擾。

有一天，眾多敵人群集在部落的防禦大門，雲豹早已在那裡把守。只看到雲豹用自己的尿液沾濕尾巴，輕輕一揮，就把敵人的眼睛全部打瞎了，族人隨後跟進收拾敵人。從那之後，外族再也不敢侵犯他們。

What's more?

舊好茶（Kochapongane，古茶布安）：指的就是屏東縣霧台鄉的舊好茶部落，擁有全台灣最大最多的傳統石板屋遺跡，族人多在1978年遷到隘寮南溪旁的新好茶部落定居。

石柱（tamaunalhe，達瑪嗚吶樂）：立石柱表示：「這一塊地方是祖靈所賜給的，因此請守望、保護我們。」

頭蝨家族（tuakuchu ka ua chekechekele，都阿古朱卡瓦池各池各樂）：「頭上長頭蝨的家族」之意。

隘寮南溪（Maka tagaraoso ka drakerale，馬客大客爾阿蘇卡拉客兒樂）：指的是「流自北大武山的溪水」。

過了相當長的一段時間，族人覺得獵犬雲豹已經漸漸衰老，不應該再負擔工作，因此想把牠送回原來的故鄉，讓牠過著更快樂、更自在的生活。

於是，全族人開始籌備，首先是動員狩獵，將獵到的比較細嫩的山羌給雲豹享用，做為惜別禮物；較普通的山鹿則給族人作為送別途中的糧食。

留守的族人一個個用手撫摸雲豹告別，並反覆的提醒：「千萬不要暴露在別族的地盤，以免受到不敬或傷害。」

護送雲豹的獵人們一路上細心的照顧牠，由於雲豹年紀很大了，體力明顯不如當年，行走速度頗為緩慢。

但是，當他們翻過榕樹林，也就是現在魯凱族的聖地巴魯冠時，雲豹突然以閃電般的速度衝入叢林，獵人們根本來不及呼喚。

不久卻聽到不遠處傳來山鹿的悲鳴聲，獵人們隨後追尋，只見雲豹坐在血淋淋的山鹿旁邊等候他們。

「這顯然是牠與我們離別之前，給我們的最後禮物。」

一位經驗豐富的老獵人說。

獵人們趕緊讓雲豹享用山鹿的鮮血、肝臟和心臟，其他的肉則留在原地，等護送雲豹回來經過這裡的時候，再帶回去給族人分享。

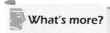

What's more?

聖地（tau-lhisisiane，島里希希阿尼）：意思是因為神聖所以是禁地。

巴魯冠（Balhukuan）：為人死後靈魂的歸宿、永恆的居所，也是祖靈所在，魯凱族人視為聖地，現址在北大武山和霧頭山之間的稜線，也就是茶部岩山的北方台地。

祖先（kuna-chuchungulane，古那祖祖烏蘭或mubalhithita，母巴里滴達）：前者意指「很久之前的祖先」，後者意指「被我們輪替的先人」。

他們繼續往前行，走到知本溪東邊一處寬闊的台地，這個地方終年雲霧，氣候濕潤，綠草嫩葉繁茂，獵物種類數量眾多，猶如享用不盡的宴席，雲豹的食物必然永不匱乏。

老獵人爾部祿，就是那一位陪伴著雲豹度過一生的人，緊緊的抱著牠、親牠，並唸唸有詞的說：

「你是我們所有魯凱人永遠的獵犬。我們會永遠記得，你曾經陪伴著我們度過那艱苦的歲月。你以獵物養育我們，使我們有尊嚴；也留給我們子子孫孫一塊永不被侵犯的美地，和永不枯竭的泉源。回到你的祖先身旁和永遠的故鄉那裡去吧！」

說完之後，他們便把雲豹給放了。雲豹走了幾步便停住，轉頭不捨的再看他們一眼，接著，便匆匆躍入叢林，消失蹤影。

從此，雲豹的民族魯凱人，不殺雲豹，不穿雲豹的皮，不穿戴有雲豹牙的花冠。也以自己是雲豹的民族為榮耀，不論再惡劣的環境或再艱苦的生活，永遠憑著雲豹的精神，以堅韌的生命力，努力不懈。

Where did it come from?

本則故事由好茶的史官拉巴告（Lapagao）講述，採集自古茶布安（屏東縣霧台鄉好茶村）。

What's more?

花冠（bengelhai，伯莪萊）：一種戴在頭上的裝飾，代表一個人的人格和情操的象徵意義。

#

卡巴哩彎

> 遠古時大地渾沌，一道生命曙光直射神秘洞穴
> 中的陶壺，不分晝夜孕育著陶壺中的兩粒太陽
> 蛋，最後太陽蛋破裂生出一對男女，魯凱族的
> 始祖誕生了。
>
> 為了讓生命的延續，他們結為夫妻，歷經挫折
> 和失敗，終於繁衍出健康的子孫，也尋覓到魯
> 凱族人永遠的家鄉卡巴哩彎。

很久很久以前，魯凱族的始祖原本來自達露巴淋湖附近的卡里阿罕，這裡
正是生命第一道曙光降臨的地方。

那時候，大地一片混沌，沒有任何生命，唯獨卡里阿罕一個神秘洞穴裡頭
的陶壺中，有兩粒太陽的蛋；每當東方第一道曙光乍現，便正好照射在這
顆蛋上。

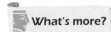

What's more?

達露巴淋（Dalupalhing）：指現在的大鬼湖，是台灣知名的高山湖泊，此處有
珍貴的台灣杉林群，位於高雄縣茂林鄉、屏東縣霧台及台東縣延平鄉三區的交
界處，屬於中央山脈南段山區。

卡里阿罕（kaliaharn）：語意是生命第一道曙光降臨的意思。

陽光日復一日的照耀著，有一天，這兩粒蛋破殼，誕生了一對兄妹：

男孩子名叫依拉伊勞，女孩子名叫阿拉優沐。他們兩人後來成為夫婦，生了一對兄妹，男孩子叫阿喇琉，女孩子叫冒都都姑。

阿喇琉和冒都都姑長大後又成為夫婦，那時，正好遭遇大地洪水氾濫，生活環境非常惡劣，所生的幾個孩子都雙目失明，相繼夭折；最後生下來唯一存活的小女兒名叫凱亞卡德，也是瞎子。

冒都都姑很想再生個小男孩許配給凱亞卡德，可是丈夫年已老邁，不能再生小孩，她很為女兒的未來擔憂。

有一天，天色朦朧，東方出現一道曙光，從天窗照射下來，隨後掉落一粒檳榔，冒都都姑撿起來往嘴裡咀嚼，於是懷孕生了蘇馬拉拉伊。

慶幸的是，凱亞卡德和蘇馬拉拉伊成為夫婦之後，生養了很多健康的子子孫孫，開始繁衍族群。

當大洪水慢慢退去，凱亞卡德和蘇馬拉拉伊夫婦帶著年邁的雙親，向東方順著洪水消退的谷地，走到洪水退盡的一處平原台地定居下來。

 What's more?

陶壺（dilung，低倫）：用陶土製造的壺，象徵一個家族的名分和地位。

蘇馬拉拉伊（Sumalalay）：即「曙光之子」之意。

里都古阿（Lhidukua）：魯凱族大南部落語，意指「平地」；也就是卑南族人稱「把那巴那揚」（Panapanayan），「可種植稻米的土地」，位於現在台東縣太麻里鄉美和村一帶。

由於洪水剛退，台地黏糊糊的，便稱這個地方叫里都古阿。

過了一代又一代，族中人數成長得很快。到了凱亞卡德和蘇馬拉拉伊不知第幾代的子孫阿東蓋亞和娥稜夫婦，生了兩個兄弟——卡里瑪勞和巴沙卡拉尼，兩兄弟都覺得族人這麼多，必須再找其他地方定居。

哥哥卡里瑪勞認為時機成熟，便對弟弟巴沙卡拉尼說：「黏糊糊的地實在不容易生存，為子子孫孫的將來，我們必須另外尋找更寬闊的地方。」

卡里瑪勞又說：「往山上走，應該比較容易尋找食物！」

於是，卡里瑪勞和弟弟巴沙卡拉尼各帶一群族人出發，找尋適合居住的土地。

卡里瑪勞這一支隊伍便到了肯都爾山。

巴沙卡拉尼所帶領的這一群人，則沿著海岸線經過古拉拉烏，起初來到瑪底阿讚，後來因為地勢不理想，又常受外來侵擾，於是又遷移到卡巴哩彎。

在魯凱人心目中，卡巴哩彎就是他們永久的家鄉。

Where did it come from?

本則故事由康英子女士（Labausu・Labuan拉娃烏蘇・達拉巴丹）講述，採集自屏東縣霧台鄉大武村。

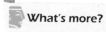

What's more?

肯都爾山（Kingduru）：山名，是魯凱族大南部落的聖山。

古拉拉烏（Kulalau）：指今屏東縣來義鄉古樓村。

瑪底阿讚（Mathiachane）：指今屏東縣霧台鄉佳暮村派出所後面的一座山丘。

卡巴哩彎（Kabalhivane）：永久的家鄉之意，在今天的屏東縣霧台鄉大武村的東北方一處台地。

多情的巴嫩姑娘

> 達露巴淋王國的蛇君王，以笛聲擄獲大頭目瑪巴琉大女兒巴嫩的芳心。不久，蛇隊們帶著琉璃珠、花冠、項鍊、手鐲許多珍貴的聘禮來迎娶，巴嫩的美麗倩影從此便消失在達露巴淋湖面中。
>
> 思親心切的巴嫩，時常讓孩子回來探親，直到今天，魯凱族人看見白鷺鷥在天空盤旋時，不禁想起美麗、多情的巴嫩。

卡巴哩灣部落的大頭目瑪巴琉，家中有三個小孩：老大是女孩，名字叫巴嫩，她還有一個弟弟、一個妹妹。

巴嫩正值適婚年齡，容貌猶如純潔嬌美的百合，吐露著幽幽芳香，令人難忘。尤其，她那柔美而清澈的眼神，宛如神秘的朝陽，見了她，眩目、心

What's more?

巴嫩（Baleng）：女子名。台灣首次以原住民神話與傳說故事為題材，開發出「巴冷公主」遊戲軟體，即取材自本故事，為表現出女主角的柔美，這裡譯音成「巴嫩」。

百合（inavalhua，憶那娃露阿）：百合象徵女性的貞潔；對男性而言，配戴百合表示是個偉大的獵人。

醉以及眷戀的心情霎時湧現，交織著意亂情迷的好感；甚至於遙遠的東魯凱、排灣以及布農，都聽過巴嫩這個美人的名字。

卡巴哩彎部落剛收完小米，豐年佳節的各項祭典和相關生命禮俗的儀式即將展開，這個時候正是男男女女相親的最好時機。因為剛收完小米，釀製小米酒和搗製小米黏糕送禮給女方，是收穫節重要項目之一。

從各地慕名而來的客人，早已使巴嫩的家裡座無虛席了。

夜晚明月當空，正是豐年祭「被滿足之日」的最高潮，部落的年輕人及遠道而來的客人都聚集在巴嫩家，歡樂的歌聲，貫穿整個山谷。巴嫩穿著華麗的盛裝，坐在女孩子們的中央，顯得格外出眾。

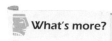 **What's more?**

妹妹（agiagi，阿給阿給）：發音和稱呼弟弟是一樣的；哥哥和姐姐的發音也相同，（kaka，嘎嘎）或（takataka，大嘎大嘎）。

小米（becheng，泊正）：小米為魯凱族的農作物中最重要的一種，除了是主食，黏糕、釀酒之外，許多祭典儀式都少不了它。

小米酒（bava，葩娃）：是以小米為主，紅藜做為發酵粉所釀製而成的酒。

小米黏糕（abaye，阿拜）：小米黏糕形狀如蛋，裡頭包肉。

生命禮俗（lhisi ki niake，里希給尼阿各）：魯凱人一生中從出生到死亡，每一個階段都有一次為生命成長舉行的儀式。如嬰兒的十天祭、童年的背肩袋祭、少年的成年禮，獵人的戴百合祭等等。

豐年祭（kala-lhilhisane，卡拉里里希安）：也叫收穫祭，是收穫小米之後的祭典，如同漢人的過年。

石板（lhenege，勒尼格）：堅固牢靠之意。

笛聲（kulhalhu，咕拉露）：故事中所用的是竹子製成的直笛，音色柔和而哀怨。

這樣深受大家喜愛，讓巴嫩感到非常榮耀。但儘管如此，無論大家如何想盡辦法表達情意，她也不知道為什麼，卻始終都不為其所動。

午夜已過，歌聲依然嘹亮，不覺中，從擋風石板牆的縫隙間吹來陣陣微風，伴著幽遠的笛聲，牽動巴嫩的心思進入奇幻的情境。

奇妙的是，眾人高亢的歌聲竟然壓不住笛聲扣人心弦的傾訴，它猶如一隻孤獨的熊鷹，忽而展翅在蔚藍壯闊的天海，忽而又若隱若現穿梭在浪花與浮雲間，然後漸漸遠去。

巴嫩的心情迷戀的追隨著尾音，一時無法拉回現實。

而這一段不可思議的歷程，旁邊的女孩子們以及眾多客人完全沒有發現。

第二個夜晚，巴嫩的家比前一個晚上更熱鬧，歌聲更宏亮、動人，男男女女的情歌掀起另一波高潮。

月光悄悄的向西方傾斜，熱情的歌聲也逐漸進入慢板的詠嘆：

「愛情雖是喜悅的，奈何人生如朝露。」

悠揚的歌聲中充滿著離情的韻味，莫非這是巴嫩的最後一夜，預示她即將要和親人分開？

這個同時，石縫裡又吹來陣陣微風，動人的笛聲，幾乎奪走了巴嫩的靈魂。

突然，笛聲像熊鷹爬升高空翱翔，然後瞬間俯衝下來、突然而止；陣陣涼風從大門吹進，越來越強烈！眾人驚嚇，紛紛奪門而出，只剩巴嫩的父母以及陪她的女伴。

 What's more?

熊鷹：這裡以熊鷹比喻笛聲悠揚。熊鷹是鷹科鳥類，俗名赫氏角鷹、大花雕，為台灣留鳥中最雄壯的鷹；（aadrisi，阿低希），因其羽毛上有七個斑點，像百步蛇的斑紋，所以魯凱人視熊鷹為百步蛇的化身。

他們發現一條粗大而華麗的蛇緩緩滑行，來到巴嫩的正前方，但巴嫩眼中看到的，卻是一位非常英俊瀟灑且有威儀的男子。還未開口交談，巴嫩就已經愛上了他了。

這名男子向巴嫩表明愛意之後，立即消失無蹤。巴嫩的父母和女伴們，驚慌得說不出話來。

這件事很快在部落傳開，遠道而來的客人再也不敢接近巴嫩了。大家完全不知她所見到的，正是達露巴淋王國的君王卡瑪瑪尼阿尼。

不久之後的某一天，突然閃電雷聲大作，穿過層層烏雲，彷彿狂風暴雨即將到來。奇怪的是，說是狂風，卻不見樹木起舞。隨著沙沙的聲音愈來愈近、愈來愈刺耳，族人們突然看到，原來是蛇族們簇擁著卡瑪瑪尼阿尼前來迎娶巴嫩。

事實上，蒞臨大頭目瑪巴琉家迎親的事情，卡瑪瑪尼阿尼早已託夢給巴嫩的父母親，而巴嫩本人也非常明白並欣然接受。

蛇隊們帶著很多的禮物，包括最貴重的陶壺及珍貴的琉璃珠等，做為對地位崇高的巴嫩的聘禮；還有許多華麗的衣裳、花冠、項鍊、手鐲、耳環，做為獻給巴嫩的禮物。巴嫩的父母見到這麼隆重的安排，女兒又一見傾心，只好無奈的看著他們的愛女嫁給達露巴淋王國的君王。

巴嫩出嫁前的最後一夜，族人來到大頭目瑪巴琉家參加惜別舞會，達露巴淋王國的君王卡瑪瑪尼阿尼威風的端坐在石柱前的寶座，其他大大小小的蛇伴則爬到大榕樹上，數量多到讓高大榕樹的莖葉都垂了下來。

What's more?

蛇（dula都籟）：魯凱族人認為蛇是靈界的魂所呈現的一種方式。

卡瑪瑪尼阿尼（Kamamaniane）：即「那一位」之意。

迎親（ua-malhamalha，瓦馬拉馬拉）：迎接新娘到新郎的家的一種活動。

託夢（kia pasipi，給阿巴希比）：夢是魯凱人與祖先溝通的唯一方式，所以有夢占。

因為巴嫩這一嫁出去，再也不能回來，大家離情依依卻又忐忑不安，跳舞跳到天明，實在捨不得結束。

迎親日的早晨，替巴嫩送行的人多如濃霧，大部分的人只送到部落郊外的山頭，而體力好的便陪著一路隨行到巴嫩的夫家。

當他們到達露巴淋湖時，送行的家屬站在湖邊，巴嫩一一向父母及親友握手話別：「生離死別是永恆的開始，我只是先走一步而已，請不要替我擔心。」

巴嫩輕聲叮嚀族人：「當你們來到山上打獵，一定要記得經過湖邊，我必定為你們準備食物，摸一摸若是溫的，就拿去享用；若是冷的，那是陌生人家煮的，要小心！不可以吃，務必記住。」

最後，巴嫩含淚說：「你們在這個地方目送著我，當你們看到為我遮陽的榕樹枝葉，慢慢從湖面消失時，表示我已經進到夫家了。」

隨後，微風帶著淡淡的薄霧吹向湖面，把巴嫩和送行的人拉開，在緩緩離去的同時，她一面揮手一面說：「代我問候我們的族人以及其他親朋好友！也請你們多珍重！唉依！唉依！」

巴嫩的身影在親友的目送下，緩緩消失在湖中央。

巴嫩離開之後，依然非常想念愛護她的族人，於是選擇在豐年佳節時，派她的兩個孩子到卡巴哩彎，拜訪他們的外公、外婆和族人。

巴嫩在安排兩個孩子前往故鄉之前，預先託夢給她的父母，告知兩個孩子即將來訪。

 What's more?

寢台(delepane，特樂板)：石板屋靠窗戶中央的活動空間，也是接待貴客的地方。

有一天，巴嫩的父母剛從田裡回來，發現兩條卡瑪瑪尼阿尼的小孩宿於靠窗的寢台，兩位老人家非常尊敬的以美酒和鮮肉來供奉。那天晚上，兩兄弟託夢給他們的外公外婆說：「是母親派我們來看你們的，謝謝外公、外婆對我們的禮遇。」

第二天醒來，兩兄弟已經不見了。

巴嫩的後裔代代都是如此探望親人。

有一天，一個不認識這個家族的媳婦，抱著嬰孩想放進搖籃，突然發現卡瑪瑪尼阿尼的小孩在搖籃裡，驚慌中將搖籃給踢翻了，卡瑪瑪尼阿尼的小孩毫無尊嚴的掉落地上而消失。

巴嫩聽到這個消息非常難過，託夢給族人說：「我再也不派我的後代來拜訪你們了，因為你們已慢慢不認識我了。」

又說：「往後，當你們看到白鷺鷥飛翔在部落的上空時，就表示我對你們的無限懷念。」

有關巴嫩託夢的事被族人知道了，於是大家在豐年祭的時候特別舉行祭拜儀式，希望得到寬恕，並盼望在祭典期間，巴嫩能夠再度顯現。但，一切似乎都太遲了。

豐年祭的最後一天，夕陽西下時，只見一隻白鷺鷥孤零零的在卡巴哩彎的上空飛翔盤旋。族人看了之後，也感嘆的說：

「巴嫩，我們的祖母啊！我們也非常懷念您啊！」

Where did it come from?

本則故事由康英子女士（Labausu・Labuan拉娃烏蘇・達拉巴丹）講述，採集自屏東縣霧台鄉大武村。

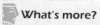

What's more?

白鷺鷥（daladalathe，達拉達拉特）：象徵思親的意義。

部落百寶盒 │ │ 傳授哈「原」秘笈，搖身變成魯凱通

一、穿越洪水開闢新家園

遠古時期，在大洪水侵襲之前，在大鬼湖（也就是達露巴淋湖）附近，一處稱作「卡里阿罕」（意思是「生命第一道曙光」）的地方，誕生了一對魯凱族的始祖。那個地方高山峻嶺，環境險惡，生存不容易，但是魯凱人自己發明了在高山上生存的方法、溝通情感的語言，以及共同生活的倫理道德，稱自己為「高山民族」或「住在山地的人」。

魯凱人分為三大族群，分布在不同的地方，以下將個別特色做簡要說明：

▶ 魯凱族的分布範圍

東魯凱族群 （台東縣卑南鄉）	這一群受到卑南族的影響很深，使得原來的特色已漸模糊，但是傳統的達魯瑪克語則保留得很好。 ・大南部落（Tarumake 達魯瑪克） ・太平部落（Tamalakao 達馬拉告）
西魯凱族群 （屏東縣霧台鄉、三地門鄉青葉村）	1. 古茶布安系：這一群自稱雲豹民族的子民，曾經和矮人一起過生活，後來矮人神秘失蹤。其特色是石板文化的精神還保存完整，木雕、刺繡、音樂、舞蹈等等也都十分出眾。 ・好茶部落（Kochapongane 古茶布安），位於霧台鄉好茶村。 ・阿禮部落（Adiri 阿低禮），位於霧台鄉阿禮村。 ・上霧台部落（Kavedathane 卡發地森），包括佳暮（Karame-desang 卡拉馬地撒），位於霧台鄉佳暮村。 ・下霧台部落（Kabalelhathane 卡玻利喝甚），包括卡烏達丹（Kavathanane）、古的魯莪魯（Kudrengere），位於霧台鄉霧台村。 ・達都古魯部落（Tatukulu），位於三地門鄉德文村。 2. 去露（Kinulane 給怒朗）：自稱是不屬任何系統，位於霧台鄉吉露村。 3. 大武（Tailabuane）和達德樂（Dadele）：自認為是東魯凱族的達魯瑪克系，又自稱是百步蛇的民族，因為山中美人巴嫩是從這裡嫁給達露巴淋的百步蛇。其中，大武部落位於霧台鄉大武村；但是，達拉瑪告和達德樂在日本時代被合併，並且遷移到現在屏東縣三地門鄉的青葉村。
高雄下三社族群 （高雄市茂林區）	他們自稱是從岩石誕生的；雖然分布區域分散，語言也顯然和其他族群不同，但他們還是保有魯凱族的社會制度、道德觀念及文化習俗。 ・茂林部落（Taruladrekane 達魯拉樂幹）。 ・多納部落（Kingdavang 京大彎）。 ・萬山部落（Oponohu 歐布諾伙）。

※ 魯凱族主要分佈圖，請見封面裏頁。

二、階級制度和百合花冠

魯凱族社會以部落為自治單位，每個部落各有屬於自己的土地領域和頭目等領導者。魯凱族的階級分明，主要分為貴族與平民兩個階級，並從貴族中再推選出頭目。部落裡每隔一段時間，會從全部落族人中推選出最有智慧或是最勇敢的人做為首領，這是因為貴族世襲制的關係，推舉出來的頭目不見得都有能力，所以必須再選出一個首領帶領族人。

▶ 世襲的貴族

頭目的主要責任是維持部落秩序及團結，並擁有許多特殊權利，例如掌管土地、獵區與河域。所以，平民必須將農、漁、獵所得的部分納貢給頭目，不過頭目也會將部分的納貢品送給需要的平民，或是在祭典中和族人一同分享。

世襲制的貴族階級，通常由長子繼承；如果家中沒有男丁，則可由長女繼承地位與財產。雖然女子也可以繼承頭目的地位和頭銜，但是能夠在社群間行使政治權的仍是男性，通常會由女繼承者的丈夫代替。貴族的階級也會因為婚姻關係而提升或下降，男性會希望以婚姻來提升自己的家世、地位，但是這通常必須以高價值的聘禮換得。

魯凱族的階級制度讓社會有秩序、人人各盡本分，但是族人謹守應盡的義務之外，更極力取得佩帶百合花的資格，因為象徵堅貞、純潔的百合花代表著榮譽，男子佩帶表示他身手矯健、狩獵技巧高，女子佩帶則表示有婦德及高尚的操守。

▶ 真正的英雄

魯凱族男子必須獵獲六隻大山豬，在大頭目和長老們的核定之後，經由佩帶百合花許可儀式，才可以佩帶一朵百合花。獵獲幾十隻獵物者，可佩帶一朵百合及一朵未開的花蕊和葉片。對魯凱族男人來說，公開佩帶百合花，不只表示他的勇氣，更代表他願意與族人分享，是真正的獵人，也就是英雄。

當女子通過象徵成年禮的買百合花儀式（魯凱語稱作給阿里芳kia-lidrao）之後，並且賢慧、清白、擁有好手藝又會處理家務，才具有資格佩帶百合花。另外，魯凱女子有了佩帶資格，卻在貞潔操守上犯了過錯，需自行取下花冠；若依然在公共場合戴著花冠，大頭目以及佩帶百合花的族人，可以將她的花冠取下，以示懲罰。

三、歡樂的擺盪鞦韆

魯凱族傳統製作的鞦韆，是用一種野蔓藤的莖，捆成像胳臂那麼粗，底部編成環形，以便套上雙腳中任何慣用的一隻腳，就這麼直接吊在樹上，中間繫著一條蔓藤方便左右拉擺，魯凱語稱做「達拉依西」（talaisi）。

另外一種鞦韆是用四根粗壯的長竹或木材作為支架，把四根支架的頂端捆綁在一起，並留下環節，再套一條粗蔓藤以便於擺盪，這種鞦韆比起吊在樹上的還要高，擺盪的距離也會比較遠。

這是魯凱人從大自然中學到的一種習俗，包括育嬰所用的搖籃也是一樣。嬰孩在搖籃中擺盪，除了感覺輕盈舒服之外，也像是在母親的臂膀中搖晃。

▶ 牽起佳偶良緣

盪鞦韆是貴族女子的權利，男性是不可以盪鞦韆的。過去只有貴族大頭目的女兒結婚的時候，才有盪鞦韆的儀式。要嫁人的那一天，部落所有的人會來到寬廣的大廣場，圍起大圓圈跳舞，中央架設鞦韆，女子們輪流盪鞦韆，由男人拉繩子擺盪。對要娶她的人來說，其重要的意義就是：「因為愛妳，所以永遠擺盪妳。」

魯凱族人的豐年祭中，盪鞦韆活動是祭典的高潮，這時大頭目會將所擁有的盪鞦韆特權，分享給全族人參與，以安慰並鼓勵族人一年來的辛勞。另外一個目的，是讓青年男女能夠藉著盪鞦韆活動的湊合，牽起另一段佳偶良緣。

▶ 女子的專利

不過，在豐年祭中這個饒富趣味的盪鞦韆活動，只有女子才可以盪鞦韆 —— 魯凱族人認為從女子盪鞦韆的姿勢和儀態，可顯示她的氣質、素養和婦德，同時也可以看出這位女性的未來是否順利平安；而魯凱男性則負責搭設鞦韆及拉動繩子擺盪鞦韆，若有男子盪了鞦韆，會被認為缺乏男子氣概！

除了在婚禮及豐年祭等既定的場合和時節之外，嚴禁盪鞦韆，否則會招來災害和不幸，所以不要以遊樂的心態輕慢魯凱族人的盪鞦韆活動。

四、傳統石板屋

魯凱族的傳統建築是石板屋，以前的結構比較簡單，大小是以主人的身體為標準，寬度大約是雙手伸開的兩倍半，長度又比寬度大一些，屋簷很矮。牆壁以石片砌成，橫樑由木材架成，屋頂是樹皮、蘆葦，地面則鋪了石板。

後來建築形式有了改進，屋頂為一半石板、一半蘆葦。最後才逐漸演進到石板屋頂，簷桁與中心柱也加上雕飾。石板屋的耐久性高，而且冬暖夏涼，不容易被強風吹垮，也是良好的防禦基地。

一般石板屋的空間，從前面窗戶到後面共分三個格局：

‧前面靠窗的台面：這裡通常比中間的活動空間高出約5寸，並設有寢台，寢台又比台面高約5寸。這個地方因為空氣良好，光線充足，是女性刺繡編織的地方，也是照顧嬰兒的場所。如果家中有待嫁姑娘，這台面也是傳情歌唱、談情說愛的地方。此外，此處床位地底下約1.5公尺處，是埋葬女性的地方。

．中央活動空間：這裡是民生事務忙碌的地方，包括家族協商議事，也是祭拜祖靈的場所，因為祖靈柱正好位在最後方的神聖空間和中央活動空間之間。另外，這裡的地底下也是埋葬男性死者的場所。

．最後方的神聖空間：這個地方設有米倉，也藏放貴重物品和祭拜道具。祖靈柱是人頭蛇形，頂著屋脊橫樑，所有祭儀都以這柱子為重心。而所有的武器也都繫在柱子上，任何人趁黑夜來犯，屋主摸黑都可以取得武器來防衛。

如果是頭目住屋，屋外的前庭廣場會樹立石柱，這是頭目權威象徵，也是全部落開會地點。家屋外的大榕樹，可供夏日遮蔭休憩，也是盪鞦韆的地方。

對這一群石板文化的子民而言，石板屋除了可以遮陽避雨，也是愛情的溫床、生命永續的暖房，同時更是代代活人、死人的永久居所；所以，魯凱人稱「家」為「巴里屋」（balhio），意思是「永遠的居所、永恆的歸宿」。

▶ **石板屋內部示意圖**

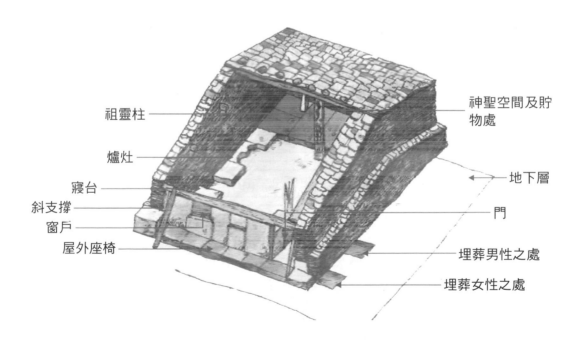

(資料提供：王應棠先生／繪圖：劉素珍)

五、魯凱族的傳統祭典

魯凱族人從台灣東部遷移到西部，穿越中央山脈南系開闢家園，目前主要居住的三個地點，除保留了共同的魯凱族傳統與認知，也分別發展出各具特色的文化。參與祭典活動，就是我們認識魯凱文化最好的途徑之一。在此分別以三個魯凱族地區的重大祭典為例，讓大家更了解魯凱文化的精神與內涵。

東魯凱族的買沙呼魯祭，主要在大南部落（台東縣卑南鄉東興村）舉行，因為是在除草季節舉行，所以又名除草祭。雖然除草祭是台灣各原住民族都有的祭典，但是因族群的習慣、傳統不同，活動的形式也有不同。小米收穫祭又稱為豐年祭，慶祝一年的豐收，並祈求來年依舊順利平安；小米收穫祭也是一年的分界點，提醒著生命的週而復始。黑米祭的背後有著一則溫暖的傳說，是下三社部落(位於高雄市茂林區)一項特別的傳統。這些祭典都有著豐富的意義和象徵，請懷著尊重和愉悅的心，親身參與體會。

▶ 買沙呼魯祭

東魯凱大南部落的買沙呼魯祭（maisauru）是生命禮儀的一種，魯凱族少女在13歲到結婚之前，都必須參加買沙呼魯祭，以表示開始進入社會，並學習魯凱族的傳統美德。過去在小米收成前的最後一次除草工作時，魯凱族較年長的女性們會開始傳播消息，提醒少女們加入買沙呼魯的行列，為小米進行最後一次的除草工作，以迎接收穫時節到來。這時候，少女們紛紛主動加入，以互助、輪流的方式，共同完成除草的工作。因此，買沙呼魯祭又被稱為除草祭。

祭典一開始，由部落巫師祈求祖靈保佑儀式能夠平安進行，並且希望今年能夠豐收。參加買沙呼魯祭的少女們，在工作中除了飲水之外，不可以吃中餐或其他食物；午間休息過後，族人會檢查其唾液，確定沒有偷偷進食，否則便會受到處罰。在除草工作過程中，通常會和著童謠或情歌，在歌聲中將耕地內的工作完成。此時，少男們會派出數名勇士，以搖晃臀鈴的方式，迎接少女工作成員回到部落。到了晚間，便是跳舞高歌的歡樂時刻了，少男少女們會藉此機會互訴情意，待買沙呼魯祭結束，也就是少男少女們追求異性的開始了。

▶ 小米收穫祭

小米收穫祭魯凱語稱為卡拉里里希安（kala-lhilhisane），是魯凱族最重要的祭典，這是為了感謝農作物豐收、祈求平安而舉辦的慶祝活動，舉辦的時間約在每年8月左右。

祭典開始，由主祭者吟誦祈禱文，感謝上天與祖先護佑，讓族人能夠豐收，同時也希望來年依舊平安、富裕。在祭儀進行中，不可以大聲喧嘩、打噴嚏、放屁、隨便與人打招呼等等，必須保持嚴肅。對於魯凱族人來說，小米收穫祭是一年一度的重要祭祀活動，相當於漢人習俗的「過年」，其所祭祀的對象，除了祖先之外，也包含創世的神祇、自然界神祇、各地守護神、惡靈等。在嚴肅的祭祀、祈求過程之後，會有一些娛樂、競賽與生命禮儀的活動，例如盪鞦韆比賽、勇士舞、射箭比賽、背物競走等，這時候通常也是收穫祭的高潮。

不同地區或許會有些許不同的活動內容，然而收穫祭的重要性都是一樣的，即使時代變遷、人口外移，但到了小米收穫祭，離家出外的魯凱子弟們就會由各地返家，在族人的環繞下，進行一次次傳統的洗禮與保護。因此，不管參與何處的收穫祭，都不要以觀光的心態看待，若是願意實際參與，並且感受雲豹子民對天地的敬意與感謝、對維護傳統與生存的深厚意義，或許你也更懂得如何與自然相處，與多元的文化環境誠敬相待。

▶ 搭巴嘎饒望黑米祭

一般人知道的「黑米祭」，是「搭巴嘎饒望」祭典活動之一。這是高雄縣茂林鄉多納村的西魯凱人每年固定舉行的祭典，時間在每年的小米收穫祭之後。

關於黑米祭的由來，有一則古老且感人的傳奇故事。古時候，魯凱族婦女為了到田裡種植黑米，必須將孩子放在田邊。孩子會因孤單而哭泣，母親們只要聽得到孩子的哭聲，就知道孩子還在，便可以放心工作。然而有一次，有一位婦女在接近中午的時候，突然聽不到孩子的哭聲了，她趕忙跑到田邊去找，卻發現孩子已經不見了，只剩下一個石頭。在四處奔忙卻無法尋獲之下，她只好回到部落中，請求族人幫忙尋找，但是也沒有結果，族人以為完全沒有希望了。當晚，這位失去孩子的母親卻做了一個夢，她夢見濁口溪的水神告訴她，因為水神不忍心看母親必須一邊耕種，還要一邊照顧孩子，於是將孩子帶走，等他長大後再送回。但是族人必須和水神合力種植更多的黑米，其中一半要用來祭祀水神。

這位母親將夢境告訴族人，族人雖半信半疑，卻還是幫忙種下更多的黑米。收成的時候到了，待全部的黑米曝曬完之後，大家才發現有些黑米竟然不見了！之後，每年的情形都一樣。許多年過去了，那個被水神收養的孩子真的回來了，並且成為英俊的勇士，回到母親與族人身邊，一起為族人的生活而努力。

從那個時候起，族人會在黑米收成的時候祭拜水神，感謝水神幫忙照顧孩子。演變至今，黑米祭同時也被賦予感謝祖先、神靈保佑的意義。遠古的傳說，也就一直護佑族人至今。

買沙呼魯祭	3 月	台東縣卑南鄉東興村	卑南鄉公所 電話：089-381368
小米收穫祭	8 月	台東縣卑南鄉東興村、高雄市茂林區、屏東縣霧台鄉	卑南鄉公所 電話：089-381368 茂林區公所民政課 電話：07-6801045 轉 32 霧台鄉公所 電話：08-7902234
搭巴嘎饒望黑米祭	11～12 月	高雄市茂林區多納村	茂林區公所民政課 電話：07-6801045 轉 32 茂林風景區管理所 電話：07-6801441

六、孤巴察峨的傳說

在高雄茂林境內的「萬山岩雕」有三處遺址，是台灣原住民少見的巨大岩雕，其中以「孤巴察峨」（gubatsaeh，語意是「有雕刻的大岩石」）的岩雕圖案最壯觀，雕有幾十個各種渦旋紋、同心圓、百步蛇、人頭像、雲鉤紋等等。關於這些神奇的圖案，魯凱族人流傳著一段淒美的傳說。

相傳萬山舊部落（高雄市茂林區萬頭蘭山一帶），歐布諾伙（Oponohu）頭目家族長男娶了一個妻子，她是布農族雁爾社的女子，名字叫做荷絲（有一種說法認為荷絲是卡那卡那富族人），夫妻非常恩愛。荷絲平日負責燒飯挑水，卻從不和家人一進吃飯；而荷絲所煮的飯菜，家人吃來卻總有一股怪味道，家人也因此漸漸消瘦。這使得荷絲的公公感到懷疑，於是找一天故意不到田裡工作，留下來偷看荷絲做飯。

▶ 招來百步蛇

原來荷絲在煮地瓜和芋頭時，竟然吹口哨招來百步蛇，將百步蛇放到灶裡一起烤。對於魯凱族人來說，百步蛇是祖靈的象徵，侵犯不得。荷絲的公公發現了自己的媳婦竟然做出這種事，立刻將這嚴重的情形告訴家人，並且責備荷絲。荷絲知道自己做錯了事，向大家道歉，然後撿起百步蛇，離開了家人。

荷絲一邊走著，一邊吃著蛇肉。她將蛇骨吐在地上，而掉在地上的蛇骨，竟然變成活生生的蛇。她邊走邊想著疼愛她的丈夫一定會來帶她回家的，走到平日經常與丈夫相會的「莎那奇瑙」（sanaginaeh）大石頭等候，一邊唱歌，一邊用手在石頭上畫畫。她的手指一碰到石頭，石頭就變軟了。

等不到丈夫的荷絲，繼續走到「孤巴察峨」大石頭，在一處平坦的地方，又用手指畫了許多圖案。但石頭都畫滿了，心愛的丈夫還是沒來。

▶ 大石上的人影

她繼續走過溪流，到了「周布里力」（tsubulili）大石頭，還是一邊吃著蛇肉，一邊吐著蛇骨，地上出現越來越多的百步蛇，可是仍舊等不到丈夫。傷心的荷絲絕望的靠在岩石上痛哭，「周布里力」的那塊大石上便印下了她的輪廓。

荷絲就這麼一路走回雁爾社，她的族人認為這是莫大的恥辱，於是萬山社的魯凱族人與雁爾社的布農族人因此結下仇恨，廝殺不斷。至於荷絲經過的路，也成為百步蛇最多的地方。

參考書目：

《山海文化雙月刊：萬山岩雕專輯》（山海文化雜誌社，1996）。《歐布諾伙與孤巴察峨的研究》（高雄縣立文化中心，1996）。《高雄縣六大族群傳統歌謠叢書》（高雄縣立文化中心，1999）。《萬山岩雕—台灣首次發現摩崖藝術之研究》（屏東師院）。

造訪部落　**部落藏寶圖，來挖魯凱寶**

看過了美麗的慕阿凱凱與多情的巴嫩姑娘，你是否也嚮往雲豹的子民徜徉在山林間的那分自在？想不想隨著慕阿凱凱的鞦韆擺盪，深入魯凱傳說的神秘境地呢？

魯凱族人的活動範圍，大約在海拔700公尺到2400公尺之間，目前人口數約一萬人。魯凱族分為東魯凱群和西魯凱群，以及高雄市下三社。東魯凱族人多聚居在台東縣卑南鄉大南部落（東興村）；西魯凱族人多聚居在南北隘寮溪沿岸，也就是屏東縣霧台鄉及三地門鄉青葉社區；高雄市下三社則在高雄市茂林區的萬山、多納、茂林三個部落。高雄下三社除了語言上和其他二族群有所不同之外，在社會制度、文化習俗、道德觀念等方面都有一致性。

現在，透過這分精心編製的「魯凱族部落文化導覽圖」，陪伴身歷其境，盡情挖掘部落文化寶藏，保證不虛此行。

當然，造訪部落時更不能錯過魯凱族豐富的祭儀活動，像是每年三月在台東縣卑南鄉東興村舉行的買沙呼魯祭（除草祭）；八月分在屏東縣霧台鄉、高雄市茂林區等地都會舉行的小米收穫祭；以及高雄市茂林區多納部落在十一月、十二月間舉行的搭巴嘎饒望祭（黑米祭）。

心動想要行動之前，最好先確定時間及地點，詳情請洽：
・台東縣卑南鄉公所　電話：089-381368
・屏東縣霧台鄉公所　電話：08-7902234
・高雄市茂林區公所　電話：07-6801045轉32
・茂林風景管理處　　電話：07-6801441

魯凱族
文化導覽圖

族語開口說　**入境隨俗的魯凱語**

您好嗎？
Mua dringadringai su？
很　好嗎　　　您？

是！我很好。
Unu！mua dringadringath aku.
是　很　好　　我

您是誰？
Sia aneane su.
是　誰　　您？

我叫奧威尼。
Sia auvinnie aku.
是　奧威尼　我。

您住哪裡？
Sua ainu su.
住　哪裡　您？

我住古茶布安
Sua kochapongan aku.
住　古茶布安　　我。

這是什麼？
Manemane kikai.
什麼　　　這個？

這是狗。
Kikai taupung.
這個　狗。

您們的午餐是什麼？
Manemane ku kudrali numi？
什麼　　　是　午餐　您們的？

我們的午餐是地瓜。
Lhi tu　kudrali　nai　　ku vorasi.
(前置詞)午餐　我們(的)　是　地瓜。

你們什麼時候舉行豐年祭？
Lhi tulhisisi　　numi luigane？
(前置詞)豐年祭 你們 什麼時候？

我們在收完小米的時候舉行豐年祭？
Lhi tulhisisi　　nai　lu maka kibecheng.
(前置詞)豐年祭 我們 收完　　小米。

您們要去哪裡？
Lhi　　muinu numi？
(前置詞)哪裡　您們？

我們要去烤餅祭。
Lhi ka　tuase nai　chapi.
(前置詞)去　　我們 烤餅祭。

我很喜歡您們的部落。
Ma dalam aku ki　　chekele numi.
很　喜歡　我(前置詞)部落　　您們(的)。

感謝您來。
Maelane-nge la kela su.
感謝　　　　能 到來 您。

很高興見到你。
Matia ki ragai la drel-aku musuane.
很　　　高興 能 見到　　你。

希望下次再相見。
Ta madresengenga ki bibilhili.
希望 相見　　　再 下次。

我要走了。
Nau ka tuasenga.
(我) 就要走了。

一路順風。
Lhi ka　　la hualhuai　su.
(前置詞) 能 平安順利　您。

族語開口說　魯凱族稱謂的介紹

umu	阿公	agili	弟弟
kaingu	阿媽	ama	爸爸
ina	媽媽	la-ama	伯、叔、舅舅
la-ina	阿姨和姑姑	kaka	kaka
kaka	哥哥	agili	agili

學習加油站　**本書漢語與魯凱語名詞對照表**

故事01：美麗的慕阿凱凱

用漢字拼讀	魯凱語	漢語名詞
塔瑪	tama	父親
依娜	ina	母親
池歌樂	chekele	部落
拉拉格	lalake	兒子
馬塔塔哦樂哦樂	matataelhelhe	夫妻
達爾拉柏	daralape	榕樹
沙烏瓦拉伊	sauvalai	男孩
阿芭芭伊	ababai	女孩
達魯勞烏朗	tarudraudrang	老人
阿嘎呢	agane	孫子
拉白白姨	la-baibaie	妻子
瑪喳	macha	眼睛
樂屎	lhese	眼淚
阿拉伊	ngalhai	檳榔汁
阿里馬	alhima	手
大跋勒	drapale	腳
查里繫	chalhisi	繩子
瑪路朗	marudrange	長老
莎意拉那呢	sangi-ragelanane	首飾
莎嘎池歌樂	saka-chekele	族人
卡巴里瓦呢	ka-balhivane	故鄉
給娜達拉瑪呢	kinadalaman	愛人
瓦意牙呢	kaviyiane	日
馬翁	maunge	夜
米阿樂阿樂	mialhealhe	早上
樂拉給瓦伊	ledrea ki vaie	陽光
烏古陸	ukudru	拐杖

故事02：雲豹的頭蝨家族

用漢字拼讀	魯凱語	漢語名詞
德樂泊	delebe	洪水
拉馬阿大卡	lama-ataka	兄弟
大嘎大嘎	takataka	哥哥、姊姊
阿給阿給	agiagi	弟弟、妹妹
拉都阿哥哥呢	la-tuagagane	子孫
馬依里路固	ma-ililuku	首領、頭目
淘蹦	taupung	獵犬
達部阿里卡阿啦灣	Tabuali-kadravane	太麻里溪
都立比	dulipi	夕陽
達阿伯稜安給樂喀樂喀	tabelengane ki lhegelhege	高山
達爾拉泊	daralape	榕樹
拉大呢	dratane	台地
喀大灣	kadravane	山川
底哦那哦那	tienaenale	叢林
樂瓦路	valhu	溪谷
拉歌喇樂	drakerale	水源
達巴朗阿呢	tabalangane	鞍部
卡樂歌樂客呢	ka-lhegelhegane	山頂
漏露	luru	尿液
奧盧給烏馬烏馬斯	aulhu ki umaumase	人頭
道吐	tauthu	尾巴
阿客隻	akeche	山羌
傻牢安	salungane	山鹿
打爾阿鹿捕	tara-alupu	獵人
阿兒阿伊	eraii	鮮血
阿大伊	athaii	肝臟
阿娃娃	avava	心臟
馬卡卡查奇布路卡卡拉灣	Maka-kachachipulu ka kadravane	知本溪

用漢字拼讀	魯凱語	漢語名詞
伯莪萊	bengelhai	花冠
藍伊幾給里古洛	lhangichi ki lhikolao	雲豹皮
瓦里希給里古洛	valisi ki lhikolao	雲豹牙

故事03：卡巴哩彎

用漢字拼讀	魯凱語	漢語名詞
達巴塔給朗伊拉特哥	tapathagilane ngiratheke	始祖
裡必	libii	洞穴
瓦伊	vaye	太陽
巴度古	batuku	蛋
麻目給棄	ma-mukichi	瞎子
達拉烏安	talhauane	東方

故事04：多情的巴嫩姑娘

用漢字拼讀	魯凱語	漢語名詞
伊阿娥莎丹卡阿菡菡依	ngiaesathane ka ababaiu	美人
達都里希里希安	tatulhislhisane	祭典
達拉馬呢	dalamane	愛情
拉慕	lamu	朝露
阿巴格	abake	靈魂
哦默哦默	ememe	雲
里喀茲	lhikache	閃電
瓦里給	valhigi	颱風
馬樂得樂卡拉都籟	maredele kala dulai	蛇隊(蛇群)
莎伊拉客拉南	sangi ragelanane	華麗的衣裳
卡拉特	kalathe	手鐲
里丁	lhiding	耳環
阿持博	achebe	禮物
達給馬拉尼卡哇伊	taki malhane ka vaye	迎親日
達尼給夏希拉安	daane ki siailangane	夫家
麻初露	machulu	溫的

用漢字拼讀	魯凱語	漢語名詞
麻德司	matetese	冷的
都姆吾低那	tumu ngo tina	外公
該娥吾低那	kaingu ngo tina	外婆
馬答里里卡葩娃	mathariri ka bava	美酒
莫阿里埃卡布都陸	muadringai ka butulu	鮮肉
給樂哦卡阿巴派	kiare ka ababai	媳婦
胎尼	dainie	嬰孩
紐古	niuku	搖籃
巴阿慈泊	pa achepe	寬恕
蓋烏	kaingu	祖母

部落百寶盒：階級制度和百合花

用漢字拼讀	魯凱語	漢語名詞
給阿里芳	kia-lidrao	買百合花儀式

部落百寶盒：傳統石板屋

用漢字拼讀	魯凱語	漢語名詞
巴里屋	balhio	家

部落百寶盒：魯凱族的傳統祭典

用漢字拼讀	魯凱語	漢語名詞
買沙呼魯	maisauru	除草祭
搭巴嘎饒望	tapakarhauan	黑米祭

部落百寶盒：孤巴察峨的傳說

用漢字拼讀	魯凱語	漢語名詞
孤巴察峨	gubatsaeh	有雕刻的大岩石
歐布諾伙	Oponohu	頭目家族名
莎那奇瑙	sanaginaeh	大石頭名
周布里力	tsubulili	大石頭名

排灣族
Paiwan

▶小筆記▶

・住在石板屋，屋前都會種植檳榔樹。
・蔡英文總統的祖母是屏東獅子鄉的排灣族。
・採行頭目制，依階級而分工。

．撒古隆・巴瓦瓦隆、撒伐楚古・斯羔烙、撒可努、烏瑪斯等都是著名的藝術 家、 文 學家。

．為什麼辦喜事要溫鞦韆？

．善死者蹲坐埋在家屋正廳，面向大武山。

故事導讀　檳榔、陶壺與百步蛇

檳榔在排灣族和若干台灣原住民族群（例如魯凱族、卑南族、阿美族和南部平埔各族等）當中，是非常神聖的。這不只可以做為日常社交場合交換的禮物，也是結婚聘禮中不可或缺的項目。尤其更重要的是：檳榔更是巫術行為中的法器，陣勢的排列，有賴一顆顆檳榔做為攻防的象徵。如今檳榔文化在台灣的惡質發展，大概是原住民祖先始料未及的吧！

在早期的原住民經驗中，部落或庭園周邊種植高高的檳榔樹，通風又遮蔭；月上樹梢，更添萬種風情。結實纍纍的檳榔，除了一部分取用外，我們寧願讓它們在樹上長大、變老、變黃、變紅，然後散落一地，又長出一株株樹苗。那個過程往往令人感動……

巴里紅眼睛的故事，讓我們對變老、變紅的檳榔，有了更豐富的想像。保浪樸素的童心，既溫厚又窩心，閃爍著友誼的光輝。相對於一般人的粗心、冷漠、自私、現實和猜忌，也只有像保浪那樣單純的心靈，才能真正了解巴里的寂寞，並慷慨地給出自己的友誼。巴里雖然具有天上賜予的稟賦，但他卻是孤獨、敏感且又自抑的，他多麼希望和一般人一樣走出戶外，和小孩子一同嬉戲。童心是真正友誼的基礎。忘情地與巴里玩在一起的，都是小孩子；工於算計的大人，只想到利害，只懂得歸罪；他們的友誼是論斤論兩的。

悲劇終於還是無法避免，敵人砍下了巴里的頭顱。有趣的是，巴里並沒有因此怪罪族人。就在埋葬巴里的地方，長出了檳榔樹，樹上結出紅色大粒的檳榔，猶如巴里厲害的眼睛。紅眼巴里繼續守護、看顧著部落和族人。

正如大家所知道的，排灣族是一個有貴族階級的社會。但貴族卻不是高高在上的統治階級，他必須有功於社會，並且有責任照顧他的子民。人類的貪婪，破壞了人與天神的約定，招來了災難。幸有老人巴勒法法吾、紅嘴鳥、百步蛇和從陶壺所生的人的幫助，才使排灣族人免於滅絕。這些有功於族人的存在，便成了貴族的神聖系譜，代替天神掌理人間的秩序，看顧芸芸眾生。

而盪鞦韆的愛情故事，也顯示貴族與平民間的界線並不完全是無法挑戰的，忠貞的愛情，勇往直前的勇氣，依然是感動天神的偉大力量！

Reader's Guide　Betel Nuts, Clay Vessels and Vurung

Betel nut is sacred among the Paiwan. Some Taiwan indigenous peoples (for example Rukai, Puyuma, Amis, and Southern Pingpu ethnic groups). Not only is it as a gift casually exchanged in daily social intercourse, it is an indispensable item of the wedding dowry. More importantly, the betel nut is a magic weapon used in witchcraft, and in devising the strategies of warfare, the betel nut is used to divine both offense and defense. The negative aspects of betel nut culture that developed in Taiwan must be quite unexpected by the ancestors of our indigenous peoples!

For indigenous peoples, the tall betel palm trees planted around their settlements or in their gardens, bringt ventilation and shade, and the moon peeking through the betel palm treetops is but one of a thousand scene to which the trees contribute. In addition to a portion of the betel nuts that we use, we prefer to see the fruit grow up on the tree, grow old, turn yellow and red, and then scatter to the ground where it begins to sprout, and the process begins anew, and again, and again..

The story of "Pali's Red Eyes" gives us an even richer picture of the palm betel nuts as they age and redden. Baleng, who befriends Pali, has a simple childlike innocence that is both tender and heartwarming, shining with the brilliance of friendship. Unlike the ordinary person's indifference, selfishness, faux-realism and suspicion, only a person with a pure heart such as Baleng was able to truly understand Pali's loneliness and generously offer his friendship. Although Pali has the heavenly gift of the red eyes, he is lonely, fragile and reproaches himself. How he hopes to go out and play with others as an ordinary child. A child's heart the foundation of true friendship. Those who interact with Pali in a carefree manner are all children; the shrewd adult only thinks in terms of their interests and who they can blame when something goes awry: for those people friendship is a matter of what they think are practical considerations and calculations.

Tragedy was inevitable and his enemies cut off Pali's head. Interestingly, Pali did not blame his people for this, rather at the place where he was buried, Pali grew into a palm betel tree, with enormous red betel nuts - Pali's powerful eyes. Red-eyed Pali continued to guard and take care of his village and its people.

Paiwan is known as a society with an aristocratic class. But these nobles do not constitute a superior class of rulers, they must make a contribution to society and are responsible for taking care of the people. The avarice of humans has broken the covenants with the gods and brought forth disaster. Fortunately, we can thank for their assistance to the Paiwan the elder Paljevavaw and his wise counsel, the black bulbul retrieving the fire, the vurung, and the man who emerges from a clay djilung, all of whom contributed to the survival of the Paiwan. So we can say that the nobility of the Paiwan came to mitigate the disasters that people brought upon themselves after losing the order due to their estrangement from the heavens and nature.

This section on the Paiwan ends with "The Tests of Love", a love story that includes the Paiwan's swing, but also shows that the boundaries between the nobility and the common people can be challenged. And the gods can be moved to initiate their great powers when they see the power of abiding love and the courage to forge ahead.

01

巴里的紅眼睛

巴里在紅眼睛貼上竹子薄膜,族人就不用怕巴里,又可以在需要時利用他厲害的紅眼睛殺死敵人;但是,土蜂取走了巴里眼睛上的薄膜,害死了許多小孩。

灰心喪志的巴里,最後被敵人用計殺害,埋葬他的地方長出檳榔樹、結出紅檳榔。日後,排灣族人看到紅檳榔,深信那是巴里的紅眼睛在守護著族人。

傳說中，排灣族古時候有個叫巴里的人，他的眼睛非常厲害，只要被他雙紅的眼睛看到，任何動物和植物都會馬上死去。

就因為巴里有著一雙紅眼睛的關係，他只好待在昏暗的屋子裡生活，並且總是低著頭或背對著人說話。

不過，巴里的紅眼睛也常成為抵禦外敵入侵的利器，鄰近部落聽到有巴里這麼一號人物，只好遠遠的繞過他的部落，不敢接近；當有人喊著：「巴里來了！」每個人都會快速的跑開。

有一次，巴里聽到屋外孩子們的嬉戲聲，很想走出去和他們一起玩，可是又怕他的出現和紅眼睛，會把孩子們嚇跑或傷到無辜的人。於是，巴里便解下腰帶矇住眼睛，這樣一來就能走出屋外，傷不到別人了。

矇住雙眼的巴里，看不見屋外的情形，一個人獨坐在屋簷下，用耳朵聽著孩子們的嬉笑聲。巴里可以感覺到孩子們玩得很開心，自己好像也加入其中，跟著笑開懷。

但是，巴里的笑聲卻引來一些小孩的注目和疑問：「你是誰，為什麼要將你的眼睛矇住？」當巴里說出自己的名字，在屋外的孩子們就像偷食小米被趕走的小鳥般，驚慌失措的跑散開來。

What's more?

植物（cemel，卡米）：像是南瓜植物、地瓜這些植物，被巴里看到後，都會爛掉。

小米（vaqu，發古）：排灣族人的傳統主食，可釀製小米酒。

沒多久，屋外變成巴里所熟悉的情景——只有他孤獨一個人，像是早被遺忘了。

巴里哭泣著，被躲在石板後面一位叫做保浪的小孩看到。「巴里好可憐，為什麼他沒有朋友。」保浪心想。

於是，保浪大膽的走向前，對巴里說：「我們做朋友好不好，我跟你一起玩。」

巴里聽到了非常高興。從此，保浪每天黃昏之後，都會來找巴里玩。

有一天，巴里對保浪說：「我只聽到你的聲音，我好想看到你的臉和外面的世界喔！」

於是，保浪想出了一個能讓巴里看到外面世界的方法，就是將竹子裡的薄膜取出，貼在巴里的眼睛上，巴里的紅眼睛隔著薄薄一層的薄膜，看到保浪的樣子，也看到外面的世界，周圍的東西不再受到「死亡」的威脅了。

保浪將巴里帶回家，族人一看到他來，全躲起來不敢看，唯獨保浪已經失明的祖母，拿出地瓜和肉乾給巴里吃。

What's more?

石板（qaciljai，卡拉里哥）：石板分為公石、母石，石板可以拿來蓋房子，當做立柱或圍牆，甚至也能拿來做為石棺的材料；詳見「部落百寶盒：認識排灣三寶和石板屋」。

死（macai，馬才伊）：詳見「部落百寶盒：排灣族的喪葬習俗」。

「為什麼只有妳不怕我？」巴里對著保浪的祖母說。

祖母慈祥的對巴里說：「我的眼睛雖然看不到，但我的手卻能感覺得到，這不是也一樣能看見嗎？但是你有眼睛，卻不能看到你想看的東西，有眼睛和沒眼睛不是一樣嗎？相信造物者給你的那雙眼睛，一定有祂的道理。」

之後，族人知道巴里的紅眼睛不會再傷人，便開始接受他。平時，巴里還是要將竹子的薄膜貼在眼睛上，一旦發現敵人接近，或是族人結婚到遠處遇到危險，走在最前面的巴里，只要將貼在眼睛上的薄膜拿開，前來出草的敵人或兇猛的野獸，都逃不過巴里的紅眼睛。

巴里的能力受到族人的肯定，享有崇高的地位。

有一天，巴里跟著一群小孩子到山谷放牛，中午的太陽非常大，大家都到河裡游泳，唯獨巴里一個人在大樹下小睡。

What's more?

地瓜（vulasi，夫拉西）：小米、地瓜、芋頭都是排灣族人的傳統主食，族人相信吃了這樣的食物之後，比較有力量。

肉乾（rjinasi，令那西）：排灣族人將肉放在高架的平台上，用溫火及煙燻等方式，慢慢的燻烤。

祖母（vu vu，夫夫）：排灣族人稱祖母為「夫夫」（vu vu），為長者之意，代表生命經驗和智慧的來源。

出草（kiquluqulu，給古魯古魯）：過去的出草是一種成年儀式，象徵已經是有擔當的人了。

結婚（puvaljau，布法了吾）：詳見「部落百寶盒：排灣族的傳統婚禮」。

太陽（qadau，嘎道吾）：對排灣族人而言，太陽是賦予生命和力量的來源。

不知道哪裡飛來的土蜂，將他貼在眼睛上的薄膜取走，睡醒後的巴里並不知道，起來時很自然的張開眼睛，這時候，巴里看到的牛和植物都死光了，剛好爬上河岸休息的小孩子，因為被巴里看到也都死了。

只有幾個還在潛水抓蝦的小孩子，躲過了巴里紅眼睛的目光，當他們游回河岸邊，才知道出事了，趕緊逃回部落。

大人帶著逃回部落的孩子們前來，向巴里追究責任，不過他們也不太敢接近巴里，這時候保浪帶著祖母，慢慢的走到巴里的面前，對著眾人說：

「巴里的紅眼睛沒有錯，不要忘了他經常用紅眼睛幫助我們，卻從未邀功；而我們不但沒有感謝他，還只記得他的不好。更何況，這次的錯不在他，他並不是故意的！」

不過，族人還是決定把巴里趕到部落的後山。

被趕到後山的巴里又變得孤獨了，唯一讓他覺得欣慰的是，每天下午，都會聽到保浪在遠處叫他的聲音。

「巴里，我是保浪，我帶吃的來了。」

巴里知道保浪來了，非常高興，但他還是小心翼翼的倒著走出來，不讓紅眼睛傷到保浪。

自責的巴里每天都在懺悔，想著不該再讓族人受苦，所以，每次保浪提議要帶他出去玩，巴里總是喪氣的說：「我早已經習慣待在這裡了。」就這樣巴里再也沒有走出後山。

直到有一天，敵人知道了巴里住的地方，便在遠處模仿著保浪的聲音叫著：「巴里，巴里，我來了，我帶了你愛吃的食物！」

巴里不疑有他，背對著且低著頭走出來，就這樣，敵人便趁機將巴里的頭砍下。

這一天，還不知情的保浪來到後山，同樣在很遠的地方叫著：

「巴里，我是保浪，我帶來祖母煮的地瓜給你吃，巴里--巴里--」

當保浪走進屋裡時，發現巴里被人害死了，傷心難過的保浪，默默的將巴里埋在屋外。

What's more?

食物（kakanen，嘎嘎能）：排灣族的傳統食物十分豐盛，主食有小米糕、烤蕃薯、小米粥，湯品有芋頭乾煮湯、芋頭莖湯、溪魚湯、長豆湯，配菜有芋頭粉腸、石板烤肉、山萵苣、芋頭莖，點心有用葉子包著豐富材料的吉拿富（ci-naun）、南瓜糕（siak）等等。

族人聽到巴里死掉的消息，不知道是要難過，還是高興。

非常想念巴里的保浪，有一天獨自來到後山，說也奇怪，埋葬巴里的地方，竟然長出檳榔樹，樹上都結了又紅又大的檳榔。

保浪走到檳榔樹下，抬頭看著樹上的檳榔時，總有一種熟悉又懷念的感覺。

直到保浪將手親碰著檳榔樹時，突然從手的觸覺傳來巴里的聲音：

「雖然我沒有眼睛，但我能感覺到是你！保浪，我是巴里啊！」

保浪抱著檳榔樹哭泣，又聽到巴里說：「我死後變成了檳榔樹，而樹上結的紅檳榔就像我的紅眼睛。」這時候保浪才想起來，為什麼剛才看到樹上的紅檳榔時，是那麼的熟悉。

族人知道埋葬巴里的地方長出檳榔樹，便撿拾掉落的紅檳榔，種在住家四周。有一次，敵人來攻擊，看到有那麼多的巴里紅眼睛，都不敢進犯保浪的部落。

這也是為什麼排灣族人寧願讓檳榔樹上的檳榔一直長大，變老、變黃、變紅，也不把它摘下，因為老人會告訴年輕人說：

「那是巴里的眼睛，能守護部落、看顧族人。

Where did it come from?

本故事採集自台東縣大武鄉大竹部落，由亞榮隆‧撒可努的外婆講述。

What's more?

埋（葬）：人斷氣後，家人不可哭泣，必須先將亡者未僵硬的軀體擺成蹲坐姿，再用長揹帶及頭巾綑綁住，完成一切程序之後，家屬才可以放聲大哭，向親友們宣告；詳見「部落百寶盒：排灣族的喪葬習俗」。

檳榔樹及檳榔（saviki，撒非給）：檳榔樹是部落識別的地標；檳榔象徵著友情，更是結婚的重要聘禮之一。

02

頭目的故事

天神震怒，利用一場洪水淹沒貪婪的人
類，接受天神旨意的一群人造舟儲糧逃過
一劫；雖然有紅嘴鳥幫忙取火種，又傳來
有陸地的消息，但是食物總會吃完！人們
想起天神的預言，天洞口放著小米種子，
等有膽識、有能力的人取走，他便是由陶
壺所生的人，之後被排灣族人奉為頭目，
從此一切生活開始有了秩序。

頭目的故事之一

◆ 大水淹沒陸地

大地自從有了人們看顧之後，排灣族人稱自己為「阿底旦」，也就是土地的朋友，或是照顧土地的人。那時候只有家族的區分，還沒有所謂的階級制度，也沒有部落的觀念。排灣族的社會制度，就好像剛在破土發芽的種子一樣。

長久以來，土地上的人始終遵守與天神的約定，但時間久了，人性的貪婪帶來了許多紛爭，也產生仇視和敵意。人們慢慢的忘記當初與天神的約定，不再燃燒小米梗，讓裊裊上升的煙燻，飄向天神處祈求平安，也不相信風、雷電、雨神的能力了。

數年過後，大地時而久旱乾渴，時而傾盆大雨。往往，清晨便雷聲作響，雷電打出的雷火，把大地燒成黑灰色；黃昏颳起的強風，讓許多植物連根拔起；久旱的大地塵土飛揚，還挾雜著燒過的灰燼，整個天空都變得灰濛濛的。

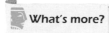
What's more?

階級制度（papapenetan，巴巴本呢當）：詳見「部落百寶盒：排灣族團結的基礎」。

阿底旦（adidan，阿底旦）：在排灣族階級制度當中「阿底旦」指的是平民。

家族：指的是同一家名的人。

部落：部落是由人、土地、領域所形成的，是一群享有共同利益的人所組成。

小米梗（singilje，希英樂）：小米梗是用來請示天神或招喚祖靈，排灣族人視為是寫給天神和祖靈的文字。

天神（cemas，吃馬斯）：天神的名字為Dagalaus，達告拉斯。

這時候，土地上的人才開始為自己的貪婪行為感到後悔，但這時候就算燃起小米梗的煙，再也得不到天神的回應了。

有一天，大雨又開始傾盆降下，落下的雨滴幾乎快跟芋頭一樣粗大，很快的，連下數個月所累積的雨水，高漲到快要頂到天空。

早在大水還沒來之前，有些人在天神的指示下，先砍收芒草，綁成大腿般粗細的一把、一把草束，並將地瓜、芋頭和小米等糧食藏在芒草束裡。

那些沒有被告知的人，竟然取笑他們說：「放著小米不收，去收那些不能吃、又沒用的芒草做什麼？」

經天神指示的人不受影響，繼續努力綁好更多的草束，並將綁好的拉到大樹頂端放。當大水漲到一個高度後，眾人便爬到樹上，將預先準備的芒草，成把、成把的集結在一起，綁成如同一塊在水上浮起的陸地，這些人在慶幸逃過一劫的同時，才知道天神的用意。

What's more?

法撒（vasa）：芋頭的統稱。芋頭分旱芋和水芋，旱芋可製作成芋頭乾，作為預備過冬的糧食。

芒草（ljaviya，拉非呀）：芒草可用來蓋房子，芒草梗更可拿來做火把使用。

火種（paudalj，保吾達）：傳說中，它是一塊發紅的白石，意義為延續生命和力量。

吉拿富（cinaun）：泛指用葉子包裹的食物。排灣族傳統點心，製作方式如下：1.五花肉加芋頭粉，用一點水和鹽拌勻，2.酸菜葉4-5片交疊，取3-5塊五花肉捲成長圓形，3.蒸煮30分鐘即可食用。

阿法伊（a-uai）：排灣族的傳統食物，製作方式如下：將肉片拌小米打成粉狀後，加上芋頭莖，再用月桃葉包成長條狀，蒸熟即可。

天神還指示要收集芒草、農作物、大鍋子、火種等等，也有人帶了乾肉、吉拿富、阿法伊三樣食物，以及乾材、三顆當火灶的礫石和墊在火灶下的石板。

可是，有一天，某家的小孩將尿灑在火灶上，天神聞到尿騷味般的燻煙，對這般不敬的舉動極為震怒。

天神鄭重告誡土地上的人：「土地上的人啊！你們燃燒後飄起的煙霧，是往返天界的使者，不但會說話，也是火灶從天界往返陸地的地標，非常神聖且莊嚴。」

天神說完，便將人們用火的權利取回。

大人們為了懲罰灑尿在火灶上的小孩，便用生芋頭塗在他尿尿的地方，讓小孩的下體發癢得不能尿尿。

排灣族老人常說：「千萬不能將尿灑在火灶上或是用水澆熄，這是對天神不禮貌的舉動。」

不過，如果火是自己熄掉，便認為是：「火休息了，去睡覺了。」

大家正為了沒有火種而煩惱，一位叫巴勒法法吾的老人抽著煙斗走來，對

What's more?

火（sapui，撒布伊）：象徵生命的延續。

水（zaljum，加侖）：象徵力量。

巴勒法法吾（Paljevavaw）：人名，也有將物品拿高之意。

煙斗（qungcu，屋出）：抽煙用的器具，也有「來吧！咱們來抽煙吧！」的意思。

煙絲（tjamaku，加馬古）：用煙草的枯葉製成。

著全部的人說：「如果你們問我帶來什麼，我說沒有，但是天神指示，離開時記得將煙斗裡的煙絲裝滿。」這時候老人巴勒法法吾用力吸著煙斗，從嘴裡緩緩的吐出幾口煙，眾人才知道天神指示他的用意。

老人巴勒法法吾將煙斗裡的火種取出放在手裡，遞給闖禍的小孩，對他說：「將火升起吧！在大水退去之前，你要一直看顧著火種，擔任守火之人。」

小孩用力點頭表示願意。

於是，小孩以實際行動感謝老人巴勒法法吾：當他需要點煙，小孩會很快的飛奔到火灶前；他口渴了，小孩便會趕著去取水；看他揹重的東西，小孩也會搶著分擔。

尊敬老人，是排灣社會的重要禮儀和傳統。排灣族老人常說：

「我的智慧和經驗，要給懂得尊敬和有禮貌的小孩；我在等待，等待一個我想要傳承的人。」

老人又說：「長者的智慧是要用拿的，而拿的過程就是在學習並了解和自己族群的關係。」

Where did it come from?
本故事採集自台東縣大武鄉大竹部落，由亞榮隆‧撒可努的外公講述。

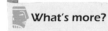

What's more?

老人、小孩：在排灣族人的觀念中，老人是尊敬與學習的對象，小孩必須將老人的生命智慧傳承下去，所以當老人叫小孩，或小孩稱呼老人時，就可以用（vuvu，夫夫）互稱。

頭目的故事之二

◆ 紅嘴鳥取回火種

大水還是沒有消退的跡象，潮溼的芒草梗吸入了大量的水；眾多芒草縱橫交疊所連結的陸地，因為吸水嚴重而越陷越深了。

老人巴勒法法吾僅留的火種，也隨著被打濕的芒草，一起熄掉了。於是，人們又怪罪小孩。

老人巴勒法法吾面色凝重的對大家說：「大水淹沒了這一切，是因為人心的貪婪！由於天神的憐憫，我們有幸聚在這裡，你們不懂得珍惜，卻只會起爭執。」

老人巴勒法法吾又說：「遇到問題，不去設法解決，反而製造更多的紛爭，實在太沒有智慧了。要知道，今天發生的這些事情，是天神對我們的考驗啊！」

於是，有人提議要去取火種回來，但好幾次都無功而返，不然就是差那麼一點。

有一次，派了烏鴉去，在回程的路上，正當快要到達芒草陸地時，烏鴉的嘴巴因為被火種燒到，「啊-- 啊-- 啊--」大叫地哭號起來，火種就這麼從嘴邊放掉。

What's more?

烏鴉（qaqa，嘎嘎）：對排灣族人而言，烏鴉是天界的使者。

大武山（Tjagaraus，加卡拉吾斯）：當大水淹沒大地，排灣族人逃到了大武山，在那裡打獵、耕作。之後，大水退去，排灣族人才慢慢往下遷移，所以大武山是他們的發源地，視為聖山尊敬著。

最後，派紅嘴鳥去取火種，才順利的取回來。不過，紅嘴鳥付出極大的代價，因為原本牠的嘴巴和雙腳都是黑色的，為了不讓火種落水，牠用嘴巴和雙腳輪流保護火種，卻被燒成了紅嘴巴和紅腳的紅嘴鳥。

紅嘴鳥取回火種，同時也帶來在不遠處有陸地的消息；傳說中，那塊陸地就是現在的大武山。

經由紅嘴鳥的指示，人們朝著陸地的方向划去，划了很久才終於到了紅嘴鳥說的陸地。原本以為到了陸地之後，會有很多東西可以吃、可以用；令人失望的是，這裡不但荒蕪一片，還為了要補充這趟旅程所消耗的體力，大家吃了太多而讓食物變得更少。

Where did it come from?

本故事採集自台東縣大武鄉大竹部落，由亞榮隆・撒可努的外公講述。

頭目的故事之三

◆ 百步蛇‧陶壺‧頭目

又過了很久，大水還是不見消退的跡象。有一天，大武山山頂上出現了一只發亮的陶壺。於是，人們到山上察看，但不太敢接近陶壺，因為附近都有百步蛇守護著，只好待在遠遠的地方觀望。

經過一段時間之後，躲在樹林後觀察的人覺得奇怪：為什麼陶壺在太陽照射之後，裡面好像有什麼東西在動。

有一天，陶壺突然破了，走出來一個人，在陶壺外蟠伏的百步蛇馬上自動讓出一條路來。看到這種景象，躲在樹林後的人覺得非常不可思議，馬上跑回去告訴其他人。

說也奇怪，就在陶壺破裂的同時，大水也開始慢慢的退去。可是，人們又開始著急，因為食物就快要吃完了。

當人們商議要到哪裡找吃的東西時，天空又開始打雷、颱風；這時候，有人想起天神曾經說過的話：「天神曾預言，在某一天將開一個天洞，會把小米種子放在洞口，要請有膽識、有能力的人爬到天洞，才能順利帶回。」

果然，人們找到了天洞，合力把竹子砍成一大截、一大截，一根接一根地升到天神所指示的天洞，還派了一個最強壯的人爬上去，但到了洞口，卻因為他的肩膀太寬塞不進去，卡在洞外。

 What's more?

　　陶壺（djilung，基命）：陶壺過去為貴族家所有，象徵地位、權力及財富。陶壺分為公壺、母壺、陰陽壺、祭祀壺，也是結婚下聘時是不可缺少的聘禮。

　　百步蛇（vurung，夫命）：排灣族人稱百步蛇為「長者」，是一種尊榮的稱呼，百步蛇圖形是頭目特有的裝飾。

於是，決定改派小孩子，原以為能夠順利的進入天洞，但小孩子個子小力量也小，根本沒有力氣爬到天洞，所以還是無功而返。

許多人試過了幾次，就是沒有人能將小米取回。

天神所指示的人，又夢見了很多百步蛇；天亮後，他急忙告訴其他人，大家才想起由陶壺所生的人，可能是他們最後的希望。

當人們正要去請求陶壺所生的人，卻看見一隻粗大肥短的百步蛇正向他們爬行而來，並緩緩的將蛇頭昂起，看著連接天洞外的竹竿，意有所指的說：「這件事，我會讓你們的頭目知道。」

有人就好奇的追問：「什麼是頭目？」

百步蛇吐信著，並未再開口說話，但四周卻傳來天神說話的聲音：

「如果陶壺所生的人，能夠順利將放在天洞的小米種子取回，他就是你們的頭目。因為你們已經變得貪婪，又忘記當初與我的約定，因此所有的權利將交由頭目管理，你們必須遵從。」

幾天後，陶壺所生的人出現在天洞下的竹竿邊，人們看到便取笑：

「那麼瘦小的人，營養不良，我看不用爬了，他的腳連捉住竹竿的力量都沒有。」

眾人帶著輕蔑、瞧不起的眼光盯著陶壺所生的人。

「如果我真的能帶回小米種子，有幾個約定希望你們能答應。」陶壺所生的人如此說。

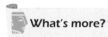

What's more?

頭目（mazazangiljan，馬展展伊郎）：頭目為部落的管理者，具有各項特權，例如土地的農作物、獵區的獵物、河流漁獲等專利特權，以及服飾和服裝上的裝飾權。頭目制度是世襲的，由長子繼承。現在，排灣社會一一瓦解，頭目只是文化層面的象徵，不再有任何的權力了。

眾人討論之後，承諾只要能將小米帶回來，都將答應他的要求。於是，陶壺所生的人吹著鼻笛，用鼻笛發出的聲音和百步蛇交談，就在這時候跟來許多百步蛇，一隻接著一隻纏繞著連接的竹竿，陶壺所生的人便踩在百步蛇的身上，輕輕鬆鬆爬到了天洞。大家張著嘴、瞪大眼睛，看著陶壺所生的人將小米取回。

從天洞下來的時候，陶壺所生的人用力搖晃竹子，一瞬間，小米散落一地；於是，女人拉起裙襬、男人張開披風，興奮的將一粒粒珍貴的小米給接住。

陶壺所生的人回到陸地上之後，眾人看著他手上只拿了一串結實飽滿的小米，非常生氣的對他說：「你那一把小米怎麼夠我們吃，要我們如何答應你的要求呢？」

陶壺所生的人說：「我將你們食用的小米種子帶回來了，散落掉下的種子是留給你們栽種的。」

「從天洞落下的小米種子，如果肯耐心照顧，有一天也會像我手上成串結穗的小米；如果有人等不及小米種子發芽結穗，就將我手上的小米拿去吃吧！」陶壺所生的人高舉著手上的小米說。

當陶壺所生的人將小米拋向空中，人們便急忙搶著，像偷食小米的小鳥般爭先恐後。

奇怪的事情發生了，搶食小米的人隔天都變成小鳥，這時候人們才領悟到陶壺所生的人曾說過：「可以等待並照顧一粒小米種子長大結穗的人，只要辛苦耕種就能得到溫飽；但是，那些急著立刻吃飽的人，只會坐享其成，從不付出；變成小鳥，是對他們的懲罰。」

What's more?

鼻笛（kulalu，古拉魯）：排灣族人的直笛分為口笛及鼻笛。鼻笛只有貴族才能使用，口笛與鼻笛又有單管及雙管的分別。

披風（itung，依洞）：男子的衣服多半有披風的設計，方便他們外出打獵過夜時，當做被子或毯子使用。

陶壺所生的人所說的這段話，得到眾人的讚許，人們也決定遵守之前的約定。

陶壺所生的人說：「雖然你們擁有土地，但如果沒有了小米，土地又有何用呢？現在，小米我帶來了，你們的子子孫孫將繁衍下去。」

接著又說：「洪水帶走了一切，現在要有新的秩序，我用小米跟你們交換土地，小米歸你們，土地歸我，等到收成之後，我只要一隻手能抓取的小米就夠了。另外，百步蛇幫助我順利取回小米，你們以後就把牠視為權力、才幹、智慧的象徵吧！」

陶壺所生的人讓大家心服口服，便奉他為頭目。

頭目走向大石頭便站了上去，之後他用力甩動身體和頭髮，只見小米散落。

「這些小米是給無依無靠沒有家的人！從今以後，讓我們共同分享喜悅，也一起承擔苦難。」陶壺所生的人對著人們說。

頭目訂定了階級制度，大家的生活開始有秩序；平民為了感謝頭目的照顧，便讓頭目享有住屋、衣服等裝飾上的特權。

頭目雖然擁有這些特權，但是和平民的地位平等，不會因此改變；甚至可以說，平民是頭目的父母，要是沒有平民的辛勤勞動，頭目就沒有榮耀和收穫。

自從頭目用小米交換土地，頭目和平民的互動便密不可分，因為只有小米，沒有土地，小米就會長不出來；若只有土地，沒有小米，土地又有什麼用？

平民開墾栽種付出勞力，頭目全心管理而勞心，分工和參與帶來了族群延續的力量和秩序，這就是排灣族最早的階級制度概念。總之，排灣族不能沒有頭目，更不能沒有平民。

Where did it come from?
本故事採集自台東縣太麻里鄉新香蘭部落。

盪鞦韆的愛情故事

身為平民的本仍，和排灣族頭目的女兒露古相愛，頭目卻百般刁難。

即將要嫁給別人的露古，相信本仍一定會通過考驗趕回來娶她；果然，雄鷹羽毛、雲豹牙齒、刻有百步蛇紋飾的刀，以及琉璃珠，一樣也不缺。

日後，在排灣族人的傳統婚禮中，少不了這四樣愛情見證物，也會擺盪鞦韆邀請天神和祖靈一同歡樂。

每當排灣族頭目家有人嫁娶，就會盪鞦韆邀請天神和祖靈參加。因為族人相信：鞦韆是天神和祖靈來到人間的樓梯，重要的喜事當然要邀祂們同樂。

架設鞦韆的雕刻及裝飾，會因頭目家族的大小而不同；鞦韆架上擺盪的粗繩，也會繫上能發出聲響的鐵管和響鈴。

老人總是說：「鐵管和響鈴繫得越多，代表著小米越豐收，也是在告知鄰近部落前來參加我們的收穫祭。而且，天神和祖靈也會被召喚前來，坐在鞦韆架上觀看。」

排灣族有個關於盪鞦韆的美麗故事。

從前，卡古力古家族有個女孩，名叫露古，她是頭目的女兒，和身為平民的本仍相愛，由於雙方家族地位差距太大，遭到女方家極力反對。不過，他們還是常在一起，這個秘密只有露古的祖母知道。

有一天，突然有人到家裡來提親，但露古就是不答應，並在祖母的通風報信之下先躲起來，提親的人只好回去。

事後，祖母告訴露古：「這樣子不是辦法，總有一天妳還是要出嫁的。」

露古搖著頭就是不願意，表明只愛本仍。

祖母回答說：「本仍是平民，就算我答應了，妳的父母親呢？他們絕對不會答應的。」

之後，還是有很多人來提親，但露古就是不喜歡。

直到有一天，露古的父親知道了女兒不嫁的原因，便對著本仍說：「如果你能答應我要求的四件事，便把女兒嫁給你。」

「第一件事，就是帶回雄鷹的羽毛；第二件事，拔下雲豹的牙齒；第三件事，將百步蛇的小孩帶回來。」

What's more?

鞦韆（ljukai，流該）：在排灣族的傳統婚禮和收穫祭，都可以看見族人架設鞦韆，不過只有結婚的女子和建立戰功的男子，才可以上去擺盪。過去，只有頭目才能架設鞦韆，象徵地位、階級，而收穫祭所架設的鞦韆則是豐收的象徵。

收穫祭（venalasaq，分那拉散）：排灣族人認為當小米收成時，象徵「越過」或「過一個年」，又稱「收小米祭」（masu vapu），每年在七月底八月初舉行。過去，排灣族是以「小米」為文化發展中心，如今小米文化已慢慢轉變為凝聚部落情感的活動。

祖靈（tjalje tjalj，打裡打）：指死去的祖先。

說到第四件事，頭目想了一下，便說：「那就到神界的地方去拿琉璃珠中最貴重的珠子。如果這幾樣東西你都拿到了，就穿著貴族的服飾前來迎娶我的女兒吧！」

本仍聽完之後，心想：「要帶回雄鷹的羽毛，那是不可能的；拔下雲豹的牙齒，一定會讓人喪命；要將百步蛇的小孩帶回來，比登天還難啊！」

「要我到天神的地方，取回高貴、漂亮的琉璃珠，根本就是強人所難；更別說要穿著貴族般的服飾前來迎娶露古。」

本仍雙腿發軟跪坐在地上，流下眼淚，恨自己無能為力。

排灣族人視雄鷹為天神派來巡視土地的使者；雲豹是土地的鬼魅，因為雲豹的皮毛就像土地的顏色，不易讓人發覺；神聖的百步蛇是族人的守護神，光是提到百步蛇就讓人感到敬畏，別說要帶牠的小孩回來；高貴又漂亮的琉璃珠，更是遠在天神住的地方，沒聽過誰到得了。

本仍知道這一去，不可能順利又安全的回來，也知道頭目這般刻意刁難，只為了阻止自己和露古在一起。但是他心意已決，立刻準備清晨出發的東西，並且盤算著要如何帶回這四樣寶物。

在天色微亮的清晨，本仍出發了，一去數年。

What's more?

提親（kisudju，給書九）：詳見「部落百寶盒：排灣族的傳統婚禮」。

雄鷹（qarjis，卡迪斯）：對排灣族人而言，雄鷹的羽毛象徵著身份、地位與能力。

雲豹（likuljua，里古獠）：排灣族人認為雲豹是獵人死去的靈魂變成的，死後不願離開，仍繼續留在凡間。傳說中，雲豹是神明的寵物，一般人不可以獵取，隨便獵取雲豹的人會引起神明的憤怒。依照排灣族的傳統習俗，能夠穿著雲豹皮衣的人，公認最具尊貴地位，而且是連神明都默認的勇者。

本仍憑著一股無人能及的毅力，走到了土地的盡頭，卻始終找不到通往神界的路。他感到十分內疚。

在回程的路上，忽然感覺有東西遮住了太陽，他抬頭看天空，只見一隻展翅盤旋的雄鷹；這時候，天空竟然掉落了幾根羽毛，當本仍再抬頭看，早已不見雄鷹的影子，本仍便順手將雄鷹羽毛裝進竹筒裡收好。

取得了雄鷹羽毛之後，本仍越過了高山稜線，在太陽下山處看見一位穿著雲豹皮衣的老人，本仍很高興的走上前：「請問你身上的雲豹皮衣，是你的嗎？」

老人家點著頭。本仍繼續問：「請問哪裡可以找得到雲豹？」

老人回答：「不用再四處奔走了，我已經在這裡等你很久了。」本仍聽了非常驚訝。

老人不說話，很快的從口中拿出一件東西握在手上，要本仍接著，他接過老人手裡的東西時，嚇了一跳，怎麼會是雲豹的牙齒！就在本仍想問個究竟時，老人卻化成了雲豹，伸出利爪，在他的身上亂抓，把本仍嚇得暈了過去。

 What's more?

琉璃珠（zangaq，喳安恩克）：排灣族人的琉璃珠是代代相傳的。每顆琉璃珠都有其象徵意義，分別代表階級、地位、財富、性別、美感、生命禮儀的強化、宗教神靈的色彩、風俗信仰的特色。排灣族人也因為琉璃珠的豐富性，強化了族人的向心力及其文化深層的特殊性和內在精神。

最貴重的琉璃珠（mulimulidan，母力母力當）：有太陽之光的意思，是琉璃珠中最貴重的珠子，代表了漂亮、美麗與高貴。「母力母力當」種類很多，名稱也不太一樣，通常位於項鍊的中央位置，珠子以白色為底，帶有藍、紅、黃等紋彩，而紋彩會決定珠子的貴重程度。當頭目結婚時必須有「母力母力當」作為聘禮，才能顯示出婚禮的隆重和地位的尊貴。

守護神（naljemakve a cemas，那勒馬克分 阿 吃馬斯）：排灣族除了有守護神，還有創造神、保護神、戰神，以及管理土地和掌管播種、收穫等神明。

本仍在昏睡中，夢見變成雲豹的老人對他說：「你身上的傷，是證明拔下我的牙齒的戰功，雲豹皮送你當禮物，牙齒和雲豹皮一起帶回去吧！」

本仍清醒後半信半疑，但身上的痛和傷，以及地上的雲豹牙和雲豹皮，讓他不得不相信。

在過去排灣族的習俗，只要族人得到雲豹，就會將利牙和雲豹皮先交給頭目挑選，剩下的便歸獵得雲豹的人所有。本仍從來沒想到自己竟然可以得到這麼尊貴的禮物。

本仍充滿感謝的將雲豹牙齒收好，穿起了雲豹皮，踏上歸程。在路上，一不小心踩到了百步蛇。

百步蛇昂首將利牙刺入本仍的身體內，本仍走了幾步，便昏昏沈沈倒在一棵大樹下，恍惚之中好像聽見百步蛇對他說：「咬你，是要你回去告訴族人，別想捉捕我們的小孩；以後對我們還這麼不敬的話，後果將不堪設想。」

百步蛇在離開前又說：「不過，我將變成一把利刀，取代你帶回百步蛇小孩的約定。」

果真，本仍醒來後雙手正握著一把刀身極像蛇形的短刀。這也是排灣族人為什麼會將自己的配刀刻劃蛇身的由來。

本仍有了這三樣東西，就獨缺高貴、漂亮的琉璃珠。

本仍的真誠與毅力讓天神非常感動，便將高貴、漂亮的琉璃珠繫在一只陶壺上，但陶壺裡卻裝滿了奇奇怪怪的昆蟲，放在本仍回程的路上。

當本仍走著走著，見到遠處有發亮的東西，在好奇心的驅使下前去察看，發現了陶壺和琉璃珠。不過，他對於不勞而獲取得琉璃珠和陶壺，覺得非

What's more?

夢（sepi，斯比）：夢對排灣族夢 人而言，是祖靈傳達訊息的一種語言。

常心虛，呆站在路邊想了很久，最後想到心愛的露古正等著他帶這些禮物回去，還是決定用大紅布包起來帶回家。

露古的父親趁本仍一去多年都沒下落，強迫她嫁給別人，但她還是愛著本仍，而且相信本仍一定會平安回來。因此，露古把希望放在結婚時所舉行的盪鞦韆活動，一心想要將鞦韆擺盪得又高又遠，讓在遠方的本仍看到。

排灣族人認為：「女孩子盪完鞦韆後才算真正的嫁人，沒有盪鞦韆之前還是可以退婚。」

露古始終相信，只要本仍看到她，本仍一定會快快奔跑回來的。

婚禮的盪鞦韆活動開始了，對本仍充滿信心和期待的露古，果真看到本仍從遠處回來了。

長途跋涉回來的本仍，帶著約定的東西，立刻來到了頭目面前。頭目一一檢視了雄鷹的羽毛、雲豹的牙齒後，轉過頭問：「百步蛇的小孩呢？」

這時候，本仍手上拿的刀，一下子變成了百步蛇，圍觀的人都發出驚叫聲，不敢置信。

接著，頭目接過陶壺，對陶壺裡有許多昆蟲正感到納悶，突然頭目手上的陶壺掉在地上，陶壺裡的昆蟲幻化成了一顆一顆的琉璃珠。

頭目將他對本仍要求的東西，雄鷹羽毛、雲豹牙齒、百步蛇紋飾的刀、琉璃珠，一樣一樣的呈現在眾人眼前。於是，頭目遵守和本仍的約定，在大家的祝福聲中，露古高興的擺盪鞦韆，順利嫁給本仍了。

日後，本仍娶露古的這四樣寶物，也成為排灣族人結婚時一定要有的聘禮。

Where did it come from?

本則故事採集自台東縣太麻里鄉新香蘭部落。

What's more?

聘禮（gingking，金肯恩）：詳見「部落百寶盒：排灣族的傳統婚禮」。

部落百寶盒 ││ 傳授哈「原」秘笈，搖身變成排灣通

一、大武山下的排灣族

關於排灣（Paiwan）一詞的由來，因為歷史久遠，說法各有不同。大致上，排灣族人流傳的共同說法是，祖先起初發祥於大武山的某個地方，並把這個地方稱做「排灣」，後來逐漸演變成為今日的族名。

排灣族分布的地區主要在台灣中央山脈南段，地理位置北起武洛溪上游大母母山一帶，南到恒春半島，東南則包括山麓與狹長的海岸地區。在高度方面，排灣族所有的部落都在海拔一千五百公尺以內，並且以一百至一千公尺的淺山為主要分布區。

受到地理環境位置及接臨其他族群的影響，排灣族各群在文化、物質上也都相當豐富且多樣。

排灣族分為拉瓦爾亞群（Raval）和布曹爾亞群（Butsul）二大群，拉瓦爾亞群又稱北排灣；而布曹爾亞群分又可分為四群，其中巴武馬群、查傲保爾群、巴利澤敖群，位在大武山的西側，稱為西排灣；位在大武山東側的巴卡羅卡羅群，稱為東排灣。除此之外，還有少數族人居住在花蓮縣卓溪鄉與高雄縣三民、桃源鄉境內。

排灣族各群分布情況，請參見「排灣族各群分布圖」，可以讓大家有較全面性的了解。

▶ 排灣族各群分布圖

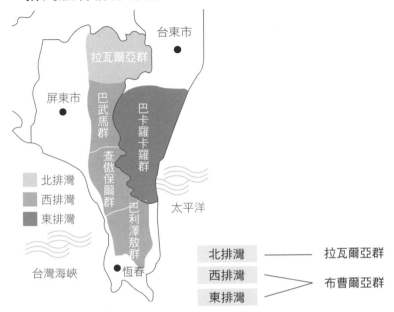

拉瓦爾亞群：分布於屏東縣三地門鄉，由於三面被魯凱族圍繞，風俗習慣受到很深的影響。

巴武馬群（Paumaumag）：分布在屏東縣的瑪家、泰武、來義鄉。

查傲保爾群（Chaoboobol）：分布在屏東縣的春日、獅子鄉。

巴利澤敖群（Palidalilao）：分布在屏東縣的牡丹、滿州鄉；地處最南端，文化又受當地平埔族和阿美族的影響，自成一格。

巴卡羅卡羅群（Pagalogalo）：分布於台東縣的達仁、金峰、太麻里、大武、卑南鄉，在卑南、阿美等其他族的摻雜，以及東海岸新環境的影響之下，發展出多元的文化系統。

＊ 排灣族主要分佈圖，請見封面裏頁。

二、排灣族團結的基礎

過去，排灣族的政治單位為「部落」，由同一個部落的人齊心共同防守抵禦外敵；至於社會單位稱為「團」（通常具有血緣關係），是一個經濟和治安的群體，團主必須擔起維持團內和諧的責任。團與部落單位不一定一樣，可能一個部落有好幾個團，或是一個部落就是一個團，也有一些團是由幾個部落共同組成。

排灣族的財產除了極少數的自然財產及公用財產之外，極大部分的財產都是私有的，包括山林、河流、土地、森林，平民和一般貴族無論是耕地或造屋，事先都必須徵求地主的許可；對排灣族而言，團主便是擁有宅地及居民的地主。而在單團的部落內，團的功能就可能和部落的功能合而為一了。

排灣族的社會階層制度是建立在土地制度與長嗣繼承上，換句話說，土地所有權是由長嗣繼承。過去，排灣族的社會階層分為貴族、士族、平民，共三個階級，以下將做簡單的介紹：

（1）貴族階級

排灣族因為有嚴謹分明的階級制度，形成某種程度的特權，包括地主或團主和他們近親的貴族。貴族又可分為地主、核心貴族、二級貴族、邊緣貴族等等。貴族在過去具有不可侵犯的神聖性，家名及人名都有特定尊號，而家屋中的雕刻石柱及簷桁、橫樑和檻楣等也都刻有特定的標幟，還享有特殊服飾，例如豹裘、琉璃珠等等，並行紋身習俗；另外，使用的器物也有專用的紋飾，如人頭、百步蛇圖騰等。

（2）士族階級

介於貴族與平民之間，在各社群中分別具有極為不同的意義與特徵，可享有免稅、若干紋身以及名號的特權。

（3）平民階級

平民是以勞力換取生活所需的階級，包括追隨貴族的族人、團族的團民，以及邊緣貴族和士族的後代。

由於現代文明的衝擊，排灣族階級制度已被政府行政體系所替代，貴族階級喪失了地位和權力，雕刻及服飾的使用也漸漸地普遍而平民化了。不過，昔日排灣族在家屋、服飾等傳統表現方式，經由現今多位排灣族藝術工作者，以新的方式詮釋，已呈現出另一種美感，並推向藝術創作層次了。

三、排灣族的宗教觀和五年祭

想要深入排灣族人的內心世界，一定要先認識排灣族人的宗教信仰，以及排灣族傳統的五年祭。

排灣族人對超自然的觀念有兩個特點：

第一個特點，他們認為無論神或鬼都一樣，只是有善惡之分。

第二個特點，他們相信超自然世界和人類世界，是同時存在且真實的。排灣族社會普遍相信，神雖然會保護人，但是也要求人必須完全遵守神的規律，如果不聽從神的指示，就是觸犯禁忌，會遭受傷害、生病等各種懲罰。不過，超自然世界有時候也會無緣無故的迫害人，這便是惡神、厲鬼在作祟。

▶ 傳統祭儀很豐富

在排灣族的社會裡，祭司和巫師相當重要，祭司是宗教的執行者，擔負祭祀工作，祈求風調雨順、年年豐收；巫師會在一些祭儀中唸咒以祈求神祇降臨，以及在人生病時為人治病，或是用占卜為人解惑。

排灣族的宗教活動十分豐富，各種傳統的祭祀很多，例如豐收祭、播種儀式、入倉儀式、收穫祭，還有捕魚祭、五年祭等。但是，隨著時代的演變，排灣族人的宗教信仰起了變化，加上西方教會的進入，絕大多數的族人已經改變原有的傳統信仰，現在祭司和巫師的的宗教意義減少許多，反而是文化意義較濃厚。

▶ 五年祭由來

五年祭是排灣族傳統祭儀的一大特色，但它的由來和說法都不太一樣。傳說中，排灣族頭目家的先祖雷門很喜歡雕刻，有一天，他在院子雕刻後，燃燒著剩餘的木屑，輕煙緩緩上升，飄到了靈界。當時，正好有一位女神在曬衣服。她很好奇的跟著煙跡來到人間，看到了人們吃的地瓜、芋頭都那麼小，土地如此貧瘠，便很仁慈的告訴雷門種植的方法和技巧，並賜給他小米的種子。在女神安排之下，雷門進出了靈界好幾次，也陸續學會所有祭祀的方法及禮儀。女神又和雷門約定，要他將所學來的祭儀在固定的時間舉行，做為凡間與靈界溝通訊息的橋樑。

每當五年祭時，祖靈和天神會從大武山南下尋訪各部落，然後又折回大武山，來回總共需要五年的時間，所以有五年祭之說。

▶ 祈求五穀充盈和獵物豐收

有關五年祭的祭儀內容簡單說明如下：

準備期：問神確定舉行祭儀的日期，主祭女巫師選定擲球的男巫師及助理，上山砍伐竹子、相思樹皮及葛藤，並準備製作祭竿、祭球，布置祭球場。

正式祭祀：在雷門神座前插上一顆祭球，恭請雷門回來參加；勇士們在祭屋前手牽手齊唱英雄頌及迎送祖靈歌；之後，主祭女巫師點燃小米梗，在輕煙中召請祖靈和天神回來與族人團聚，共享盛會。

至於五年祭儀式活動的高潮：「刺球」，便是族人利用長達三、四層樓高的竹製祭竿，去刺中拋擲在半空中的祭球（以樹皮或藤皮製成），真正意義是為了祈求五穀糧食豐收、獵物源源不斷，以及個人、家庭與部落平安幸福，所以排灣族人每隔五年就會舉行一次這樣的祭典。

想多認識並了解原住民文化，親臨現場參加他們的祭儀活動是最直接的方式了。只不過對於排灣五年祭，我們還要多具備一份耐心，因為每五年才舉辦一次。著名的五年祭，目前以屏東來義鄉古樓部落和台東達仁鄉土坂部落較為人所熟知。

四、排灣族的傳統婚禮

排灣族不論男女都能自由選擇娶妻或入贅、出嫁或招婿。不過，由於階級有別，平民、貴族與頭目的婚禮雖然過程及方式相同，但禮數及儀式卻大大不同。一般而言，排灣族人的傳統婚禮分為：探訪、提親、訂親、搭設鞦韆，最後才正式舉行婚禮。

當情投意合的男女相互定情之後，就要由男方家長央請媒人到女方家提親，並攜帶聘禮前往，女方若願意收下聘禮，便表示同意。

▶ 結婚是家族大事

對排灣族人而言，家族中有人結婚可真是大事，所以當訂親完成之後，男方便會向自己的親戚家徵集聘禮。過去的聘禮以鐵器為主，如鐵鋁、鐵耙、刀和數件由女方要求的東西，經分類後再用繩索繫綁在一起。聘禮的數量和地位階級的高低成正比。

在結婚之前，新郎必須邀約同伴二、三人砍伐數根樹木，運回女方家搭設鞦韆架。鞦韆架的兩根主柱頂會保留樹梢的葉子，象徵生命力；另由四根交叉的柱子作為支架，象徵男女雙方家族的結合與相互扶持，之後再架上短橫木，而鞦韆便掛在短橫木上，並以繩索綑綁固定。鞦韆架上還會掛上木刀、槍、服飾，象徵著財富。

▶ 宣布喜訊了

婚禮當天，男方會邊走邊唱，走到女方家去送聘禮；到女方家後，男方會先大聲高呼，才將準備好的聘禮交給女方。聘禮有酒、陶壺、山豬肉、檳榔、香蕉、小米、芋頭、小米糕、布料等等。接著，雙方圍著圓圈跳舞，女方一一清點聘禮，並向觀禮的族人報告。男方藉著聘禮證明有足夠的能力照顧新娘，希望女方同意這門親事。若女方願意接受聘禮，代表認同這門婚姻，此時男方便會向所有人宣告這項喜訊，最後舉行宴會大家一起慶祝。

順帶一提，由於排灣族人的傳統命名方式是本名連家名，所以當婚後有新生命誕生時，家族便會討論這個嬰兒的行為或特徵，比較像過去的哪一位祖先，或是直接依循祖先的本名，替新生兒立下本名。至於家名的封立，都是經由長老、部落會議決議，再請頭目賜封；而且，家名只傳給長子或長女。以本書故事採集者「亞榮隆・撒可努」的名字為例，「亞榮隆」是家名，意思是雷聲；「撒可努」則是本名，排灣語的意思為「動物從未停止奔馳」，另一個意義則是「植物從未停止成長」。

五、排灣族的喪葬習俗

在排灣族人的觀念中，在家病亡稱為善死；如果猝死在野外，像是遇到天災、被敵人殺死或自殺，就是惡死。

▶ 善死和惡死的埋葬方式不同

善死者的喪葬儀式過程，經由裝殮、訃告親戚、行告別祭、下葬、改火驅靈、服喪、行招靈祭、慰問遺族、除喪祭，最後行滿月驅靈祭，才算完全結束。惡死者的喪葬過程就較為簡略了，經由收殮、安祭幽靈、慰靈祭、分肉除忌、禳祓祭，最後進行祖靈祭。

排灣族的埋葬方式有室內葬和室外葬兩種，只有善死者才有資格葬在家裡的正廳，以布條綑綁住身體成為蹲坐的姿勢，挖洞葬下，之後在上面覆蓋四塊石板。等完成一切程序之後，家屬才能放聲哭泣，向親友們宣告親人死去的消息。

▶ 亡靈不要再回家！

排灣族人會在部落附近特別劃一塊地做為墓場，當成室外葬的埋葬地。下葬時，先由親戚中的男性前往墓地挖掘墓穴，然後由最近親男性，例如父親或兄弟，從家中將屍體抬運至墓地埋葬；死者蹲坐在穴內，面向東方，並以石板覆蓋後再覆土，最後在地面上再蓋上石板，由長老用豬皮、豬骨對亡靈進行告別儀式。

埋葬完畢，參加喪葬者會返回喪家。喪家必須預先準備清水三盆，讓參加喪事的親友手上沾水後，以手潑灑在喪家門前的地上，並祝告亡靈「不得再回家」；之後，喪家撿拾灶中剩餘柴燼，丟棄到屋外，再由男性家長用打火石點燃薪火，稱為改火驅靈。

通常親人下葬後三日，要舉行招靈祭，第五日再舉行除喪祭，由男性親族一起上山打獵，等獵獲獵物回來後，再除去喪家門口的竹枝，表示停止禁忌；一個月後再舉行驅靈祭。喪家從親人去世開始，便要改穿喪服百日，有時候因為太思念去世的親人，會穿著喪服長達半年之久。

排灣族人深信，善死者的靈魂為善靈，可以歸返大武山成為祖靈；惡死者的靈魂將淪為惡靈，徘徊在自己死去的地方，向相遇的生人作祟。

六、認識排灣三寶和石板屋

排灣族人有三寶，分別是青銅刀、陶壺、琉璃珠；而依山而建的石板屋，更別具特色。

▶ 排灣第一寶：陶壺

排灣族人認為，陶壺是祖先在人間居住的地方，象徵祖先的遺體。陶壺可說是頭目家專屬的珍藏品，數量的多寡與好壞，都可以看出頭目家族的地位。

陶壺的種類很多，有結婚用的壺、祭祀用的占卜壺，以及盛裝各種器物的壺（例如放粟物種子、收藏琉璃珠的陶壺等等）。陶壺又分公壺、母壺、陰陽壺，紋飾又可分為太陽紋、人形紋及蛇紋三種。有著太陽紋飾的是母壺，有蛇紋的稱為公壺，而結合二者紋飾的叫做陰陽壺。

▶ 排灣第二寶：青銅刀

傳說青銅刀是宇宙的柺杖，排灣族人把青銅刀看做宇宙神的器物，屬於全部落所有，由頭目保管。男人佩帶青銅刀，代表著力量和權威，所以排灣族人認為青銅刀象徵男人。

▶ 排灣第三寶：琉璃珠

琉璃珠代表財富，並且也象徵女性的貞節與美麗。排灣族的琉璃珠又分為頸飾及長鍊，男女所戴的頸飾及長鍊又有區分，名稱也不同；尤其，由於部落不同，對琉璃珠的意義和解釋也不盡相同，例如有太陽的光、有眼睛之珠、土地之珠等等。

▶ 依山而建的石板屋

過去的排灣族男子在成家之後，蓋屋所需要的材料都必須自己準備，當所有的材料準備妥當之後，才請家族的人幫忙。西部的排灣族人多以石板為材料，石板分為公石和母石，公石較黑，質地較硬，用來蓋屋頂和地板；母石色澤較淺，質地軟，用來砌石牆。而東部的排灣族人因石材取得不易，大都以茅草為材料。當家屋蓋好後便封立家名，由母家移來火種，在屋內燃燒七里香的葉子或小米穗，宣告家屋種在土地上，並立竹竿綁上小米、豬骨、紅布、鐵器，象徵穀物豐收、獵物滿滿和永遠被庇佑，這樣家屋才算正式完成。

排灣族的石板屋一棟接一棟，依山而建，屋頂上一片片的石板，遠看就像百步蛇的鱗片，排灣族人說那是百步蛇的衣服。過去，在頭目、貴族家的屋前，通常設有石雕的立柱和榕樹，做為家屋的象徵。據說，以前排灣族石板屋的正面還設有門楣，各階級都有屬於自己的圖案，也有一些動物圖案。其中，動物圖案代表狩獵的能力，像是捕獲山豬象徵搏鬥的能力，獵到水鹿表示能跟水鹿跑得一樣快，而獵獲黑熊則代表和黑熊一樣擁有其大無比的力量。至於，人頭圖案則表示出草的紀錄，百步蛇及神明的頭像象徵祈求祖先庇佑，人形與蛇紋複合的圖像則是興盛、繁榮的象徵。

造訪部落 部落藏寶圖，來挖排灣寶

看過了排灣族的神話與傳說故事，很想身歷其境，和排灣族人一起仰望聖山大武山，認識陶壺、百步蛇、琉璃珠，感受傳統婚禮吧！

傳說中，排灣族發祥於大武山一處稱為「排灣」的地方，現在主要分布在屏東、台東等地區，目前約有六萬多人，大體可分為北排灣，以及以大武山為界的東排灣和西排灣。

北排灣族人多住在屏東縣三地門鄉，由於三面都有魯凱族圍繞，風俗習慣深受影響；西排灣族人聚居在屏東縣瑪家鄉、泰武鄉、來義鄉、春日鄉、獅子鄉、牡丹鄉、滿州鄉；東排灣族人則主要分布於台東縣達仁鄉、大武鄉、金峰鄉、太麻里鄉，並且在卑南、阿美等其他族摻雜及緊臨東海岸環境的影響之下，發展出多元文化。

現在，透過這份精心編製的「排灣族部落文化導覽圖」，陪伴身歷其境，盡情挖掘部落文化寶藏，保證不虛此行。

當然，造訪部落時更不能錯過排灣族豐富的祭儀活動，像是每五年一次的五年祭、七月及八月份的小米收穫節。心動想要行動之前，最好先確定時間及地點，詳情請洽各地縣市政府或鄉公所。

洽詢電話：

・台東縣政府原住民行政局教育文化課 電話：089-320112
・屏東縣政府原住民行政局輔導行政課 電話：08-7320415分機246

排灣族
文化導覽圖

族語開口說　**入境隨俗的排灣語**

你健康嗎？
davadavai，natalivak sun？
（註：見到新朋友的招呼語）

是的，我很健康。
davadavi,ui natalivak a ken.

你叫什麼名字？
tima su ngadan？

我叫撒可努。
ti sakinu a ku ngadan.

你家住哪裡？
inuan a su umaq？

我家住在拉勞蘭部落。
i laraulan a u umaq.
（註：拉勞蘭部落位在台東縣太麻里鄉
新香蘭部落。）

你中餐吃什麼？
anema nu cengelj？

我吃小米飯
vaqu a nia cengelj.

你們部落的收穫祭什麼時候舉行？
nu ngida a masalut itua nu qinaljan？

我們部落的收穫祭在每年的七月舉行。
a nia si taliduan tua masalut,pinitua sika pitju a qiljas.

你們要去哪裡？
sema I nu mun？

我們要去山上。
sema I nu mun?

我很喜歡你們的部落。
tjengelaya ken aravac tua nu qinaljan.

感謝你們的到來。
masalu tua nu pinatjezan.

很高興能見到你。
maleva ken tua tja sincevungan.

希望下次再見面。
ulja tjen a mecevucevung nanan nua tjaivililj.

我要走了。
vaikanga ken.

祝你平安。
katalivalivaku.

族語開口說　排灣族稱謂的介紹

vuvu a uqaljai	阿公	kina	媽媽、阿姨、姑姑
vuvu a vavayan	阿媽	kaka a uqaljai	哥哥、弟弟
kama	爸爸、叔叔、舅舅	kaka a vavayan	姐姐、妹妹

學習加油站　本書漢語與排灣語名詞對照表

故事01：巴里的紅眼睛

用漢字拼讀	排灣語	漢語名詞
巴里	Pali	人名
古里基	quljizilj	紅色
馬查	maca	眼睛
卡米	cemel	植物
撒卡米	sacemel	動物
魯那依	lunain	腰帶
查里那	calinga	耳朵
發古	vaqu	小米
嘎洋嘎洋	qayaqayam	小鳥
卡拉里哥	qaciljai	石板
保浪	Balan	人名
卡哥里洋	kakerjiyan	小孩
卡里	qali	朋友
馬才伊	macai	死
母丁尼安	mudingan	臉
法西告吾	vasikaw	竹子
夫拉西	vulasi	地瓜
令那西	rjinasi	乾肉
夫夫	vu vu	祖母
里馬	lima	手
吃馬斯	cemas	天神
給古魯古魯	kiquluqulu	出草
布法了吾	puvaljau	結婚
嘎拉	qalja	敵人
嘎道吾	qadau	太陽
哥馬法卡	kemavakav	游泳
芬拉里	venelalje	土蜂
古恩	gung	牛
谷斬	guzang	蝦
法夫魯安	vavurungan	大人

用漢字拼讀	排灣語	漢語名詞
嘎嘎能	kakanen	食物
吉拿富	cinaun	泛指用葉子包裹的食物
西殼	siak	南瓜糕
古魯	qulu	頭
冷門哥冷	lemegelje	死訊
馬布法輪	mapuvarung	難過
馬勒法	maleva	喜悅
撒非給	saviki	檳榔樹或檳榔
給那查法查法	kinacavacavan	身體
拉馬冷	lamaleng	老人

故事02：頭目的故事 之一：大水淹沒陸地

用漢字拼讀	排灣語	漢語名詞
巴巴本呢當	papapenetan	階級制度
阿底旦	adidan	平民
嘎九那安恩	kadjunangan	大地或土地
排灣	Paiwan	族名
加拉洋	tjaljayan	種子
希英樂	singilje	小米梗
吃馬斯	cemas	天神
達告拉斯	Dagalaus	天神的名字
查吾查吾	caucau	人類
馬拉米樂	malamilje	貪婪
吃夫樂	cevulje	煙
法里	vali	風
吃拉拉	celalaq	雷電
古加依	qudjalj	雨
卡加滿加滿	kadjamadjaman	清晨
馬書樂書冷	masulesulem	黃昏
法撒	vasa	芋頭
拉非呀	ljaviya	芒草
卡樂弗樂曼	kalevelevan	天空
拉立茲加崙	laljiz zaljum	大水
卡西吾　阿　嘎古拉古樂	kasiv a kurakural	大樹
保吾達	paudalj	火種
阿法伊	a-uai	小米糕
巴里吾克	Paliuk	大鍋子
嘎西吾 啊 那馬達的	kasiv a nametad	乾材
嘎嘎夫灣	qaqavuan	火灶
嘎起來	qaciljai	礫石、石頭
撒布伊	sapui	火
加崙	zaljum	水
伊西哥	isiq	尿
巴勒法法吾	Paljevavaw	人名；也有將物品拿高的意思
屋出	qungcu	煙斗
加馬古	tjamaku	煙絲

頭目的故事 之二：紅嘴鳥取回火種

用漢字拼讀	排灣語	漢語名詞
嘎嘎	qaqa	烏鴉
安阿勒	angalj	嘴巴
古拉	kula	雙腳
古刺恩刺恩	qucengcenglj	黑色
古里基 阿 安阿勒	quljizilj a angalj	紅嘴巴
古里基 阿 古拉	quljizilj a kula	紅腳
加卡拉吾斯	Tjagaraus	大武山

頭目的故事 之三：百步蛇‧陶壺‧頭目

用漢字拼讀	排灣語	漢語名詞
基侖	djilung	陶壺
夫侖	vurung	百步蛇
卡度	gadu	山
夫給的	vukid	樹林
嘎勒分勒凡 阿 魯法	kalevelevan a ljuva	天洞
法西告吾	vasikaw	竹子
嘎凡	qavan	肩膀
馬展展伊郎	mazazangiljan	頭目
古拉魯	kulalu	鼻笛
法法洋	vavayan	女人、女孩
吾嘎來	uqaljai	男人
依洞	itung	披風
哥馬加拉	kemazala	讚許
弗那屋	venaung	洪水
吾法	uva	頭髮
吾馬克	umaq	住屋
嘎法	kava	衣服

故事03：盪鞦韆的愛情故事

用漢字拼讀	排灣語	漢語名詞
流該	ljukai	鞦韆
分那拉散	venalasaq	收穫祭
查里西	calis	粗繩
角鈴	tjaurjing	響鈴
打裡打	tjalje tjalj	祖靈
打當	tadal	樓梯
卡古力古	Kaquliquli	頭目的家族名；卡古力古
阿拉克 阿 法法洋	aljak a vavayan	女兒
露古	Ruku	人名
本仍	Benaq	人名
給書九	kisudju	提親
卡馬	kama	父親
給那	kina	母親
卡迪斯	qarjis	雄鷹
里古獠	likuljua	雲豹
喳安恩克	zangaq	琉璃珠

用漢字拼讀	排灣語	漢語名詞
母力母力當	mulimulidan	最貴重的琉璃珠
卡郎安恩	kalangan	貴族
阿里斯	aljis	牙齒
那勒馬克分 阿 吃馬斯	naljemakve a cemas	守護神
卡拉	galalj	鬼
布度	putut	竹筒
古馬刺	gumac	利爪
斯比	sepi	夢
拉達伊 阿 打給	ladjai a takid	利刀
嘎九非伊	qadjuvi	蛇身
拉給	takid	刀身
該法分吾溫	qaivavung	昆蟲
金肯恩	gingking	聘禮

賽夏族
S a i s i y a t

▶ 小筆記 ▶

・巴斯達隘（矮靈祭）兩年一次在南庄、五峰輪流舉行，外族只允許參加第二階段的娛靈Kisitomal。
・紋面：女子僅上額；男子與泰雅同，獵首二個可紋身。

‧同姓、同住(包括無血緣)、同外祖父的表兄妹禁止通婚。

‧父系社會，子連父名。例：伊德‧阿道‧撒萬：伊德是自己的名字，阿道是父親的名字，撒萬是姓(世系)。

故事導讀　感恩與信靠

在台灣所有的原住民族群中，賽夏族的矮靈祭（巴斯達隘）是相當具有特色的，不單是祭儀本身，更重要的是它背後有一個完整且複雜的傳說故事，內容觸及賽夏族與矮人（異族）間一段糾纏難斷的恩怨情仇。每一首祭歌，每一個儀式，每一個動作，從芒草到山枇杷樹，都充滿隱喻和象徵的意義，反映深邃的民族心理。

賽夏族夾在泰雅、客家兩大族群之間，長久以來面臨複雜的族群關係。矮人的故事，其實就是賽夏族人面對異族的心理狀態。互惠和競爭、歡迎和排斥、敬佩和妒嫉，原來就是人類和異族相遇時共同的矛盾情緒，賽夏族人用一個龐大的祭儀將其淨化了，希望族人永遠懂得感恩，追求族群的和諧。

其實在賽夏族的巴斯達隘祭歌中，也有一個段落敘述到雷女的故事。如果說矮人的情節觸及人和異族間橫向的關係，那麼雷女下凡則關涉到人與天的縱向關聯。雷神畢瓦同情賽夏人生活的艱難，責請自己的女兒娃恩攜帶盛滿小米種子的葫蘆來到人間，並和賽夏人結為夫妻，慷慨地教導人們學習農耕技術。但人的好奇、多疑和不滿足，破壞了天人之間應當有的界線；雷女被迫返回天界，只剩下一株還冒著煙的芭蕉樹。

因此，按賽夏人的祖訓，感恩和信靠應當是本族與異族之間、人與天之間，最首要的倫理和誡律，猜忌、仇恨、自我中心，既破壞和諧也造成毀滅性的災難。無論情況如何，永遠保持感恩和信靠的謙懷，才能夠成為一個有福的人。

歐倍那伯翁在這一方面為我們樹立了典型！在〈白髮老人的預言〉裡，歐倍那伯翁對夢中白髮老人的交待，不論別人怎麼懷疑、取笑，他始終堅信不移，全然信靠。狂風暴雨來襲，他不顧自己的安危，遵照白髮老人的指示將自己的船讓給曾經譏笑他的族人。這種信靠和交託，不但讓他和他的妹妹安然渡過大洪水的災難，也因此繁衍子孫，成了賽夏族人的再造先祖，並幻化為大霸尖山、小霸尖山，守望著賽夏子民。

Reader's Guide   Gratitude, Trust, Reliance

The pas-taai or "rites to the spirits of the little people" is unique and distinctive within Taiwan's indigenous cultures. Not only is the ritual itself distinctive, but the stories behind the ritual are rich and complex, implicating the entangled love-hate relationship between the taai (the "foreigners") and the Saisiyat. In the pas taai ceremony, every sacrificial song, every ritual, every action, from the razor grass to the loquat tree, is full of metaphor and symbolic meaning, a reflection of Saisiyat's profound consciousness.

The Saisiyat reside in an area sandwiched between the Atayal and Hakka and has long faced complex relations with these other peoples. The story of the little people can be seen as metaphor for the mental state of the Saisiyat as they come face to face with alien tribes. Reciprocity and competition, welcoming and discrimination, admiration and wariness are the ambivalent emotions that all humans experience when confronting the "other" or the "foreigner." The pas-taai, is really a huge ceremony developed by the Saisiyat to come to terms with the contradictions, in the hope that their people will adopt attitudes of grace and gratitude, and pursue harmony between different groups.

One part of the pas-taai ceremony recounts a story of Biwa, the lightening spirit. We can say if the story of the little people illustrates horizontal inter-human relations, this story of the "The Lightening Woman's Visit to the Saisiyat" is about the vertical relations of humans and the gods. In the story, Biwa, feeling sorry for the Saisiyat's toil and struggle to survive, dispatches her daughter waaung to take a gourd full of millet seeds to the human realm. Here she generously shared agriculture techniques with the Saisiyat and even married a young man of the Saisiyat. But human curiosity, suspiciousness, and failure to understand satisfaction, eventually severed the connection between the heavenly and earthly realms: waaung was forced to leave and return to the heavens, only a smoking plantain tree remained.

Thus, we learn from the ancestors of the Saisiyat that gratitude and trust must guide the relations between different peoples and between people and the cosmos. We learn that suspicion, hatred, and self-centeredness, both destroy harmony among humans and cause destruction of and disaster for the natural order upon which humans depend. Regardless of the situation, the blessed will always maintain the humility of gratitude and trust.

And with the opening story of the Saisiyat collection, "The Prophecy of the Great Storm", we have a model for this. To carry out the mission posed by an old white haired man who came to him in a dream, oppehnaboon disregarded the ridicule and humiliation of others and stayed true to his purpose. When the prophesied storms arrived, with no regard for his own safety, oppehnaboon followed the instructions of the white-haired old man to cede his boat to the people who had ridiculed him. This kind of trust and fidelity not only allowed him and his sister mayanaboon to survive the disaster of the great flood, but also allowed them to procreate and lay the foundation for their Saisiyat descendants. They became the revered ancestors of the Saisiyat and transformed respectively into the two mountains known Da Ba Jian Mountain and Xiao Ba Jian Mountain, protectors of the Saisiyat.

01

白髮老人的預言

由於一名白髮老人的告誡及上天的垂憐，歐倍那伯翁和瑪雅那伯翁兄妹，借助織布機載浮載沉，奇蹟似在歷經洪水浩劫後倖存，讓賽夏族人得以世代延續。

兩兄妹在賽夏族人心中，猶如大霸尖山和小霸尖山，守在白雲深處護佑他們。

從前，有個名叫歐倍那伯翁的年輕人，一天晚上夢見了一位白髮老人，告訴他再過不久會有暴風雨來襲，要他告訴賽夏族人，趕快做好事先的準備。

當時，的確常有狂風暴雨，但一般人習以為常，並不在意。白髮老人的夢喻強調這次的風雨將特別大，會淹沒整個大地，要求大家造船，以便逃生。

歐倍那伯翁將自己的夢告訴了族人，卻招來一陣嘲笑，沒人理會他。不過，他抱著寧可信其有的想法，自己造了一條小船。

沒多久，天上突然烏雲密布，刮起狂風，天色暗得跟黑夜一樣，接著滂沱大雨傾盆而下，這時人們才知道事態嚴重，開始覺得害怕，後悔不聽歐倍那伯翁的警告，現在狂風暴雨真的來襲，已經來不及防範，只有聽天由命了。

歐倍那伯翁還是非常關心大家的安危，晚上他又夢見了白髮老人。白髮老人吩咐歐倍那伯翁把小船讓給別人，然後要他領著無船可搭的人逃往高地。

歐倍那伯翁醒來後，立刻照辦。

雨越下越大，水越漲越高，陸地漸漸的被淹沒了，來不及逃命的人一個一個被洪水吞沒。

What's more?

賽夏（sai-siat）：族稱。賽（sai）在賽夏語中有所在、地方的意思，「賽夏」就是指住在「夏」這個地方。現在，「夏」的確切位置已不可考。

歐倍那伯翁（oppehnaboon）：指大洪水故事裡浩劫後僅存的兄妹中的哥哥，在賽夏族神話中他是一位先知、創世者，象徵大霸尖山守護族人；而妹妹瑪雅那伯翁（mayanaboon）則象徵小霸尖山。

歐倍那伯翁帶領族人拼命向高處逃命，但是大水還是追上來了，一個大浪就把所有的人捲入洶湧波濤中。連嗆幾口水的歐倍那伯恩拼命掙扎，不放棄任何求生的希望。

慌忙中，歐倍那伯翁抓到了一架織布機，他牢牢的抓住。就在這個時候，他看見妹妹瑪雅那伯翁在旁邊載沉載浮，眼看就要滅頂了，歐倍那伯翁立刻一把拉住妹妹，兄妹倆就這樣抱著織布機漂流在大水當中。

不知漂流了多久，就在他們精疲力盡絕望得快要放棄求生意志時，陸地在遠方出現了。他們奮力向前划爬上陸地保住了性命。這塊浮出的陸地，便是現在的大霸尖山。

兄妹倆環顧四周，全被大水淹沒，只剩下自己所站的這塊陸地。所有族人都被洪水吞沒無蹤，整個世界只剩下他們兄妹兩人！

當晚，歐倍那伯翁又夢見白髮老人，他說：「歐倍那伯翁！現在只有你們兄妹倆活著了，為了繁衍後代，你們必須結婚生子！」。

歐倍那伯翁雖然覺得和自己的妹妹結婚是違反倫理的，心裡百般不願，但是又不敢違背，因為白髮老人的預言非常靈驗，他的決定是不會錯的。

於是，歐倍那伯翁就和妹妹瑪雅那伯翁結為夫妻，不久以後，就生下了一個小孩。

What's more?

織布機（o:ko'，偶固）：世界各民族中，以大洪水的神話做為創世或人類起源的故事非常多，基督教的聖經有諾亞方舟的故事，賽夏族故事的逃生工具便是織布機（也有人認為是葫蘆）。賽夏族使用的是水平背帶織布機，所編織的服裝有長衣、腰裙、遮陰布、胸衣及披風等。

大霸尖山（pakpakwaka，巴巴哇嘎）：是「大地之耳」的意思。大霸尖山是賽夏族創世神話的發源之地，相傳族人就是自大霸尖山逐漸遷移到周邊的桃、竹、苗各地。

夫婦倆覺得世界上只有他們一家三口很孤單，應該多一些人。於是就把小孩切成肉塊，丟到水裡，肉塊立刻變成了人！歐倍那伯翁在切肉塊時就已經把姓氏分好了，他們因而成了賽夏族現在各姓氏的始祖。

現在，每個孩子都有了姓氏，如果忘記了，歐倍那伯翁還會反覆教導。大家都記住自己的姓氏之後，大水逐漸退去，一家人便順著河流下山，一直走到海邊才開始定居，不過後來他們還是又慢慢的向大霸尖山遷移。

賽夏族人曾經住過苗栗縣的後龍、頭份、三灣，現在大部分的族人則住在南庄、五峰和獅潭一帶。

歐倍那伯翁和瑪雅那伯翁兄妹倆一直留在大霸尖山生活，大霸尖山成了歐倍那伯翁的化身，而瑪雅那伯翁就是小霸尖山。千萬年來，他們屹立在白雲深處，守望著他們的賽夏子民。

Where did it come from?

本則故事是由苗栗縣南庄鄉東江新村的朱新欽先生所講述。

 What's more?

肉（bori，玻立）：分肉變人在現實社會中不太可能實現，故事中肉塊變成人是想像的境界，世界上有許多民族的神話或傳說都有類似的例子，讀者對於最後一段情節不必用太寫實的眼光去看待。

作者註：賽夏族的神話及傳說都是全族性的，並非專屬某個部落，每個故事在不同的部落會有些內容上的差異，但仍維持整個故事的精神及基本架構，講述者都是賽夏族的長老，朱阿良先生及潘金旺先生還分別擔任巴斯達隘（向天湖）及祈天祭的主祭。

02

雷女下凡

> 天上的雷神畢瓦不忍心看到賽夏族人過苦日子,派他的女兒娃恩帶著小米種子下凡來,小米成了族人的珍貴糧食。
>
> 由於雷女娃恩和賽夏青年達印相戀成婚,她不但幫助達印維持全家生計,也讓達印的父親重見光明。眷顧賽夏族人的雷神和雷女,至今仍受到族人的崇敬。

蠻荒時期，賽夏族人只知道打獵，或到山上採野菜、摘果實裹腹，對於農耕技巧一無所知，過著簡單而清苦的生活。

天上的雷神畢瓦看到這種情形，便把女兒叫到跟前來：「娃恩，賽夏族人到現在還不懂如何種植農作物，生活太艱苦了，妳就帶著小米下凡到人間，教導他們吧！」。

於是，雷女娃恩帶著裝滿小米種子的葫蘆來到人間。

雷女娃恩一到人間便巧遇正在打獵的賽夏青年達印，兩人一見鍾情，達印把雷女娃恩帶回家裡，當晚就成了親。

第二天，雷女娃恩把葫蘆剖開，拿出小米種子給達印，開始教他種植小米。從那時開始，賽夏族人就以小米為主食，進入農業生活。

達印的母親很早就過世了，父親也雙目失明。雷女娃恩恢復了他的視力，使他重見光明。

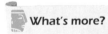 **What's more?**

雷神（biwa，畢瓦）：這則故事的時空比達隘來到賽夏社會更古老，那時賽夏社會剛進入農業社會，小米的種植需要雨水的滋潤，傳說中雨水的多寡都是由雷神決定，因此，雷神是非常重要的農業神，包括賽夏族在內的許多民族也都把雷神當作雨神來崇拜。

雷女（waaung，娃恩）：雷神畢瓦派雷女娃恩下凡幫助賽夏族的農業發展，族人感念至深，直到現在，雷女還被奉為賽夏族最重要的神。

結婚（yinra，因拉）：賽夏族是氏族外婚制，同姓氏絕不可結婚，傳統婚姻有幾個過程，如許婚、求婚，訂婚及結婚等。賽夏語沒有結婚一詞，是以「女子到男家住」來形容結婚。

達印的父親見到兒子娶了雷女娃恩，心裡非常高興。但是為了顯示自己家長的地位，便對雷女娃恩說：「依照傳統，女人結婚後要料理家務，妳最好不要隨便出門。」

雷女娃恩回答說：「父親，我不能碰鍋子，還是要麻煩您老人家在家煮飯，至於田裡的事就交給我和達印就好了！」

達印的父親見她如此堅持，也就不便多說什麼。

雷女娃恩上山工作時，帶著二十把鐮刀和二十把柴刀。到了田裡，娃恩要達印每六步放一把鐮刀和一把柴刀，並要他放好之後，就先回家。達印心裡覺得奇怪，但也沒多問。擺好鐮刀和柴刀後，一個人就先回家去了。

達印剛回到家就聽到田裡發出好大的雷聲，以為發生了什麼事，跑回田裡一看，竟然在短短的時間內，田裡的草已經割完了，地也整理好了。

回到家裡後，達印把經過情形告訴了父親，父親非常高興。回想從前艱苦的日子，自從娃恩來了之後，似乎一切都變得那麼順心，不但自己眼睛重見光明，達印田裡的工作也很順利，這都是娃恩帶來的好運。父親便一再吩咐達印，要多多善待娃恩。

達印夫妻轉眼間度過了三年幸福平靜的日子，父親對他們感到很滿意。唯一美中不足的小小遺憾，就是達印夫妻結婚都三年了，卻還沒有生下兒女。

What's more?

過世（masay，馬塞）：從前賽夏族的喪葬必須以死者是善死或惡死來決定埋葬地點及方式，在家死亡為善死，喪禮較隆重；意外或被獵頭而死亡者為惡死，只能草草埋葬在死亡地點。現在則大都以漢式葬禮送別死者，清明節也掃墓。

達印的父親開始憂慮傳宗接代的問題：「這三年多虧了娃恩！她什麼都好，可惜不生小孩。到底是什麼原因呢？對了！記得她從一進門開始就不曾進過廚房，也說過不能摸鍋子；嗯，一定是沒有摸過鍋子，所以才生不出小孩！」。

達印的父親越想越有道理，覺得只要媳婦能下廚房，就能解決傳宗接代的問題。於是他把雷女娃恩叫來，假借說自己餓極了，一定要她趕快下廚煮飯給他吃。

雷女娃恩見公公的心意很堅決，已無法推辭，於是就對公公說：「現在我就去煮飯，請在外面等，煮好了之後，再請您老人家進來吃。」

雷女娃恩說完後進了廚房。不久，廚房裡傳出一聲巨響，父親連忙進去一看，雷女娃恩已經不見了，只剩下一株芭蕉樹，伸出窗外的葉子還冒著煙。

其實，當達印的父親勉強雷女娃恩煮飯時，她心裡明白已經不能久留人間，於是就趁這個機會回到天上去了。

Where did it come from?
本則故事是由苗栗縣南庄鄉蓬萊村大湳部落的潘金旺（武茂達印）講述。

巴斯達隘傳說

> 達隘教導賽夏族人耕作，但卻調戲賽夏婦女，族人由敬重、忍辱到反抗，設計消滅達隘。
>
> 事後，倖存的達隘對賽夏人下了詛咒，唯有學會他們教的祭歌、祭舞，虔誠祈求原諒，才能平安、豐收。
>
> 巴斯達隘祭典可以說是賽夏族和達隘之間，和解彼此長久以來恩怨情仇的一種儀式。

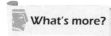

What's more?

巴斯達隘（pas-taai）：賽夏族全族性祭典之一，過去稱為矮人祭，也有人稱為矮靈祭，為了避免爭議，便直接音譯，以巴斯達隘命名。達隘是賽夏族人對矮人的稱謂，巴斯是祭典的意思，巴斯達隘就是祭祀矮人（靈）的祭典。每兩年（公元的雙數年）舉行一次，每十年一次大祭，時間大約在農曆的十月中旬。地點有兩處，分別在苗栗縣南庄鄉的向天湖及新竹縣五峰鄉的大隘。

很久以前，住在賽‧吉拉巴的賽夏族人，靠著農耕和狩獵生活，但耕作技術不發達，成熟的穀物又不時被老鼠、小鳥偷吃，一旦颱風來襲，常常歉收挨餓。

當時，賽夏族人每年秋收後都會舉行祭典，感謝神靈及祖先的恩賜，並祈求來年風調雨順。

不知何時起，賽夏族人居住地附近遷來了一群人。他們的外表和賽夏族人不一樣，身材矮小，僅及賽夏族人的胸前。儘管如此，但他們的手臂卻強而有力，動作也很敏捷，連賽夏族的勇士都比不上，賽夏族人稱呼這些新鄰居為「達隘」。

達隘的農耕技術非常先進。賽夏族人只知道種植小米，對於稻作一無所知。達隘不僅帶來了陸稻的種子，並教導賽夏族人種植的知識。

What's more?

賽‧吉拉巴（sai-kirapa）：為賽夏族的傳統地名，即現在的新竹縣五峰鄉。學術界把「賽‧吉拉巴」視為賽夏族的北群，而南群「賽‧蘭姆頌」（sai-lam-song）則在苗栗縣的南庄鄉及獅潭鄉。

秋天（pinana'amishan，比那那阿密斯案）：賽夏族的季節只有兩個，即夏天「阿伐安」（a:bqan）及冬天「阿密斯案」（amishan），春天說成夏之初，秋天說成冬之初，在詞首加上「比那那」（pinana）即可。

達隘（taai）：賽夏族人對矮人的稱謂。

小米（tata'，打大）：小米是賽夏族由漁獵、採集社會進入農業經濟生活時，最早種植的作物，現在已成為祭典當中的獻祭品；在祈天祭舉行時，參加的族人還要分食小米飯糰。祈天祭是賽夏族祈求風調雨順及驅逐疾病的祭典，每年農曆三月中旬舉行；與巴斯達隘同年舉行的是小祭，隔年的是大祭。

達隘還會法術，只要他們施法，天氣就變得非常好，颱風、暴雨不會侵襲大地，老鼠和小鳥也不再偷吃穀物，每年的收成都比從前好很多。

更神奇的是，只要一點點米粒就能煮成一大鍋飯，可以讓許多人吃飽。賽夏族人的生活，因為達隘的幫助而大大的改善了。

賽夏族人非常高興，認為這一切都是達隘帶來的好運，對達隘充滿感激，便常邀請達隘參加秋收時舉行的祭典。暮秋的月圓之夜，大家不分彼此一起慶祝豐收。通宵達旦，盡情歡樂歌舞。

達隘能歌善舞，也把他們的歌舞帶入了賽夏族人的祭典當中。賽夏族人對達隘充滿敬畏與感激，並不介意自己的祭典因達隘的參與而有了些微的改變。賽夏族人和達隘和睦相處。

但是，和諧的日子維持不久，達隘自認對賽夏族人有恩，漸漸地露出好色的本性。在眾人熱烈慶祝豐收的祭典中，達隘有意無意地調戲賽夏婦女。受侮辱的婦女為了全族生計，忍氣吞聲，以免傷害了雙方的關係。

沒想到達隘有恃無恐，連平常的日子也開始騷擾賽夏婦女。

達隘的行徑，引起了眾人的憤怒，年輕氣盛的族人更是憤恨不平。是啊，有誰能忍受外人欺侮自己的母親跟姊妹呢？

 What's more?

法術：法術或巫術一直存在於賽夏族社會，方法以水占、竹占、鳥占居多，許多社會活動必須以占卜斷吉凶，過去的巫師也會治病；巫師以女性為主，必須經過學習。

賽夏語沒有法術一語，過去比較流行的水占有兩種，（saralom，撒拉隆姆）是生病或有疑難雜症問靈用；（ponapis，玻那比斯）是用來尋找失物或失蹤者。現在較常使用採借泰雅族的竹占，（romhaep，輪哈普），用來問事或治病。

於是，賽夏族人秘密集會，眾人圍坐在火堆旁，討論對付達隘的策略。「不行！我們不能再裝聾作啞了，一定要採取行動懲罰達隘，保護我們的姊妹！」青年武茂顧不得會議倫理，首先站出來發言，他的意見立刻獲得許多族人的贊同。

「大家稍安勿躁！對於這件事，我們千萬不可以意氣用事，必須從長計議。況且達隘過去對我們有恩，現在大家能過好日子都是達隘的功勞，不可以恩將仇報！」老成持重的第地韻氏族長老加列赫力勸眾人為本族生計，再忍耐一段時間。

「照您這麼說，我們豈不是要讓達隘予取予求，任意侮辱了嗎？」另一名青年伊德質疑長老息事寧人的態度。

加列赫說：「各位，我也是賽夏的一份子，做任何決定都會先考慮族人的利益。我不是反對你們懲罰達隘，而是想到自古以來我們的生活一直很艱苦，達隘來了以後，才有溫飽，我們要飲水思源、知恩圖報。」

「現在達隘的行為是過份了些，不過，我認為應該先跟達隘溝通看看，請他們自我約束；如果還是我行我素，再處罰他們也不遲！」

加列赫長老向來一言九鼎，深獲賽夏族人的敬重，經過他的勸說，大家才逐漸冷靜下來。

What's more?

會議倫理（ayalaihou，阿亞來浩）：每當舉行全族性祭典或有重要事務商討時，便召開長老會議，由各氏族長老參與。其他族人不分男女也都可以參加，長老首先發言，再依輩份及年齡依序發言。

第底韻（titiyun）：賽夏族傳統姓氏之一，漢姓為朱姓，是巴斯達隘的主祭氏族，南庄及五峰都有第底韻分布。第底韻在賽夏語中指的是「雞母珠」這種植物，又稱為「相思子」，其紅色鮮豔的果實有毒。

不久，加列赫長老邀約其他氏族的長老一起跟達隘談判，請他們念在舊日情份，不要再做出傷害彼此感情的事。但是，達隘不顧長老們的勸說，反而變本加厲地欺凌賽夏族人。

有些賽夏青年實在看不過去，私下找達隘理論。但達隘身手矯健，臂力奇大無比，賽夏青年往往不是對手，大都被打敗，狼狽而回。

一時之間，賽夏族人對達隘無可奈何，只得與達隘保持距離，雙方的關係變得劍拔弩張。達隘見賽夏族人對他們毫無辦法，更加得意忘形、為所欲為，賽夏婦女人人自危。

但是，衝突還是發生了。

有一天，一名賽夏女孩單獨出門被達隘看到，達隘又重施故技地對她橫加污辱，恰巧被武茂撞見，怒火中燒的武茂發了瘋似的攻擊達隘，把女孩救了回來。

事後，武茂一五一十地把經過告訴族人，所有賽夏人都義憤填膺，發誓一定要向達隘討回公道。

這時，平日溫厚的長者加列赫長老也發出了怒吼：「各位族人！我們已經給了達隘時間和機會，他們卻不能體會我們的好意，仍然一再欺負我們的姊妹，我們的耐性是有限度的。現在，該輪到我們反擊了！」

通常達隘最喜歡在賽‧吉拉巴附近一處風景絕美，但地勢險要的地方乘涼，從高山上流下的溪水將懸崖切為兩邊，懸崖的東邊長著一株高大的山枇杷樹，粗大的枝幹橫跨溪面，伸向懸崖的西邊，樹幹下便是深深的河谷及湍急的溪水。傍晚時，藝高膽大的達隘們常常列坐在樹幹上，享受著陣陣涼風吹拂。

這天晚上，武茂和伊德兩人趁著達隘已經熟睡，帶著斧頭悄悄地潛行到懸崖邊，合力將樹幹砍了一道很深的裂縫，再用泥土把裂縫塗滿。

現在，就等達隘上當了。

隔天傍晚，達隘又來到了山枇杷樹下，他們毫不懷疑的一個接著一個爬上大樹，當大部分的達隘爬上後，樹幹無法支撐重量，發出「啪啪」的斷裂聲。

「什麼聲音？」坐在樹上的達隘疑惑地問道。

「那是老太太膝蓋骨發出的聲音！」樹下的一名賽夏大嫂鎮定地回答。達隘不疑有他，繼續上樹。

最後兩名達隘還來不及爬上山枇杷樹，樹幹就已經承受不住重壓，發出一聲巨響後，直墜溪谷，坐在樹幹上的達隘們像箭般跟著掉落，不是摔死，就是溺斃，沒有一個活口。

只留下樹下的兩名達隘，眼睜睜地看著悲劇發生。

躲在一旁的賽夏族人眼見計謀成功，高興地衝了出來，想要捉住剩下的兩名達隘，可惜還是被他們逃掉了。

過了幾天，兩名達隘回到賽夏部落，對賽夏族人發出詛咒：「賽夏族人！你們竟然恩將仇報，你們會後悔的，以後你們的農作物不會豐收，颱風也會再度來到！」

What's more?

山枇杷樹（ito'，倚豆）：傳說中的懸崖及山枇杷樹迄今還在原處；還有，聽說曾有人見過賽·吉拉巴溪谷的一個石洞中（新竹縣五峰鄉大隘村附近的油羅溪河段），擺著小石床、石桌、石椅等，許多人相信這就是達隘住過的地方。

「記住，你們從此要祭祀我們的亡靈，要虔誠地學習我們的祭歌和祭舞，不然還會受到懲罰！」

但短時間之內，只有第地韻氏族的人向達隘學會了祭歌、祭舞，也因此巴斯達隘就由第地韻氏族掌理。兩位達隘交代祭典方式之後，便往東方離去。

果然，受到達隘的詛咒之後，賽夏族人無法再每年豐收，各種天災接連不斷。

這時加列赫長老想起了達隘的臨別告誡，他告訴族人：「這是我們消滅達隘的後果，為了子孫後代的生活，從今年秋天的收穫祭開始，我們改成祭祀達隘，唱達隘教的歌，跳達隘教的舞，用虔誠的心祈求原諒，也祈求平安、豐收。」

眾人沒有異議，於是巴斯達隘就這樣一年一年的傳承下來，這就是賽夏族矮靈祭的由來。

Where did it come from?
本則故事是由苗栗縣南庄鄉向天湖部落的朱阿良（加列赫伊德）先生所講述。

一、子連父名

賽夏族是父系社會，命名制度是子女名字後面一律加上父名，舉例來說，兒子的賽夏名叫iteh a atau shawan（伊德　阿道　撒萬），「伊德」是兒子名，「阿道」是父親名，「撒萬」則是姓。

賽夏人在一般場合都只稱呼自己的名字，人較多的場合，為避免同名，就會連父親名字一起稱呼，別人就知道這是誰家的小孩；如果遇到隆重的會議或祭典，參與的人更多，為了讓他人了解自己的身份，就必須把「姓」介紹給大家；「姓」是漢字的概念，賽夏語稱為shinraihou（欣來浩），意思是從同一祖先傳下來的男性血親，aehae' shinraihou（阿哈-欣來浩）更廣義，aehae'是數目字「一」的意思，阿哈-欣來浩更強化同一祖先的意涵，即使年代已久，不容易辨認世系，但仍然承認是出自同一祖先，不但禁止通婚，也有相互保護的義務。

賽夏族改漢姓時間比其他原住民族要早，根據史料記載，清朝道光六年（1826年）賽夏族就因為擔任「隘丁」有功而被「賜」漢姓，使用漢姓的歷史到現在至少有一百七十多年。日本時代後期，日本政府推行「改姓名」政策，當時的賽夏族人的戶籍登記又改成了日本姓名，像漢姓「潘」就被改為「幡田」及「幡野」。

台灣光復後，賽夏族又再一次的改漢姓，這次增加更多姓氏，既有的氏族制度幾乎被攪得昏頭轉向！還好，聰明的族人在改姓過程中，巧妙地把傳統姓氏的精神融入漢姓，讓欣來浩與漢姓找到對應，形成清楚的脈絡，現在的族人都可以知道自己的姓氏源頭。「阿哈-欣來浩」也就是同一祖先的概念在每年兩次的祖靈祭中不斷被強化，在每個欣來浩各自舉辦的祖靈祭時，有不同的漢姓一起祭祖靈的情形，那是因為他們的傳統姓氏屬於同一祖先。

近年來，政府通過了原住民恢復傳統姓名的法律，族人可依自身意願申請恢復，對賽夏族來說，由於過去傳統姓氏透過巧妙機制保留，現在要恢復傳統姓名是既正確又方便。

▶ **以下列出賽夏族姓氏的發音、漢姓及其原始意義**

氏族名	漢姓	詞　義	漢 語 音 譯
babai	風	bai是風的意思	叭拜
kaybaybaw	高	ibabaw是高的意思	改擺刨
kas'amus	根	amus是草木之根	嘎斯阿慕思
kinrakes	樟	rakes是樟樹	敏拉各斯
karkarang	解（蟹）	karang是螃蟹	嘎嘎浪
tanohila	日	hahila是太陽	打努晞剌
sayna'ase	芎	ase是九芎	賽哪阿塞
kamlalai	詹（蟬）	lalai是蟬	橄姆拉賴
botbotol	胡（狐）	botbotol是狐狸	窩窩頓
tatayshi	絲	shi閩南語「絲」	打逮系
saytibora'an	獅	say閩南語「獅」	賽底窩喇按
shawan	錢 潘	樹枝交錯	撒萬
tawtawwazay	豆	taw閩南語「豆」	導導瓦日艾
titiyun	朱（珠）	雞母珠（植物）	第底韻
hayawan	夏	ha閩南語「夏」	哈雅萬
katiramo	血	ramo是血	喇莫
tabtabiras	膜	biras是內臟的膜	比剌斯

上表十八個漢姓，其中血姓及膜姓早已絕嗣，獅姓只出現在文獻記載裡，shawan氏族又分為潘、錢兩個漢姓，所以現在實際還參與社會運作的是十四個欣來浩。

二、巴斯達隘祭（上）

賽夏族人藉由巴斯達隘的舉行，強化族人對已往生活的共同記憶。

巴斯達隘也稱矮人祭或矮靈祭，地點分為兩個地方：苗栗縣南庄鄉向天湖祭場及新竹縣五峰鄉大隘祭場。慣例上，每兩年才舉行一次，一般是在西元雙數年的農曆十月十五日左右，在祭場的祭期就要四天三夜（據耆老回憶，過去的祭期曾長達六天五夜）。而實際上，整個巴斯達隘的祭期很長，尤其是擔任主祭的第地韻（titiyun，漢譯為朱）氏族，更是要忙碌好幾個月，包括與各姓氏溝通，充分吸收各界意見，目的就是為辦好祭典，做盡可能的籌畫與準備。這個儀式叫做叭叭哖（babalon）。

叭叭哖之後，祭典前一個月左右的時間，要舉行嘎嘎哇斯（kakawas，意為約期會議），邀請南庄及五峰的各氏族長老及族人聚在一起，商定祭典的確切日期，嘎嘎哇斯由南庄及五峰輪流主辦。當約期會議完成後，平時禁唱的巴斯達隘祭歌才能解禁，部落裡總會傳來祭歌的學習聲，同時族人也開始準備參加巴斯達隘的各項用品。

祭期決定之後，還有一個重要的儀式叫做阿雅來號（ayalaihou，座談會或長老會議的意思），舉行的地點固定在苗栗縣南庄鄉南庄大橋附近往東河的河床上，時間大約在正式祭期前一週左右，這時不論南庄或五峰的長老、族人都會來參加。阿雅來號主要目的是討論巴斯達隘應該注意及改進之處。會議由擔任主祭的朱姓長老首先發言，然後是各姓長老及族人依序發言，近年來婦女發言的情形也很普遍。必須注意的是，參加阿雅來號之前，各家各戶都要開始綁芒草，因為自嘎嘎哇斯後，達隘（即矮人）的祖靈就已來到，為了避邪，在農具、獵具、廚房、門窗及每個人身上，都必須綁上芒草以保平安。

阿雅來號結束後，有關巴斯達隘的準備工作大致就緒，而各氏族也各自製作參與祭典時象徵本氏族的吉啦吉嗯（kirakil，舞帽），主要功能是在祭典的歌舞儀式中，滿場不停的舞動，以娛樂達隘；吉啦吉嗯的形狀有兩種：扇形的象徵棕櫚葉，長形的象徵芭蕉葉，各氏族都有固定的形狀，不能隨意更改。

早期的吉啦吉嗯較小，重量較輕，可以戴在頭上舞動，所以又名舞帽；近年來盛行製作較大型的舞帽，但因重量已不適合戴在頭上，改為扛在肩上舞動，仍不影響吉啦吉嗯在祭典中的象徵意義。

三、巴斯達隘祭（下）

當所有準備工作完成，巴斯達隘約定之期也到了，整個祭典分為幾個部分: 首先，在農曆十月十三日，以吼瑪本斯（homabes）儀式告祖請神，由朱姓主祭帶領其他姓氏的長老，拿著豬肉串及竹杯酒面向東方獻祭，除了邀請達隘降臨，也祈求祭典期間風和日麗，一切順利進行。

接著，農曆十月十四日清晨，舉行巴紹儀式（paksau，薦晚餐，請達隘吃晚餐的意思），由朱家媳婦舂米、男子打糯米糕做為祭品。擔任主祭者在達隘靈前放置煙斗、魚和泉水，迎接古固酉奧（koko　yuaow，女性達隘）蒞臨。然後，下午行吉西瑙浪（kisinaulang，會靈），各姓氏代表迎接達隘之靈到祭場旁的祭屋；這是最神聖的地方，外人不能接近，有關祭典的事務及儀式程序都在祭屋中決定及指揮。日前完成的舞帽也在這天上場了，當會靈儀式開始，巴斯達隘歌舞正式展開，由打叭阿尚（tabaa'sang，漢譯臀鈴或背響）的節奏帶領歌舞進行，由各姓青年扛著的舞帽跟著全場巡行跳躍。若到十年一次的大祭（年份是遇到公元的六，如1986年、1996年及2006年），還可以看到大祭旗（tinaton），這是在一根長約五、六公尺的竹竿上，綁著紅、白色的布條（紅、白色的比例約為1：4，紅色在頂端），由三個人一起揹著繞行祭場。

到了農曆十月十五日，舉行吉西篤曼（kisitomal，娛靈），歌舞儀式通宵達旦，近年來，這個儀式已漸開放若干時段給外族人進場共舞。當歌舞上場一個多小時後，另有揮打樹皮做成的蛇鞭（註1）的儀式，由朱姓派男子代表護送蛇鞭進場，呈交給主祭及朱姓長老在祭場中央揮動，發出很大的聲音。這個儀式有祈求天氣晴朗之意，這時賽夏族婦女都會抱著新生兒觸摸揮動蛇鞭者的背部或手臂，祈求孩子健康成長。

農曆十月十六日，舉行吉西巴巴那瓦尚（kisipapatnawasak，逐靈），歌舞儀式從傍晚開始，到午夜暫時停止，這時眾人仍要維持手牽手、圍圓圈，在圈子中央放著一個米臼，由主祭站到臼上訓話後開始巡迴敬酒——把本族傳統的比努撒幹（pinosakan，糯米酒）放在舞圈中間，主祭先敬長老，然後是跳舞行列的每一個人，最後是場外的人，接著歌舞再持續到天亮。這晚的儀式是在宣示達隘祭典即將完成，大家可以準備回程了。

最後一天，也就是農曆十月十七日的清晨，進行吉西巴巴伍薩(kisipapaosa，送靈儀式)，這是整個巴斯達隘的最高潮。整個儀式分為幾個部分：

▶ 巴巴西比令（papasibilil，餽糧）

由朱姓和風姓青年各一人吃下糯米糕後，到山上砍竹子；祭屋內兩位朱家媳婦抱著芒草結及用葉子包好的糯米糕，等砍竹青年快回到祭場時，迅速跑出繞祭場一週，之後跑到面東的場邊丟棄芒草結和糯米糕，這時所有參加典禮者都要將身上的芒草結丟棄，砍竹子的青年隨後也跑到丟棄芒草的地點丟棄竹枝。

▶ 數瑪瑪（sumama，塗泥）

芒草結丟棄後，祭場中再擺上糯米糕和酒，兩位青年吃完後繼續到山上砍樹，另兩位青年在場內挖一小坑，加上水攪成泥漿，把原來盛酒和糯米糕的米籩（註2）割裂，並將今年及上次使用過的蛇鞭，塗上泥漿；這時本族病弱的婦女可以披上方巾，讓兩名青年把塗過泥漿的米

割裂米籩，塗上泥漿

米簻擦婦女背部　　　　　　　　　　伐回榛木，綁上芒草結，接著進行墮架

簻擦過她們的背部，據說可以袪除病痛。使用過的米簻和蛇鞭也要丟棄在丟芒草結的地方。

▶ 瑪類 嘎 喜窩（mare ka sibook，砍伐榛木）

太陽出來後，達隘已經離開，這時主祭派兩位青年到山上砍榛木（即台灣赤楊），場內歌舞的節奏開始加快，榛木伐回時，樹身綁了許多芒草結，青年把樹頭架在祭屋的屋頂上，樹尾則以另一支架撐住，歌舞在此時停止。接著進行墮架、跳抓芒草結、毀架等最後儀節，各姓青年在架好的榛木下跳躍努力抓下芒草結，等芒草結剩一半時，榛木會逐漸放低，青年們會去搶帶有葉

放下榛木，青年跳搶枝葉，向東方丟棄　　賽夏傳統祭典，就這樣大手牽小手薪傳下來

子的樹枝，然後把搶到的枝葉向東方丟棄。這時主祭下令把榛木放下，砍榛木的兩位青年躲回祭屋中，其他青年合力折斷榛木，再折成若干小段，支架也折斷，同樣的向東方丟棄，祭典便在高潮中結束。

註1.「蛇鞭」：用樹皮製成，每兩年做一條，只有南庄祭典才有，配合上次祭典留下的，這次揮完後，丟掉舊的留下新的，每兩年替代下去。

註2.「米簁」：用來淘去稻穀的農具。

▶ 賽夏族傳統服飾穿著圖解

男子頭飾 6

無袖短上衣 7

遮陰布 8

1 女子頭飾

2 女子耳飾

3 頸飾

4 無袖短上衣

5 腰裙

▶ 巴斯達隘祭典圖解

1 舞帽

舞帽音與賽夏男子名武茂雷同,祭典前幾天開始,由各姓氏製作,過去的質地輕較小,能戴在頭上,現在的變大變重,只好扛在肩上,所以又稱肩旗,形狀類似芭蕉葉或山棕葉,因為舞動時十分消耗體力,各姓氏肩旗需由同姓青年輪流背負。

2 服裝

布料以麻為主,棉布次之,顏色以紅白為主,紋飾為菱形、三角形、卍字形或十字型,卍字代表雷女,菱形則指海龍女,點狀橫紋象徵矮靈。祭典時男女均穿著長及小腿的無袖長衣。

巴斯達隘:賽夏族全族性祭典之一,並非朱家獨有祭典,朱家只負責主祭,全族都要深入參與,而且負責其中重要工作,例如風姓是祭典顧問,有任何疑問都要向他們請教,而章姓則負責在祭典的最後砍斷榛木。每兩年(公元的雙數年)舉行一次,每十年一次大祭,時間大約在農曆的十月中旬。地點有兩處,分別在苗栗縣南庄鄉的向天湖及新竹縣五峰鄉的大隘。

3 日月

舞帽音與賽夏男子名武茂雷同,祭典巴斯達隘前三天從晚上六點進行到早上六點,在天剛亮太陽升起、月亮還未落下時,歌舞仍持續著。

4 隊形

逆時針方向行進,蛇狀隊形,有蛇崇拜的意思,引隊伍出來的是朱家長老,但之後這名長老會在隊伍中間,並不在第一個位置。

5 臀鈴

又名背響。一種樂器,在巴斯達隘祭典中具有領舞作用,一般說來,只有章家的男性與媳婦才能背,女兒不能背。

7 米椿

薦晚餐時椿糯米,然後製成米糕,於祭典結束後分給族人,由朱家負責。

6 火堆

布料以麻為主,棉布次之,顏色以紅為達隘引路用。

巴斯達隘禁忌:賽夏族人相信在祭典中如有不敬的行為,將會受到矮靈懲罰。祭典期間,人人都要綁上芒草結,器物也要,以免惡運上身;參與祭典的外族人也該以敬畏的心情對待,除了身上,連相機或攝影機都要繫上芒草結。此外孕婦也不能看,否則會帶來惡運。

四、回娘家

賽夏族的生命禮俗正如同世界各民族，是牽繫著個人與家族、民族，乃至於與超自然世界關係的儀式；然而，隨著時代的變遷，有些不合時宜的禮俗難免必須修改或被淘汰。舉例來說，早期賽夏族的男子必須完成「獵頭」才能舉行成年儀式，才能進行缺齒、拔毛（註1.）、蓄長髮、紋面及結婚；女子也必須學習織布等各項技藝，被族人認可後，才有資格談論婚嫁。到了飽經現代文明洗禮的今天，當然不可能再遵照古俗，把這些標準做為成年的標記，因此，有關的生命禮俗便日漸在人們記憶中淡去。

但值得一提的是，賽夏族的「回娘家」是台灣原住民中獨有、而且奉行至今的生命禮俗。賽夏族的「回娘家」並不是春節大年初二的回娘家，而是男女結婚後，夫婦兩人終其一生總共只有四次回娘家的儀式，藉著儀式維繫出嫁女兒與娘家的關係，四種回娘家的形式如下：

▶ 婚後回娘家（monsaesae'p，門撒撒）

結婚後二、三天，新婚夫婦帶著糯米糕及少數親人一起回門，一般會在娘家住一晚，第二天新郎要替岳家做些勞動工作，有考驗新郎體力及賠償女方損失的意思（這項勞動現在已經省略了），而娘家會準備一些糯米糕讓女兒帶回夫家。

▶ 新生兒回娘家（malakazaza，瑪拉嘎乍乍）

女兒生完第一胎的滿月後，不論生男生女都必須帶回娘家通報；如生男孩，要送給岳家一枝箭簇，女孩就送麻線；進門前夫妻雙方要各找一位沒有被蛇咬過的健康男孩交換吃糯米糰，吃完才可進門祭告祖先。新生兒自出生起就與母親娘家關係密切，終其一生都會獲得娘家的照顧與祝福。

▶ 子女成人後回娘家（maspazau，瑪斯巴繞）

這是賽夏社會最受重視的回娘家儀式，不論任何情況都必須要做，當女兒出嫁一段長時間，小孩已經長大，同時經濟環境也已改善，這時夫妻兩人就會帶著所有的小孩回娘家，祈求女方祖先保佑全家平安幸福。如果女子出嫁後忘了做這次的回娘家，女方祖先很可能會透露一些徵兆，或許是一種警告，讓出嫁多年的女兒不會忘記娘家。這次回娘家所攜帶的物品有豬肉、糯米糕和酒，是分給娘家前來參加的親友，儀式雖簡單，意義卻相當深遠。賽夏族出嫁的女子謹遵傳統要求，不敢懈怠。

▶ 喪偶後回娘家（mazau，瑪繞）

依照賽夏族傳統禮俗，丈夫在喪偶後，必須由本家的長輩帶著他及子女回到妻子娘家。過去的儀式較繁複：首先，丈夫會在妻子娘家前大哭，由娘家人勸止後進屋，接受娘家長者說一些惋惜的話，而後夫妻雙方的代表合飲（註2.）；最後，娘家人領著喪偶的女婿到田裡象徵性的工作，這是意味著喪偶的丈夫從此刻起，可以正常工作及生活了。這個禮俗現在演變成，不論夫妻任何一方逝世，配偶都要攜子女回娘家，以表示生者的哀慟之情。總而言之，瑪繞儀式對賽夏人而言，是希望表達不因妻子故去，夫家就忽略了與娘家關係的互動連結。

> 註1.「缺齒」、「拔毛」：成年標記，也就是拔掉2枚上門牙及若干陰毛，才能算成人。
>
> 註2.「合飲」：ainomi（艾努米），兩人共飲一杯酒之意，通常在婚喪、和解、會議及友好氣氛時，才會合飲。

五、祈天祭

祈天祭是與農事及天候相關的祭典，目的是在播種農作物後，祈求風調雨順。過去賽夏族有關天氣的祭典包括祈晴祭、祈雨祭、鎮風祭及驅疫祭，都是分開舉行的；現在已經都合併在一起，稱為祈天祭（a'uwalr，阿伍萬）。

祈天祭是賽夏族全族性祭典，每年農曆三月十五日前後，以占卜決定舉行日期，分大祭和小祭，兩個逐年輪流。小祭的祭期一天，與巴斯達隘同一年舉行；隔年就是大祭，祭期三天。

賽夏族祭典的一大特色是各由不同氏族司祭，例如巴斯達隘是由朱姓司祭，祈天祭就由潘姓司祭。不過，潘姓氏族在賽夏族傳統姓氏裡稱為撒萬（sha-wan），包含潘、錢兩個漢姓，再加上嘎斯阿慕思（kas'amus，漢譯為根）也是過去由撒萬分出的，因此，祈天祭的祭團（sa'pang，撒棒）成員便包括潘、錢、根三個漢姓。此外，祈天祭儀式的運作雖然是撒棒主導，但是在儀式開始前必須由敏拉各（minrakes，漢譯章）氏族發起，並決定祭期，同時在叭拜（babai，漢譯風）氏族見證下，才能正式進行。

祈天祭的神話來源為雷女奉雷神之命，攜小米種子到人間幫助賽夏族，因此雷女在賽夏族傳統信仰中的地位崇高，而小米就成為祈天祭的象徵作物。儀式中，主祭者處理小米時，新生兒或是一般成人都可以去碰觸主祭的背部，祈求健康平安。除了小米，貝珠（siloe喜露）也是祈天祭儀式裡，獻給祖靈及神靈的象徵物。

為期三天的大祭，第一天是河邊會議，與巴斯達隘的河邊會議性質相同，地點在大南河畔；第二天為殺豬儀式，地點在大南河靠蓬萊處，由各氏族長老持豬肉串與酒向東方獻祭；第三天在蓬萊村的大湳部落祈天祭場，參與儀式的族人要分食小米糰、糯米糰及豬肉，並且不能喝水，傍晚由主祭獻祭小米糰、豬肉及貝珠。

祈天祭有幾個明顯的傳統禁忌必須注意：

一、由於祈天祭同時具有祈晴、祈雨及祈求農作物順利生長的性質，因此祭典期間對水有時親近（前兩日在河邊），有時又是禁忌（第三日在祭場）。

二、在分食小米糰及糯米糰時必須緊閉門窗，以避免疾病入侵。

三、因為祈天祭是農業祭典，在祭典期間對植物新芽的摘砍也有嚴格限制，以現代觀念來看，這正是生態保育的具體表現。

四、孕婦和她的丈夫都不能參加祭典，以免對小孩不好。

現在的祈天祭除了仍然維持賽夏族傳統信仰中有關農事、天候的祭典性質外，同時更是賽夏族傳承古老文化、凝聚族群意識的傳統祭典之一。

造訪部落　部落藏寶圖，來挖賽夏寶

看過了賽夏族的神話與傳說故事，和賽夏人一起仰望發源地大霸尖山，親探神秘的巴斯達隘儀式，感受雷女下凡帶來的恩澤，覺得意猶未盡吧！

賽夏族分布在新竹、苗栗兩縣交界山區，大致可以鵝公髻山和橫屏背山為界，分為南北兩大群。南賽夏居住於苗栗縣南庄及獅潭鄉，以南庄最多，主要在東河、蓬萊、南江三村，獅潭則多集中在百壽村。北賽夏則在新竹縣五峰鄉一帶，包括大隘村以及花園村。

賽夏族原分布地極為廣闊，南自大安溪，北至大嵙崁溪，東到大霸尖山。後來受到客家人及泰雅族擴展的壓力，退縮到山區，成為原住民活動範圍最狹窄的一族，人口數與蘭嶼達悟族差不多，是本島人口最少的原住民，目前不到五千人。南賽夏與客家人互動頻繁，北賽夏則長期與泰雅族混居，深受其影響。現在，透過這份精心編製的「南庄鄉賽夏族文化與旅遊導覽圖」以及「新竹縣、苗栗縣文化與旅遊導覽圖」，陪伴身歷其境，盡情挖掘部落文化寶藏，保證不虛此行。

當然，造訪部落時更不能錯過賽夏族獨有的祭儀活動，除了兩年一小祭、十年一大祭的巴斯達隘祭，農曆三月十五日前後舉行的祈天祭，也是賽夏族傳承文化、凝聚族群意識的傳統祭典。心動想要行動之前，最好先確定時間及地點。

詳情請洽：

苗栗縣政府（電話：037-322150 網址http://www.miaoli.gov.tw/）

新竹縣政府（電話：03-5518101 網址https://hsinchu.gov.tw）

賽夏族
文化導覽圖

族語開口說　　**入境隨俗的賽夏語**

早安！
so'o kimizemzemay！
叟噢 吉米稔稔唉

你好嗎？
so'o kayzahay？
叟噢 改日阿唉
. . . .
你吃飯了嗎？
so'o sominialilaay？
叟噢 叟米按以啦埃

我從＿＿來。
yako mialay ＿＿moiy.
雅構 米亞賴＿＿模埃亦

我很高興遇見你。
yao kinsiya komitasoen.
瑤 葛引喜亞 吉米大叟恩

我的名字是伊德‧阿道。
inmanaa'raro：o iteh a atau.
尹滿那阿 啦羅歐 伊德 阿道

巴斯達隘祭場在哪？
hano ka pas-taaiyan.
哈努 嘎 巴斯 達隘恩

你幾歲了？
so'o pizaila tinaomah？
叟噢 比日阿以啦 底那伍瑪？

我＿＿歲了。
yako＿＿tinaomah.
雅構＿＿底那伍瑪

你在做什麼？
so'o ampowa？
叟噢 安姆部瓦

這是什麼？
hini kano？
呵以膩 嘎努
. . . .
那是什麼？
hiza kano？
呵以日阿 嘎努

我們要去參加巴斯達隘祭。
yami am rima ka pas-taaiyan.
雅密 阿姆 里瑪 嘎嘎 巴斯達隘恩

你歌唱得真好。
so'o rammatomalan motolr.
叟噢 蘭姆瑪斗瑪蘭　抹豆恩

. . . .

你舞跳得真好。
so'o rammatomalan homiyon.
叟噢 蘭姆瑪斗瑪蘭 吼米用

謝謝。
Ma'alo'.
瑪 阿洛

再見！
pinawan.
比那萬

你好帥(美)！
so'o kaizahtomalan ka tinola:a.
叟噢 改日阿斗瑪蘭 嘎 頂伍拉阿(本句男女通用)

族語開口說　賽夏族稱謂的介紹

baki	叭給	阿公
koko	古固	阿媽
yaba	亞爸	爸爸
oya	伍婭	媽媽

賽夏語發音原則：

1.本書使用的音韻符號主要是以教育部訂定之南島語音韻賽夏語部分。

2發音時，請將重音放在每個單詞的最後一個音節。

3.p、t、k是不送氣的清塞音，發音時比較接近注音符號的ㄅ、ㄉ、ㄍ。

4.喉塞音以逗點記音，本身不發音，遇此記號時，以喉頭阻擋氣流。

5.「：」表示長音。

6.「l」表示兩個母音間的滑音；「i」在字尾時發音為「n」。

學習加油站　本書漢語與賽夏語名詞對照表

故事01：白髮老人的預言

用漢字拼讀	賽夏語	漢語名詞
依斯畢	'ishpi'	夢
卜奧	pongaw	白髮
打砥膩	tatini	老人、長老
歐倍那伯翁	oppehnaboon	男祖先名
玻羅努	polono'	船
瑪亞該以	ma'ya kai'	告訴
撙阿伍然惡夢	tal'ae'oeralemom	烏雲
歐姆伍然	omoral	大雨
來以	rai:	陸地
叟米窩	somibo'	洪水
撒西窩	sasibo:	水災
拉羅阿	laloa	大浪
偶固	o:ko'	織布機
米那砥膩	minatini	兄姊
米那以弟	mina'iti	弟妹
瑪雅那伯恩	mayanaboon	女祖先名
巴巴哇嘎	pakpakwaka	大霸尖山
哇散	wasal	大海
敏那漢	mina:hael	子孫
玻立	bori	肉
賽‧瓦洛或賽‧蘭姆頌	Sai-waro 或 sai-lamsong	南庄
賽‧吉拉巴	sai-kirapa	五峰
賽‧撒衛	sai-shawe	獅潭

故事02：雷女下凡

用漢字拼讀	賽夏語	漢語名詞
本歐	per'oe	野菜、生菜
卜外	boay	果實
巴地椏以	patiay	耕田
嘎哇斯	kawas	天上
比哇	biwa	雷神
娃恩	waaung	雷女
嘎拉列	kalali'	葫蘆
達印	tain	人名
導案	tawan	家
因拉	yinra	結婚
底娜	tina	母親
亞爸	yaba	父親
阿奈	anay	媳婦
馬薩	masa'	眼睛
倚瑪玻奧	imapoaw	失明
馬塞	masay	過世
來刨	raibaw	大鍋
掃給	sawki	鐮刀
巴拉鋯	palakaw	柴刀
比那底椏以	pinatiyay	田
陡莫比哇	tomobiwa	打雷
古薩	kosa'	草
達達瑪	tatama'	夫
橄姆哈麗	kamhali'	妻
喜欸	siae	幸福、快樂
嘎打樂淦	katalekan	廚房
叭給	baki	公公
導莫	tawmo'	芭蕉樹
依努哈斯	inoehaes	窗
比葉	biye	葉子

故事03：巴斯達隘傳說

用漢字拼讀	賽夏語	漢語名詞
巴斯達隘	pas-taai	巴斯達隘
賽夏	sai-siat	賽夏
瑪倚亞	ma'iyah	人
撢伍禖	taloemaeh	農耕
撢窩佑	talboyo	打獵
叭佑斯	bayosh	颱風
熬害斯	awhaesh	老鼠
玻厄斯	poes	麻雀
比拿納阿密斯案	pinana'amishan	秋天
阿伐安	a:bqan	夏天
阿密斯案	amishan	冬天
伍瑪玻斯	omabes	祭典、獻祭
嘎叭給	kabaki'	祖先
亦亦喇案	ir'iray'an	矮
伍伍喇案	o'ola'an	小
首把瑞	soparey	大
嘎臘	kaara	胸
呵以瑪	hima'	臂
阿膩許	angish	勇敢
阿尚	a'sang	鄰居
達隘	taai	賽夏族人對矮人的稱謂
打大	tata'	小米
把日艾	pazay	稻米
比引系	binsi	種子
撒拉隆姆	saralom	生病或有疑難雜症問靈用
玻那比斯	ponapis	用來尋找失物或失蹤者的占卜法
輪哈普	romhaep	用來問事或治病的占卜法
阿伍日暗	a'oral	雨
阿酩	alaw	魚
姆亞以喇	mya'ila	喜歡（高興）
瑪阿露	ma'alo	感激（謝謝）
倚喇斯	ilash	月亮
魯哈難	rohanan	夜晚
敏古玲案	minkoringan	婦女

用漢字拼讀	賽夏語	漢語名詞
阿亞來浩	ayalaihou	會議倫理
安阿喇	al'alak	青年
武茂	umau	人名
第底韻	titiyun	賽夏族傳統姓氏，漢譯朱
加列赫	kaleh	人名
伊德	iteh	人名
吉杜亞恩	kitoya'en	艱苦（窮）
叭窩	bobok	飽
阿立嘎	alikah	快
瑪斯橄嘎該以	mashkanka:l	語言約定（發誓）
撒守叭多	sasobato'	埋石為誓
倚豆	ito'	山枇杷樹
苟苟恩	ko:kool	山
叭阿喇	baala'	溪
嘎吼以	kahoi	樹
倚亞散瑟	iya:samsek	傍晚
阿武莫	a'omo'	斧頭
霞瑪	shama	泥土
欣欸	shil'l	重
該以	ka:l	聲音
玻厄	poe'oe'	膝蓋
得哇奈	twanay	大嫂
巴斯	pas—	祭祀（前置）
巴達比爾	paspatabir	儀式
哈汶	habun	亡靈
阿日阿日姆	az'azem	心
欣來浩	shinraihou	相當於漢人的「姓」
阿哈—欣來浩	aehae' shinraihou	比「姓」更強調源自同一祖先
阿哈	aehae'	一（數字）

部落百寶盒：巴斯達隘祭（上）

用漢字拼讀	賽夏語	漢語名詞
叭叭哢	babalon	祭前儀式
嘎嘎哇斯	kakawas	約期會議
阿雅來號	ayalaihou	座談會或長老會議
吉啦吉嗯	kirakil	舞帽

部落百寶盒：巴斯達隘祭（下）

用漢字拼讀	賽夏語	漢語名詞
吼瑪本斯	homabes	告祖請神儀式
巴紹	paksau	薦晚餐（請達隘吃晚餐）
古固酉奧	koko yuaow	女性達隘
吉西瑙浪	kisinaulang	會靈儀式
打叭阿尚	tabaa'sang	臀鈴或背響
吉西篤曼	kisitomal	娛靈儀式
吉西巴巴那瓦尚	kisipapatnawasak	逐靈儀式
比努撒幹	pinosakan	糯米酒
吉西巴巴伍薩	kisipapaosa	送靈儀式
巴巴西比令	papasibilil	饋糧
數瑪瑪	sumama	塗泥
瑪類 嘎 喜窩	mare ka sibook	砍伐榛木

部落百寶盒：回娘家

用漢字拼讀	賽夏語	漢語名詞
門撒撒	monsaesae'p	婚後回娘家
瑪拉嘎乍乍	malakazaza	新生兒回娘家
瑪斯巴繞	maspazau	子女成人後回娘家
瑪繞	mazau	喪偶後回娘家
艾努米	ainomi	合飲

部落百寶盒：祈天祭

用漢字拼讀	賽夏語	漢語名詞
阿伍萬	a'uwalr	祈天祭
撒萬	shawan	賽夏族傳統姓氏，漢譯潘、錢
撒棒	sa'pang	祭團
敏拉各	minrakes	賽夏族傳統姓氏，漢譯章
叭拜	babai	賽夏族傳統姓氏，漢譯風
喜露	siloe	貝珠

邵族
Thao

▶小筆記▶

· 於2001年正名，是台灣第10族原住民。

· 日治時代曾將邵族視為鄒族之一。

· 當時的阿里山包括今天彰雲嘉的淺山丘陵，當時稱「曹族」。

．吳沙開墾水沙連造成衰落；日本人興建日月潭水庫，淹沒了絕大多數邵族棲地⋯，
　目前人口僅300多人的邵族，仍有族群意識、母語與信仰祭儀。

．祖靈籃又稱公媽籃，相當於祖先神位，每家戶都有。

．愛唱歌的民族，目前日月潭表演的杵歌主要是打獵歌與迎賓歌。

故事導讀　　大自然是走向祖靈的路

和賽夏族比較，邵族傳說中的小矮人顯得有些滑稽，他們住在山洞裡，還長著尾巴。
有關長尾巴的人的故事，在其他族群中也有一些傳述，他們不一定是小矮人，且住在
地底下；和上天界一樣，要和地底下的人交通，也有一定的規矩。但在邵族這裡，顯
然小矮人和地底下的人的故事版本被編織在一起了。

邵族眼中的小矮人更早來到日月潭，聰明、擅長各種工藝且精於農作，邵族人從他們
那裡獲益良多。衝突的發生，仍然起源於人類的好奇心。做為異族的小矮人，長有尾
巴，從邵族人的眼光看，這或許是尚未完全進化的象徵。邵族人之強行探訪小矮人的
住處，事實上就是把小矮人趕走了。

漢人的到來，是另一個強勢異族的入侵。大茄苳樹既象徵邵族的祖靈，也代表自然；
獠牙精以現代工具的威力，鋸倒了茄苳樹，破壞了大自然，也決定了邵族步入衰微的
命運。

祖靈與大自然精神的合一，可以在〈白鹿傳奇〉的故事中得到印證。白鹿若即若離的
引導，使邵族人的祖先發現了日月潭，來到了美麗的「普吉」，並世世代代繁衍至
今。因而對大自然的破壞，即是對祖靈的褻瀆，就像獠牙精鋸倒茄苳樹一樣，我們同
時切斷了走向祖靈的路。這種情況，最具破壞性的一面，不只是因像漢族這樣強勢族
群的入侵，而是族人本身無知、貪婪所引發的誘惑。日月潭的長髮精怪即是大自然的
反撲，激戰三天三夜之後，精怪達克拉哈對邵族的勇士努瑪說：「日月潭裡佈滿了密
密麻麻的漁具，如果將魚蝦全數打盡後，那麼我們大家還能活下去嗎？」這正是邵族
人也是台灣原住民各族的文化智慧，他們代替大自然不斷地追問人類：沒有了地球、
消滅了萬物，我們將往哪裡去？

雖然我們無法確定視雙胞胎為不吉祥的觀念，如何演變成祖靈籃的信仰？被沈溺在日
月潭的為什麼是黑嬰而不是白嬰？黑嬰託夢的隱喻到底代表著什麼？它和祖靈之間
存在著什麼樣的關係？這些複雜的問題，當然還需要我們更進一步的探討。但，至少
〈黑白孿生子和祖靈籃〉的故事，提供了一個線索，藉以說明一個在現今邵族社會中
普遍存在的信仰形式。如何經由這個線索去連接邵族的大自然信仰？並透過其和異族
（如漢族）深刻的互動歷史探究其信仰變遷？這當然有待來者。

Reader's Guide　　## Through Nature is the Way to the Ancestral Spirit

We have heard of the Saisiyat's experience with the little people. By comparison, the ihiltun of the Thao are more amusing. They live in caves and have long tails. There are also stories about people with long tails in other ethnic groups but they are not necessarily dwarfs nor necessarily live under the ground. Whether underground, above ground, or in the heavens, there are certain norms for communicating with people.

The Thao believe that the ihiltun arrived at Sun Moon Lake long before them. The ihiltun were intelligent, adept craftsmen, and good at farming. The Thao benefited a lot from the ihiltun. Ultimately, the conflict between the ihiltun and the Thao was due to human curiosity. The Thao may have believed that these peoples' tails indicated they were not fully evolved, but their forcible visit to the home of the ihiltun drove them away.

The arrival of the Han Chinese shows us an example of yet another powerful invasion by an alien people. The giant pariqaz tree in the story of the same name, not only symbolizes the Thao ancestor spirits, but also represents nature; the use of the lhalhikhlik , a saw, to slay the ancient pariqaz shows how a powerful technology may lead to the devastation of nature and the natural order, it also portended the decline of the Thao.

The unity of nature and the ancestral spirits is demonstrated in the "The Legend of the White Deer". Guided by the deer, the Thao ancestors discovered Sun Moon Lake and came to the beautiful "puji", where they have lived for generations to this day. The destruction of nature is tantamount to the desecration of the ancestral spirits, just like the lhalhikhlik sawing down the pariqaz, we also severed the path to our ancestral spirits. But the destruction of nature was not just due to the invasion of the powerful alien Han Chinese, but also by the ignorance and greed of the Thao themselves. The Long Haired Spirit of Sun Moon Lake tells about nature's counterattack. After a fierce battle lasting three days and nights, the spirit Taqrahaz said to the Thao warrior Numa: "Sun Moon Lake is full of abandoned fishing gear and other junk; this overfishing and reckless exploitation will spell the end of our shrimp, fish and other life. How then can we live?" This cultural wisdom of the Thao people and indeed, of all Taiwan's indigenous peoples can be summed up by the their question, posed on behalf of the natural world: "when the earth is gone and all life disappears, where will we go?"

Although we cannot be sure about the notion that giving birth to twins is inauspicious, how can we explain its evolve into the Thao conviction as to the ancestral basket? Why was the black infant twin thrown into Sun Moon Lake to be drowned rather than the white infant twin? What does the metaphor of the black infant's appearance in Hinaluma's dream represent? What does it have to do with the ancestor spirits? Of course, these complex issues need to be further explored. However, at a minimum from the story "The Black and White Twins and the Origins of the Ancestral Spirits Basket" we have some clues understand a belief system that remains prevalent in present Thao society. But how do we use this clue to find the connection with Thao faith and belief in nature, or the connection to the profound impact which historical interaction between the Thao and other peoples (for example the Han Chinese) had upon these beliefs? In this regard we can only say, much remains to be done by those who succeed us.

01

白鹿傳奇

> 究竟是白鹿有意引路,還是祖靈的眷顧?因為
> 不斷追逐白鹿,邵族人尋找到了豐美的日月
> 潭,決定就此定居;並將首次抵達的地方,稱
> 作「普吉」,是白色的意思,以感念白鹿。

初秋原野，芒草陸陸續續抽出幼嫩的穗莖。天邊一片蔚藍，乾爽的風兒吹拂著雪白耀眼的菅芒花，散發出一股淡淡的青草香味。應該是邵族出獵的時候了！

 What's more?

芒草（茅草）（Ihimza，斯林拉）：茅草和菅芒一樣是野外最常見的草本植物，由於葉緣呈現細鋸齒狀，所以在草叢中鑽行時，外露的皮膚常會被割傷。

菅芒花：故事中指的是五節芒，屬於禾本科植物，在秋天開花結籽，能適應乾燥貧瘠的惡劣環境；常見的芒花還有好幾種，包括蘆葦、甜根子草、高山芒等等。

邵族（Thaw或 Thao）：邵族的正確讀音為「thaw」，後來約定俗成變為「Thao」，學界也都以「Thao」來稱呼邵族。

為了出獵，邵族部落好幾天前就蓄勢待發。長老不斷提醒年輕人：要把弓弦搓實、把有缺角的矛頭磨順、不能忘記獵袋裡該有的火石和蕉絨。其中，蕉絨是山上過夜和烘乾獸肉時用來生火的，一定要很乾燥，不能帶有一點點濕氣，族人這幾天不停的在火塘邊烘製，已經準備充分。

年輕人壓抑住即將外出打獵的喜悅，在長老的指導下，勤快地整理獵具，成群的獵犬也被這個奇妙的興奮氣氛感染，不斷在族人的膝邊腳下哼哼唉唉著。

再過不久就要舉行每年例行的祖靈祭典，因為長達二、三十天的祖靈祭典中，需要祭獻許多獸肉，每到此時，族人總會一起出獵，滿載而歸。

 What's more?

部落（taun，達恩）：邵族的「部落」和「家」都是一樣的說法。

長老（apu，阿部）：老人都可稱呼為阿部，邵族人非常敬重老人家，是部落裡重要事務的詢問和請教對象。

把弓弦搓實：弓弦是用苧麻纖維搓成的繩子，一定要搓得密實堅固，才不致於被弓板彈斷。

矛頭（shinabunan，西拿布南）：是一種投射擲遠的獵具或武器。

火石（fatu，發度）：以前邵族人拿堅硬的白石頭用力相互碰擊以產生火花，再引燃蕉絨，用來生火煮飯或取暖。

蕉絨：指香蕉樹的樹皮纖維，曬乾後是很好的點火材料。

獸肉（bunlhaz，本薩）：狩獵和漁撈是邵族人獲得蛋白質以維護健康的生活技能，但必須遵守一些禁忌，在固定的時間做這類工作，獵捕對象和數量也有規矩，不能濫殺濫捕，以維護生態資源的平衡。

火（apuy，阿布依）：火是非常重要的東西，用來烹煮食物、照明、禦寒，通常家中的火塘終年不熄火，即使是外出工作打獵，火塘中的火種也是煨在灰燼當中，以便隨時取用。

火塘（aynuz，艾努）：生火煮東西及烤火取暖的地方。

獵犬（atu，阿度）：狗是邵族人的好朋友，差不多家家戶戶都養狗。狗陪邵族人上山打獵，也擔任部落的警戒工作，保護部落的安全。

眼看到部落附近丘陵與縱谷間的鹿群長得又肥又壯，年輕人個個磨拳擦掌，就等族長一聲吆喝，出發一展身手。

對於這次的狩獵，族人興致高昂。因為最近有不少族人在附近的林野中，親眼看見一隻頭上頂著分叉的巨角、昂首闊步、高大俊偉，而且一身雪白的鹿。人人都希望能與牠相遇，這隻白鹿正是獻給祖靈最好的禮物啊！

終於出獵了。獵隊奔馳在芒葉高度可以割臉的平野溪畔，露宿於繁星罩頂的小丘上。長老的指揮吆喝聲和著獵犬的奔吠聲，使初秋的原野好不熱鬧！

一天、兩天、數天過去了，族人已經獵得了不少山禽和野獸，在豐獵的歡愉下，大家喜孜孜地正要回到部落。忽然一道白色的身影從眼前飛奔而過——那不正是大家心中期盼著的白鹿嗎？

長老的第一支箭「嗖——」一聲，間不容髮地射出，獵犬狂吠著追了過去，獵隊也緊跟在後。

追呀追，繞過小溪，翻過小山，鑽過榛林芒原，獵人們再怎麼快速奔馳，就是追不上白鹿。到了夜晚，大家累得呼呼而睡。

What's more?

祖靈（qali，嘎里）：邵族認為死去的先人都變成祖靈，會庇佑家人和族人的平安和健康。

祭典（mulalu，模拉祿）：主要的祭典有：農事祭典、狩獵祭典和祖靈祭典，目前都仍依照古禮實施，並未因年代久遠而廢止。其中以陰曆八月的祖靈祭最為隆重，有時祭典的時間甚至於長達一個月之久。

鹿（lhkaribush a qnuwan，斯嘎列布斯 阿 克奴彎）：台灣以前的原野到處可見鹿的蹤影，是原住民的主要獵物和生活所需。後來因為荷蘭人將鹿皮列為主要貿易商品，漢人墾民又大量濫墾、濫捕，以致於台灣的野生鹿已經將近絕跡。

Jun 01.9.16

天亮時，又是一道白影從大家面前一閃而過，於是大夥兒又開始了一天的追逐。

就這樣追著追著，眼看著似乎要追上，但是就差那麼一點點，白鹿又跑到不遠的前方去了。漸漸地，族人發現他們已經離部落愈來愈遠，但白鹿又往更深的山中奔跑。

阿里山周圍與鄰近的淺山丘陵是大家熟悉的家園，但是白鹿奔逃的方向卻是東北邊的內山，那是族人從來沒有到過的地方。滾滾的濁水從那裡發源流出，深邃蓊鬱的群山中似乎埋藏著不可知的神秘。

帶隊的長老認為白鹿應該已經耗盡體力，而且領頭的獵犬正在前面不遠處吠叫著，也許白鹿就在不遠的前方，再過不多久就可以追上了。於是，大夥兒又抓起了弓、箭、長矛，鼓起勁往前追。

族長一路在樹身上劈削樹皮做為記號，以便回家時有跡可循，不會暈山迷路。

這樣子又辛苦地追了幾天，但白鹿總是若即若離，和獵隊保持一段微妙的距離。

就在精疲力竭的族人隨著白鹿登上一座險峻的陡坡時，只見一潭波光粼粼

What's more?

箭（shpazishan，斯巴利山）：箭身以山上的箭竹為材，取挺直而少節的箭竹修製而成，箭鏃最早應該是以適當的石材磨製而成，後來有了鐵器才使用鐵鏃。

阿里山：阿里山是一個大地域的泛稱，不一定指單獨一座山，邵族的原居地很可能在西部平原的某地，和鄒族、布農族及平埔族毗鄰而居。

滾滾的濁水：指濁水溪。邵族分布的領域，在南邊係以濁水溪為界，再往南就是鄒族的領域了。濁水溪因為發源於粘板岩地質的山地，黑色的細岩碎屑和泥土被沖刷而下，形成滾滾的濁水。

的大湖出現在眼前，而白鹿竟然奔向湖邊，族人就這樣眼睜睜地看著白鹿躍入湖中、游泳到縹渺的對岸，從此消失蹤影！

也許是祖靈的旨意吧！族人驚喜地發現環湖四周綠樹茂密，有山有水，湖邊土肥草長，湖裡有數不清的肥美魚兒，這真是一個居住的好地方啊！

一部分的族人於是趕緊循著記號趕回部落，揹著芋苗、帶著粟穀，扶老攜幼地來到湖邊定居，世世代代綿衍至今。族人將這個湖稱作「仁頓」，也就是現在的日月潭，而白鹿帶領族人來到的美麗地方則叫做「普吉」，現在漢人稱「土亭仔」。

 What's more?

弓（futulh，夫度斯）：邵族人善射，所使用的弓有木弓和竹弓兩種，都非常強勁有力。

劈削樹皮：原住民在深山中打獵時，為免迷失方向，常會用砍刀劈削樹皮做記號，以做為路途的指引。

暈山：在原始森林中，常因高大濃密的樹木遮蔽，而使人失去方向感，以致於在森林中迷失方向，找不到回去的路。

大湖（vazaqan，瓦乍甘）：邵族人以此稱呼大面積的潭或湖，有時甚至指稱「海」。

山（hudun，呼崙）：日月潭附近都是重重的峰巒，蘊藏著豐富的生態資源，提供邵人日常的生活所需。

芋頭（lhari，砂列）：可以種在水邊或山坡地上，是原住民的主食。

粟（kamar，嘎瑪）：俗稱小米的植物。

日月潭（zintun，仁頓）：日月潭因為日潭和月潭的形狀得名，二、三百年前的清朝文獻就已經這樣稱呼了，這裡是邵族人的母社，社名叫「水社」，因為有水環繞於四周，所以稱為水社。

土亭仔（puzi，普吉）：即白色之意。邵族的祖先們因為追逐白鹿而到了日月潭，為了紀念這件事情，族人把這個第一次抵達的地點就叫做「白」，漢人來了以後又起了「土亭仔」的地名。

02

長尾巴的小矮人

聰明和善的小矮人什麼都願意與邵族分享，就是不願意邵族來拜訪自己在山洞的家。

邵族的年輕人終於禁不住好奇而私自闖入山洞，赫然發現小矮人想要隱瞞的天大秘密——他們長著一條長尾巴，卻也因此失去小矮人的友誼，從此再也見不到好朋友的芳蹤。

日月潭除了有邵族人居住之外，其實還有一群個子短小的矮人，他們比邵族人更早來到日月潭。

小矮人喜歡住在森林深處，樹叢濃密的山洞裡，他們非常聰明，擅長製造各種工具，種植許多稀奇古怪的農作物。

邵族人和小矮人很快的成為好朋友，並且從小矮人那兒學會了很多製造器物和耕種的技巧。

儘管小矮人和邵族人相處融洽，但是邵族人卻從來不曾到過小矮人的部落，因為小矮人不喜歡邵族人去拜訪他們位在山洞裡的家。

「我們的家又濕又暗，恐怕會讓你們絆倒、滑跤，實在不方便招待你們！」

「我們的家又窄又矮，恐怕會讓你們撞到頭，不方便招待你們！」

小矮人以各種理由拒絕，反而讓邵族人更加好奇。於是，部落年輕人自己下了決定：「我就去突訪小矮人的家，探個究竟吧！」

有天傍晚，邵族年輕人終於成功地闖入了小矮人聚居的山洞。火炬乍現，正準備休息的小矮人驚慌地四處竄跑，急著要找個角落躲起來。

What's more?

矮人（Ihilitun，斯立頓）：傳說邵族人曾經和小矮人一起居住在日月潭，可惜現在日月潭附近沒有任何有關小矮人的遺跡留傳下來。

木臼（runu，魯奴）：以整截樹幹剚挖而成，有相當的重量，和杵配合，用來舂搗穀物的器具。另外也有用很大塊的石頭打製的，重量就更可觀了。

邵族人在炬火照射下定睛一看，發現這些小矮人的屁股竟然都長著一條長長的尾巴。

情急之下，小矮人趕忙坐到木臼上，想把尾巴藏入木臼中，情急間有人摔了下來，尾巴壓斷了，痛得當場哇哇大叫。

原來小矮人在出門前，總是小心翼翼將長尾巴藏好，沒想到邵族年輕人魯莽的闖進來，讓他們非常生氣。

不久，小矮人便遷居到別的地方去了，從此再也沒人見到他們的蹤影，邵族人也因而失去了一群善良且多才多藝的好朋友。

日月潭的長髮精怪

日月潭裡的魚蝦千百年來彷彿取之不盡,然而最近邵族人怎麼捕也捕不到魚蝦?

邵族勇士努瑪縱身躍入潭中一探究竟,發現原來是長髮精怪達克拉哈在破壞漁具。

向來與邵族人和平相處的達克拉哈為什麼這麼做?又帶給努瑪與邵族什麼啟示?

日月潭的水底曾經住著一種奇怪的生物，他們的上半身和人沒有兩樣，不過下半部卻是魚的身體，頭上烏亮的長髮蓋住臉孔，垂在胸前和背後，終日在潭底悠游嬉戲。邵族人稱他們為達克拉哈。

邵族人自從住在日月潭邊以來，和這些水中的長髮精怪達克拉哈一直維持著和諧的關係。

精怪達克拉哈和邵族人都是依靠潭中的魚、蝦、螺、蚌等維生，千百年來日月潭的水邊、水面與水中所有的動植物還是綿衍繁盛，並沒有因為精怪與邵族人的捕撈而減少。

不過，邵族人最近卻常常捕不到魚。

老頭目排達沐憂心的說：「我們的祖先因為日月潭豐碩的魚蝦，過著衣食無缺、自在快樂的日子，也和達克拉哈和平地共享日月潭中的東西，但是這一陣子突然連續發生許多奇怪的事……」

「咦？我的網怎麼破了？」

「啊！捕筒裡的鰻跑掉了！」

「唉！我的蝦籠又被塞口了！」

 What's more?

達克拉哈（Taqrahaz）：邵族的傳說故事人物達克哈拉，是潛藏於日月潭水中的人首魚身精怪，平常和邵族人和平共存，並不會傷害人畜。又傳說以前族人常常看到這精怪在潭中浮出的小嶼上曬太陽、梳理頭髮呢！

排達沐（Paytabu）：是古代邵族頭目的名字。

網（davaz，達瓦茲）：一種架在木排上的魚網。

捕筒（lhalhutha，薩斯薩）：一種捕魚的魚籠，也就是一般稱做魚筌的器具。

剛開始時族人們都非常疑惑，怎麼回事呢？潭中捕不到魚蝦了，這還得了！

「讓我到水中看看是怎麼回事吧！」勇敢的族人努瑪說。

努瑪是個善泳的好漢，天生一副魁梧的身材，他的魚叉射得又快又準，潛入水中還可以大半天不用浮出水面換氣。

勇敢的努瑪縱身躍入潭中，一下子就潛到最深邃幽藍的地方。他游過每一個灣岬，檢視所有的魚網和漁具，發現潭中密密麻麻堆積著各式各樣的漁具，有很久很久以前就廢棄的，也有最近才設置的。

就在最深的潭底處，努瑪看見精怪達克拉哈正在破壞鰻筒。

「喔——原來是這麼一回事！」努瑪頓然了解為什麼族人這一陣子總是捕不到魚！

努瑪和精怪達克拉哈在潭中展開了一場非常激烈的打鬥，掀起的浪花飛濺到水社的山頂，打了三天三夜還分不出勝負。

兩人都因激烈戰鬥而疲累不堪，努瑪不滿的質問精怪達克拉哈為何要破壞

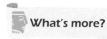

What's more?

善泳的好漢：邵族人世居日月潭旁邊，生活和水有密切的關係，所以幾乎每個人都識得水性，有些人甚至可以潛水很久，擁有在水中佈陷捉魚的絕活。

魚叉（rapu，拉部）：邵族人捕魚的方式除了用網和陷阱之外，也直接用弓箭或魚叉捕魚，通常是在岸邊或船上密切觀察魚群的動態，伺機刺出魚叉，用這種方式捉到的都是大一點的魚。

鰻筒（taqan，達敢）：邵族人常把筆筒樹的樹林砍下，挖空心材的部分，做成鰻筒，因為它的質地較重，可以沉到水底，鰻魚常會鑽到裡面棲息。

漁具，達克拉哈則是憤慨的反問說：「日月潭裡佈滿了密密麻麻的漁具，如果將魚蝦全數打盡後，那麼大家還能活下去嗎？」

努瑪原本以為自己才是擁有正當理由的一方，聽了精怪達克拉哈的話以後，這才知道那麼多年以來，族人已經不知不覺的在日月潭中製造並埋藏了一些問題。

了解發生爭端之後，努瑪和達克拉哈轉戰為和、把肩言歡，因為他們都已經知道應該如何解決長久以來的問題了。

經過這次的事件，邵族人終於體悟到維持萬物永續生息的重要性，因而嚴格約束族人要在固定的時間才能捕捉特定的魚種，網子的疏密和魚筒的半徑也要限制，不可再有「一網打盡」的做法。

邵族人還特意讓日月潭特有的水草在潭面糾集蔓生成一塊塊的水上浮嶼，讓魚蝦們有更多獵食、下卵、繁衍的空間。

這樣一來，不但維持了日月潭中的魚蝦的繁殖，長髮的精怪達克拉哈從此也不再作怪，族人還能常看到他們悠閒地在浮嶼上梳頭曬太陽呢！

What's more?

網目、筒徑：邵族人絕對不用孔目太細的魚網或筒徑過小的筌籠捕魚，並在潭面上設置浮嶼，供魚蝦產卵棲息，平常也會按季節捕撈，這種種的做法使日月潭裡的資源常保豐裕，陪伴邵族人走過悠悠的歷史歲月。

浮嶼：是一種由水草糾結叢生而形成的水上漂浮體，有時會又寬又大、又厚，變成浮島的模樣

黑白孿生子和祖靈籃

邵族每戶人家非常虔誠供奉著自家的祖靈籃，凡是家中大大小小的事情、或是部落裡舉行祭典，都會恭敬地向祖靈籃稟告。

雖然這個敬祖的傳統究竟延續多少年已不可考，但孿生子的禁忌故事仍在族人之間流傳。

「普吉」的生活環境豐沃，加上邵族人辛勤的工作，部落人口因此快速成長，這個地方已經不夠族人居住了。

日月潭中有一個很大的島，邵族人稱為「拉魯」。由於有潭水環繞，形成一個天然屏障，不必擔心野獸和敵人的侵擾，很適合居住；於是部分族人搬到拉魯島上，建立另一個家園。

日月潭真是個好地方，不但山青水綠，而且到處是飛禽走獸和游魚，提供了邵族人豐富的生活資源，族人在島上無憂無慮地住下來，並發展成邵族最大的聚落——水社。

邵族傳統習俗認為，生出雙胞胎是個很大的忌諱。然而有一天，頭目希那努馬的妻子卻生下一對雙胞胎男嬰，而且一個黑臉、一個白臉。族人相當驚恐並且議論紛紛：

「會不會是不祥的預兆？」

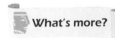

What's more?

拉魯（Lalu）：是日月潭中的一個島嶼，這個島也是邵族祖先早期居住的地點之一，由於位於湖的中間，四周有水的環繞保護，所以曾經是邵族最主要的大聚落 。後來由於瘟疫和漢人侵擾等種種原因，邵族人才搬離拉魯島。拉魯島在清代時被漢人稱為「珠仔山」，日治時代稱為「玉島」，國民政府遷台以後，改稱為「光華島」。

水社（Sazum，沙連）：水社是邵族最主要的大聚落，因為是在大湖之中，所以叫「水社」，在古代的文獻裡，水社又被稱為「沙連」或「水沙連」，邵族的語言稱水就叫做沙連，所以不管是沙連或水沙連，其實指的都是水社。除了水社之外，邵族的其他聚落還有頭社、貓蘭社、審鹿社等等，都是以日月潭為中心，散處於日月潭附近一帶。

頭目更是痛苦萬分，因為這件事關係著整個部族的吉凶安危。

在惶惶不安中，頭目希那努馬趁著妻子不注意時，忍痛將黑臉男嬰兒投入日月潭中。

第二天夜裡，頭目在睡夢中竟然夢見黑臉男嬰。這個男嬰哭著說：

「我的死並不能消除災厄，長久的辦法是每一家都必須準備一個祭籃，將祖先用過的衣物和珠鍊飾品放進裡面，當做祖靈居住的地方。家中有任何大小事情或部落中有重要祭典，都必須恭敬地稟告，否則將會有災禍發生。」

頭目醒來後立即把這個消息告訴所有的族人，大家都非常懊惱後悔，並連忙備妥祖先的衣飾放在籐籃之中——這就是邵族人從視雙胞胎為不吉祥，演變成祭拜祖靈籃的故事。

一直到今天，每個邵族家中仍然虔誠地供奉著自家的祖靈籃。祖靈籃裡面裝著祖先從前遺留下來的衣物飾品，代表祖靈的靈在。家中或部落大大小小的事情，族人都恭敬地向祖靈籃稟告，不敢有任何怠慢。

What's more?

災厄（makarman，麻葛曼）：小災厄如個人的災病、受傷、不順；大災厄可能是洪水地震或瘟疫傳染病。

祖靈籃（祭籃）（ulalaluan，巫拉拉魯安）：又稱為「公媽籃」，邵族人把祖先穿戴過的衣物和珠鍊放在籐編的籃子裡，當作祭拜祖靈時的象徵對象。

05

大茄苳

> 庇護邵族的大茄苳樹被漢人鋸倒後，紅色的樹
> 汁染紅整個日月潭，不久後就遭到瘟疫侵襲，
> 人口大量減少，根本無法抵抗漢人的入侵、佔
> 地開墾。
>
> 甦醒吧！最高祖靈「巴薩拉」，請撫慰邵族人
> 心，讓族人命脈延續下去。

邵族居住的日月潭邊有一棵很大很大的茄苳樹，長老認為大茄苳上面居住著邵族最高的祖靈巴薩拉，保祐著邵族興盛壯大；而邵族人也深信，茄苳樹上茂密的每一片綠葉，代表著邵族的每一個人。

「要小心呵護這棵茄苳樹啊！」老人們一再地仔細叮嚀年輕的族人：

「茄苳樹每萌生一片新葉就代表著我們族裡又增添了一個新的生命！」

春去秋來，茄苳樹的老葉凋落了，又抽出新芽，一年又一年，族人和茄苳樹一起茁壯茂盛。

大約三百多年前，族裡出現了一位雄才大略的頭目骨宗，他率領著族人東征西討，使邵族成為台灣中部水沙連地區最強大的族群。

這時正是清朝政府取代鄭成功家族，統治台灣的初期，漢人由南部持續往台灣中北部拓展，骨宗率領的族人在水沙連山區力抗漢人的推進，漢人因而無法再繼續向內山拓墾。

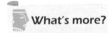

What's more?

茄苳樹（pariqaz，巴列嘎）：台灣的原生樹種之一，以前遍生於全台灣的平地、丘陵及中海拔山地，樹齡可以活得很老，往往變成聚落的守護象徵。全台灣有不少地方以「茄苳腳」為地名。

巴薩拉（Pathalar，巴薩拉）：是邵族各姓氏共同始祖的名字，從開天闢地起祂就是邵族的造物主，是最具權威的祖靈，祂掌管所有善靈和惡靈，祂能降福給族人，也可以驅除邪魔；邵族人每逢歲時祭典，或是遇到困難時，就會準備豐盛的酒食虔誠地向祂祈求。

水沙連地區（Sazum，沙連）：分布區域詳見本書第228頁部落百寶盒中的說明。

漢人們想盡辦法要解決這個令人苦惱的大障礙，在費盡心思、百般探聽之後，終於打聽到日月潭邊大茄苳樹的傳說；於是漢人們就想：「如果能把大茄苳砍倒，這個麻煩的『番人』就可解決了！」

於是一群漢人趁著邵族出外征伐、疏於注意時，帶著斧頭偷偷潛入日月潭邊，打算把這棵邵族人心目中和性命相關聯的大茄苳砍倒。

他們來到潭邊，拿出斧頭用力的砍，但奇怪的是砍完這邊的樹身，再砍另一邊的時候，剛才砍下的傷口竟然又復原了！漢人使盡力氣，大樹卻依舊完好，好像什麼事情都沒發生。

有一天晚上，當中一位漢人實在太疲累了，不知不覺倒在茄苳樹下睡著了。迷迷糊糊間他聽見了大樹絮絮叨叨地對一旁的小樹說：「他們是砍不倒我的！我什麼都不怕，就只怕獠牙精而已！」

漢人醒來後半信半疑的將聽到的話告訴其他人，但是什麼是獠牙精呢？起初大家百思不得其解，後來靈光一現，莫非獠牙精指的就是「鋸子」？

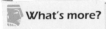 **What's more?**

獠牙精（lhalhiklhik，撒西克西克）：也就是鋸子的意思。

漢人於是改以鋸子來鋸樹身，唏唏嗦嗦，到傍晚就把大茄苳樹給鋸倒了。
當大樹倒下後，漢人唯恐它再復活，又用早已準備好的長銅針釘住樹頭，
並潑上黑狗血，再以大銅蓋把整個樹頭覆蓋住，才滿意的罷手。

大茄苳樹被鋸倒後，紅色的樹汁流滿了整個日月潭的水域。邵族失去了大
茄苳樹的庇護，不久就遭到瘟疫的侵襲，人口大量減少，根本無法抵抗一
批又一批的漢人侵入，原本茂盛的樹林也被漢人砍倒，開墾為水田；邵族
人覺得拉魯島不再是可以長住之地，只好陸續遷到日月潭周圍的其他地
方。邵族的勢力從此再也無法像以前那麼興盛了！

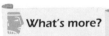

What's more?

長銅針、黑狗血、大銅蓋：漢人的宗教習俗裡，認為這三樣東西經過祭拜加持
之後，可以用來鎮煞及壓制精怪，為了不讓茄苳樹復活，特別用了這三件東西
加以壓制。

覆蓋樹頭：大茄苳雖被砍倒，但仍有可能再萌生孽芽，為了徹底防止樹神再度
復活，用大銅蓋覆蓋住樹頭，阻絕陽光照射，連發芽機會都斷絕了。

紅色樹汁：茄苳樹的樹汁剛流出來時原本是白色的，但是一旦和空氣接觸以
後，會產生氧化的現象而變成紅褐色。

部落百寶盒 ││ 傳授哈「原」秘笈，搖身變成邵族通

一、水沙連的邵族部落

▶ 邵族正名

經過漫長的尋根之旅，邵族申請正名，終在2001年9月21日，獲陳水扁總統於日月潭正式宣布：「邵族」為政府認定的台灣第十族原住民。從此，邵族恢復了原本族稱，不再被誤稱為鄒族或平埔族了。

根據南投縣魚池鄉公所2001年度的統計資料，邵族總人口數不超過三百人，是人數稀少的原住民族群之一。

▶ 天壤之別的邵族與鄒族

早昔大多數人對邵族的了解是很模糊、含混的，首先會混淆的是把邵族當成鄒族，這或許是因為邵（Thaw或Thao）和鄒（Cou或Tsou）的發音非常接近，而且邵族的傳說故事裡又說祖先是在打獵的時候，從「阿里山」（鄒族分布的領域）一路追逐白鹿到日月潭畔才定居下來的。其實「阿里山」在古代是一個籠統的大地名，範圍很廣；包括今天彰化、雲林、嘉義一帶的丘陵淺山地區，都屬「阿里山」的範圍，不像現在專指「阿里山的山區」。

日治時代日本政府把邵族人歸併在「曹族」裡，當時日本人認知的曹族也就是現在的鄒族；「曹族」是以河洛話發音的族稱，「鄒族」則是國語發音，所以曹族就是鄒族。但事實上，邵族和鄒族（曹族）是兩個完全不同的族群，他們的語言、風俗習慣、宗教祭儀等等都有很大的差異性，即便從現代生物科技的血液遺傳因子分析來看，邵族和鄒族兩族群之間的親屬關係也是很疏遠的。

▶ 邵族的聚落演變

邵族勢力強盛之時，分布領域縱橫整個水沙連內山，就是今天的南投縣集

集、水里、魚池、埔里這一帶山區，跨烏溪以北到濁水溪以南的區域，在清代初期，邵族曾是台灣中部內山最有影響力的族群。根據文獻記載，迨至清光緒年間，水沙連六社除了眉社以外，其他五社——埔社、沈鹿社、貓蘭社、水社、頭社應該都還是屬於邵族的勢力範圍。

三百年來，邵族人和漢人的關係錯綜複雜，先是康熙時的輸貢納賦，接著是雍正時的武力對抗，並且因此遭清廷圍剿，乾隆末年納入番屯制之後，漢人就不斷地用各種方式向邵族的領域侵墾，加以瘟疫肆虐，到清光緒末年，邵族人的聚落就只剩下日月潭附近的幾個舊社而已了。光緒21年以後，日本人統治台灣，大正末年和昭和初年，日月潭水力發電工程施工，築壩蓄水的結果，原來日月潭畔的邵族舊部落均淹在潭中了，日本人遂把全部邵族人集中遷至卜吉社（邵語Barawbaw，河洛話取其諧音叫「北窟」，即今之魚池鄉日月村，又俗名「德化社」，不過「德化社」的名稱因有「以德教化」、鄙視原住民的意思，最好不用）。現在還有邵族人聚集的地方，另外有水里鄉頂崁村的大平林社區仍約10戶邵族人家聚集，這是目前兩個邵族人居住的聚落。

邵族人口少，力量單薄，而且長期以來又處於極度觀光、商業化的地區，照理說，他們的固有傳統文化應該已被同化而消磨殆盡了才對，然而令人訝異的是，邵族人還保有相當完整的傳統歲時祭儀：祖靈崇拜的觀念仍然依舊，族群意識清晰明確；母語的傳承雖然有危機，不過五十歲左右的邵族人仍能以母語溝通交談，從歷史演進的軌跡來看，邵族人的堅持和強韌實在令人欽佩！

清末以前，邵族系統的分布地區一直有「水沙連」的稱法。其實「水沙連」源自於邵語「沙連」（sazum），水的意思，狹義的說也就是「水社」。但是水社因為曾經勢力強大，所以「水沙連」也被廣義的當作整個區域的代稱。

▶ 邵族部落名詞釋義

名詞釋義	廣義的「水沙連」＝水沙連內山			狹義的「水沙連」＝水社
分布	北港 （烏溪以北）	中港 （烏溪以南、濁水溪以北）	南港 （濁水溪以南）	南投縣魚池鄉日月潭周邊
部落	眉社 至霧社（現在的霧社） 平了萬社 （現在的萬大）等	集集社、社仔社頭社、水社、貓蘭、沈鹿、埔社…	鸞社、卓社、卡社、丹社…	水社
種族	泰雅族	邵族	布農族、鄒族	邵族

廣義的「水沙連」指的就是「水沙連內山」，分為北港、中港、與南港三區，其詳細分布如上表列。早期因為漢人對原住民的族群分法不甚了解，故有文獻記載整個水沙連內山（包含水沙連六社）皆屬於邵族系統的部落。但據後來研究發現：居住於北港的眉社部落原住民臉上皆有紋面，應屬於泰雅族而非邵族；位於中港的原住民才是真正的邵族人，另在濁水溪以南的南港區域，則是布農族與鄒族的分布領域；而狹義的「水沙連」則專指日月潭周圍的「水社」。

▶ 邵族部落分布示意圖

＊ 邵族主要分佈圖，
　請見封面裏頁。

二、農漁狩並行的邵族生活

▶ 居住在得天獨厚的魚米之鄉

邵族居住的日月潭周邊地區，因依山傍水，故其生態資源得天獨厚，邵族的祖先因此能兼營農耕和漁獵生活，並從事狩獵；從過去的歷史資料可知，在漢人還未大舉入墾水沙連內山之前，邵族曾經享有一段富庶風光的歲月。

▶ 採典型的火墾刀耕

邵族的傳統農耕方式屬於典型的「火墾刀耕」：先在部落附近的山上選妥一塊大小適當的墾地，然後在墾地外圍開出能隔絕火勢、不讓火勢延續竄燒到墾地之外的防火巷，接著放火燒山，把墾地上的樹林全數燒掉，等火熄滅了以後，再把地面上的石塊和沒燒盡的樹幹整理好，堆疊成一段一段的矮牆，以防止表土流失。邵族人就在這墾成的山園裡種植陸稻、小米（粟）或其他旱作的農作物，地面上的灰燼就是現成的肥料。大約種了二、三年以後，土地的肥力已經消耗得差不多了，再換地方開墾，原來的土地則休耕任其荒蕪，以自然的方式恢復原來樹林的樣貌；和漢人的水田定墾精耕的土地利用方式完全不同。

傳統邵族社會的土地是全體族人所共同擁有，所有的族人都可在部落的領地範圍裡墾地種植或狩獵。

▶ 最擅長設陷捕獵

邵族人除了農耕之外，狩獵也是主要的生活方式。一般都是在夏秋兩季上山出獵，除了直接以弓箭或槍射殺之外，有時也動員全部落的人，用驅趕圍獵的方式捕捉野獸。邵族人也很擅長裝設陷阱誘捕獵物，如套索、路槍、壓陷、誘籠……等都是常用的方式，不費吹灰之力，就能輕易捉到獵物。

邵族主要獵捕的獵物有山豬、水鹿、山羊、松鼠等獸類，和森林裡大大小小的飛禽。以前邵族人喜歡把大型動物的頭骨或下顎骨吊掛在屋內或簷下，以誇耀自己的勇敢，獵得大型動物如山豬、水鹿的族人，更是部落裡人人稱羨的英雄好漢！

▶ 漁撈網蝦是較特殊的生活技能

邵族人住在日月潭邊，所以漁獵也是族人的主要生活方式。捕魚的方法很多，一般常用魚網捕撈，較大型的魚類就用魚叉直接射取；邵族人還擅長以籐皮和竹篾製作大大小小的魚笭、蝦籠、鰻筒，裝上誘餌放在岸邊靠水的草叢裡，第二天清晨就有滿筐滿簍的魚蝦等著收取。

以前日月潭還沒有修建發電水壩的時候，水位比現在還要低二十幾公尺，日月潭的湖邊是一大片的淺水沼澤，魚、鰻、蝦、螺、蚌等各式各樣的水產應有盡有，在岸邊隨便裝個圈欄陷阱就可輕易豐收。

▶ 水上浮嶼使魚群生生不息

在清代文獻中有多處記載的「水上浮田」，是往昔日月潭中很特殊的景觀。邵族人將籐編的竹網拋浮於水面，任由浮生的水草聚集叢生之後，再糾結串連、形成大浮嶼；其雖名為「水上浮田」，但實際上並不能夠種田，倒是一種可供水中各種生物遮蔽聚生的大浮體。魚群可以在浮嶼下產卵、攝食、繁衍，也是邵族人放置魚笭捕魚的好處所。

自從日月潭築壩發電後，原有的湖泊沼澤完全消失，水域的生態環境也已經徹底改觀，電力公司因恐水上浮嶼會堵塞進水口而將之全數銷毀。現在日月潭成為著名的觀光區，邵族人也已經不太捕魚了，可見的水上浮嶼景觀僅存位於拉魯島附近，專供觀賞用的塑膠網製浮嶼，邵族老人們都相當緬懷昔日夕陽下泛舟漁唱的情景呢！

三、敬畏感恩的邵族祭典

▶ 特殊的祖靈籃祭拜

邵族和所有台灣的原住民族群一樣，都是以「祖靈崇拜」做為傳統的信仰基礎，而邵族人更把抽象的祖靈形象具體化為「公媽籃」來祭拜。「公媽籃」在學術研究上或稱「祖靈籃」，邵族人把古代祖先穿戴過的衣物和珠鍊等飾物放在籐編的籃子裡，當作祖靈祭拜時的象徵對象，凡是家中或部落裡有重要的行事及祭典，都要恭敬地請出祖靈籃，由女性祭司——先生媽（邵語shinsh'i，這可能是源自於河洛話的「先生」或日語「先生」的外來語，指有一定身分地位的人）主持祭告、祝禱的儀式，恭謹戒慎，不敢稍有怠慢。

▶ 播種祭首先登場

邵族的傳統歲時祭儀較隆重的，首先是農曆3月初一的「播種祭」。為了避開邵族用來做鳥占依據的「繡眼畫眉」鳥（邵語shmashuni）來攪局，初一清晨天色才朦朦亮的時候，家中的長輩就要帶著播種的小孩出發到山上的旱園去，一路上必須禁聲，不可以交談，也不能攀折花木。小孩子拿著小鍬，挖土把陸稻的種籽播種在幾天前就準備好的2公尺見方的墾地裡，祝禱、彈灑祭酒敬祖。婦女們則在家裡備妥祭飯，取下吊掛在牆壁上的「公媽籃」，到部落祭場去祭拜祖先。以前在播種祭之後的3天裡，所有的人都只能吃不加鹽的淡食，言行也都要自我約束，務求莊重，其意義在於從外在形式到內心世界一致體現肅穆敬謹、莊嚴慎重的心情，希望在播種的開始有個平安順利的好兆頭。

▶ 盪鞦韆慶移苗祭

農曆3月12、13日左右，播下的陸稻已經長到大約10公分的高度，這時就要實施「移苗祭」了。如同象徵性播種一樣，移苗祭要把稻苗從2公尺見方的墾地裡移種到其他較大的墾地，各家的公媽籃也要集中在祭場做祭拜儀式。以往做移苗祭的時候，還有一個重要的活動是——盪鞦韆。邵族人的鞦韆架是以四枝粗大的麻竹和藤蔓綑製而成，高度大約10公尺，他們以盪鞦韆來預祝山園裡的陸稻能長得像竹幹那麼粗壯，將來稻穗纍纍、飽滿結實，迎風招展就像擺盪中的鞦韆一樣，所以能把鞦韆盪得愈高，大家就愈高興。

▶ 狩獵祭

農曆7月初，邵族人開始做「狩獵祭」。由於邵族人生活在日月潭附近，尋獵的內容除了山上的飛禽走獸之外，還包括日月潭中的魚鰻蝦蟹漁獵；老人們說，鰻魚渾身滑溜有勁，耐力十足，是日月潭中最凶猛慓悍的魚類，所以邵族的狩獵祭，最奇特的是以糯米麻糬捏成的白鰻當做祭供物，因此也稱為「白鰻祭」或「拜鰻祭」，有別於其他原住民族群以百步蛇作為狩獵的代表圖騰。

▶ 熱鬧非凡的八月祖靈祭

做了狩獵祭之後，男人們就陸陸續續地分批結隊上山打獵，準備8月祭典要用到的大量獸肉。從農曆8月1日的前一天晚上開始，歷經2、30天的盛大祭典，是邵族的「祖靈祭」。不但要以飯和甜酒對祖靈獻祭、也有擦手禳祓、除穢祈福的儀式（長老以棕葉、飛禽的羽毛綁成的束狀掃刷，為族人擦拂手臂以驅除邪穢、祈求平安），另外還必須到每個族人家中喝酒祈福。擔任祭主的，整個8月裡更是熱鬧非凡：要搭建祖靈屋給祖靈歇宿，每個晚上還得在祖靈屋前的祭場唱歌跳舞；族人們利用這個機會溫習古傳的祭歌和舞步，氣氛溫馨感人。祭典的最後一天，幾乎所有的族人都穿戴盛裝，結伴輪流到每個族人的家中歌舞慶賀，往往持續到天亮。

近幾十年來，由於時代變遷，邵族人的傳統農耕及狩獵生活早已沒落式微，但祖靈信仰與傳統祭儀卻都還清楚地保留著，非常可貴而且不容易！

四、邵族祭司「先生媽」

自遠古時代邵族有黑白孿生子的故事流傳開始，邵族人幾乎每一家戶都設有一個「公媽籃」，有的掛在大廳的牆上，有的放在供桌的一側，所有邵人都相信自己家族的祖靈就在這個籃子中，每個家人莫不敬謹有加，倍極尊重。祖靈籃平時不得隨意搬離或翻動，只有在重要的行事或祭儀時才可以取出，是祭祀時的主要祭告對象。而執行祭告的人則是女性祭司，邵族人稱為「先生媽」。

▶ 先生媽必須得到祖靈的認可

2002年時邵族部落裡一共有6位先生媽，她們都是年高德劭，深為族人敬重的女性長者。擔任先生媽的人要有一定的資格和學習的過程，並非人人都可勝任。在學做先生媽之前，首先必須是丈夫健在、家庭生活幸福圓滿的人；其次必須是擔任過8月祭典的主祭。最後更重要的是，必須由老先生媽陪同到祖靈之島「拉魯」（邵語Lalu），尋求祖靈的首肯及確認，才算完成。

在拉魯島上時，新的先生媽人選如果有特殊的感受，比如聽到奇特的聲音、看到奇怪的異象…等，那就是象徵祖靈已經答應此人入門學做先生媽，然後就可回家，由老先生媽親自傳授唸誦祝禱詞和主持祭儀的方法。

▶ 邵人虔誠信仰祖靈籃和先生媽

古代的先生媽除了主持祭儀之外，還得為族人做驅邪收魂、治病解惑的服務，在部落裡享有崇高的地位。邵族人平常家中若有重要的行事，如婚喪喜慶、建屋置產、出獵旅行…等，都會取出祖靈籃置於門前，獻上一碗濁酒以為祭禮，請先生媽向祖先報告，祝禱一番。而一年中的幾個重要祭典如：播種祭、狩獵祭、祖靈祭，其儀式就更為隆重，每家的祖靈籃都要集合到部落裡固定的祭場，請所有的先生媽一起向共同的祖靈祝禱祈福。即使到21世紀的今天，邵族的家庭有諸如：新購大型傢俱、買了新車、家中有久住的客人…等事情，老人家還是會拿出祖靈籃，請先生媽做簡單祝禱，將事情稟明，以免祖靈忌諱疑猜。

邵族居住的水沙連是很多族群相互交會、接觸極為頻繁的地區，邵族人生活周遭充斥著外來的宗教信仰（如佛、道、基督教…）和其他種種的異文化，文化的衝擊和影響是相當激烈的，但邵族卻還能夠保有傳統的民族文化精華和特徵，研究者認為，祖靈籃的信仰和對先生媽的敬重堅持是兩大關鍵！

五、孿生禁忌與傳統習俗

▶ 禁忌源自於敬畏心理

人類在原始大自然環境中，經常要面對水災、火災、颱風和地震等等不可抗力的天然災害，而且生活資源的生產與交換處於封閉狀態，加上醫療衛生落後貧乏，生活中可以說處處充滿危機，稍一不慎就面臨個人、甚至整個社群或聚落的生存威脅。因此，人們對於不可知的奧妙世界油然產生敬畏的心理，進而更由於生活經驗的累積，歸納出日常生活必須遵守的法則。原住民社會沒有文字，這些規矩法則就化約成習俗或禁忌，在無形中規範約束族人的生活言行。

▶ 合乎優生觀念的孿生禁忌

邵族的習俗中忌諱生育雙胞胎，這在醫藥衛生不發達的古代是可以理解的，因為雙胞胎常常造成難產，不只嬰兒存活不易，還可能危及母體生命，而且即使一時存活，在生活資源不充裕的環境裡，後續的養育也往往造成困難。

邵族的婚嫁習俗非常現代化，規定同氏族的男女不相婚嫁，也就是說同姓不婚，因為從經驗法則可以知道：血統太接近的婚配可能會生育出不良遺傳的後代，最合乎現代的健康優生觀念。

▶ 狩獵有時的永續觀念

邵族人上山打獵有一定的時間，忌諱在冬季和春季出獵，老人或許會告誡年輕的族人，說是在這段時間出獵會觸犯山中的精怪、可能被山豬咬傷、或跌落山谷受傷……等等，其實背後的真正原因是：冬季和春季是母獸懷孕、生育幼獸的時期，如果在這段時間打獵，可能使獸群的數量不再成長，將來會更難獵到野獸，那就不再經常有獸肉可吃了！可見其中蘊含並體現了生態保育、永續利用的觀念。

▶ 莊重敬仰自然的賜與

邵族人在實施重要祭典時，都會要求族人把飲食改為不加鹽巴的淡食，禁吃複雜不潔的食物，從飲食的清淡以體現莊嚴慎重的心情；老人家甚至還會要求禁聲慎言，認為這樣子才不會得罪精靈，播下的稻子才不會枯萎、埋置的陷阱才不會落空……這些無非是要族人從外在形式上莊重起來，以嚴肅謹慎的態度去從事播種與狩獵的行為，如此才不容易因輕慢而造成失誤或傷害。

▶ 「鳥占」透露生活智慧

邵族還有「鳥占」的習俗，以名字叫「繡眼畫眉」的鳥鳴聲來判斷吉凶。這種小型鳥類喜歡群居，從平地到高山都是牠們活躍的領域，往昔邵族人外出或行獵的時候，都會很在意這種鳥的鳴聲；如果繡眼畫眉在某個方向成群煩躁地啼叫時，即認為是不吉祥的徵兆，此時必定中止行動，儘速回家；反之，若繡眼畫眉是成群地在某個方向，以和悅平順的聲音鳴叫，那就被視為吉兆，可以放心的出發。這種以飛禽的動靜反應偵知安危的做法，隱含了邵族人對環境豐富的觀察力和生活經驗的智慧累積。

大自然界的力量神祕偉大而又不可預測，邵族的祖先們融合長時間與自然環境奮鬥的智慧，延伸祖靈的觀念，發展出具有族群特色的神話傳說、禁忌禮俗和社會規範。雖然有些做法以今天的知識來看，或許夾雜些許迷信的味道，但是，生命經驗和民族智慧的傳承，正是藉著種種的禮俗禁忌、傳說故事，得以代代相傳延續下來，它們的背後自有其維繫人與自然和人與群體之間和諧穩定的意義。

六、山水中的杵音歌舞

日月潭有山有水、風景秀麗，再加上邵族原住民「杵音漁唱」的文化特色，自古以來就是詩人墨客歌頌吟詠的對象，在世人心目中印象鮮明。從清末以來，歷經日本統治到國民政府遷台迄今，日月潭始終是個名聞遐邇、膾炙人口的觀光景點，遊客到日月潭旅遊，都把觀賞邵族的杵音和歌舞當作一大樂事。

▶「舂石音」展開8月祭典序幕

邵族的杵音有兩種形式，一種是和傳統祭儀有關的儀式性杵音，通常稱為「舂石音」，是由7到8支長杵輪流撞擊埋在地面的石頭，配合3支低音竹筒，組合成叮叮咚咚、富有變化又非常悅耳動聽的節奏。這種儀式性杵音是邵族最隆重的8月祭典序幕，參與的人只製造舂石音而已，並不唱其他的歌曲，一年之中只有農曆8月1日的前一天晚上在頭目家舉行。

按照傳統規矩，舂石音是婦女的專責工作，男人是不碰長杵的；舂石音的當天晚上，所有的男人都要在部落附近的路口和要道守衛過夜，稱為「眠山」，讓婦女們能安心地舂石音。婦女們則整夜在頭目家舂石音，直到凌晨天色朦朧亮起時，才回家準備8月初一祭祖的供飯，隆重的8月祭典就此展開。

▶「杵歌」成為邵族的觀光特色

另一種杵音純粹是表演給觀光客看的，正確地說應該是「杵歌」才對！把祭儀的「舂石音」配合觀光的需要，逐漸演變成表演的「杵歌」，這種杵歌除了以長杵和竹筒來表現節奏音律的美感之外，中段還配合有邵族歌謠的演唱，通常唱的是「打獵歌」和「迎賓歌」，這也就是目前大家最常看見的杵歌表演。

邵族的器樂除了杵音之外，也有口簧琴和弓琴，可惜已經失傳，部落裡找不到會成曲演奏的人了。

▶ 祭典歌謠喚祖靈

至於口唱的歌曲則數量眾多、內容豐富，有哄小孩入睡的催眠歌、趣味性的兒歌、情歌、工作歌、即興感懷歌…等，充分顯現出邵族也是愛唱歌的民族。比較特殊的是邵族還有數十首「有禁忌的歌曲」，這些歌曲在平常是絕對不准隨意亂唱的，只能在「有主祭的8月祭典」時才准教習和傳唱，否則就會被當作是冒犯祖靈、觸犯禁忌的大事。這些歌曲都是年代久遠的古調，歌詞大部分只存字音而不能了解涵義。邵族人把這些歌謠歸類為「祭典歌謠」，是只唱給祖先聽的歌，一旦唱出來就是召喚和邀請祖靈蒞臨聆賞的意思，如果有人不是在8月祭典的期間而隨便亂唱，當祖靈蒞臨而又沒有祭典或重要的原因時，祖靈不悅就會招惹出許多不可預測的事端來。

因為有這樣的禁忌，所以每當隆重的8月祭典舉行時，每個晚上族人不分男女老少，都會圍聚在祖靈屋前，珍惜傳唱及學習傳統祖靈歌曲的時機，用心地唱著這些平常禁唱的歌曲，當族人的內心深處和祖靈有所契合及感應時，經常有淚流滿面、令人感動莫名的畫面出現。

▶ 融合祭典創新舞蹈表演

舞蹈方面，一般情形，邵族人在日常生活中跳舞的場面其實是難得一見的，真正的舞蹈也只見於8月祭典時；晚上唱祖靈歌到深夜，有幾首歌曲節奏變快，年輕的族人會手牽著手，繞著圓圈，配合節奏做扭腰和大跨步的跳躍，或者肩搭著肩，做急速踏步繞圈的跳躍動作，表現出節慶歡愉熱鬧的氣氛。

至於現在到日月潭旅遊時所看到的舞蹈表演，是在日治時代才發展出來的觀光性演出。可以說，邵族是全台灣最早擁有觀光產業的原住民族群，這種有意排演的舞蹈，還是加入了原住民特有的文化因素，成為一種新的原住民舞蹈表現模式，也算是創風氣的鼻祖吧！

打獵歌

簡史朗記音
張正華記譜

kaw kaw kaw pin tu si yu tang ri syu syu ri

kaw kaw kaw pin tu si yu tang ri syu syu ri

rung ti qa nu ti qa nu ba hi qi

i ya hay yu~~ hay yu

man su si ma si qu na hi

備註：本譜採用IPA（International Phonetic Alphabet）國際音標記音。

造訪部落　部落藏寶圖，來挖邵族寶

看過了邵族的神話與傳說故事，想不想到白鹿所指引的日月潭，這個美麗的地方一探究竟呢？看看長髮精怪達克拉哈平日曬太陽、梳頭的小島——水上浮嶼；還有庇護邵族人的最高祖靈巴薩拉的居所——大茄苳樹；循著小矮人的足跡，造訪原始森林？

邵族在台灣原住民族中，人口最稀少，全族總人數不超過三百人，都聚居在南投縣魚池鄉日月潭的日月村。現在，透過這份精心編製的「邵族部落文化導覽圖」及「南投縣自然與文化導覽圖」，陪伴身歷其境，盡情挖掘部落文化寶藏，保證不虛此行。

當然，造訪部落時更不能錯過邵族豐富的祭儀活動，像是農曆3月的「播種祭」，農曆7月的「狩獵祭」，還有熱鬧的8月「祖靈祭」。獨特的邵族杵音、祭典歌舞，精采可期！每年還有浩大的萬人泳渡活動，心動想要行動之前，最好先確定時間及地點，可與邵族文化發展協會、或交通部觀光局日月潭國家風景區管理處查詢。

洽詢電話：
邵族文化發展協會　電話：049-2850298
交通部觀光局日月潭國家風景區管理處
電話：049-2855668
網址：http://www.sunmoonlake.gov.tw/

邵族
文化導覽圖

族語開口說　　**入境隨俗的邵語**

你好嗎？
maqitan ihu？
馬改旦　伊乎？
好　　你

我很好！
Maqitan yaku！
馬改旦　雅固
好　　我

你叫什麼名字？
kuzan mihu a lhanaz？
估染　咪虎 阿 薩拿日
什麼　你　的 名字

我叫做地延(典)
Tian nak a　lhanaz.
地延 納嘎 阿　薩拿日
地延 我　的　名字

你住在哪裡？
kanantua ihu？
嘎南都哇 伊乎？
住哪裡　你

我住在日月潭。
itusi　zintun yaku.
伊都西 仁頓　雅固
住在　日月潭 我

你來做什麼？
numa s akalawan nuhu munai？
怒嘛　斯 阿嘎拉萬 怒虎 目耐？
什麼　做　　你　來

我是來玩的。
Qinaquash　yaku.
嘎伊那固哇西 雅固
玩　　我

這東西用邵語怎麼說？
haya wa anyamin ya mashth'aw a kuzan？
海呀　哇　阿尼呀明 呀 嘛斯邵　阿 估染
這　　東西　　用邵語説 要如何

我聽懂了，
mafazak yaku tunmaza,
嘛法乍　雅固　頓嘛乍
懂　　我　聽

請你再慢慢地說。
Undawdauk kuan ihu　malhinuna.
穩牢牢　　固彎 伊虎 嘛西怒拿
慢慢　　請　你　説

你要去哪裡？
amuntua ihu？
阿門都哇 伊虎
要去哪裡 你

我要去日月潭。
Amuntusi zintun yaku.
阿門都西 仁頓　雅固
要去　　日月潭 我

這東西要多少錢？
lapiza tuali　haya anyamim？
拉必惹 度阿里 海呀 阿尼呀明
多少　錢　這　東西

一百塊錢。
Tata shaba.
大搭 沙吧
一　百

這麼多錢(貴)，我不要買。
manasha tuali, ani yaku fariw.
麻那沙 度阿里 安尼 雅固 法留
多　錢　不要 我　買

就到這裡為止，我要回家了。
amushayza yaku mutaun pyazithuyza.
阿木賽惹　雅固 木大穩 比阿利速伊惹
要走了　我　家裡 到此為止

讓你這麼忙真不好意思！
anuniza ka min'ihun ukashawan!
阿奴尼惹 嘎 明尹混　烏嘎沙彎
不好意思 阿 使你　沒空(很忙)

一點也不，再來玩吧！
ingkayza! Uqthawan munai qinaquash!
英蓋惹　沃克沙彎　目耐　嘎伊那固哇西
不會啦　再　來　玩

再見啦！
uqthawan mapariqaz!
渥克沙彎　麻巴列嘎日
再　看見

太陽出來了。
mu'apaw wiza tilhaz.
木阿寶　維惹 帝煞日
出來　已經 太陽

今天是好天氣。
maqitan thuyni a qali.
馬改旦　速伊尼 阿 嘎里
好　今天　的 天氣

下雨了。
kusazin niza.
沽沙林 尼惹
雨　已下

你有帶傘嗎？
itiya　mihu tamuhun?
伊地亞 咪虎 搭木混
有　你　傘(斗笠；帽子)

我有帶傘。
itiya　yaku tamuhun.
伊地亞 雅固 搭木混
有　我　傘(斗笠；帽子)

請來吃吧！
izau a makan!
伊勞 阿 瑪幹
來　吃

我已經吃了，我很飽！
kminaniza　yaku, mabuqshu wiza!
克米那逆惹 雅固 麻沐克休　維惹
已吃了　我　飽　已經

我不要吃。
ani yaku a makan.
尼 雅固 阿 瑪幹
不 我　吃

【備註1】以上邵語音標乃使用IPA國際音標。

【備註2】邵語的詞序和漢語不同，一般是動詞或形容詞放在前面，而把主詞放在後面，開頭第一句就是典型的例子。

學習加油站　　**本書漢語與邵語名詞對照表**

故事01：白鹿傳奇

用漢字拼讀	邵語	漢語名詞
斯林拉	lhimza	芒草=茅草
毛列布斯	muribush	打獵
邵	Thaw 或 Thao	邵族
達恩	taun	部落
阿部	apu	長老
西拿布南	shinabunan	矛頭
發度	fatu	火石
本薩	bunlhaz	獸肉
阿布依	apuy	火
艾努	aynuz	火塘
阿度	atu	獵犬
嘎里	qali	祖靈
模拉祿	mulalu	祭典
斯嘎列布斯 阿 克奴彎	lhkaribush a qnuwan	鹿
麻普吉普吉	mapuzipuzi	白色
斯巴利山	shpazishan	箭
夫度斯	futulh	弓
希那布南	shinabunan	長矛
瓦乍甘	vazaqan	大湖
呼崙	hudun	山
沙連	sazum	水
露掃	rusaw	魚
仁頓	Zintun	日月潭（潭名）
普吉	Puzi	土亭仔（地名）
砂列	lhari	芋頭
嘎瑪	kamar	粟

故事02：長尾巴的小矮人

用漢字拼讀	邵語	漢語名詞
斯立頓	Lhilitun	矮人
達恩	taun	家
阿布伊	apuy	火炬
魯奴	runu	木臼
哇維斯維斯	vavishvish	尾巴
巴給	paqi	屁股

故事03：日月潭的長髮精怪

用漢字拼讀	邵語	漢語名詞
達克拉哈	Taqrahaz	水中精怪
布諾	punuq	頭
富克伊虛	fukish	頭髮
設克伊虛	shakish	臉孔
巴固	paku	胸
累固虛	rikush	背
固孫	kuthun	蝦
度度固	tuktuku	螺
累亞茲	riyaz	蚌
排達沐	Paytabu	古代邵族頭目的名字
達瓦茲	davaz	網
薩斯薩	lhalhutha	捕筒
度札	tuza	鰻
拉部	rapu	魚叉
努瑪	Numa	古代邵族勇士的名字
達敢	taqan	鰻筒
帝煞日	tilhaz	太陽

故事04：黑白孿生子和祖靈籃

用漢字拼讀	邵語	漢語名詞
拉魯	Lalu	拉魯島（日月潭中島嶼名）
沙連	Sazum	水社 水沙連
森必亞克	lhumpiyak	雙胞胎（孿生子）
達陸	daduu	頭目

用漢字拼讀	邵語	漢語名詞
希那努馬	Hinaluma	古代邵族頭目的名字
麻葛曼	makarman	災厄
巫拉拉魯安	ulalaluan	祖靈籃 公媽籃（祭籃）
胡露斯	hulus	衣物
麗那	lina	珠鍊
丹那都嘎斯	tanatuqash	祖先

故事05：大茄苳

用漢字拼讀	邵語	漢語名詞
巴列嘎	pariqaz	茄苳樹
巴薩拉	Pathalar	邵族各姓氏共同始祖的名字
骨宗	Qutsung	古代邵族頭目的名字
巴給特	paqit	斧頭
撒西克西克	lhalhiklhik	獠牙精 鋸子
勒普努	ripnu	水田

部落百寶盒：水沙連的邵族部落

用漢字拼讀	邵語	漢語名詞
鄒	Cou或Tsou	鄒族
巴勞寶	Barawbaw	卜吉社 北窟 日月村（地名）

部落百寶盒：敬畏感恩的邵族祭典

用漢字拼讀	邵語	漢語名詞
辛系	shinshi	先生媽（邵族的女性祭司）
斯瑪速尼	shmashuni	繡眼畫眉（邵族人用來做鳥占依據的鳥類）

製作群亮相

用漢字拼讀	邵語	漢語名詞
地延（典）	Tian	簡史朗（本書作者）
巴厄拉邦	Pa'labang	孫大川（本書總策劃）

信心滿滿，魯凱、排灣、賽夏、邵族
大小事輕鬆答！

▶ 魯凱族

1. 在「被滿足之日」之中，最受歡迎的節目是什麼？怎麼玩呢？

2. 壞心腸老人大惡勒為了什麼因素，竟然綁架慕阿凱凱？他又使出了什麼詭計才得逞呢？

3. 在魯凱的社會當中，貴族和首領（頭目）各是如何產生的？

4. 你知道「雲豹」的魯凱語怎麼說嗎？為什麼魯凱族人要稱自己為「雲豹的民族」？

5. 負責養育雲豹的家族是誰？他們除了聰明善良，還有個什麼樣的大特點？

6. 檳榔是許多原住民族不可或缺的日常食物，但它在魯凱族的傳說中還具有其他意義，你能說說它代表了什麼涵意嗎？

7. 許多原住民族都有屬於自己祖先的傳說；從「卡巴哩彎」這則神話故事中，你知道魯凱族的祖先是從哪裡來的嗎？

8. 美麗的巴嫩姑娘在哪個慶典中遇見了心上人？這位心上人又是用什麼樂器吸引了巴嫩的注意？

9. 你能說出魯凱族的獵人祭和豐年祭各在什麼時候舉行嗎？

10. 這些發生在台灣遠古時代的神話與傳說故事，看完之後有什麼心得？

▶ 排灣族

1. 巴里有一雙紅色的眼睛，任何東西只要被他看到，你知道會發生什麼事情？

2. 巴里的好朋友保浪，為了幫助巴里看到外面的世界，想到了什麼好辦法？

3. 當巴里被敵人殺害之後，他的身體變成了什麼？紅眼睛又變成了什麼？

4. 有一位小孩闖了大禍，將尿灑在火灶上，天神大怒收回人們用火的權利，事後大人如何懲罰這位小孩？

5. 黑嘴鳥帶回火種的時候，同時也帶來在不遠處有陸地的消息，據說那塊陸地就是現在的哪一座山？

6. 人們願意將陶壺所生的人奉為頭目，聽從他的領導，是因為陶壺所生的人從天洞取回了什麼東西？

7. 排灣族人邀請天神和祖靈，來到凡間參加收穫祭和婚禮，請問他們是如何招喚天神和祖靈的？

8. 身為頭目的女兒露古和平民本仍相愛，露古的父親希望本仍找到哪四樣寶物，才肯將露古嫁給本仍？

9. 本仍離開部落尋找寶物，一去數年，最後他發現一只陶壺，陶壺裡面裝滿了奇奇怪怪的昆蟲，最後這些昆蟲變成了什麼？

10. 看完本書故事之後，你知道排灣族有哪些傳統食物嗎？請試舉二樣。

▶ 賽夏族

1. 賽夏人最早起源於哪座大山？後來遷移到哪裡？現在分布在何處？試著一一在地圖上指出來。

2. 賽夏祖先歐倍那伯翁兄妹在大洪水中，緊緊抓住哪樣東西，得以生存下去？

3. 賽夏人大致分為哪幾個姓氏？試列舉二、三個。

4. 請試著列舉你認識的賽夏族人？

5. 雷女娃恩下凡帶來了哪樣農作物，大大改善賽夏人生活？雷女為了善盡孝道為公公下廚，結果變成什麼植物回到天上去？

6. 賽夏青年想到什麼曠世奇謀，終於消滅身手矯捷的達隘？

7. 想一想，達隘百般欺凌賽夏人，為什麼賽夏人在消滅他們之後，反倒要祭拜他們呢？

8. 賽夏語中「矮靈祭」怎麼說？大祭小祭分別在什麼時候、在哪兩個部落舉行？

9. 如果你要參加矮靈祭，一定要繫上哪樣植物，以免惡運上身？

▶ 邵族

1. 初秋時分，邵族人總會搓實弓弦、磨順矛頭，帶著獵袋與成群的獵犬一起興奮出獵。請問他們是為了什麼祭典而準備？

2. 傳說中的白鹿，把邵族人從西部帶到豐美的日月潭定居，這個具代表性的地方，邵族人稱作「普吉」（Puzi），就是現在漢人所稱的什麼地方？

3. 住在森林深處山洞裡的小矮人，比邵族人先來到日月潭，還是更晚？他們教邵族人學會做些什麼？

4. 山洞裡有什麼秘密嗎？小矮人為什麼就是不讓人拜訪他們的家？邵族年輕人莽闖入，最後小矮人會怎麼辦？

5. 邵族人最近常補不到魚，原來是精怪達克拉哈在破壞漁具，達克拉哈為什麼這麼做？

6. 邵族頭目希那努馬家生下了一對黑白臉的雙胞胎，族人們都相當恐慌，因為他們認為這是什麼樣的預兆？

7. 頭目希那努馬狠心將黑臉男嬰投入潭中，後來男嬰哭泣託夢，告訴頭目必須家家戶戶準備什麼東西才能避過災禍？

8. 在邵族居住的日月潭邊長著一棵很大的樹，樹上居住著邵族的最高祖靈巴薩拉，保祐著邵族的興盛壯大，請問這棵樹是什麼樹？

9. 漢人打算把這棵庇護邵族的樹砍倒，他們拿了斧砍都砍不倒，聽到大樹跟小樹說它只怕獠牙精，獠牙精指的是什麼？

10. 看完了邵族的神話與傳說故事，有什麼心得與啟示嗎？

E 網 情 報 站

輕鬆上網搜尋，「原味」超靈通

這些團體默默耕耘，收集整理了有關原住民文化、原鄉風光等等豐富內容，趕快上網共享！

1 魯凱族多納社區發展協會

提供高雄茂林魯凱族部落「多納村」的旅遊資訊，並有魯凱族的石板屋、傳統祭儀和各種傳統工藝等介紹。

2 屏東縣政府

屏東縣有山有海，地理環境與人文歷史多樣且豐富，網站上資訊多采多姿，值得流覽。

3 夢想之家

提供霧台鄉的旅遊、住宿資訊和地圖，以及各村風景照片，可供人一窺霧台的美麗風光。

4 台東縣政府全球資訊網

詳細介紹台東縣的地理環境及人文歷史、觀光景點，並提供全年度的文化觀光資訊。

5 台東市公所全球資訊網

提供台東市政服務訊息，其中觀光資源選項有許多貼心外來遊客的資訊，像是享受台東的十二個方法、遊樂地圖、花東觀光導覽等。

6 台東永續發展學會

秉持推動環境與人文永續發展的理念，凝聚社區共同意識，推動生態保育、促進地方無害環境產業發展、增進族群人文關懷為組織目的，並辦理原住民各部落知性之旅等相關活動。

7 行政院原住民族委員會/原住民資訊網

舉凡原住民權益、法規、族群及文化介紹等等，十分豐富。

8 順益台灣原住民博物館

館內主要蒐藏、研究並展示台灣原住民文物，藉教育活動之推廣來呈現台灣本土文化之樣貌。

9　台灣原住民文化園區

有原住民園區風采介紹、山海的精靈（原住民介紹）、原鄉藝文、兒童園地、母語教室等，相當值得瀏覽。

10　九族文化村－原住民文化

網頁中有原住民文化介紹、部落景觀、歷史照片、音樂，以及傳統手工藝的概述。

11　公共電視原住民新聞雜誌

提供有關原住民新聞、活動訊息、原住民資料庫。

12　山海文化雜誌社

以維護並發展原住民文化、促進社會對原住民的了解與尊重為宗旨；網站提供協會簡介與消息、山海出版社出版資訊。

13　幸福綠光股份有限公司

【台灣原住民的神話與傳說】透過生動的故事，搭配精緻彩繪圖畫，勾勒出原住民信仰、儀式、禁忌、圖騰、生活智慧與技能，並透過中、英文對照，希望讓國人以及海外讀者能認識台灣原住民寶貴的生活文化遺產，也讓台灣這段遠古歷史變得清晰、鮮活、可親。

14　交通部觀光局日月潭國家風景區管理處資訊網站

針對日月潭自然景觀、文化歷史軌跡，提供包含景點的介紹、行程安排、日月潭自然生態及水庫興建原理與歷史發展等內容，以為遊賞參考。

魯凱族
R   u   k   a   i

The Story of Muakaikaiaya

Thrown from a swing by a magical wind, the life of beautiful *Muakaikai* life would never be the same. She was kidnapped from her village by a mean old man to be his grandson's wife. Although she resisted at first, she eventually resigned herself to her fate. Miraculously, she did finally return to her village.

This is a story that has been passed down for many generations. *Dalapathane* was one of the aristocrats of the *Rukai*. He had but one child, a daughter that was both beautiful and filial. Her name was *Muakaikai*. She was loved not only by her parents, but also by everyone in the tribe. Her beauty and charm were such that if a young man saw her he would collapse as if a drunken stupor.

Also in the *chekele* there was a handsome young aristocrat named *Kuleleele*. Although the status of his family was slightly lower than that of *Muakaikai*'s family, everyone in the village, including the parents of both children, thought that it was a natural match for *Kuleleele* and *Muakaikai* to marry. All the young people of the village took it for granted that when the two grew older they would become husband and wife. But for some reason when they were old enough for marriage, their parents did not raise the issue. *Kuleleele* became very anxious and worried that someone else might ask to marry *Muakaikai*.

Just after the end of *kiapa-alupu* came the day of the year that is eagerly awaited by all the young people in the village. This day, known as *taki-pakadralhuane,* or "the day of being satisfied", included an activity of playing on a swing. The young men and women of the village went out to the mountains early in the morning to gather rattan. From the rattan they made a long and wide swing. This year they hung the rattan swing from a huge old banyan tree that was in front of *Dalapahthane's* house.

What's more?

talialalaye: *Rukai* follow a system whereby the eldest son is first in line for succession; the eldest was *talialalaye* or the big aristocrat, the second and third sons were second and third rank aristocrats respectively.

Dalapathane: the name of one of the aristocratic *Rukai* families. From the name one can determine a person's social status, standing and character.

chekele: for the *Rukai* whenever two or more families settle in a place it can be considered a *chekele* or tribe. The word *chekele* to the *Rukai* signifies not only the center of their daily lives, but also the home of their souls.

kiapa-alupu: this "rite of the hunter" was performed for each male but once during their life: as rite of passage. It would generally take place around the middle of the eighth month at the time of the second full moon following the millet harvest.

taki-pakadralhuane: "the day satisfaction" came each year after the *kiapa-alupu*. A day was selected on which young women would wear a crown of white lilies. In the afternoon the swinging event would take place. *taki-pakadralhuane* literally means "consolation" or "satisfied".

talaisi: this is a special privilege enjoyed by female aristocrats whereby during the swinging event she would bestow wellbeing on the members of the tribe for their hard work during the year.

The ceremony began after mid-day. All the men and women of the village wore their most festive clothes. They danced about and played on the swing. Each young woman tried to top the others by being the most graceful and elegant on the swing, while all of the men tried to outdo one another by finding out who could demonstrate the greatest strength and who could go the highest and the furthest in the swing.

When it was *Muakaikai*'s turn everyone else stopped singing and dancing. All eyes were on *Muakaikai*. Hundreds of the young men lined up to push the swing, while the women all looked at her with admiration. Everyone in the village really loved *Muakaikai*.

Muakaikai swung high and far. She was thrilled as she went higher and higher, rocking back and forth and kicking her legs to the rhythm of the swing. Her ascent seemed endless.

All of the villagers watched in wonder as she demonstrated her skill. There was no doubt as to who was the most elegant and charming of all the women in the village. Everyone couldn't help but cry out with joy as they watched her. *Kuleleele* was also watching, enchanted by *Muakaikai*'s swinging.

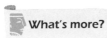 **What's more?**

vaedre: *Pueraria montana* is gathered and used by the *Rukai* to make thick rope. The rope is then hung from a tree with the lower part fashioned into a loop which can accommodate one's feet, and a vine is tied in the center for swinging. This is how the swing was constructed for this activity.

daralape: the presence of the banyan or *ficus* tree in the front courtyard of a house in the *Rukai* community signified the house belonged to members of the aristocracy and the thus the *Rukai* name for the tree literally means "shade of the noble". Daughters of the aristocracy when attending the farewell party on the eve of their marriage and separation from their family, wipe their tears with the leaves of the *daralape*.

ngia-ragelane: a kind of ceremonial dress worn only by those of special standing and class, and worn only on special occasions such as weddings and festivals.

But hiding not far from the crowd, was an old mean-hearted man named *Taevele*. He planned to steal *Muakaikai* away from her village and force her to wed his grandson. *Taevele* whispered a curse:"I wish for a wind to blow you away."

Just then, a whirlwind came over the crowd and caught *Muakaikai*'s swing. She was thrown from the swing high into the air.

When the winds died down the villagers went back to the banyan tree but all they found was an empty swing swaying back and forth. There was no trace of *Muakaikai*. Everyone went into a panic, calling out her name, running about searching for *Muakaikai*.

The festival came to a close, but the parents of *Muakaikai* had lost their daughter and they cried for many days. *Kuleleele* was heartbroken and whenever anyone in the tribe mentioned *Muakaikai*, he lowered his head and sighed. It seemed he would never laugh or be happy again.

Muakaikai was carried away by the winds and she finally landed in a place totally unfamiliar to her. The mean old man was waiting for her, and before *Muakaikai* could catch her breath, *Taevele* had tied her up and blindfolded her. Thus was she whisked off deep into the forest.

Gradually *Muakaikai* regained consciousness and realized that she couldn't move. She used all her strength to open her eyes, but all she saw was darkness. Terrified, she cried out:

What's more?

Taevele: the old man, also of the *Rukai,* was upset that none of the female aristocrats paid attention to, or would accept his grandson's advances. His jealousy turned to spite and hatred and he constantly was thinking of ways to trag *Muakaikai*.

alhilhaogo: in *Rukai* this word literally means "cyclone" but it may also be used as a general term for many sorts of disasters such as plague, infestation of crops leading to famine, or anything that brings disaster within a very short period of time.

"Ina, Ina, Please, won't you hurry and come help me?!"

Flustered, the old man quickly took out a betel nut and gave it to her. With anything but sincere concern for her wishes, he tried to console her, saying:

"Granddaughter! Don't worry! I will not hurt you. I am taking you to a place that I promise will make you happy!"

Muakaikai chewed on the betel nut but she couldn't stop crying. Whenever they stopped to rest *Muakaikai* spat betel nut juice to her left and right so that her parents might follow her trail.

From the juices she spat grew different kinds of betel nut trees and other plants. On the right were the *Daramuane* Betel Nut Tree and the *Lauviu* Piper Betel, and on the left were the *Pakulhalhia* Betel Nut Tree and the *Tavaovalo* Piper Betel.

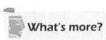

What's more?

sabiki: in *Rukai* tradition a story is told: "all of a sudden as if from nowhere, a ray of light shone through the skylight and a betel nut rolled out on to the woven mat. A curious woman picked it up. With her index finger she applied a touch of ash from the fireplace to the betel nut and then popped it into her mouth … and then, she became pregnant!" From this story it is easy to see why the betel nut symbolizes the male and how the phrase in the *Rukai* language for "one night stand" literally means "a mouthful of betel nut love".

ina is the *Rukai* word for "mother", *Muakaika*i is calling out for her mother to rescue her.

drangao is a kind of vine, the edible leaves of which *Rukai* use to wrap betel nut. Sometimes a slice of the *drangao* stem is inserted into the betel nut along with lime.

silu: there are many grades of glazed beads, at least ten from the highest grade to the lowest grade, and some necklaces may contain as many as ten different grades.

sabathane "in exchange for the daughter's life": traditional *Rukai* betrothal gifts include 1. jewelry, 2. ceremonial clothing, 3. ceremonial knife, 4. necklace, 5. shoulder sash, 6. ceramic vessel, 7. iron cooking pot, 8. axe, 9. shovel, 10. sickle, 11. rucksack, 12. jewelry box, 13. butcher knife, 14. a piece of land, 15. spirit (lifetime love).

Finally, they stopped under a banyan tree on the outskirts of another village. She was untied and the blindfold was removed. *Muakaikai* rubbed her eyes as the crowd of strangers standing before slowly came into focus.

All the people had been eagerly waiting for *Muakaikai*, not the least of which was the mean old man's grandson for whom she had been kidnapped. But *Muakaikai* would have nothing to do with these people. She just stared out blankly and would not look at or listen to any of them. Loathing and disgust welled up in her chest.

Muakaikai had love only for her parents, her childhood friend *Kuleleele*, and the people of her village with whom she had grown up. Never had she given a thought to living with anyone else. Even though the aristocrats and elders of this village were very kind to *Muakaikai*, and even though every day they treated her well, brought her azurite beads and all kinds of other ornaments as gifts for the bride-to-be, tried to make her comfortable and continuously asked her to forgive them, she couldn't get used to living with them. She missed her family and refused to eat and sleep. But after a long time of holding out, she was so tired and hungry that she had to give in. She had no choice, she would join their village and become the wife of *Taevela's* grandson.

What's more?

marudrange: the *marudrange*, or elders, are leaders jointly selected by the common people and ordinary aristocrats to keep the aristocrats' capriciousness in check, or to discuss strategies for important internal matters or matters involving outsiders.

Carried on the back: in Rukai tradition, this all important event of marriage involved the groom carrying the bride home on his back.

Having been taken from her home and forced to marry a stranger *Muakaika* spent her days in tears. Although her husband was very kind and loving, *Muakaikai* constantly longed for her parents, her loved ones, and her village. Every morning when she saw the sun *Muakaikai* would quietly pray that her people would find her and take her back to her village.

The months and years passed, and before she knew it *Muakaikai* had been away from her home for more than ten years. She had given birth to several boys and girls. Although she never forgot her family and her village, she was a good wife and a good mother. One day her husband came to her and told *Muakaikai* that in order to show their appreciation of her sacrifices over the years, their entire family would go back to *Muakaikai*'s village with some very precious gifts.

The husband, wife and children took the original route that *Muakaikai* had travelled when she was first taken from her village so many years ago. Along the way *Muakaikai* noticed that in all the places where she had spat out the betel nut juice, betel nut trees and piper betel had grown tall, flowered and borne fruit.

The villagers saw from afar that many strangers were coming towards their village. They waited quietly for their arrival. When *Muakaikai* announced who she was they let out a shout:

"She's still alive, *Muakaikai* has returned!"

Soon everyone had heard the news and came out to greet her. When *Muakaikai*'s parents finally hobbled out to join the crowd, they could hardly believe their eyes.

Muakaikai noticed her parents' hair was white from age, she saw the *kalhemeane* cloth that was hung to commemorate her death and she received the well wishes from hundreds of villagers. She exchanged hugs and tears with her people. Although fate had been cruel and she had suffered many years, there was great consolation in this warm welcome from her family and villagers.

Where did it come from?

This story was told to the author by his mother Senethe, from the village of *Kucapungane* in Pingtung County, Wutai Township.

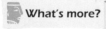 **What's more?**

kalhemeane: whenever a member of one's family or village dies the entire family or village will wear the *kalhemaeane* (black cloth) as a symbol of mourning.

02

The Cloud Leopard People

The people of the *Arubulu* clan were known for two things: raising the cloud leopard and having lots of head lice! The *Rukai* considered the cloud leopard to be their sacred hunting companion. It was on account of the cloud leopard's great tracking skills that the *Rukai* discovered their homeland in *Kochapongane*. Here they placed a sacred stone and asked for the spirits' protection. The Rukai people always understood the limits of human power, and they accepted, embraced and protected the natural environment as the way to sustain themselves.

Long, long ago just after the great flood three tribes, the *Amis*, *Puyuma* and *Rukai* all lived together on the eastern coastal area of *Panapanayan* which is around the present day Mei Ho Village in Taitung County.

 **What's more?**

Panapanayan: a village near present day Taimali Township, Taidong County.

Tarumake: Also spelled *Taromak*, located in Beinan Township, Taidong County.

Dadele: is present day Chingye Village, Sandimen Township, Pingdong County.

Kochapongane: located in Wutai Township, Pingdong County.

Amis, Puyuma, Rukai: *Amis* settlements are to the northeast of *Tugngalan* or Dulan Mountain, *Puyuma* settlements to the southeast of *Tugngalan*, while there are *Rukai* settlements in the vicinity of Kigndurn mountain.

The *Rukai* were comprised of three smaller groups, the *Tarumake,* the *Dadele*, and the *Kochapongane*.

There were two brothers that were leaders in the tribe. The elder brother *Pulaluthane*, and the younger brother *Pakedrelhase*, were worried that the place they lived in, Shikipalhichi, was not large enough for their growing tribe. They decided to seek out new lands to meet the needs of thriving future generations.

They set out with their cloud leopard bidding farewell to the members of the tribe. Everyone was sorry to see them leave. The brothers responded: "*Aye! Sabao*! Farewell, we will meet again soon!"

Amidst the clamor of the well-wishers the two brothers set off.

The two walked along the banks of the *Tabuali-Kadravane* River heading upwards towards its source. They hunted along the way as they kept a constant look out for a new place they could settle.

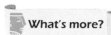 **What's more?**

ma-ililuku: in *Rukai* this means the strategist or leader. The position of chief came from the aristocracy and could be passed down. Since the chief did not necessarily represent all of those in the village that had management skills, every so often a ma-ililuku would be selected to make up for the shortcomings of this system.

shikipalhichi: this pronunciation from the eastern *Paiwan* language, means "corner" and is located in the basin of the Taimali River in Taidong County.

lhikulao: the *Rukai* believe that the pattern of the cloud leopard's appearance is like the mysterious misty clouds, and so the name of the animal also has the meaning of extraordinary power.

Aye! Sabao: Aye in the *Rukai* language means "see you again" and *Sabao* means, "you have been put to so much trouble". In the story the brothers are saying "we are sorry to have to leave you, but we will meet again."

Alupu: in the past people loaded bows and arrows on the backs of their hunting dogs and went into the forests in search of quarry, so now the word for hunting also means to seek or to find.

They continued in the direction of the setting sun. Every time they crossed a forest or went over a mountain, yet another forest and mountain awaited them. The land seemed to go on forever.

They passed over many mountains until they came to an area that was totally deserted. They were thirsty, hungry, and so exhausted that they could hardly move. The cloud leopard was also very tired, but all of a sudden it briskly bounded off into the forest.

Night was falling and the two brothers were looking for drinking water when all of a sudden the cloud leopard leapt out of the woods. The cloud leopard was covered in water. As it shook off the water it led the brothers to the source of the river, a small clear lake in a beautiful little valley.

The cloud leopard drank its fill of water from the banks of the lake and then laid down to sleep. No matter how the brothers called out they couldn't wake up the cloud leopard. The elder brother *Pulaluthane* then said:

"Perhaps this is the place where the spirits want us to settle."

The brothers carefully checked out the area along the river and they found that the natural surroundings were very favorable for a settlement. They selected an area on a saddle at the west side of the lake which also was easily defensible. This area was to be their new home. They called it *Kochapongane* and it is now known as the village of Chiuhaucha (Jiuhaocha).

 What's more?

ku mubalithita: the spirits that manage the mountains.

Kochapongane: or "old hau cha"is a village in Wutai Township, Pingdong County it has the largest number of stone houses of any village in Taiwan. In 1978 the villagers were moved to a new settlement named "new hau cha" on the banks of the Yiliao River.

tamaunalhe: when erecting the *tamaulhe*, the *Rukai* say: "this place was given to us by the ancestors, please take care and protect us."

The brothers found a *tamaunalhe*, a long pillar-shaped stone, and with great effort moved it up to the peak of the saddle where they had settled. The stone pillar was a statement that "This land is our home!"

The two brothers returned to their village along their original route. They then returned with five families, a total of about twenty-five people, to settle at the lake.

One of the families that came back with them was known as the *Arubulu* clan. The *Arubulu* clan had been entrusted by the tribe to take care of the cloud leopard. The members of the *Arubulu* family were very upstanding and kindhearted. They knew the temperament of the cloud leopard, and the animal was like a member of their family.

Every generation of the *Arubula* clan had had serious problems with head lice, and for this reason they became known as the "*tuakuchu ka ua chekechekele*". But all the members of this clan were very intelligent. They all had nice personalities and the young men and women of the clan were very attractive and were always favored as marriage partners.

A group from another tribe that lived below *Kochapongane* on the other side of *Maka tagaraoso ka drakerale* watched as the people moved in and developed the area. They continuously attacked and harassed their new neighbors.

One day a group of the enemy tribe gathered at the entrance to *Kochapongane* preparing for an attack on the village. The cloud leopard was waiting for them. The cloud leopard dipped its tail in its urine and then wagged its tail at the enemy tribe shaking the urine into their eyes. All of their eyes were stinging and the people of the cloud leopard's village had no problem in defeating their attackers. From that time on no one dared attack their village.

After a very long time the people of the tribe began to feel that the cloud leopard was getting old and should not have to take on so much responsibility. They de-

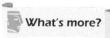

What's more?

tuakuchu ka ua chekechekele: the clan of people upon whose heads grow lice.

Maka tagaraoso ka drakerale: this is reference to the Ailiaonan River literally meaning "the river waters running from the north of Tawu Mountain."

cided to send the cloud leopard back to its original home so that it could pass a more carefree life.

They began preparing for a farewell party. First they hunted the tender and delicate muntjac and this they gave to the cloud leopard as a parting gift. The more ordinary mountain deer they gave as food for the tribesmen who would accompany the cloud leopard on his journey.

All of the tribe's people that stayed behind patted the cloud leopard and wished it the best. They reminded the cloud leopard:

"Be sure not to wander into the area of the other tribes. They will not respect you, and you may be injured!"

The people who accompanied the cloud leopard took very good care of it. The cloud leopard was old and was not able to walk like a young leopard so the journey took quite a long time.

They entered a banyan forest in what is now the *Rukai* Tribe's sacred area of *Balhukuan.* Before anyone could say a word, the cloud leopard suddenly bounded off deep into the forest.

Before long they heard the cries of a mountain deer being killed. The hunters quickly followed the sound and came upon the cloud leopard covered in blood. It was lying next to the mountain deer as though it was waiting for the hunters with a gift.

One of the experienced older hunters said: "This obviously is the cloud leopard's farewell gift to us."

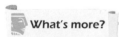 **What's more?**

tau-lhisisiane: a sacred place on account of the presence of spirits.

Balhukuan: the resting place for the spirits of dead persons and considered by *Rukai* people regard it as a holy land. It is located on the ridgeline between North Dawu Mountain and Wutou Mountain, which is also the northern terrace of Chabuyan Mountain.

kuna-chuchungulane; mubalhithita: *Rukai* classify ancestors into the *kuna-chuchungulane* which means "those from long ago", and *mubalhithita* meaning "those whose places we have taken."

The hunters let the cloud leopard enjoy the fresh blood and organs of the deer. They left the rest of meat at this place so that they could bring the meat for their tribe's people.

They continued on their journey until they came to the east bank of *Maka-kacha-chipulu ka Kadravene,* or what is now called the Chipen River. The place was a wide open grassy area that had mild weather and lots of game for the cloud leopard to hunt. One will never go hungry in such a place.

An old hunter from the *Arubulu* clan who had been with the cloud leopard all of his life hugged and kissed the leopard and said to it:

"You will be the hunting companion of the *Rukai* forever. We will eternally remember you and the difficult times we shared. You fed us with game and let us live with dignity; you gave us for generations to come a beautiful land that no one can attack and an endless supply of water. Now, it is time for you to return to the everlasting place of your ancestors!"

After he finished speaking, the cloud leopard was free to go. After a few steps the leopard stopped. Turning around to take one last look at the hunters, it was as though it could not bear to leave them… Then, all of a sudden, the cloud leopard bounded off and disappeared deep in the forest.

From this time on the *Rukai,* or people of the cloud leopard did not kill cloud leopards or wear anything made of the hide, or wear *bengelhai* with the teeth of the leopard. They are honored to be the people of the cloud leopard. No matter how difficult their situation, the spirit of the cloud leopard sustains their tenacity and vitality.

Where did it come from?
This story comes from the hau cha history gallery in the village of *Kucapungane* in Wutai Township, Pingtung County.

 **What's more?**

bengelhai: this is a kind of headdress worn that symbolizes the wearer's character and personality.

Kabalhivane: Our Eternal Home

In ancient times when the world was in chaos, a ray of light shone upon a ceramic vessel hidden deep within a cave. The two eggs in the vessel hatched and gave birth to a man and a woman, the original ancestors of the *Rukai*. So there would be future generations, they married and initiated the beginnings of the tribe. Despite many hardships their descendants were strong and healthy ensuring the prosperity and longevity for future generations of the Rukai from *Kabilhavane*.

Long, long ago the original ancestors of the *Rukai* Tribe came from a place known as *Kaliaharn,* near *Dalupalhing* Lake. This is the place where all life originated.

At that time the world was in chaos. There was no life at all except two eggs in a ceramic vessel nested deep in a mystical cave at *Kaliaharn*. Every day when the sun rose from the east, the two eggs were the very first place to be touched by is rays of the sun.

What's more?

Dalupalhing: refers to the current Daguihu or "Great Ghost Lake", a well-known alpine lake in Taiwan surrounded by exquisite cedar forests. The lake is located in the southern part of the Central Mountain Range bordered by three townships in three counties: Maolin Township of Kaohsiung County, Wutai Township in Pingtung County, and Yanping Township in Taitung County.

kaliaharn: the coming of first light of life.

After many days of absorbing the sunlight, the eggs hatched and a man and woman emerged. The man's name was *Gilagilau* and the woman's name was *Alayiumu*. They later became husband and wife and gave birth to a son, *Adralhiu*, and a daughter, *Maututuku*.

When *Adralhiu* and *Maututuku* grew older they became husband and wife. It was the time of the great flood and living conditions were extremely harsh. The children they produced were blind in both eyes and all died very young. Finally, they gave birth to a child that survived. Her name was *Gayagade* but she was also blind.

Maututuku wanted to have another child, hoping for a boy so that *Gayagade* would have company. But her husband was now too old to have another child. *Maututuku* was very worried about her daughter's future without a husband.

One day the sky was very hazy when suddenly a flash of light appeared from the east. Through the clouds a ray of light shone upon the ground. A betel nut fell behind the light. *Maututuku* picked up the betel nut, put it in her mouth and began chewing. She then became pregnant and gave birth to a son *Sumalalay*.

When *Sumalaly* and *Gayagade* grew up they became husband and wife. They had many sons and daughters, fortunately, all of whom were healthy and strong. These children also produced strong and healthy offspring. This is the origin of the *Rukai*.

The floodwaters gradually receded. *Sumalalay* and *Gayagade* took their elderly parents to search for lands beyond the reaches of the floodwaters. They settled on a terrace at the edge of the waters.

As it had not been long since the waters had receded and the area was quite marshy, they named their new home Lhidukua which means "flat land".

With every generation the tribe grew in numbers. Countless generations after *Gayagade* and *Sumalaly*, *Atungaya* and *Elhengn* gave birth to two brothers,

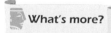

What's more?

dilung: pots made of clay are symbolic of a family's status and standing.
Sumalalay literally means the son of the dawn.

Kalhimadrau and *Basakalhane*. When the brothers grew older they thought their settlement was too crowded, so they decided to seek out a new place to live.

When the elder brother *Kalhimadrau* thought the time was right, he said to *Basakalhane*: "It is not so easy to make a living in this marshy area. For the sake of our future generations we need to find more space."

Kalhimadrau said: "Let's go into the mountains. It will be easier to find food there!"

The two brothers each took a group of people in search of a new place to settle.

Kalhimadrau's group went to Kingduru Mountain which is the sacred mountain for the *Rukai*.

Kingduru is the name of a mountain sacred to the *Rukai* of *Taromak*.

With *Basakalhane* in the lead, the group went along the sea past *Kulalau* and into *Mathiachane*. But because the land conditions were not ideal and they were often invaded by outsiders, they moved to *Kabalhivane*.

In the minds of the *Rukai*, *Kabalhivane* is their eternal ancestral home.

Where did it come from?

This story comes from the Hau Cha History Gallery in the village of Kucapungane in Wutai Township, Pingtung County.

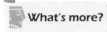 **What's more?**

Lhidukua literally means "flat land" and is known to the *Puyuma as Panapanayan* meaning "the place where one can plant rice". It is located in the area around present day Meihe Village, Taimali Township, Taidong County.

Kulalau is a village located in present day Lai Yi Township in Pingdong County.

Mathiachane refers to a mountain that lies behind the police station in Karamumudisane village, Wutai Township, Pingdong County.

Kabalhivane literally means "the eternal home". It is a plateau located in present day Labuwan village, Wutai Township, Pingdong County.

Baleng and the Snake

Kamamaniane was a snake king or a handsome young prince? The sound of his bamboo flute entranced the beautiful *Baleng* of the *Rukai Mabalhiu* aristocrats. With luxurious gifts they celebrated a marriage and Baleng went off to marry *Dalupalhing*. Later she would send her children and their children back to her village to visit her relatives and friends. For the people of the *Rukai*, the egret now symbolizes the return of *Baleng*.

In the village of *Kabalhivane* there was a family named *Mabalhiu*. They had three children, the eldest of which was a daughter named *Baleng*. *Baleng* had a younger brother and a younger sister.

Baleng had become a very beautiful young woman by the time she reached the age to marry. Her charm and beauty were such that not only the distant tribes of the Eastern *Rukai*, but also the *Paiwan* and the *Bunun* all had heard about her legendary beauty.

 What's more?

Baleng, a woman's name became well known when the computer game "Princess Baleng" came on the market, one of the relatively early examples of indigenous culture exploitation in Taiwan. That game was based on the story told here. To underscore *Baleng's* delicate beauty, the Chinese transliteration of her name includes the character for "tender" （嫩） pronounced nen`.

inavalhu: the lily is a symbol of chastity for women and signifies great hunting prowess when worn by a man.

In the village of *Kabalhivane* the millet harvest had just ended. This was the time for the annual harvest celebration and all the other festivities. It was also the most opportune time for the young men and women of the village start to begin to get to know one another. The millet had just been harvested, and at this time an important custom was for the men's families to brew millet wine and make millet cakes as gifts to the women's families.

Baleng had so many admirers. Visitors to her home couldn't even find a place to sit.

The full moon covered the evening sky on the taki-pakadralhuane, or "the day of being satisfied". This was the most exciting day of the harvest festival. All the young people of the village and guests from far away gathered at *Baleng*'s home. Their songs filled the valley. *Baleng* was dressed up in her most festive clothes and was by far the prettiest and most charming of all the women.

What's more?

Eastern Rukai: these *Rukai* were heavily influenced by the *Puyuma* and many of their original attributes became less pronounced, however the *Tarumake* preserved their *Rukai* language very well.

agiagi: the pronunciation for "little sister" and "little brother" is the same, as is the pronunciation for "elder brother" and "elder sister" - kaka or *takataka*.

becheng: millet is the most important of agricultural products for the *Rukai*. It is a staple grain, used for making millet cake and millet wine and is an essential element for many ceremonies.

bava: millet wine uses millet as its basic ingredient and red quinoa is used for the fermentation.

abaye: the *Rukai* millet cakes are egg shaped with meat inside.

lhisi ki niake: for every phase of his life the *Rukai* has a rite of passage. For example the infant has the "ten day ceremony", the child a "shoulder sash ceremony", the teen a "maturation ceremony", a hunter the "lily celebration" and so on.

Kala-lhilhisane: the *Rukai* festival following the harvest of millet is similar to the lunar new year celebrations of the Han.

Balen felt deeply honored from so much love and attention. But for some reason, no matter how much attention or gifts people lavished upon her, *Baleng* wasn't particularly moved by or attracted to any of her suitors.

It was past midnight but the singing was still loud and clear. Suddenly through a crevice in the stone wall used to block the wind came a light breeze accompanied by the sound of a bamboo flute. The music took *Baleng* off into a state of enchantment.

The strange thing was that even though everyone was still singing, the sound of the bamboo flute came through very clearly and distinctively. Gradually however the music faded away into the distance.

Baleng was in a trance and could only follow music of the bamboo flute. She was off in another world.

All this time, the other women and the other guests had no idea of what was happening.

On the next evening *Baleng*'s home was even more festive than the night before. The singing was louder and the emotions of the young men and women were brought to yet another climax by the love songs.

As the moon softly settled in the west the rousing love songs became gentle and tender refrains.

"Love is joy, how life is like the morning dew."

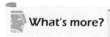

What's more?

Ihenege: this *Rukai* word for stone plate represents strong and sturdy.

Kulhalhu: a strait flute made of bamboo the sound of which is soft and somber.

aadrisi: the melodious sound of the flute is used here as a metaphor for the *Nisaetus nipalensis* (Mountain Hawk-eagle) the most majestic of large raptors resident in Taiwan. *aadrisi* has seven spots on its feathers, resembling a hundred-pace snake such that *Rukai* people consider it an incarnation of the snake.

Melodius songs full of the charm of love filled the air. Could it be that this would be *Baleng*'s last evening among her people, was this a sign that she would depart from her dear family tonight?

Once again, the breeze emerged from the crevice in the stone wall, and the music of the bamboo flute captured *Baleng*'s soul.

Suddenly the music from the bamboo flute became louder and came to a crescendo. And then just as suddenly, the music stopped altogether. A cold wind started blowing, lightly at first, but then it became stronger and stronger. All the guests were quite worried and nervous. One by one they scrambled out of *Baleng*'s home. Only *Baleng*, her parents and some of her female attendants stayed behind.

They discovered a very large but colorful snake had slithered up in front of *Baleng*. But what *Baleng* saw was not a snake lying on the ground, but rather a strong and handsome young man standing before her. Before anyone could say a word, *Baleng* had fallen in love with him.

As soon as the young man expressed his love to *Baleng* he vanished into thin air. *Baleng*'s parents and her attendants were shocked and speechless.

News of this event quickly spread throughout the villages near and far. No longer did visitors come to visit *Baleng*, indeed, no one dared to see her. No one had any idea that the person *Baleng* had seen was none other than *Kamamaniane*, the king of the *Dalupalhing* Tribe.

One evening not long thereafter, the sound of thunder shook the heavens and lightening pierced through all the black clouds. It looked as though they were in for a really big storm. The strange thing was that although the wind was blowing wildly, the trees did not move at all. A rustling sound came closer and closer and became louder and louder. Suddenly, they could see all of the members of the snake tribe clustered around *Kamamaniane* coming to take *Baleng* as his bride.

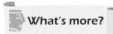 **What's more?**

> **dula:** *Rukai* believe that snakes are one kind of manifestation from the spirit world.
> **Kamamaniane:** means "that one".

In fact, *Kamamaniane* had already spoken to *Baleng*'s father in a dream about this visit to the Mabalhiu family. *Baleng* herself knew about everything that was happening and she was very pleased to receive her suitor in this way.

The snakes brought all manner of gifts for *Baleng*'s dowry including precious ceramic pots and amber beads. They also brought very colorful clothes, flowery hats, necklaces, bracelets and earrings for *Baleng* to wear. When *Baleng*'s father saw all the gifts and the elaborate arrangements that had been made for his daughter, and when he saw how much *Baleng* cared for her suitor, he finally accepted the fact that his dearest daughter would marry the king of *Dalupalhing*.

On the last night before her wedding all of her villagers came to her father's home to dance and sing. The king of the *Dalupalhing*, *Kamamaniane*, sat in the seat of honor in front of the stone pillar. All of the other snakes, large and small, crawled up into the banyan tree. There were so many that their weight brought the branches down close to the ground!

Because once *Baleng* married, she would go away and would not return to her village, so everyone wanted to make the most of this celebration. They danced and sang all through the night. No one wanted the night to end.

The next morning there were crowds of people gathered to see *Baleng* off. Most of the people accompanied her to the outskirts of their village but some went all the way to her new home.

When they arrived at *Dalupalhing* Lake, they stood on the shore and one by one shook *Baleng*'s hands for the last time. *Baleng* said:

"Birth and death are but beginnings. I am just taking one step. Please don't worry about me."

She encouraged her fellow villagers: "When you go out hunting you must remember to pass by the lake for I will prepare food for you. If it feels warm, then it is

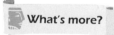

What's more?

ua-malhamalha: a ceremony welcoming a bride to the groom's home.

kia paspi: *Rukai* believe that dreams are the only way to communicate with ancestors. This gave rise to dream divination.

for you to take. If it feels cold, it was cooked by a stranger and you should be careful! Don't eat that. Remember this well!"

With tears in her eyes, *Baleng* said: "You are all standing here before me. When I disappear from your sight into the thicket of the banyan tree, you will know that I have arrived at my new home and we will not see each other again."

A soft wind came up and brought a light mist over the lake separating *Baleng* from her family and friends. As they departed one by one, she waved and said: "Give my best to all the family and friends in the village! Take care of yourselves! Aye, aye!"

Baleng's shadow gradually went out of sight as she disappeared into the lake.

Baleng missed her family and friends so much that every year at the harvest festival she sent her two children to *Kabalhivane* to visit their grandparents and other members of the tribe.

Before the children left to *Kabalhivane*, *Baleng* would communicate with her parents through their dreams telling them that their grandchildren were coming to visit.

One day when *Baleng*'s parents were returning home from the fields they discovered two of *Kamamaniane*'s children sleeping in special beds next to the window. They very respectfully prepared wine and meat as an offering to the two snakes. That evening the two brothers contacted their grandparents through their dreams and said: "Our mother *Baleng* sent us to see you. Thank you grandparents for your special care."

The next day the two were gone.

All of *Baleng*'s children and their children visited her relatives this way.

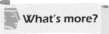 **What's more?**

delepane: the activity space in slate houses next to the central window which was also used for greeting distinguished visitors.

However, one day a young woman who didn't know *Baleng*'s family, discovered *Kamamaniane*'s children in the sleeping basket as she was about to put her own baby in to rest. With great surprise she tipped over the basket and the children fell to the ground and disappeared.

When *Baleng* heard the news of this mistreatment of her children she was very sad. Through the dreams she communicated with her villagers:

"You are gradually forgetting about me. I will no longer send my children or their children to visit you."

She continued: "But even so, when you see an egret soaring in the air above the village, it represents my eternal memories about you."

After the villagers all knew from their dreams about how *Baleng* felt, they began to perform a special ceremony every year at harvest time. They hoped for blessings and longed for the day that *Baleng* or her descendants might appear. But alas, it was too late. *Baleng* was gone.

On the last day of the harvest festival as the sun set in the west, there was a lone white egret soaring high above the village of *Kabalhivane*. When the villagers saw the egret they said with a sigh:

"*Baleng* our matriarch! We all miss you so much!"

Where did it come from?

This story was narrated by Labausu Labuan, collected from Tawu Village, Wutai Township, Pingtung County.

 **What's more?**

daladalathe: this word for egret also symbolizes nostalgia.

排灣族
Paiwan

01

Pali's Red Eyes

Pali's friend *Balan* taught him to place thin sheets of bamboo over his eyes so that their people wouldn't shun him for fear of being killed. When needed, they could remove the bamboo and *Pali's* red eyes could vanquish their enemies. One day a wasp carried away the bamboo sheets and *Pali* accidentally killed many children. A sad and dejected *Pali* was then killed through the trickery of his enemies. Palm trees grew out of the ground in which he was buried. The fruit of this tree is a bright red betel nut so when the *Paiwan* see a red betel nut they know they are being protected by *Pali's* red eyes.

The *Paiwan* tell of a man in ancient times named *Pali*. His red eyes that were so powerful that animals or plants would instantly die when his eyes caught sight of them.

Because of this pair of red eyes *Pali* passed his days confined to a dark hut and whenever he met with people he would bow down his head down or turn his back.

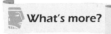
What's more?

Plants: the *Paiwan* word is *cemel* which describes gourds or yams, which when they came into *Pali's* sight, would become rotten.

But *Pali*'s eyes were also a very effective defense against the tribe's enemies. As soon as neighboring villagers knew they were approaching *Pali*'s village, they would go far out of the way to avoid it, not daring to get close. And whenever anyone shouted out "*Pali* is coming", everyone ran for their lives.

One time *Pali* heard the sounds of children playing outside of his hut. He very much wanted to go and join them, but he was afraid that his eyes would frighten them or that he might accidentally harm them. Determined to go and play, *Pali* covered his eyes with his belt so that he would not see or harm others.

With his eyes covered *Pali* could not see what was going on outside the hut so he just sat under the eaves listening to the children play. He could feel their joy as though he were playing and laughing along with them .

But *Pali*'s laugh made the other children take notice and sparked their curiousity. "Who are you?" they asked, "why are your eyes covered?" As soon as they heard *Pali*'s name the children ran away as though they were crows that had just been caught stealing the millet!

It wasn't long before the emptiness of the area around the hut became very familiar to *Pali*. He was all alone. It was as though everyone had forgotten him.

Pali began to cry. A boy named *Balan* who was hiding behind the *qaciljai* near the hut heard the crying and felt sorry for *Pali*. He thought to himself, "Poor *Pali*, why doesn't he have any friends?" He summoned up his courage to approach *Pali* . He said: "Could we be friends and play together?"

Pali was overcome with joy. From then on, every day after dusk *Balan* would come to play with *Pali*.

One day *Pali* said to Balan "I have only heard your voice. I would really like to see your face and also let you see the world in which we play!"

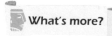

What's more?

vaqu: millet is a staple food for the Paiwan. It can also be fermented to make wine.

qaciljai: *Paiwan* for stone plate. *qaciljai* are divided into male and female and can be used in building houses, as pillars or fences, or even as coffins

Balan then devised a way that *Pali* could see the world without causing harm. He took the thin film from inside a piece of bamboo and placed it over *Pali*'s eyes. With just this thin film over his eyes *Pali* could see *Balan* and also everything around them. And he could do this without killing anyone.

When Balan took *Pali* to his home, all of the people in the village hid and did not dare look at him. Only *Balan*'s blind *vu-vu* was not afraid. She would even give *Pali vulasi* and *rjinasi*.

Pali asked her, "Why are you alone not afraid of me?"

The old woman responded to *Pali*, "Although I cannot see with my eyes, I can feel with my hands. Isn't this the same as seeing? Even though you have eyes, you are not always able to see that which you want to see. Isn't that the same as having no eyes? I am sure the creator has a purpose in giving you this pair of eyes!"

After this the people of the tribe knew that *Pali*'s red eyes would not harm people and they began to accept him. Usually *Pali* would wear the strips of bamboo film over his eyes. But when enemies were near, or when the people of his tribe had to travel far to attend a *puvaljau* and encountered danger from animals or *kiquluqulu* along the way, *Pali* would simply remove the bamboo film covers from his eyes and the hostile headhunters or dangerous animals could not escape from his lethal red eyes.

At last *Pali*'s special ability was recognized by his tribe and they honored him with respect and high status.

One day *Pali* went with a group of children to take the cows into a valley. At noon *gadau* was shining intensely, so it was very hot and all the children went to the river to play in the water. Rather than join the others, *Pali* took a nap under a big tree.

While he was sleeping, a wasp flew by and carried away the bamboo strips. *Pali*, on awakening, naturally opened his eyes without realizing that the eye covers were gone. Cows and plants that came within his sight died immediately. He also unintentionally killed many children who were resting on the banks of the river.

There were just a few children who were in the river catching shrimp who escaped *Pali*'s eyes. When they swam back to the shore, they discovered the tragedy and ran home to their village.

The village adults went with the children back to the river to find out what happened. But they dare not get too close to *Pali*. Only *Balan* and his grandmother risked approaching *Pali*. They faced the crowd and said:

"*Pali's* red eyes did not cause this trouble. Don't forget how he always uses his eyes to help us but never asks for anything in return. Not only do we not thank him, rather we keep attributing bad goings-on to *Pali*. Particularly with regards to this incident, he is without fault. What happened was not his intention!"

But the people of the tribe decided that Pali should be banished far into the mountains.

Pali was all alone once again. The only comfort he had was every day in the afternoon he would hear *Balan* calling out:

"*Pali*, this is *Balan*, I have brought you *kakanen!*"

Pali was very happy to see *Balan* but he would turn his back so his red eyes would not harm *Balan*.

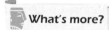

What's more?

maci: *Paiwan* word for death.

vulasi: this is the *Paiwan* word for yam, with along with millet and tarot is the staple food of the Paiwan who believe a person's energy will be enhanced by eating these items.

rjinasi: the *Paiwan* term for dried meat prepared by placing it on a high platform over low heat letting it roast and smoke.

vu vu: the *Paiwan* word for grandmother which also means elder and represents the source of life experience and wisdom.

kiquluqulu: in the past headhunting was a rite of passage, signifying that one had become a person of substance.

puvaljau: traditional *Paiwan* wedding.

gadau: the *Paiwan* revere the sun as the source of life and energy.

Pali blamed himself for the problems and was despondent all day about his sorry state. He didn't want to cause any more problems for his people, so every time that *Balan* suggested that he come out and play, Pali said to him: "It's okay, I am used to being alone here." This situation continued and Pali never came out from his isolation in the remote mountains.

One day enemies found where *Pali* was living. They disquised their voices to sound like *Balan*. Approaching *Pali's* hut they called out: "*Pali, Pali*, it's me *Balan*. I have brought you some of your favorite *kakaken*!"

Not suspecting a thing, *Pali* came out with his back to them and his eyes to the ground. Seeing their opportunity, the enemies chopped off his head.

The same day, *Balan* came as usual to the mountain. Having no clue about the tragedy, in his usual manner he called out:

"*Pali*, it is *Balan*. I have brought some *vulasi* that *vu vu* prepared especially for you.... *Pali, Pali*...."

When he entered the hut he found that *Pali's* dead body. Stricken with sorrow he found a proper place and somberly buried *Pali*.

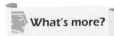

What's more?

kakanen: the food of the *Paiwan* is very rich and varied. Staples include millet cake, roasted yam, millet porridge; for soups *Paiwan* have tarot with dried fish, tarot root soup, freshwater fish soup, long bean soup; for side dishes tarot sausage, stone cooked meat, mountain lettuce and tarot stalks; and for snacks they wrap all manner of ingredients in leaves to make *cinaun* and *siak*, or pumpkin cake.

Burial: once life is over the family should not cry but must first place the deceased in a crouching position and use a strap and head scarf to bind the body. After these procedures are completed, the family may begin wailing and announce the death to friends and family.

saviki: Areca palm, and its fruit the betel nut, are an integral part of Paiwan tradition. *Paiwan* villages are distinguished by the *saviki* growing there. *saviki* is both a symbol of friendship as well as an essential betrothal gift at marriage.

When the people of the tribe heard that *Pali* was dead they didn't know whether to be happy or sad.

Balan greatly missed his friend *Pali*. One day when visiting the burial place of his lost friend, he was astonished to discover a palm tree growing right where he had buried *Pali*. The tree was bearing large red betel nut fruit.

Balan walked under the tree and looked up at the fruit. Suddenly he sensed something. It was familiar, yet at the same time it was distant.

Just as *Balan* was about to touch the palm tree, he heard *Pali's* voice:

"Although I have no eyes, I can feel you. *Balan*, it's me, *Pali*!"

Balan began crying as he hugged the tree. He felt *Pali* speak again:

"When I died I became a *saviki* and my red eyes became the red fruit of the tree." *Balan* now understood why the red betel nuts he had just seen seemed so familiar to him.

When the tribe's villagers learned about the *saviki*, they collected the fruit and planted trees all around their homes. Their enemies seeing the red eyes of *Pali* would not dare come into *Balan*'s village.

Now we know why *Paiwan* do not pick the fruit of the *saviki*, but rather let it grow large, age and turn yellow or turn red. The *Paiwan* elders of the tribe say: "Those are the eyes of *Pali*. He is protecting our village and taking care of our tribe."

Where did it come from?
This story was told to *Yaronglong Sakinu* by his maternal grandmother in Tjacupu village, Dawu Towship, Taitung County.

02

The Chief and Other Stories

Witnessing the voracious greed of the human race, *cemas*, the gods, became livid and brought on great storms and floods to put an end to the humans. There was one group of people that took the spirits' intentions to heart. They built boats and stored provisions to ride out the calamity. Despite help from haipis, the winged creature that brought them fire and led them to land, they were running out of food. It was then that they recalled the prophecy of *cemas*: at the gate of heavens cave lies the seed of *vaqu*. The brave and able soul that finds the *vaqu* is he who was born of the clay pot. This would be *mazazangiljan*, the Paiwan leader or chief. The *mazazangiljan* finally brought order into their lives.

Stories of the mazazangiljan (1)

⬥ The Great Flood

When people first began to look after the earth, *Paiwan* called themselves *adidan* which means friends, or stewards of the land. At that time the only differences among people were based on their family relations. There was no *papapenetan* or so-called class system and there was no concept of village or tribe. *Paiwan* social organisation at this time was like a seed just sprouting out of the soil.

For a very long time the people of the land abided by their pact with *cemas*, taking care of themselves and their surroundings. But after a time human avarice gave rise to many feuds, confrontations and hostilities. The people gradually forgot their pact with *cemas* and no longer used *singilje* to seek advice from *cemas*, no longer believing in the powers of the of the wind, thunder, lightning and rain spirits.

After so many years of peace and tranquility, the situation had completely changed. Now they were in a state of constant calamity, facing severe drought or colossal floods. With dawn came the roaring thunder, and lightning that set everything aflame; with dusk came the fierce wind, uprooting trees and battering everything else; the charred remains of the land resulted in dust storms that blackened the sky.

Finally, the people began to regret their errant ways. But it was too late. *cemas* ignored their attempts at communication by using the *singlje*.

One day it began to pour rain with the drops as large as taro. Soon this deluge, combined with the rain from previous months flooded the entire earth.

Before the flooding began, there was a group of people who received guidance from *cemas*. They were to gather *ljaviya* and lash it together in bundles thick as a person's thigh. Within these bundles they were to place *vulasi*, *vasa*, and *vaqu*.

Those people who had not received guidance from *cemas* laughed and ridiculed the others: "So you are leaving the *vaqu* behind while you go and collect the *ljaviya* which you can neither eat nor find other uses for!"

The people instructed by *cemas* were not bothered by this ridicule. They just went on making their bundles of *ljaviya*. The bundles were placed high up in the trees. When the floodwaters rose, they climbed up into the trees and tied the bundles together to make a raft on which they could float to safety. Now they understood the purpose of the instructions from *cemas*!

In addition to *ljaviya*, *cemas* had also instructed them to collect, their harvest foods, large cooking pots, tinder, and so on. People also took along dried meat, *cinuan*, and

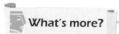

What's more?

papapenetan: the class system of *Paiwan* is the foundation of their solidarity.

adidan: in the class system of *Paiwan*, adidan are the common people.

Family: refers to people with the same name.

Tribe: the tribe is comprised of people, land and realms, it is made up by a group of people sharing common interests.

singlije: *Paiwan* believe the stems of millet plants are the language for communicating with the gods or summoning ancestral spirts.

cemas: the spirits or gods, one name of which is *Dagalaus*.

a-uai as well as all the stone implements for starting a fire and cooking.

Then, one day a little boy from one of the families peed on fire. *cemas* was infuriated when catching the acrid stench of extinguished fire's urine and smoke. Such disrespect!

cemas solemnly warned the people:

"People of the land! The smoke of your fire is the messenger between the heaven and the earth. Not only can the smoke speak, it is also the marker of the ways between the heaven and the earth. It is sacred and to be respected."

When *cemas* finished the people's right to make fire was revoked.

Tribe members punished the child who peed on the fire by applying raw taro to his penis so that his body became very itchy and he could not urinate.

Paiwan elders often say: "It is disrespectful to *cemas* to pee on or even put out fire with water."

But if a fire goes out on its own they say: "The fire is resting, it has gone to sleep."

Just as all people were agonizing over how they could get along with no fire, an old man smoking a *quncu* named *Paljevavaw* said to the crowd: "If you ask me what I have brought I will say I have brought nothing. However, *cemas* instructed me that

 What's more?

vasa: this is a general name for tarot. *Paiwan* distinguish between dry tarot and water taro, with the former often being made into a dehydrated product which can be stored for winter use.

ljaviya: razor grass, a species within the genus Miscanthus, is used for building houses and its stems can be used as torches.

paudalj: legend has it that what is normally translated as "tinder" is actually a white stone that gives a red glow, a symbol of continuity and power.

cinuan: food wrapped in leaves. Traditional *Paiwan* snacks are made as follows: 1. combine pork belly, tarot powder, a little water and salt and mix well, 2. wrap the ingredients in four to five pickled vegetable leaves, 3. steam for about 30 minutes – ready to eat!

a-uai: another traditional Paiwan food made by pounding strips of meat and millet into a paste, adding tarot root, wrapping in moon peach leaves and steaming.

when I leave, I should remember to fill the *quncu* with tobacco. " Whereupon, the old *Paljevavaw* took a long draw on the pipe and slowly let out several puffs of smoke. The people then understood the purpose of *cemas'* instructions.

The old *Paljevavaw* put the tinder from his pipe into his hand and gave it to the child who had peed on the fire, saying: "Keep the fire burning! Before such time as the waters recede, you are the keeper of the fire and must not let it go out."

The child eagerly nodded his head in acknowledgement of his task.

From then on the child did many things to show his gratitude to the old *Paljevavaw*: when he needed to light his pipe the child would run to the stove, when he was thirsty the child would fetch water, and when the old man was carrying a heavy load the child would rush to share the burden.

Respect for elders is one of the most important traditions of the *Paiwan*. *Paiwan* elders often say: "My wisdom and experience are to be given to children who understand respect and courtesy. I am waiting, waiting for a person to whom I can pass on this on experience and wisdom."

The elders also say: "The wisdom of the elders is to be received. The way of receiving is by studying, and by understanding your relationship with your fellow tribespeople.'

Where did it come from?

This story was told to Yaronglong Sakinu by his maternal grandfather in Tjacupu village, Dawu Towship, Taitung County.

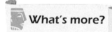 **What's more?**

sapui: Paiwan for fire symbolizing the continuation of life.

zaljum: Paiwan for water, symbolizing power.

Paljevavaw: a person's name which also means to "take something higher"

quncu: this is an implement used for smoking and is also an expression for "come!" as in the phrase, "come, lets have a cigarette!"

tjamaku: tobacco made from dry leaves.

vuvu: Elders, children: in the views of Paiwan, the elders are to be respected and learned from and children must succeed to the life wisdom of the elders, so whether an elder is calling a child, or a child is speaking to an elder, the two may both use *vuvu* to address the other.

Stories of the mazazangiljan (2)

◆ The Black Bulbul Returns with the Fire

The waters showed no signs of receding and the razor grass raft was getting heavier and heavier as it absorbed the water.

Everything was so damp, the fire brought by *Paljevavaw*'s eventually went out. When there was no fire everyone blamed the child.

Paljevavaw turned to the people and warned them: "The floods came and destroyed everything on account of the people's greed. *cemas* took pity upon us and gave us another chance, but none of you have cherished this opportunity. All you do is squabble!"

He continued, "When you are faced with a problem, you don't try and solve it, rather you just create more problems. Is there no one among you who can see this? All these trials and tribulations that we are experience are a test from *cemas*."

Someone then suggested that they try to restore the fire. Many attempts, were made, all with no success.

One time they dispatched *qaqa* to fetch fire. *qaqa* was returning with the fire and had almost reached the raft, but when the qaqa's beak was burnt by the fire, qaqa opened its beak shouting: "Ah Ah Ah", and the fire fell away.

Finally they sent a Black Bulbul. For its success in bringing back the fire the Black Bulbul made a huge sacrifice. Originally her beak and feet were as black as the rest of her body. In order not to drop the fire, the Black Bulbul swapped the fire back

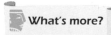

What's more?

qaqa: Paiwan believe that the black crow is an emissary of heaven.

Tjagaraus: In the time of the great flood, the Paiwan escaped to Dawu Mountain where they hunted and raised crops. After the floodwaters receded the *Paiwan* gradually began to migrate to lower altitudes but they consider *Tjagaraus* to be their place of origin.

and forth between her beak and feet, until she made it back to the raft. The heat from the fire turned the Black Bulbul's feet and beak from black to red.

Not only did the Black Bulbul bring back the fire but she also brought back news that land was close at hand. That land is *Tjagaraus*, or what many people now know as Tawu (Dawu) Mountain.

They followed the directions of the Black Bulbul and paddled toward the land. When they arrived they expected that there would be an abundance of food and everthing else they needed for their daily lives. Imagine their disappointment when they found the land empty! They were physically and mentally exhausted. Having spent extra effort to get to land, they used up more food than expected, and now hardly any remained.

Where did it come from?

This story was told to Yaronglong Sakinu by his maternal grandfather in Tjacupu village, Dawu Towship, Taitung County.

Stories of the mazazangiljan (3)

◆ vurung, djilung and the mazazangiljan

A long time passed but the waters did not recede. One day *djilung* appeared, a shiny clay pot at the top of Dawu Mountain. They wanted to check it out but they dared not get too close because the vessel was being guarded by *vurung*. They could only view *djilung* from afar.

After some time watching the vessel from the safety of the distant forest, they noticed something peculiar: whenever the sun shone on the clay pot something seemed to move inside.

One day *djilung* suddenly broke open. A man appeared! The multitude of *vurung* surrounding the vessel instantly parted to make a path for him. The people watching from the forest were astounded and ran back to tell the others.

Extraordinary! Just djilung broke open, the floodwaters began to recede. Nevertheless, the people were still very concerned because they were nearly out of food.

Just as they were discussing how and where to find food, the skies suddenly shook with the roar of thunder and a fierce gale. Someone recalled a prophecy:

"*cemas* has said that one day a cave in the heavens will appear. Millet seeds have been placed near the cave entrance. One of you, one who is both brave and wise, will climb up to the cave and bring back the seeds."

Now that the cave had appeared, they hurried to fashion a ladder from bamboo on

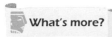

What's more?

djilung: pottery, or ceramic containers are owned by the aristocracy and signify status, power and wealth. The *djilung* may be male, female, ying-yang, and ceremonial. *djilung* are also among the essential betrothal gifts.

vurung: This is *Deinagkistrodon acutus* also known as the hundred pace pit viper. *Paiwan* use the honorific "elder" when speaking of this animal. The pattern of the *vurung's* colors and symbols is used exclusively by the *mazazangiljan*.

which they could climb to the cave. They sent their strongest man up the ladder to retrieve the millet, but when he got to the cave, his shoulders were too broad for him to squeeze through.

Next they tried sending a child. The child's body was small enough to fit through the cave, but had nowhere enough strength for the task.

Many more attempts followed. No one succeeded in retrieving the millet.

One night, the man who had recalled *cemas'* words about the millet and the heavenly cave, dreamt about a large gathering of *vurung*. The next morning when he told the others about his dream they realized that the man who emerged from the clay pot on *Tjagaraus* was the one to bring back the millet. They were desparate now. This could be their last hope.

When they went to find the man they were interrupted by a very fat *vurung* slithering toward them. The snake slowly raised its head and looked knowingly at the bamboo ladder reaching up to heaven's cave and said: "I will let your *mazazangiljan* know about this."

Puzzled, they asked: "What is a *mazazangiljan*?"

The *vurung* spat and hissed, but said no more. Then all around them they heard the voice of *cemas*:

"If that man can go to heaven's cave and bring back the millet, then he is your chief, your *mazazangiljan*. You have forgotten the pact that we made. You have become an insatiable and wasteful lot. So, all rights and privileges of your people will be for the *mazazangiljan* to manage and dispense. You must follow and obey."

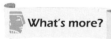 **What's more?**

> **mazazangiljan:** for the Paiwan, the chief is the manager of the tribe or village with special exclusive rights and power over everything, such as the produce of the land, the animals that are hunted, the fish in the streams, the decoration on clothing, and clothing itself. The *mazazangiljan* system is hereditary with the eldest son succeeding. With the collapse of the Paiwan society the *mazazangiljan* has become just a cultural symbol with no special rights.

After several days the man born of the clay pot appeared at the foot of the ladder to heaven's cave. People jeered and mocked him:

"Such a skinny person! He looks as though he has never eaten. No point in his even trying to climb the ladder. There's no way his legs are strong enough."

Everyone glared at him with revulsion and contempt.

Undeterred, he responded to their hostility by saying: "If I can really bring back the millet seeds from heaven's cave, there are a few things I want you all to promise me."

After some discussion they agreed that if he brings back the millet they will comply with his requests. He then began playing the *kulalu* to communicate with the *vurung*. Behold! Never had anyone seen such a large gathering of *vurung*. One by one they encircled the bamboo ladder enabling him to easily and quickly ascend to heaven's cave. The people watched transfixed, eyes and mouths agape. Miraculously he returned from the cave carrying the millet.

On his way down the ladder from heaven's cave he shook the ladder with great force and the millet grains began to rain down on the people gathered below. Excitedly, the women lifted their skirts and the men spread their *itung* catch the falling grains.

Upon his return the people saw but one bunch of ripe millet in his hand. Angrily they shouted out: "How can one measly handful of grain be enough to feed us? How can you expect us to agree to your requests?!"

He replied: "I brought back the seeds for your millet and spread it over the ground for you to cultivate."

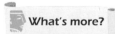

What's more?

kulalu: *Paiwan* have two general types of direct-blown flutes: those blown with the mouth and those blown with the nose. The nose flutes are exclusively used by the aristocracy. Both type of flutes, those blown with the mouth and those blown with the nose, may be single or double bodied.

Itung: cape.

He held up the millet and continued: "The millet seeds that came from the heavens will grow into great harvests of millet for those who are patient and who tend to the crops. If you cannot wait for the plants to grow and mature, why don't you take what I have in my hand and eat it!." Whereupon he flung the millet into the air.

Everyone scrambled to grab what they could, just like so many little birds trying to be the first to steal the millet from the fields.

Something strange then happened. The next day those people who had greedily snatched up the millet all turned into birds. The others then remembered the man's words: "For those of you who are patient and willing to tend the millet plants you will be rewarded with plentiful harvests and you will have enough to eat, but, for those of you who are anxious to eat your fill now and want just to reap grain but not put in any effort, your punishment is for you become little birds."

His words were finally understood and the people decided to abide by the terms of their agreement.

He went on: "Although you all have land, of what use is land without millet? I brought you the millet. Your progeny will prosper for many generations."

He then said: "Everything was washed away by the flood. Now we will begin with a new order. I will exchange millet with you for land. The millet belongs to you, the land belongs to me, when the millet is harvested just give me a few handfuls. I ask for no more. One more thing, *vurung* helped me bring back the millet. From now on you shall make this snake the symbol of authority, ability and wisdom!"

Everyone was persuaded by the man from the clay pot and they proclaimed him their *mazazangiljan*, the chief of the tribe.

The *mazazangiljan* walked to the great stone wall and began shaking his body and hair with all his might so that the only thing people could see was a cloud of millet.

He said to the people: "This millet is for those people who have no family or friends to rely upon! From this day on, let us all share our joys and happiness, and let us all take on adversity and hardship together."

The *mazazangiljan* set up the class system for the *Paiwan* and their lives began to have order. To show gratitude to the *mazazangiljan*, the people gave him special privileges for the decoration of his house and clothing.

Although the *mazazangiljan* had these privileges, status among common people remained equal and did not change. One could even say that the common people are the parents of the *mazazangiljan* - if there were no hard work and labor by the ordinary people, there would be no honor for the *mazazangiljan*.

From the time the *mazazangiljan* exchanged the millet for the land his relationship with the common people became much closer. They both needed each other, for without the land of what use was the millet, and without the millet of what use was the land?

The common people used their labor to plant and cultivate the fields and the *mazazangiljan* used wisdom and introspection to manage the customs and ways of the society. This separation of responsibilities is the basis for *Paiwan* society's power and order. This "class system" was the *Paiwan* way of life since the earliest times. In a word, the *Paiwan* could not be without their *mazazangiljan*, nor could they be without their common people.

Where did it come from?
This story was collected from the village of Lalauran, Taimaili Township, Taitung County.

03

The Tests of Love

Benaq was of the commoner class. He and *Ruku*, daughter of the *mazazangiljan*, fell in love. This posed a big problem for the chief of the village. Could *Benaq* pass the tests in order to marry *Ruku*? He did indeed come up with the feathers of an eagle, the tooth of a cloud leopard, the knife carved with the Hundred Pace Snake design, and crystal beads. From that time on these four items became essential symbols of love according to *Paiwan* marriage custom. Later on, in the *Paiwan* traditional marriage ceremony playing on the *ljukai*, or swing, was adopted as a way of inviting cemas and the *tjalje tjalj*, or ancestral spirits, to join in the festivities.

When members of the *Paiwan mazazangiljan*'s family marry, they use a *ljukai* in a swinging game to invite the *cemas* and *tjalje tjalj* to come down from the heavens and join in the celebrations. *Paiwan* believe that this *ljukai*, or swing, is the stairway connecting the heavens and the earth. Naturally, for important events they must invite the spirits to join in.

How the *ljukai* is constructed and decorated differs from family to family. It is fitted out with tubes and bells attached to the swing's thick ropes which make all kinds of singing sounds as the game proceeds.

The elders had a saying: "The more tubes and bells attached to the swing, the more abundant will be the millet harvest. It is also an invitation to the other villages to come and join the celebration. And it lets *cemas* and *tjalije tjalj* know they are welcome to sit upon the *ljukai* to watch over the festivities."

Paiwan have a beautiful story about playing on the *ljukai*.

Long ago, *Ruku*, a young girl in the *Kaquliquli* clan and daughter of the *mazazan-giljan* was in love with a commoner named *Benaq*. Because of the status gap between the two families, *Ruku's* parents adamantly opposed any talk of their marriage. Nevertheless, the two frequently found ways to meet and spend time together. The only other person who knew their secret was *Ruku's* grandmother.

One day someone showed up at *Ruku's* home to propose marriage *(kisudju)*, but *Ruku* would have none of it. With her grandmother's assistance, *Ruku* was able to evade her suitors and they eventually went away.

"This won't do." said *Ruku's* grandmother, "You can't go on like this forever. Someday you have to get married."

Ruku shook her head. She would not have anyone except *Benaq*. Her grandmother said: "*Benaq* is a commoner, even if I were to agree with your marrying him, your parents would never consent."

Many people continued to call on *Ruku's* family to be considered for her marriage, but *Ruku* remained true to *Benaq*, spurning all suitors.

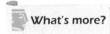

What's more?

> **ljukai:** during a *Paiwan* wedding or harvest celebration one will always see the *ljukai* but it is only those who are to be married or the man who has shown outstanding merit that are allowed to play on this swing. In the past it was only the *mazazangiljan's* family that used the *ljukai* as a symbol of position and class status. The *ljukai* is also a symbol of an abundant harvest.
>
> **venalasaq:** this word is used by the *Paiwan* to symbolize abundance or the passing of another year. *masu vapu* is also used to mean the harvest that takes place every year in the seventh or eighth month.
>
> **tjalje tjalj:** the *Paiwan* word for ancestors who have passed away.
>
> **kisudju:** elaborate preparations are involved in the five stages of traditional Paiwan weddings.

One day *Ruku's* father discovered the reason his daughter would not consider marrying any of multitude of candidates. He found *Benaq* and told him: "If you can accomplish four things, I will agree to your marriage with *Ruku*."

"First you must bring back a feather of *qarjis*; second you bring me a tooth from *likuljua*; and third, you must bring me the baby of the Hundred Pace Snake."

When he got to the fourth item, the *mazazangiljan* thought for a moment, and then said: "For the fourth item you must go to the realm of the gods and bring back the *mulimulidan*, the brightest and most precious bead among all their *zangaq*.

If you can accomplish these tasks, you may wear the clothes of the upper class and take my daughter as your bride."

What's more?

qarjis: Paiwan consider the feather of a male eagle a symbol of identity, status and ability.

likuljua: Paiwan believe the clouded leopard (*Neofelis nebulosi*) is the incarnation of a hunter who was killed but refused to leave the human realm. Legend has it that the animals were pets of the gods and could not be hunted by ordinary people. Casual hunting of the animals enrages the gods. People who wear the skins of *likuljua* are recognized as being of great status and deserving of the utmost respect, and this is tacitly endorsed by the gods.

zangaq: *Paiwan* treasure crystal beads and hand them down from generation to generation. Each bead has its symbolic meaning representing class, status, wealth, gender, aesthetics, enhancement of ritual, the color of religious gods, and special characteristics of customs and beliefs. The richness of the colored glass beads has been an important part of the *Paiwan* solidarity, cultural distinctiveness and inner spirit.

mulimulidan: The name of this most precious bead among all the *zangaq*. It means the "light of the sun" and represents, brightness, beauty and grandeur. There are many kinds of *mulimulidan* each with a slightly different name. They are usually located in the center of the necklace and have a white background with blue, red, and yellow patterns. The pattern determines the value of the beads. When a *mazazangiljan* is married, the *mulimulidan* is an essential dowry gift symbolizing the grandeur and the noble status of the wedding.

When *Benaq* heard this he thought to himself: "It is impossible to get an eagle feather and one would surely lose his life trying to take a tooth from a cloud leopard. Bringing back a baby Hundred Pace Snake is more difficult than climbing to the heavens!"

"And he wants me to go to the heaven to retrieve the *mulimulidan*. That is something no man can do! Alas, I think I will never wear the clothes of the upper class nor be marrying *Ruku*!"

This realizstion was too much for *Benaq*. His knees weakened and as he fell to the ground tears streaming, he blamed himself for being so incompetent.

Paiwan believe that the eagle is an emissary from the heaven and that the cloud leopard is the soul of the earth. Because the colors of the cloud leopard are the colors of earth, these animals were very difficult to find and are rarely seen. The sacred Hundred Pace Snake is the *Paiwan* peoples' *naljemakve a cemas* and people tremble simply at the mention of the name "Hundred Pace Snake": no one would ever consider trying to bring back a baby snake. The crystal beads are so far away in the remotest place of the heavens that no one has ever been able to find them.

Benaq knew that if he tried to get these things he would never return. But he also knew that *Ruku's* father was purposely making things difficult for him so that he and *Ruku* would be forever separated. Despite the enormity of the mission, he resolved to set out the next morning and immediately made preparations for his quest to bring back the four treasures.

He was off at the first light of morning: the beginning of a journey that would last many years.

Benaq used all his will power and determination and followed every path to the ends of the earth, but was unable to find the road that would take him to the realm of the spirits. He hung his head low in remorse as he continued on.

What's more?

naljemakve a cemas: Paiwan have many spirit gods. In addition to this "guardian angel" spirit, they also believe in a creator spirit, a protector spirit, and a war spirit as well as spirits that manage the land, sowing crops and the harvest.

As he was walking back to his village he suddenly felt as though something was blocking the sun. Looking up saw a great eagle, wings spread and circling above. Just at that moment several eagle feathers wafted down from the sky. *Benaq* looked up again, but the eagle was gone. *Benaq* gathered up the feathers and placed them in a bamboo tube for safe keeping.

After collecting the feathers he was walking along a high mountain ridge. In the place where the sun sets, he saw an old man wearing a cloud leopard pelt draped over his shoulders. Excitedly, *Benaq* ran up to him: "Excuse me, does the pelt you are wearing belong to you?"

When the old man nodded his head, *Benaq* asked: "Do you know where the cloud leopard can be found?"

The old man said: "You need go no further, I have been awaiting your arrival here for a long time." *Benaq* was very startled.

The old man said nothing but quickly took something from his mouth and held it in his hand. He then handed it to *Benaq*. When *Benaq* looked in his hand he was shocked to see a tooth of the cloud leopard. How did the old man get this? Just as *Benaq* was about to ask, the old man transformed into a cloud leopard and struck at *Benaq* with his sharp claws. The terrified *Benaq* passed out.

While he was unconscious, *Benaq* dreamed that the old man who had turned into a cloud leopard said to him: "The wounds on your body from my claws are proof that you have the skills to fight and take my tooth. I am also giving you the cloud leopard skin as a gift. Take the tooth and the skin and go back to your home!"

When *Benaq* awoke he was not sure whether he had had a dream or whether this all had really happened. But when he saw the cuts on his body and saw the cloud leopard tooth and skin on the ground beside him, he knew it had to be true.

According to *Paiwan* tradition, whenever someone took out a cloud leopard they delivered the teeth and the skins of the animals to the *mazazangiljan* to let him choose which he wanted. Whatever was left over would belong to the hunter. *Benaq* never imagined he would ever obtain such precious gifts.

Full of satisfaction at having obtained a tooth of the cloud leopard, *Benaq* put on the cloud leopard skin and started his journey home. But on the way back he accidentally stepped on a Hundred Pace Snake.

The Hundred Pace Snake lifted its head and dug its sharp teeth deep into *Benaq*. *Benaq* took a few steps and then fell into a coma under a large tree. While in the trance he heard the voice of the Hundred Pace Snake: "I bit you so that you would take a message back to your people not to steal our children, for if you carry out these acts of disrespect, our revenge will be brutal."

When the Hundred Pace Snake was leaving he also said: "But for now I am going to transform myself into a knife. This will take the place of your having to steal a baby Hundred Pace Snake for *Ruku's* father."

When *Benaq* awoke his hands were holding a short knife in the shape of a snake. This is why *Paiwan* customarily inscribe snakes on their knives.

Benaq now had everything except the *mulimulidan*.

The *cemas* were extremely moved by *Benaq*'s sincerity and tenacity so they placed the *mulimulidan* in a ceramic vessel that was full of all kinds of strange insects and placed the vessel containing the crystal beads on road taken by *Benaq*'s on his way back to his village.

Benaq was walking down a path when he noticed something off in the distance that radiated light. Curious, he went up to the ceramic vessel for a closer look and discovered the *mulimulidan*. But he felt something wasn't apposite about getting the crystal beads and the ceramic vessel without having to work for it. He stood there deliberating for some time. Finally, he remembered that his beloved *Ruku* had been waiting for such a long time for him to bring back the gifts. He then decided to wrap everything up in a red cloth and it all back to the village.

While *Benaq* was away on his mission *Ruku's* father took advantage of the absence of any news and forced *Ruku* into marriage with another man. But *Ruku* only had love for *Benaq* believing that he would eventually return safe and sound. So she pinned her hopes on the *ljukai* or swinging part of the wedding ceremonies. She would swing so high that no matter how far away, *Benaq* would see her.

 What's more?

sepi: dreams are considered by Paiwan as a kind of language for transmitting information from the ancestor spirits to the dreamer.

Paiwan believe "Only after the woman has played on the swing can the marriage be considered complete. Before that the woman can change her mind and call off the marriage."

Ruku was sure that if *Benaq* saw her he was sure to come running back.

When the swinging game began *Ruku* was confident that *Benaq* would see her. She was right! *Benaq* returned from afar as she anticipated.

When *Benaq* returned to the village with the designated items he immediately went to the *mazazangiljan*. *Ruku's* father looked everything over and then said to *Benaq* : "What about the baby snake?"

All of a sudden the knife in *Benaq*'s hand transformed into a Hundred Pace Snake. Not daring to believe their eyes, everyone gasped in astonishment.

Then the *mazazangiljan* took the ceramic vessel but was puzzled to see so many strange insects crawling about. Suddenly he dropped the ceramic vessel to the ground and all of the insects turned into precious crystal beads.

Ruku's father had received all of his requests: the eagle feathers, the tooth of the cloud leopard, the knife with the Hundred Pace Snake design, and the crystal beads. He placed them in the open for all to see and announced that he would keep his promise and blessed them. Ruku completed her play in the great swing: her marriage to *Benaq* was happily consummated.

These four items that *Benaq* presented to *Ruku's* father became the essential gifts in the *Paiwan* wedding ceremonies.

Where did it come from?

This story was collected from the village of Lalauran, Taimaili Township, Taitung County.

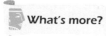

What's more?

gingking: this the word in Paiwan for betrothal gifts.

賽夏族
S a i s i y a t

01

The Prophecy of the Great Storm

The *Saisiyat* have thrived for generations thanks to the advice of an old white-haired man and a brother and sister holding on to a loom amidst the turbulent waters of the great flood. The spirits of *oppehnaboon* and *mayanaboon* live on today in the two mountains Dabajian Mountain and ShiaobaJian Mountain. To this day these mountains remain the protectors of the Saisiyat Tribe.

Long ago there was a young man named *oppehnaboon*. One night an old white-haired man came to him in a dream. The old man told him that a great storm would soon come to *oppehnaboon*'s people. The old man told *oppehnaboon* that he must alert the *Saisiyat* to begin preparations for the coming calamity.

At that time thunderstorms were so common that most people paid them little attention. But the old man of *oppehnaboon*'s dream had warned that this storm would be different. It would bring flooding all over the land. He told *oppehnaboon* that he must persuade his people to build boats or they all would drowned.

oppehnaboon told his people about the old man's warnings of a great storm. But instead of following his advice and building boats, everyone just laughed and ignored his warnings. Nevertheless, *oppehnaboon* did build his boat.

Not long after the warnings the rains came. The heavens clouded over until it was as dark as night. Torrents of rain poured down and the winds blew with a ferocity as no one had ever seen. The people of *oppehnaboon*'s tribe finally began to understand the seriousness of the situation. They regretted not having heeded the warnings of *oppehnaboon*, but alas, it was too late and they must accept their fate.

oppehnaboon was still anxious about his people's safety. That night he had another dream of the old white-haired man. This time the old man advised *oppehnaboon* to give up his boat. He told *oppehnaboon* to lead all of his people to the land above the flood waters.

When *oppehnaboon* awoke he immediately set about carrying out the instructions from the old white-haired man.

The rain continued to fall. The flooding became worse and people were drowning everywhere.

Leading a group of people *oppehnaboon* set off for the high ground. The flood waters were close behind as they tried to climb to safety. There was no escape and they were all swept away by a giant wave. Inundated and nearly drowned, nevertheless, *oppehnaboon* continued to struggle for his life, never giving up hope.

As he struggled in the rushing waters *oppehnaboon* grabbed ahold of a loom that was floating nearby. As he tightly clutched the loom he saw his younger sister, *mayanaboon*, bobbing up and down in the water barely alive. With his other hand he reached out and grabbed onto *mayanaboon*. Clinging together onto the loom they drifted out into the great floodwaters.

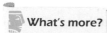

What's more?

sai-siat: the word "sai" has the meanings of "at" or "place", while the word "siat" refers to a specific place, a place which to this day no one can be sure where "siat" is located.

oppehnaboon: in the story of the great flood, following all the chaos and destruction two people remain, the prophet and creator *oppehnaboon*, and his sister *mayanaboon* are respectively considered by the *Saisiyat* to be embodied by Dabajian Mountain (*oppehnaboon*), and the smaller Siaobajian Mountain .

They drifted about for what seemed an eternity. Just as they were about to give up from exhaustion and hunger, they saw land. Using the last of their remaining energy they swam ashore. They landed at *pakpakwaka*.

All around there was nothing but water. The entire world was flooded except for the piece of land on which they were standing. All the people of their tribe were gone, only they remained.

That evening *oppehnaboon* had another dream of the old white-haired man. The white-haired man told *oppehnaboon*: "Now there are only you and your sister. For the sake of your tribe's survival you must marry and have children!"

Marry his own sister? How could he do that? It was against ethics! What should *oppehnaboon* do? Violate the rules or go against the advice of the old white-haired man? The old man had been right before. He is probably right this time too!

oppenhnaboon and his little sister *mayanaboon* joined to become husband and wife, and soon gave birth to a child.

The couple felt however that the world was a lonely place with only the three of them. There should be more people they thought, and with that, *they chopped up the little child into many pieces and threw the pieces* into the water whereupon each of the little pieces instantly became a person! While chopping up the child *oppehnaboon* had already thought of names for each of the children. The names that he gave the children are the original names of the *Saisiyat* ancestors.

All of the children now had names. If they forgot their name *oppehnaboon* would

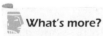

What's more?

o:ko': Around the world it is common for floods to be a part of the people's creation story. In Christianity there is the example of Noah's Ark, while the *Saisiyat* instrument of choice is a weaving loom, although there are also those who believe it was a gourd. *Saisiyat* use a horizontal back sling loom to make long gowns, skirts, shade cloth, bras and cloaks.

pakpakwaka: known in mandarin Chinese as, Dabajian Mountain. pakpakwaka in *Saisiyat* literally means "ear of the Earth". It is the sacred place of origin for the *Saisiyat* and most of the *Saisiyat* later settled in what today are the surrounding areas in Taoyuan, Hsinchu and Miaoli Counties.

teach them again. After everyone knew their clan names, and as the floodwaters receded, they gradually left the mountain and went to other places, including following the river to the edge of the ocean. Later they returned to live around *pakpakwaka*.

Saisiyat used to live in present day Houlung, Toufen, and Sanwan in Miaoli County. For the most part *Saisiyat* now live in the areas around Nanchuang, Wufeng and Shihtan.

oppehnaboon and mayanaboon lived out their lives on *pakpakwaka*. *oppehnaboon* became the spirit of Dabajian Mountain and *mayanaboon* became the spirit of Siaobjian Jian Mountain. For eons their spirits have watched over and protected the *Saisiyat*.

Where did it come from?

This story was narrated by Chu Sin-cin of Dongjianghsin Village, Nanchuang Township, Miaoli County.

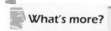 **What's more?**

bori: the *Saisiyat* word for "meat" is *bori*. Pieces of a chopped up body all turning into humans is not very realistic and is the product of an imaginary world. *Saisiyat* are not alone in this idea among world cultures as there are many other examples. The reader should not take this too literally.

A note from the author: the stories and legends of the *Saisiyat* are pan tribal, and while there are slight variations from village to village, the spirit and structure of the stories are quite similar. The narrators of these stories are all *Saisiyat* elders. Both Mr. Chu Sin-cin and Pan Jin-wang have each separately served as the ceremonial chief leader during the *pastaii* in Xiangtian Lake, and the Heavenly Prayer Rite.

biwa Visits the Saisiyat

biwa, the lightning spirit, could not bear to see the *Saisiyat* suffering so much in the toils of their daily work. She sent her daughter waaung to the world of humans. waaung carried millet seeds with her to share with *Saisiyat*. Millet later became the prized staple of the *Saisiyat* people. During this time waaung met and betrothed tain, a young *Saisiyat* man. waaung not only helped tain's family to make a living, she also helped tain's father regain his sight. In their ceremonies today the people of the *Saisiyat* still honor the lightning spirit, *biwa*, and her spirit daughter, waaung.

In the wild times of many ages ago, the *Saisiyat* lived by hunting and gathering. They collected fruits from the trees and roots from the ground. Knowing nothing about farming, their lives were simple.

The lightning spirit, *biwa*, could not bear to see people suffer. *biwa* had a daughter named *waaung*. *biwa* called *waaung* before her and said: "*waaung*, the *Saisiyat* people do not know how to plant. Their lives are too harsh. Take these millet seeds and teach them farming!"

What's more?

biwa: this story of the *Saisiyat* predates the arrival of the *taai* and tells of the beginnings of the *Saisiyat* becoming an agricultural society. Raising millet requires the moisture from rain and legend has it that all aspects of rainfall were decided upon by *biwa*. Thus *biwa* became an important god of agriculture, and along with many other cultures the *Saisiyat*, revere the lightening spirit as a rain god.

waaung: *waaung* was sent by *biwa* to help the *Saisiyat* develop agriculture and to this day is revered as their most important diety.

waaung filled her calabash with millet seed and set off for the realm of the humans.

No sooner had *waaung* entered the human world did she come across *tain*, a young *Saisiyat* man who was out hunting. It was love at first sight. *tain* took *waaung* home with him and they became lovers that same evening.

The next day *waaung* opened her calabash and gave *tain* the millet seed. She taught him how to plant. From that time on, millet became the staple of the *Saisiyat*, and agriculture became their way of life.

tain's mother had passed away long ago. His father was blind in both eyes. *waaung* used her powers to restore *tain*'s father's sight.

tain's father was so happy to have his sight and see his son's wife. However, in order to demonstrate his status as the head of the household he said to *waaung*: "Our traditions require that a married woman take care of the household. It is best if you stay at home."

waaung replied: "Father, I cannot get near the cooking pot, so I hope that you will cook the food for the family. You can leave all the work in the fields to *tain* and me!"

Seeing how determined was *waaung* to have her way, *tain*'s father went along and said no more.

waaung and *tain* went to the mountain fields carrying twenty sickles and twenty

 What's more?

yinra: *Saisiyat* have no word for marriage as such. This word yinra literally means "the woman goes to the man's house to live". *yinra* is the fourth step of what we might call the "marriage process" and is preceded by "courtship", "proposal", and "engagement".

masay: when a *Saisiyat* dies the place and manner of burial will be determined by whether the death was "good" or "bad". A "good" death typically is one that occurs at home and the attending obsequies are more ceremonious. Death by accident or say, by decapitation, is considered a "bad" death and the body will hurriedly be buried at the site of the death. Nowadays most of the *Saisiyat* have adopted the Han forms of funerals and they sweep graves at Qing Ming Festival, the Han people's celebrated day of tomb sweeping.

hatchets. When they arrived at the fields *waaung* instructed *tain* to place one sickle and one hatchet every six paces. *tain* was puzzled, but did as he was told. When all the tools were in place he returned home alone.

Just as *tain* arrived home he heard the roar of thunder coming from the fields. He ran back and saw that in such a short time the grasses in the fields had all been cut, and the land was neatly plowed.

tain told his father all about what had happened in the fields. His father was happy to hear about it. He recalled the hard days of the past and thought that ever since *waaung* joined them their lives were much better. He had regained his sight, the fields produced millet and they were blessed with good fortune in all respects. *tain*'s father told his son that he must take good care of *waaung*.

tain and *waaung* enjoyed their lives together. They were very happy and time passed quickly. But after three years they were still without children.

tain's father worried about the next generation. He said to himself, "These three years have been hard for *waaung*. Everything is fine except that she has not borne a child. What is the reason for this? Hmmm, I think I know! She has never gone into the kitchen. Although she says she can't 'touch the cooking pots'. I am sure this is the reason she has not given birth to children!"

The more he thought of this the more *tain*'s father was sure that all *waaung* needed to do was to go into the kitchen and cook. She would then have children and their problem of the next generation would be solved. He called out to waaung saying that he was very hungry: would she please go to the kitchen and make him something to eat?

He was so determined that *waaung* could not refuse him. She said, "Father, please wait outside. I will go to the kitchen. Do not come in until the food is done."

waaung went into the kitchen. Soon a loud noise came from the kitchen. *tain*'s father rushed in but *waaung* was nowhere to be found. Only a plantain tree was standing with its leaves sticking out window. Smoke was rising from the leaves of the tree.

When *tain*'s father had forced her into the kitchen, *waaung* knew her time in the human world was at an end. This was her chance to return to her home in the sky.

Where did it come from?

This story was narrated by Pan Chin-wang (Wumao da yin) of Penglai Village, Nanchuang Township, Miaoli County.

03

pas-taai: Legend of the Little People

The "*taai*", or the "Little People" were highly respected by the *Saisiyat*. From the *taai* the *Saisiyat* learned horticulture. However, the taai sometimes caused trouble and took advantage of the Saisiyat women. Gradually the *Saisiyat's* respect for the taai turned to resentment. When the *Saisiyat* could no longer bear the humiliation they laid a trap that killed nearly all of the *taai*. The last of the taai then cast a spell on the Saisiyat. Only those *Saisiyat* who learned the traditional songs and dances of the taai would enjoy peace and good harvests. These songs and dances are known as the "*pas-taai*" and became part of the peace ceremony when the Saisiyat and the taai settled their disputes.

What's more?

pas-taai: One of the ceremonies of the entire *Saisiyat* people. In the past some called it the "sacrifice to the little people", while others called "sacrifice to the little spirits", so in order to settle the controversy, it was directly transliterated and named pas-taai. "*taai*" is the name the *Saisiyat* gave to the little people, and "pas" means a festival. Thus "pas-taai" is a festival dedicated to the little people and their spirits. It is held every two years (even-numbered years in the western calendar), and a big festival is held every ten years, all in the middle of the tenth month of the lunar calendar. It is held in two locations: Xiangtian Lake in Nanzhuang Township, Miaoli County and Daai in Wufeng Township, Hsinchu County.

Long, long ago the people of the *Saisiyat* who lived in *sai-kirapa* made their living by simple horticulture and hunting. Their farming skills were not well developed. The crops might be eaten by animals or ruined by the weather before the harvest. The people often went hungry.

The *Saisiyat* performed ceremonies every year after the harvest. They thanked all the gods and the spirits of their ancestors for the gifts of nature, and they asked for fair weather and good fortune in the coming year.

One day, nobody knows exactly when, a group of people moved into an area near *sai-kirapa*. These people looked quite different than the *Saisiyat*. They were short in stature; an adult was only as tall as the chest of a *Saisiyat*. Nevertheless, they were strong, nimble, and could move very quickly such that even the *Saisiyat* warriors were no match for them. The *Saisiyat* called their new neighbors "*taai*".

At the time prior to the arrival of the *taai*, the only grain known to the *Saisiyat* was millet. The *taai* were very knowledgeable about plants and introduced *Saisiyat* to rice cultivation.

What's more?

sai-kirapa; sai-lamsong: *sai-kirapa* is the place name from *Saisiyat* tradition, is located in present day Wufeng Township, Miaoli County. Scholars consider the Saisiyat of this area to be the "northern Saisiyat" while the "southern Saisiyat" are located in Nanzhuang Township and Shihtan Township in Miaoli County.

pinana'amishan: *Saisiyat* consider there to be just two seasons in the year: summer or *a:bqan* and winter or *amishan*. Spring is called "the beginnings of summer" and autumn "the beginnings of winter", with the idea of "the beginnings of" conveyed by simply adding the prefix "pinana'".

taai: the name given by the *Saisiyat* to the "little people".

tata': the *Saisiyat's* cultivation of millet began as part of their transition from hunter/gatherer to an agricultural economy and has become an important offering as part of their ceremonies. When performing the Heavenly Prayer Rite participants are all given millet balls to eat. This rite is performed by the Saisiyat to ask the gods for good weather and to dispel disease. It is held in the third month of the lunar year and if it comes in the same year as the *pas-taai* it will be a relatively smaller ceremony, a larger ceremony being held in the following year.

The *taai* were also good at magic. They could turn away typhoons and storms to make the weather fine. The rodents, birds and other animals all stayed away from their fields. Their harvests increased every year.

The *taai's* most amazing feat was to take a few grains of rice and turn it into enough food to feed many people. The *Saisiyat* benefited greatly from the knowledge and experience shared with them by the *taai*.

The *Saisiyat* were very happy, believing that the *taai* had brought them their good fortune. They often invited the taai to join their harvest and planting celebrations and festivals. Together they gathered as one family, singing and dancing through the night.

The *taai* were outstanding singers and dancers. Many of their songs and dances became part of *Saisiyat* ceremony. The *Saisiyat* admired and were grateful to *taai*, and did not mind that their own *Saisiyat* ceremonies were changing. It was a time of harmony.

But these days of harmony did not last long. The *taai* knew they had been kind to the *Saisiyat*, but the lascivious nature of the *taai* gradually emerged as they began taking advantage of the *Saisiyat* women. One year during the harvest festival when everyone was dancing and singing the *taai* were harassing *Saisiyat* women in all manner and form. The humiliated *Saisiyat* women, in order to maintain the greater harmony, swallowed their anger kept the matters to themselves.

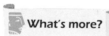 **What's more?**

Magic: magic or witchcraft was always an integral part of Saisiyat society with divination by water, bamboo or birds being the most common. Many social activities require divination to determine whether the outcome will be auspicious or menacing. The *Saisiyat* shamans also healed the sick. The majority of shamans were women. Training and study was required.

There is no word for "magic" in the Saisiyat language, but there were two kinds of water divination: saralom being the one used for curing difficult disease or illnesses and ponapis being used for finding something or someone gone missing. More common today is the *romhaep*, or bamboo divination, which has been borrowed from the Atayal and is used to answer questions or cure illness.

Before long however, to everyone's shock, it was common for the *taai* to harass the *Saisiyat* women in broad daylight.

The *Saisiyat* were outraged by this behavior of the *taai*. The young men of the tribe wanted to take revenge. Who could bear to watch their mothers and sisters humiliated like this?!

The *Saisiyat* began holding secret meetings. They gathered around the fire to discuss how to deal with *taai*. "This is intolerable!" said the young *umau*. Standing up he continued, "How can we sit around like deaf and dumb people! We must take action against the *taai* to protect our mothers and sisters!" The *Saisiyat* youth rallied to his call for action.

However, *kaleh*, an elder of the *titiyun* clan, was both experienced and cautious. He asked everyone to think about the long-term interests of their tribe. Imploring them to be patient, he said, "Hold on, hold on. Everybody calm down! We must not be hasty. We should think this through carefully. Remember what the *taai* have done for us. The good life we now enjoy is due to the gifts and teachings of the *taai*. We should not be too quick to seek revenge."

But the young man *iteh* questioned the elder's wisdom of waiting, "If you put it that way, why don't we just hand everything over to the *taai* and let them do as they please?"

kaleh responded, "Listen everyone, I am also a *Saisiyat*. Before we do anything we should consider the welfare of all *Saisiyat*. It is not that I am against punishing the

What's more?

ayalaihou: whenever the need arose to discuss a festival or other important matters came up, the elders would be summoned, with each clan sending someone to participate. All others, whether male or female were allowed to join. The elders would speak first and then the others would speak, in an order based on their generation and age.

titiyun: this is a traditional family name of the *Saisiyat*, and would be the Han name "Chu" meaning vermillion in Chinese. The family *titiyun* was the leader in the performance of the *pas-taai* ceremonies and the name titiyun can be found both in Nanzhuang and Wufeng townships. The word in *Saisiyat* is the plant "rosary pea" (*Abrus precatorius*) which has a bright red fruit (pea) containing albrin, a highly toxic substance.

taai, but we should remember that ever since ancient times we had to struggle to survive. It was only after the *taai* came into our lives that we have had enough to eat and can take care of our daily needs. We should find a way to repay the *taai's* gifts and kindness.

"The *taai's* behavior is certainly over the top and cannot be tolerated. But we should first try talk to them, requesting that they agree to restrain themselves. And if they don't? Well, there will be plenty of time to punish them!"

kaleh had long held the trust and respect of the *Saisiyat*. After his speech people's tempers cooled and they reached a consensus. They would try to reason with the *taai*.

kaleh soon called the elders of the other clans together to go to meet with the *taai* and ask them to go back to the ways of old days and to not harm one another. However, in spite of all of the *Saisiyat*s' good will and efforts the entreaties of the *Saisiyat* elders were ignored and the *taai* continued to bully the *Saisiyat*. In fact their bullying behavior became even more brazen and extreme.

Some of the young *Saisiyat* men could bear this no more and they secretly set out to deal with the *taai*. But they were no match for the *taai*. The young *Saisiyat* were thoroughly defeated and returned home in humiliation.

All the *Saisiyat* could do was to try and avoid the *taai*. The relations between the *Saisiyat* and the *taai* became worsened daily. Seeing that the *Saisiyat* were helpless to stop them, the *taai* became even more aggressive and bold in their abuse, doing whatever they pleased. The *Saisiyat* women were terrified.

The conflicts between the *Saisiyat* and *taai* continued.

One day a young *Saisiyat* woman was out alone. A group of *taai* began to harass her. Luckily *wumau of* the *Saisiyat* was in the area and was able to rescue the young girl from her attackers.

When *wumau* told his people what happened they were furious and vowed to take revenge against the *taai*.

Even *kaleh* had no more patience. He shouted out in anger, "We have given the *taai* every chance to make peace. All they do is return our goodwill with intimidation and abuse. Our women are not safe and our patience has run out. It is time to fight back!"

The *taai* liked to gather in the valley of *sai-kirapa*. *sai-kirapa* was a place of splendid beauty but also very remote. A waterfall divided the great cliffs surrounding the valley. On the eastern cliffs was a tall loquat tree whose massive trunk stretched across the river to the western cliffs. In the valley below the river ran fast and furious. Those among the *taai* with sufficient skill and courage liked to climb onto the tree trunk overhanging the river, enjoying the evenings in the beauty of the area and the cool breezes of the valley.

On this evening *wumau* and *iteh* went to *sai-kirapa*. As the *taai* were all soundly sleeping *wumau* and *iteh* quietly crept up to the trunk and used their hatchets to cut a deep gash in the tree. They covered the gash with mud.

Quietly, they waited for the *taai* to fall into their trap.

Early the next evening the *taai* prepared to make their return to *sai-kirapa*. As they approached, and were about to climb onto the loquat tree everything was as usual. The *taai* suspected nothing. One by one they scaled the tree. When nearly all of them were on, the tree gave out a loud noise: PAH!, PAH!

"What was that?" called out one of the *taai*. Nearby, an old *Saisiyat* woman calmly replied, "It's nothing, just the popping sound of this old woman's knee caps!" Oblivious to the trap, the *taai* shrugged it off and continued scampering on to the tree bridge.

All but two of the *taai* were on the tree. Under the weight of so many people, the tree suddenly collapsed. It gave out a deafening sound as it crashed into the deep gorge. The *taai* were sent hurtling below like so many arrows. Those who were not crushed by the fall were drowned in the rushing waters. Not a single *taai* who had been on the tree survived.

However, there were the two *taai* who did not make it on to the tree bridge. They could only watch in horror from under the tree as their comrades plunged to their deaths.

 What's more?

ito': The cliffs and loquat trees from this story are still in place today. It is said that near the stone cave in Sai Jilaba River Valley (the Youluo River section near Daai Village, Wufeng Township, Hsinchu County), there are small stone beds, stone tables, stone chairs, and so on which many people believe are evidence of the *taai* residence.

The *Saisiyat* were also watching from their hiding places. When they saw that their plan was a success they were overjoyed. They chased after the two *taai* survivors, but the *taai* were too fast and they escaped from the *Saisiyat*.

After a few days the two surviving *taai* went to the *Saisiyat* village and announced to the tribe: "People of the *Saisiyat*, now that you have returned our goodness with your evil deeds, you will live to regret it! Your harvests will be poor and you will be plagued by typhoons!"

They continued, "However, there is one way to avoid this punishment: As long as you honor and pay respect to the souls of our ancestors and diligently study our songs and dances, the curse will be lifted."

For the time just after they received the warnings, of the *Saisiyat*, only the *titiyun* clan learned the songs and dance of the *taai*. The two surviving *taai* stayed with the *titiyun* and taught them everything they knew of their rituals. When all had been passed on to the *titiyun*, the two *taai* departed toward the east.

After the curse of the *taai*, the *Saisiyat* did indeed suffer poor harvests every year. One disaster followed another.

After a long time of enduring hardship, the elder *kaleh* recalled the parting words of the two surviving *taai*. He called upon his people to heed those words: "We suffer because we exterminated the *taai*. For the sake of our future generations, from now on when we celebrate the harvest, we must honor the *taai*. We must sing *taai* songs and dance *taai* dances. We shall seek forgiveness of all the *taai* souls and ask that they bring us peace and abundant harvests.

All agreed with *kaleh*. These songs and dances thus became part of the most important celebration of the *Saisiyat*. Passed down from generation to generation, it is known as "*pas-taai*".

Where did it come from?

This story was narrated by Chu A-liang of raremewan villiage (Xiang Tian Lake), Nanzhuang Township, Miaoli County.

邵 族
T　　H　　A　　O

01

Legend of the White Deer

> How did the Thao come to live around Sun Moon Lake? All we know is that a white deer led their ancestors to the lake at the end of a long and exciting chase. Did the deer intend to show the Thao the area that would become their home for thousands of generations? In any event, the Thao call the place from which they first saw the lake "puji" which means the color white in the Thao language. This is one way they remember the white deer.

It was early autumn. Young and tender sprouts of the *lhimza* were just beginning to appear. The skies were a crisp blue color as the snow white silvergrass flowers danced about in the gentle winds. A faint scent of young blossoms was in the air. The hunting season for the *Thao* Tribe had arrived!

Everyone in the *Thao* village had been busy preparing for the hunt for many days. The elders repeatedly reminded the young hunters to check their bowstrings and arrow tips, and not to forget to take along their hunting bags. They must also re-member to pack the flint and tinder so they will be able to start the fires needed to dry their meat in the evenings after the hunt. The tinder must be perfectly dry, otherwise it will not catch fire from the flint. They all were gathered around the fire making sure all was ready.

The youth of the village were excited as they followed the guidance from their elders in making preparations for the hunt. Even the dogs were caught up in the anticipation of joining the hunt. Yapping and barking they ran about nipping at the legs of their masters.

This hunt was to prepare for the annual ceremonies in honor of the *Thao qali*. The celebrations would go on for twenty or thirty days and in preparation, every year they went out on a great hunt to bring back meat for the *mulalu*.

There were many well fed deer in the valleys and mountains around the village. The young men were anxious for the elders to give the word so they could start out for the hunt.

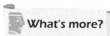

What's more?

lhimza: razor or sword grass and silver grass are commonly seen plants. The edges of the leaves are quite sharp one is often afflicted with small cuts when walking among these grasses.

Thao: sometimes spelled "thaw" which is closer to its correct pronouciation. Scholars have adopted the romanized spelling "Thao".

taun: the word for village and home is the same in the *Thao* language.

apu: A general name for old people, *apu*, or elders are accorded great respect among the Thao and play an important role in consulting on important matters and for teaching.

Firmly twisting the bowstring: made of ramie fiber, the bowstrings must be twisted very tightly so as to avoid breaking.

shinabunan: an implement that is thrown and used by the Thao for hunting or as a weapon.

fatu: a kind of stone used by the *Thao* to make fire. The velvety part of banana trees was dried and used for tinder.

bunlhaz: meat and fish were important to the Thao diet as a source of protein however there were many protocols around the hunting activities concerning the subjects hunted, amounts taken and so on. Arbitrary killing or capture or animals was prohibited so as not to disturb the balance of nature.

apuy: fire was important to the *Thao* whether for cooking, lighting or warmth, and generally the fire was never extinguished even when going out to work or hunt.

aynuz: *Thao* word for cooking place or hearth.

This time the villagers were especially excited because they had heard people talk of having seen a great white deer in the forest around their village. It was said that the deer was like no other. All of the hunters hoped they would be able to bring the deer back for the celebrations as a gift to their ancestors.

Finally, the day came for them to set out on the hunt. They went along the river where the *lhimza* was so high that it brushed against their faces. They slept in the open with the millions of stars above them. The shouting of orders by the elders the barking and yelping of the hunting dogs made for a lively and noisy group!

After several days of hunting their bags were full of game. Their spirits were high as they prepared to return home with their bounty. They were walking through the forest when suddenly a flash of white passed before them before disappearing into the trees. Could this be the white deer that they had heard so much about?

An elder let fly the first arrow - siiiieeewww! The dogs gave chase with the hunters close behind.

The chase went on over the rivers and hills, through the forests and bushes. But no matter how hard they tried, no matter how fast they ran, they could not catch up with the white deer. By evening everyone was so tired that they fell into a deep sleep.

 What's more?

atu: nearly every household raises dogs as friends, hunting companions and to guard and watch over the village's security.

qali: *Thao* believe that those who have died become spirits that protect and ensure their peace and health.

mulalu: the main rites performed by the *Thao* are for agriculture, hunting and to honor the ancestor spirits, *qali*. These are all carried on today with the most festive being held in the eighth lunar month to honor the *qali*, with the celebrations sometimes last as long as a month.

lhkaribush a qnuwan: at one time long ago deer could be seen nearly everywhere in Taiwan. As prey they played an important role in the lives of indigenous peoples. Later the deer became a mainstay of the Dutch trade, and this along with Han peoples' wanton land development and indiscriminate hunting, nearly caused the animals to go extinct.

At daybreak the white deer appeared once again. And once again they all scrambled off to give chase. They pursued the white deer the entire day.

The white deer sometimes stopped and stood still not far away from the hunters. However, as they got closer and thought they could catch the white deer, it bounded off deep into the forest. Soon they were already far from their village, but the white deer kept on leading them further and further away.

The hunters all knew the area around Ali Shan but the white deer kept leading them into unknown mountains to the northeast. They were getting close to the river source, a place none of them had been before. They could feel the mysteries surrounding them in these deep lush valleys.

The elder thought that surely the white deer must be exhausted by now, and hearing the dogs barking up ahead, it shouldn't be long before they catch up to the white deer. Readying their bows, arrows, and spears, they forged ahead.

The leader of the band had carved notches in the trees all along the way so that they would be able to find their way home after the chase.

And thus they continued for several days, but they never got close enough to the white deer. It stayed just far enough away to elude their success.

Weary from the chase the hunters climbed up on a mound to take a rest. There before them they saw the sparkling waters of a *vazaqan*. Standing on the shore was

 What's more?

Ihpazishan: the bodies of arrows were made from bamboo that was straight and had relatively few joints, while the arrowheads were likely first made of stone, and later made of iron.

Ali Shan: Here the name for Ali Mountain refers not necessarily to the mountain itself but to the area surrounding the mountain. The Thao's place of origin was quite possibly the western plains, which was also home to the Zou, *Bunun* and different plains' indigenous peoples.

Billowing turbid waters: This refers to the Zhuo Shui River whose name literally means "turbid waters" and was likely the southern border of Thao territory, with Zou territory being further south. In the upper reaches of the river it runs over black slate, the fine powder of which turns the water turbid as it flowes toward the Taiwan Strait.

the white deer! Within moments of their spotting the white deer, it bounded into the water, swam to the distant shore and was never seen again.

Perhaps it was the will of their ancestors' spirits that led them to this *vazaqan* and its surrounding *hudun*. For this was truly a land of plenty: all the water they needed, lush forests, rich soil and countless fish for their harvest.

A group of the hunters followed the signs back to their village, packed up their *ihari* shoots and *kamar,* and brought the old and young alike to settle at the lake. For generations they have lived and this lake which they named *zintun*. *zintun* is now known as Sun Moon Lake and the place they settled is known as *puzi*. The Han Chinese people called this place "Tudingzai".

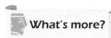
What's more?

futulh: The powerful hunting bows of the skilled *Thao* archers were made from two kinds of wood.

Carving notches in the trees: When hunting in the deep mountains, people often use a machete to cut a notch in the trees bark as a guide to avoid losing their way.

Lost!: In the primeval forests of Taiwan the lush vegetation, dense underbrush and tall trees cause people to lose their way

vazaqan: the name the Thao use for large bodies of water such as large lakes, or even at times, the sea.

hudun: the mountains in the vicinity of Sun Moon Lake are filled with lush vegetation and abundant wildlife, providing everything required to satisfy the needs of the Thao.

ihari: tarot may be planted next to the water or on mountain slopes. It is an important staple food for indigenous peoples.

kamar: millet.

zintun/Sun Moon Lake: as far back as two or three hundred years documents from the Qing Dynasty contain accounts of *zintun*, which they named for its resemblance to the shapes of the sun and the moon. This is the "mother" community of the Thao which they call "water community".

puzi: this word in *Thao* means "white" in commemoration of the chase of the white deer that led them to *zintun*. The Han people later came up with the name Tudingzai.

02

Tales of the Long-tailed Elves

The clever and good-natured Little People shared everything they had with the people of the *Thao*. But there was one thing that they wouldn't do. They wouldn't let the Thao visit them at their homes in the caves. One time, however, a daring and curious young *Thao* man couldn't restrain himself. He followed the Little People to their home. As he watched from his hiding place, he discovered their secret: they had tails! Ever since that time, the Little People wanted nothing more to do with the Thao. They disappeared and have never been seen since.

In addition to the *Thao*, Sun Moon Lake was home to another tribe of people. They were known as the lhilitun or "little people" because they were very short in stature. The lhilitun lived at Sun Moon Lake long before the *Thao*.

The lhilitun lived in caves, secluded in the deep forest. They were very, very clever. From their hands came all manner of tools, and from their gardens all kinds of strange and wonderful fruits and vegetables.

When the *Thao* arrived at Sun Moon Lake they soon became good friends with the lhilitun. The lhilitun taught them many skills for making tools, planting and so on.

However, even though they were such good friends, the *Thao* never visited the villages of the lhilitun. For some reason the lhilitun did not want the Thao to come to their cave homes deep in the mountains.

"Our homes are damp and dark and you would be most uncomfortable. We're sorry, but we really could not take care of you, so please do not visit!"

"Our homes are small and the halls are narrow. We're afraid you'll bump your heads or stumble and fall. We're sorry, but we really cannot take care of you, so please do not visit!"

The *lhilitun* came up with all kinds of reasons to reject a visit by the *Thao*. But the more they insisted, the more curious the Thao became. One young man in the Thao village was determined to go to the homes of the *lhilitun*. After he decided to go, he said to himself, "At last, I will go and see what is going on at their homes!"

One evening the young man finally found his way to the cave village of the *lhilitun*. The *lhilitun* were just about to retire for the evening when they saw the young *Thao* man in the shadows of the fading fire. They were stunned to see someone from the *Thao*, after all they had done everything possible to keep their home a secret. Upon seeing the Thao man they scampered to hiding places like so many mice.

By the light of the fire the young *Thao* man discovered that all of the *lhilitun* had long tails.

In their haste to get away the *lhilitun* put their tails in the *runu* hoping to hide them from the young man. One of the lhilitun fell over and the *runu* broke his tail. He screamed out from the excruciating pain.

The lhilitun had always been very careful to hide their tails. They had never dreamed that someone would barge in to their homes like this and discover their secret. They were furious with the Thao.

Not long after this incident the *lhilitun* moved away. The *Thao* never saw them again – gone forever were the good friends who liked to share their talents and skills with the *Thao*.

What's more?

lhilitun: legend has it that the little people once lived alongside the *Thao* at Sun Moon Lake. Unfortunately to date no traces of these people have been found.

runu: the *Thao* would hollow out a tree stump to serve as a mortar for pounding grains. This implement was already quite heavy, and when made from stone, the weight of the mortar would be even greater.

The Long Haired Spirit of Sun Moon Lake

For as long as the people of the *Thao* could remember there had always been plenty of fish and shrimp in Sun Moon Lake. So recently why were they not catching anything? The young hero *Numa* decided to find out. He went into the lake to find that the *Taqrahaz* were tampering with their fishing lines and hooks. The *Thao* and *Taqrahaz* had gotten along for such a long time. What were the T*aqrahaz* trying to tell the Thao?

There once was a time when strange beings lived at the bottom of Sun Moon Lake. The upper part of their bodies was just like a human but the lower part was like that of a fish. Their thick black hair hung over their faces, flowing down to their chests and backs. They spent all day swimming about and enjoying the waters at the bottom of Sun Moon Lake. The Thao people called the long haired beings the "*Taqrahaz*".

Ever since the Thao settled at Sun Moon Lake they got along very well with the *Taqrahaz*.

What's more?

Taqrahaz: the people of this story living in the waters of Sun Moon Lake had upper bodies of humans and lower bodies of fish. Stories abound of people seeing the *Taqrahaz* floating around in the water taking in the sun while combing their long hair!

As did the Thao, the *Taqrahaz* depended on the fish, shrimp and mollusks of the lake for their livelihood. For tens of thousands of years the flora and fauna around, in, and on the lake sustained the *Thao* and the *Taqrahaz*. For all their fishing and gathering, the abundance of life at the lake was not diminished.

Of late however, the Thao often came back to their villages without having caught any fish from the lake.

The old chief, *Paytabu*, was very worried. He thought to himself: "Ever since anyone can remember our Thao ancestors and the *Taqrahaz* shared the bounty of the lake. We had plenty to eat and our lives were carefree. Lately, however, many strange things have suddenly occurred all at once..."

"Hey, what's happening to my *davaz*? Why is it torn?"

"Hey, how did the eel escape from the bucket?"

"What happened to the shrimp traps?"

The Thao people were worried and confused. What was happening? This couldn't go on for long or else they would starve!

A brave young man, *Numa*, said, "I will go into the water and find out what is going on!"

Tall and muscular, *Numa* was an expert swimmer. He was fast with a spear and always hit his target. He could swim for a half day under the water without coming up for air.

What's more?

Paytabu: the name of a *Thao* chief in ancient times.

davaz: a kind of fish net on a wooden raft.

lhalhutha: a kind of fish trap and the word can also be used as a general term for fishing implements.

Expert swimmer: living as they did along the lake the *Thao* were all good swimmers with a good knowledge of water. Many could dive for long periods of time and developed special fishing and trapping skills.

Numa leapt into the water and swam for the deepest part of the lake. He swam through every bay, looking at the nets and other equipment for catching fish, shrimp and so on. While he was swimming he discovered all kinds of abandoned or discarded fishing equipment scattered throughout the water. There were hooks and nets, old equipment and new equipment everywhere.

At the very deepest part of the lake *Numa* saw *Taqrahaz* breaking holes in the *tagan*!

"So that's what is going on!" Now *Numa* finally understood why the Thao had been unable to catch any fish!

Numa and *Taqrahaz* fought a fierce battle. Their thrashing about stirred up the waters, the waves washing over the surrounding hills. For three days and three nights they fought, with no one emerging victorious.

While they were fighting, *Numa* asked the *Taqrahaz* why they had been ruining the Thao's fishing equipment. The *Taqrahaz* angrily replied, "For years you have been fishing in Sun Moon Lake and leaving your equipment behind. The lake is becoming filled with all sorts of your junk. Someday there will be no more fish to catch. Then how do you expect people to live!?"

After he heard the *Taqrahaz*' explanation, *Numa* realized that his people had been ruining the lake without even knowing it! For all these years they had been dumping their junk and waste into the lake. This was the cause of their problems!

Once *Numa* understood, he stopped fighting. He and the *Taqrahaz* worked together to solve the problems.

 **What's more?**

rapu: in addition to using nets to catch fish the *Thao* also used arrows and spears, which would typically be done from the shores or from a boat and this would generally be done with the larger species.

tagan: To make eel traps *Thao* hollow out the trunks of tree ferns (*Cyathea lepifera*) from nearby forests. The heavy base sinks in the water and the hollowed out core attracts burrowing eels.

From this incident the Thao people learned the importance of understanding the interconnection of all life. From that time on, the Thao strictly enforced rules as to what kinds of fish could be hunted at what times of the year. The nets, traps and other equipment were designed so that the smaller fish could get away and they no longer allowed the nets to have to fine a mesh; the time of indiscriminate fishing had ended.

The Thao took particular care to ensure that Sun Moon Lake had undisturbed areas of waterweeds where the fish and shrimp could feed and breed.

After learning these lessons, the Thao people left Sun Moon Lake to recover on its own so that all the life in the lake could flourish. For their part, the *Taqrahaz* no longer bothered the Thao's nets, traps and other fishing gear. Sometimes the *Taqrahaz* can even be seen resting on the waterweeds!

What's more?

Net and trap dimensions: if the mesh of fishing nets or diameter of the traps is too small or narrow, even the very young animals are caught, and this can pose a danger to the viability of the particular species. The Thao also place pads for shrimp and fish to lay their eggs, an example of conservation measures that can ensure the sustainability of the lake's resources.

Floating aquatic plants: providing habitat for water creatures, the floating plants often aggregate to create small islands.

04

The Black and White Twins and the Origins of the Ancestral Spirits Basket

Every family of the Thao has its "ancestral sprit basket". The basket plays an especially important role in the lives of the Thao because any matter, large or small, whether of the family or of the village, must not be undertaken unless the ancestral spirit basket has been consulted. The importance of the basket will be seen in this story which recounts the origin of the taboo against twins.

The land around *puji* was fertile and the Thao people were clever. It is no wonder then that the Thao grew in number and soon did not have enough room for all their people.

In the middle of Sun Moon Lake is a large island known to the Thao as *Lalu*. *Lalu* was the ideal place to settle. Surrounded by water. people living on *Lalu* need not fear wild animals or invasions by enemy tribes.

The area around Sun Moon Lake is blessed with pure water, green hills and an abundance of flora and fauna. The area provides the Thao with all their needs to pass carefree lives. It was in this land of plenty that the Thao established their largest settlement, known as *Sazum*, on the island of *Lalu*.

The traditions of the Thao have it that the birth of twins is a great misfortune. One day the wife of chief *Hinaluma*, gave birth to twins, one with a black face and one with a white face. Everyone in the tribe was quite frightened and could not stop talking about this event.

"Could this be a bad omen?"

The state of affairs was one big headache for chief *Hinaluma*, as it could impact the fortunes of all the Thao.

In the confusion, *Hinaluma* waited for an opportunity when his wife was not paying attention and threw the black-faced infant into the lake.

But the following night *Hinaluma* had a dream about the infant he had thrown into the lake. The infant was crying out to him: "Your misfortune will not be helped by my death. You must have every household of the Thao place the belongings of their ancestors into a wicker basket. This includes clothes and jewelry that they wore during their lives. This basket becomes the home of their ancestor's spirit. For all matters, large and small, the ancestor basket must be consulted. Otherwise the bad fortune will continue."

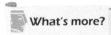 **What's more?**

Lalu: this is the island located in the middle of Sun Moon Lake and is one of the places inhabited by the *Thao's* ancestors. Because of the island's surrounding water it was secure and was one of the most important *Thao* settlements. Later, on account of disease and incursions of the Han Chinese, the *Thao* moved away from *Lalu*. During the Qing Dynasty called the island was called "Pearl Mountain" by the Chinese, while during the Japanese era it was called Jade Island, and when the Chinese again came to Taiwan in the 1940's they called it "Glorious China" Island.

Sazum: the main settlement of the *Thao*. There are many other Thao settlements scattered around Sun Moon Lake.

makarman: these are matters that are troublesome for the individual such as an illness, injury, or some other misfortune; whereas the "big problems" would be things such as a great flood or an epidemic of disease.

When he awoke and told his people of the dream they were all very upset. They scurried about searching out the belongings of their ancestors to place in their wicker baskets. This story shows how an event of misfortune became the basis of the Thao ritual.

Today, every family of the Thao keeps their ancestral spirit basket and strictly adheres to the ritual. The belongings of the deceased ancestor placed in the basket indicate that the ancestor is never far away. All matters of the family and village, large and small, are undertaken by the Thao after first consulting with the ancestral spirit basket.

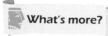 **What's more?**

ulalaluan: *Thao* place the clothes and bead chains worn by their ancestors in a rattan basket which becomes an important symbolic object when worshiping the spirits of one's ancestors.

05

The Story of the Pariqaz

The waters of Sun Moon Lake were covered in the blood red sap of the pariqaz tree that had been cut down by the Han Chinese. Soon after the death of the sacred tree the Thao were devastated by plague and were no longer able to hold their own against the assault on their lands by the Chinese. Can pathlar, the great ancestral spirit, hear the voices of their hearts and save the Thao from the holocaust!?

Near the shores of Sun Moon Lake stood the giant *pariqaz*. The Thao elders believed that Pathalar, the most revered spirit of their ancestors, lived within the tree. The *pariqaz* ensured that the Thao would have their needs taken care of and thrive. The Thao believe that each leaf of the *pariqaz* represents one of their people.

"Take care to protect the *pariqaz*," the elders would counsel the youth, "for, every new leaf of the tree means a new life is born within our tribe!"

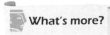 **What's more?**

pariqaz: native to Taiwan, *Bischofia javanica,* or bishop wood tree at one time could be seen throughout the plains, foothills and mid elevation mountains of Taiwan. The trees are long lived with records of over 1,200 years and the species is often a symbol of community gathering with a number of places in Taiwan being named "the foot of the bishop wood tree".

Pathalar: the common ancestor of all *Thao*; the creator of the Earth; the most authoritative diety, able to control good and evil spirits, bestow good fortune and exorcise evil. *Thao* pay tribute to *Pathalar* on birthdays, and when in need of assistance, sumptuous offerings of wine and food are prepared.

As the spring and autumn seasons came and went so would new leaves arrive and old leaves fall away. Year by year the tree and the tribe flourished together.

About three hundred years ago, *Qutsung*, a bold and gifted leader of the Thao, led his tribesmen on an expedition to the area of central Taiwan known as *Sazum*. The Thao became the dominant tribe in that region.

This was also about the time that the Qing Dynasty had wrested Taiwan from the control of Koxinga's family. The Han Chinese people first settled in the south of Taiwan, developing the land and introducing their customs. Gradually they made their way into central Taiwan. Under *Qutsung*'s leadership the Thao were able to repel the Chinese further incursion into the mountainous areas of the *Sazum* region.

Despite repeated attempts, the Chinese could not overcome the Thao. After trying all manner of attacks and strategies someone recalled that the people of the Thao worshipped the giant *pariqaz* tree standing alongside Sun Moon Lake. They said, "All we need to do to conquer these barbarians is to cut down their sacred tree!"

One day, while the Thao warriors were out on an expedition a group of Chinese secretly made their way to the lake. There, they planned to chop down the giant *pariqaz* tree. They knew that this was the heart and soul of the Thao. If they could destroy the tree they could have their way with the lands of the Thao.

When they found the tree they took out their axes and began chopping away. Strange! After they had cut away one side of the giant tree and went around to begin chopping at the other side, the first side grew back as though it had never been touched! The Chinese tried everything to chop down the tree but the great *pariqaz* withstood their efforts and remained standing.

One evening after a long day of no success in chopping down the tree, one of the Chinese wandered off to find a place to rest. Without knowing where he was going, he lay down alongside the giant *pariqaz* and fell asleep. As he was dozing off, he could faintly hear the murmurings of voices nearby. He listened closely and discovered that it was the sound of the *pariqaz* tree chatting with the little trees

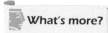 **What's more?**

Sazum is the name for much of the traditional area where *Thao* resided. Not understanding indigenous peoples, the Han Chinese mistakenly considered the *Thao* to be members of the *Tsou* tribe.

around it. "No matter what those stupid people do they can't chop me down! I am not afraid of anything... except of course the *hlahlikhlik*!"

The Chinese man woke up only half believing that he had heard a tree talking. When he told his colleagues about it they wondered what in the world is a *lhalhikhlik*? After they thought they would never figure this out, one came up with the idea that the *ihalhlikhlik* must be a saw blade!

The Chinese put down their axes and took up saws. They cut away at the giant *pariqaz* tree working all the day until twilight. Finally they sawed the tree through and it came down at last. The tree had been so difficult to cut down that the Chinese were afraid the *pariqaz* might come back to life. So they took a giant copper spike and drove it into the stump of the tree. Then they spread the blood of black dogs all over the spike and finally covered the entire stump with a copper plate. At last they were done!

When they cut the sacred *pariqaz* tree it's red sap ran like blood into Sun Moon Lake. Soon after the Thao lost the sanctuary of their *pariqaz* tree they were stricken with a plague.

None escaped infection and massive numbers died. With so few people they could no longer resist the Han Chinese who came onto their lands, cut down the rich forests, and cleared fields for rice paddy. The Thao Tribe was forced to leave the area of *Lalu* island and the sacred *pariqaz* tree, moving to more remote lands around Sun Moon Lake. Never again would they enjoy the abundance of their lives on *Lalu* island.

 **What's more?**

Red sap: when first cut the sap of the bishop wood tree is white, but after contacting the atmosphere it oxidizes and turns red.

lhalhiklhik: onomatopoeic: the sound of a saw, and in this case, signifies the tool itself.

Long copper needle, black dog's blood, large copper cover: according to the beliefs of the Han Chinese when blessed, these object are able to stifle the spirits, in this case, so the pariqaz would not come back to life.

Capping the tree trunk: unless extraordinary measures are taken a tree will often begin growth anew. Here the Chinese were taking no chances that the tree would sprout anew.

▎製作群亮相 ▎

◆ 魯凱族

故事採集者：

奧威尼・卡露斯 Auvinnie-Kadrese【漢名：邱金士】

奧威尼的名字是他母親為紀念她外公而取的。他母親的外公是部落史官：族人口述歷史、族譜和祭典的傳承者。尤其令母親難忘的是，外公常以神話故事教育小孩子。沒有想到經過四代之後，她的二兒子不僅繼承了她外公的名字，連文化傳承的工作也一併繼承了。再說到二人說話的風格和幽默，認識老奧威尼的族人，都不禁無限緬懷的說：「簡直是他外曾祖父的翻版！」

小奧威尼長住在山上的舊好茶老部落，常被人譏笑為怪人，但他自認重建魯凱族石板屋文化是自己的宿命，這或許是祖靈最好的安排，他安然接受。他唯一的嗜好是一瓶小米酒之後，微醺中拿起薩克斯風對著夕陽，或在星空月下吹奏，以排遣內心澎湃的情感；而他唱歌也如同薩克斯風一樣低沉絕對。外曾祖父奧威尼老人家若在天之靈，應該聽得到他的心聲，並對他的努力深感欣慰吧。

繪圖者：

伊誕・巴瓦瓦隆 Etan Pavavaljung

「伊誕」乃繼承外公之名，老人家說，這古老的名字有勇者的意思，代表傳承了母親先輩們所擁有的事蹟。而「巴瓦瓦隆」則是家名，意指降生於大地之家，也就是父親所繼承的家。

他的家鄉在屏東三地門鄉的達瓦蘭部落，為排灣族群最北邊，且與魯凱族人為鄰。「達瓦蘭」有「被造之地」的意思，是個山林環繞、溪谷幽靜且具有豐富人文藝術的原始部落。他十分慶幸能在這裡成長。

伊誕曾在《台灣教會公報》擔任編輯，同時也是虔敬的傳道者；並致力於以影像為原住民文化留下忠實的紀錄。在2009年創立「伊誕創蓋視界」，2017年自許坤仲藝師傳習計畫藝生結業。他常常自我期許，不論從事繪畫藝術或原住民文學，只有建立獨特風格，才能展現原真之美。他最期待的是，透過信仰的價值，看見原住民人文藝術的重建和復興。

✦ 排灣族

故事採集者：

亞榮隆‧撒可努 Yaronglong Sakunu

童年的記憶裡，我的生活方式所看、所聽到的一切，都是排灣族的概念和思維。這幾年回到拉勞蘭部落，發願用心對待部落一切人事物，找回屬於排灣族人的驕傲和尊嚴。

我預見「部落會更好、會變得美麗又漂亮」，因為我已經看到部落孩子眼神所散發出來的認同和自信心的建立，並且我也將在部落的土地上蓋「獵人學校」，傳遞獵人生命真正的原本價值，因為狩獵更是在獵取自然和土地的經驗。

我所寫下的書《山豬‧飛鼠‧撒可努》（曾獲巫永福文學獎、文建會十大文學人，並被收錄於教科書），到《走屋的人：我的獵人父親》、《外公的海》，我想說：書是我寫的，且它的真正出處，是來自排灣族、我的部落、我的父親，這是屬於他們的，我只是提筆的那人而已。

故事和文學我會繼續寫下去，部落 、孩子我會一直跟他們在一起，我深信這是一項高貴的志業。

繪圖者：

見維巴里 Chien Wei Ba-Li

百合仰望蒼穹，如大地的子民渴望性靈的甘泉。這次藉著畫作來和先祖、族人、朋友們一起分享神話故事中的傳奇，以及對各種生命現象的直指或隱喻，都在在令人興嘆自然萬物間的奧秘和其背後所要傳達的美意。

自茹素以來，結合靜坐中的靈思，從不同的角度去領會部落生活文化的精神之美，創作上也更加豐盈。透過內在、外在的感動經驗，並藉由各種素材，如雕塑、版畫、水墨、壁畫、空間規劃、舞台設計、自然觀察、生態繪畫及詩文創作來記錄自我覺醒與靈性進化的有機現象，試圖將彼此間相映的共通語言，做出有別於以往的實驗性創作。未來也有意朝服裝設計，以及建築邁進，但也順其自然，希望展現出對生命的感動與創造力。誠摯邀請大家共享這真、善、美、聖的藝術饗宴，並不吝指教後學。

◆ 賽夏族

故事採集者：

伊德 阿道 iteh a atau 【漢名：潘秋榮】

「鬥志」是他的座右銘，頑強的性格造就人生經歷多次轉折。政治大學民族所碩士、中國中央民族大學博士，當過八年兵，退伍後換過許多工作，曾在中央廣播電台擔任主持人、節目企劃約15年。

他的外表、他的口音，總會引來初見者「你是原住民嗎？不像耶？」的印象，他說：「像不像不重要，是不是才重要」，他認為原住民不一定要一個模子刻出來。

他喜歡民族音樂，會吹幾曲笛子，也聽古典音樂，過去常登山，在走完錐麓古道後，妻子「關愛」的眼神讓他不再冒險。夫妻與小貓咪「丹丹」是家庭的基本成員。

熟悉賽夏族祭典與文化習俗，曾擔任賽夏文物館館長、苗栗縣縣議員(2005~2018年)，持續致力於推動賽夏文化之傳承；並長期關注原住民族運動、的轉型期正義等議題。

繪圖者：

賴英澤

2001年秋納莉颱風夜，他剛完成「大洪水」的草圖，忽聞外頭一陣喧嘩，打開大門一看，天啊！鞋子們正載浮載沉的漂流著。

眼見水位不斷上升，只好收拾畫稿物品，抱起熟睡中的孩子，帶著家人逃出災區。雖然比起賽夏神話傳說中的大洪水，不過是小巫見大巫，但大自然的力量同樣令人難抗。

對從小喜愛觀察、塗鴉的他來說，學生時代最喜歡在課餘藉著戶外寫生到處走透透，滿足一點探險的蠢動，一度在專業油畫家和奶爸二角色間擺盪，仍不改此習性。

接下賽夏神話傳說的繪圖工作，讓他這個福佬人得以飽覽南庄、五峰的賽夏風景，也開啟了對台灣原住民的了解——不再侷限於文化村中的刻板印象，而是透過巴斯達隘祭歌中賽夏人對自然的敬畏、對台灣原生植物的歌詠，成為真實的存在。

◆ 邵族

故事採集者：

簡史朗 Tian

土生土長於埔里、十足的在地人，也是一個樂觀的在地文史工作者。他從學生時代就對本土文史有異乎尋常的興趣，常自詡擁有一顆赤子之心，對外在世界的人、事、物充滿好奇；喜歡探究到底的習性，使生活中常常有新鮮事與驚嘆。他也曾是一個「有點異類」的國中教師，常在教學內容裡加入「教科書中沒有的東西」，就是現在所謂的鄉土教材，因為是身旁周遭的史地知識，所以還頗受歡迎呢！

他花了很多時間投入在日月潭附近的邵族研究。他當是社區工作，部落裡大大小小的活動總會看到他的身影，他和邵族人熟悉到可以隨時加入家庭用餐的行列；邵族祭師給他起了一個邵名叫做Tian，漢譯為「典」，他們說，邵族部落過去也有個個兒高大，和善又會做事的人，名字就叫做典。現在的「典」和古代的「典」，或許有幾分相似吧！

繪圖者：

陳俊傑　　繪圖者在製作期間，感謝張雅琪小姐協助。

正港的台北人，不論是父系或母系，甚至他內、外祖母的家族皆然。在學校學的是美術，畢業後他嘗試過包括公務人員、老師、專業畫家、攝影記者等工作，任職的時間都不長；後來，他選擇在體制邊緣求生存，發現了另一項興趣——研究台灣歷史，特別是平埔族的歷史，從此當作志業。

1996年，他到埔里鎮做平埔族的田野調查，赫然發現母親王家的祖居地「板橋港仔嘴地區」，竟就是清代凱達格蘭族武𠟦灣社的社地！之後他在王家日治時代的戶籍資料中，真的看到好幾位女祖先的種族欄上寫著代表平埔族的「熟」字，從此對平埔族的文化傳承有了更多的使命感，並在1999年撰寫《平埔族開發的故事：平埔族現況調查報導》。

長期在埔里從事田野調查，他與鄰近的日月潭邵族，有或多或少的接觸。大膽承接邵族故事的繪圖工作，不僅是對自己繪畫風格的挑戰，更是他做平埔族研究調查的另一個想望的起點與試金石——希望有朝一日，能以繪圖的方式復原平埔族人的傳統圖像。